ONLY
TRUTH

ONLY TRUTH

A NOVEL OF SUSPENSE

JULIE CAMERON

SCARLET
NEW YORK

ONLY TRUTH

Scarlet
An Imprint of Penzler Publishers
58 Warren Street
New York, N.Y. 10007

Copyright © 2020 by Julie Cameron

First Scarlet edition October 2020

Interior design by Maria Fernandez

Library of Congress Control Number: 2020912664

ISBN: 978-1-61316-183-8

10 9 8 7 6 5 4 3 2 1

Printed in the United States of America
Distributed by W. W. Norton & Company

To my family, for their love and support

To the dead we owe only truth
—Voltaire, "Premiére Lettre sur Oedipe" in *Oeuvres*

⸎

Prologue

T he sun blazed from an unsullied sky. The leaves ceased their rustling and the blades of grass stilled. Peace once again folded itself
over the trees and the natural order was restored—except for what now
lay there, broken and bloody, sprawled on the mossy woodland floor.

A fly gently settled on her forehead and observed with interest the
clotted mess forming before its compound eyes. It shimmered like a
jewel as it dipped its head to greedily taste. Where once was beauty lay
destruction and the buttercups averted their sunny faces from the sight.

He slipped away between the trees, his every fiber singing with the
joy of what he'd done; he was transformed, the secret of who he was
and what he could be finally revealed. He was Mors, God of Death,
and the air in his wake shivered with the knowledge that something
inhuman had passed that way.

What he didn't see, as he left her there, was the bubble forming at
her parted lips, or the plucking of her fingers as they grasped at life's
thin thread.

1

NOW

"I have been bent and broken, but—I hope—into a better shape"
—Charles Dickens

I wake early with a headache. Not the kind that renders me incapable but one that throbs and threatens, spitefully jabbing behind my eyes with bony fingers. The noise from the street feels physical, each sound jarring against my skin and shrieking along the axons to my brain. The sun filters through the curtains, illuminating the dust motes and trickling languidly down the wall. The day is set to be unseasonably hot and I feel apathy settling on me like a blanket.

I lie on my back and pretend I'm alone. When we were first together, I insisted that I slept on Tom's left. That afforded me the joy of seeing him as soon as I woke, but he favored the left-hand side of the bed so eventually we swapped. Now he's on my blind side, which is convenient this morning as it means I don't have to deliberately avoid looking at him—and yes, I know I'm being petty. I turn, only to find that for once he's already up. I tend not to sleep well and am usually awake at five, well before Tom surfaces, so it's mildly disorienting to find a bed full of emptiness next to me.

He's at the counter in the kitchen already feeding his enthusiasm for the day with eggs and toast, the sight of which makes me feel nauseated. The ketchup glistens like a puddle of gore. He hasn't noticed me. I stand in the doorway and watch this man who I've been married to for the last four years.

Tom Dryland is nice. A much-underrated word that could imply insipidness or even weakness, particularly in a man, but Tom is none of these things. He is mostly patient and kind and has an unflappable strength of character that is reassuring to those around him. If he has a fault it is that he's always, always right. It's this unflinching self-belief that gives him the ability to face problems and make decisions with calm decisiveness. While not Christian Bale or Brad Pitt, he has a symmetry and evenness of features that sets him above the ordinary and I sometimes wonder why he chose me. Don't get me wrong, I don't spend my life in a state of cringing gratitude but I do occasionally wonder what exactly he saw that made him think, "Yes, this is the one for me." His mother certainly couldn't see it. Her outpouring of grief when he announced our engagement was enough to make me look around to see who'd died. I sometimes wonder if there's something about me that's inherently off-putting to parents, be they mine or someone else's. Whatever the reason, Tom calmly weathered her hysterics, and despite her objections we married the following spring on a clear and sunny day, the happiest of my life. I must remind myself of what we have and try to face today with optimism and good grace. Tom wants a fresh start for us, and I can't let who I am stand in our way.

I pour myself a coffee to try and clear the fog in my head. As I do, Tom looks up from what he's reading and I see it's a brochure for the house in Cleaver's Lane. It's the latest in our long list of maybe homes and this one has a hold on him. It's a house he remembers from his childhood; one he passed on visits to his aunt—or if not that particular house, one so much like it to make it special. Despite my best intentions I feel the familiar flutter of disquiet in the pit of my stomach and quickly look away. I'm a second too late. His eyes meet mine and he sees the expression on my face. A matching look of apprehension makes its way to his.

"God Izzy, you look so pale, are you okay? Did you manage to get some sleep in the end or not? I tried not to wake you when I got up so you could have a bit of a lie-in." He cocks his head slightly and frowns. "You're not still worrying about this are you? I've promised you we won't go anywhere until we've found somewhere we both like."

I find his tone vaguely accusatory and sigh before I can stop myself. I can't go over the same things with him again, not today. It's not fair to him or me.

I make the effort to sound distinctly more chirpy and upbeat than I feel.

"I'm fine Tom, really I am. I just woke up with a bit of a headache that's all. A coffee and a bit of toast will fix it."

I feel him watching me as I go to the fridge and I can picture the familiar concern creasing his brow.

"Are you sure you're all right? If you're still fretting about today it's going to be fine, honestly. We'll drive over this morning, find somewhere quiet to have some lunch and see the house this afternoon. Trust me, you'll love it as much as me when you see it. Please don't get all anxious about this again; wherever we live we'll be happy. You know that."

It's impossible to explain to him how I feel. Although I really don't want to leave London I'm not just "fretting" about seeing a house, it's this house I seem to be struggling with. Even the name of the road sounds sinister to me. I can't articulate what it is or why without sounding completely irrational, so I say nothing. I've dismissed so many that I'm reaching the point where I'll eventually have to give in. If this one means so very much to him, it may as well be now.

I have tried to make Tom understand my feelings about a move but a problem I find with being me is that it's sometimes difficult to have my opinion truly acknowledged, particularly where emotions are involved. I have calmly and carefully explained my reservations, which are then gently set aside. They're dismissed either as manifestations of my resistance to change, or as no more than my feelings of anxiety over the unknown.

I think I've been too honest with Tom, if there is such a thing. I wanted him to go into our relationship with eyes wide open. I now think, on reflection, I should have held some things back. We all have inner thoughts and secret fears, the things we keep inside us hidden behind the face we present to the world, but I told Tom all, so tipped the balance in his favor. He thinks he knows my innermost workings. I just guess at his. He doesn't do it intentionally or unkindly, but he tends to accept my opinions only when it suits. When it doesn't, he uses my weaknesses to diminish them.

If I become angry, I'm overstimulated. If I tear the details up and scream and cry, I'll just be exhibiting an inappropriately impulsive response. So instead I keep quiet and go with the flow. Over this I needed him to look beyond my limitations and accept what I truly feel.

Tom and I have, until now, lived and worked in the city, our rooftop apartment light and airy with its views across London to the Thames. Although I seldom venture into the disorienting thrum and jostle of the streets, I do still feel part of a bigger humanity. I'll miss the noise, the vibrancy and the feeling it gives me that I belong somewhere. It's convenient for us but, and for me it's a big but, Tom has decided the time has come for change. He wants to move out of the city, to a "delightful and sought-after rural location" where he can put down roots. Where he can breathe the air, grow things—presumably with more roots—and literally expand his horizons. The house in Cleaver's Lane is the answer to all his prayers and today we go to see it in the brick.

I've tried, really I have, but still I feel an apprehension disproportionate to the task ahead; after all we're only viewing a house. Maybe I do struggle to be the "executive of my life." Maybe certain life changes do "exceed my threshold," or maybe I've just spent too long listening to my doctors. Whatever the reason, I cannot shed the feeling that something is wrong, and I'm filled with a sense of foreboding. I'm resentful that this is being forced on me but feel I owe it to Tom to give it a chance. After all, as he sometimes gently reminds me, he's given up much to be with me. I suppose it's only fair I give up something in return.

The Cleaver's Lane brochure Tom's reading must be the new one he ordered. Once he thought it was *that* house, he had to know more. I haven't seen it before but can see it has more details, with pictures of the house's interior and its land.

"You've got to have a look at this kitchen Izzy, it's absolutely massive. It needs complete stripping out and reworking but it's big enough for an island in the middle and an Aga and for one of those big American-style fridges we've always wanted. Please at least have a look."

Tom passes me the brochure and I glance half-heartedly at the photo in front of me. I feel all the enthusiasm of a pensioner facing the prospect of snow.

Suddenly a low humming fills my head and a breaker of anxiety rolls through me, bringing in its wake a wash of nameless dread. I have the sensation that I'm no longer anchored in the present but am swirling backward through time. I've been there. I've seen this room. I can smell wood smoke and washing powder. I see tiles with carrots and onions and pepper-pot motifs, the dirt in the grout, a feeling of coldness and grit against my face.

It's a split second before the feeling passes and Tom is by my side. My teeth are chattering wildly and we look at the milk jug smashed at my feet. A tiny shard of china has speared my ankle and a trickle of bright blood runs to the floor.

"Izzy, Izzy! What is it, what's wrong?"

Tom's face is close to mine and for a moment I want to lash out at him, arms wheeling and flailing, fighting for my life. The feeling instantly passes and I let him lead me to a chair.

"No, no I'm fine; it's just that I. . ."

As I start to explain the words leave me. I can't remember what just happened or what I felt. All I feel is breathless—shaken and disoriented.

"I'm all right. Just dizzy for a moment, that's all. It's okay, don't fuss, I'll be fine in a minute."

I realize I'm still holding the brochure and I look at the picture. It's a tired kitchen, dark oak doors and dated tiles. Despite how much Tom loves it and how unique it is, I find I'm still crossing my fingers. It's definitely a project for someone, I just hope it's not one for us.

Tom fetches me a drink and I take his hand, his palm warm against my cold one.

"I'm not ill, before you start. It wasn't a seizure or anything, that's all in the past so please don't worry. I've got a headache, that's all, and I just felt dizzy. I need a plaster for my leg but otherwise I'm okay."

He goes through to the bathroom and I close my eyes and take a deep breath. I cannot have another seizure, that hasn't happened for at least four years and I've finally got a driving license. I may not often use it but I can't bear the thought of losing it or the illusion of freedom it gives me.

Tom comes back with a Band-Aid and some antiseptic and gently cleans the blood from my ankle. I lay my hand on his head and feel the softness of his hair under my fingers.

"Tom, I'm going back to bed for a bit if that's okay." My head is starting to pound now, and I really do feel sick. "Can we skip lunch? I need to take something for my head and sleep for an hour or two, otherwise I'll be good for nothing this afternoon."

He leans forward and drops a kiss on the scar at my temple.

"Of course we can; I've got some work to catch up on anyway so we can go over there later. Go on up to bed and shout if you need anything."

I hate it when he does that. There's lots of other places he could kiss me, all of which would be preferable. He doesn't realize it but each time he does it it's like a reminder of what happened to me, a reminder that I'm damaged goods.

My damage happened long ago. I was just fourteen when I was hit on the head and at least seventeen before my faculties were sufficiently restored that I would attempt to eat soup again in polite company. They found me on a sun-gilded afternoon, cracked like a hapless egg, with the secret substance of me obscenely oozing into the light.

There was apparently little evidence of a struggle but I have struggled since. I have fought and clawed, tooth and nail, to bring myself back, to be the person I am today.

I wasn't to blame. I wasn't careless with my cranium. I just happened to be in the wrong place at the wrong time, my little life colliding with someone else's madness. Some people have told me I was lucky—although I struggle with their definition—and that it could've been much worse. I could now be no more than a distant memory, a ghost occasionally troubling the minds of those that once knew me. I am of course thankful that's not the case but can't help wondering what I might have been had the events of that summer not taken place, for something, if not my life, was taken from me.

The girl who woke up in that hospital bed was not the same one who violently fell asleep, so many days before. That girl was cocky and confident, with the naivete of youth. A mixture of innocence and attitude, ready to shrug off the constraints of childhood and sail out into the world. The girl who emerged was changed; scared and vulnerable, confused and crazy, a mixture of anger and apathy cast adrift. No pearl in the world's oyster for her.

Time has healed, as the saying goes, but not completely for I am nowhere near the woman I was meant to be. I feel as if I've been two people, the me before and the me now. It's as though some part of me escaped through the hole in my head; a wisp of the essence of me floating away across the playing fields never to return. I can't put a name to what was lost yet some days I feel its absence like a missing piece of jigsaw—not a significant detail but perhaps a piece of the sky.

Even now, more than twenty years later, the events surrounding the incident remain stubbornly out of reach to me, an impenetrable blackness which time has done nothing to disperse. A deep dark hole lurks in my memory lane, which none of the therapies I've subjected myself to over the years have been able to patch and mend. I've long relinquished any real hope of knowing what happened to me or why.

My recovery, or improvement as the professionals prefer, while spectacular was not complete, and I carry with me the residual effects. At first glance I appear relatively unscathed physically but I have quirks of personality and behaviour that make me different and that have, despite my best efforts, dictated the course of my life.

If how I am now was the result of an accident I might find it easier to accept. Instead I am sometimes suffused with rage, a seething hatred that I must tamp down and set aside for no good can come of it. I could spend my life searching and wondering and obsessing about the who and the why, with the awareness of it running on an endless spool in my mind. But this would change nothing. All it would do is allow my attacker to take even more of me so, hard though it has been, I have learned to at least fake acceptance.

Thankfully Tom accepts my past, and the limitations it brings, with gentle solicitude. We don't have children and, while there is theoretically no reason why women who have suffered traumatic brain injury can't conceive, it's more difficult for us so I know I may never bear fruit. The doctor spelled it out to "manage our expectations." Irregular menses, post-partum difficulties, the "cognitive demands" of rearing a child. I swear I felt my ovaries shriveling. While Tom claims not to mind, that his life is full and he's happy, I see him looking and know his longing runs deep. His mother has helped of course; I found the link she sent me, "11 Trying to Conceive Tips the Experts Want You To Know"—and yes, there were that many capitals—particularly uplifting. Tom hopes that a change of scene, and a home we can "all" grow into, will kick my reproductive system into action. I hope so too, for the strain of this is beginning to take its toll.

I work. I am an artist, or perhaps more accurately a jobbing painter, which suits me fine as I can work from home and shut myself away from the world when I need to or want to. My paintings are abstract and have been variously described as visceral, uninhibited and thought-provoking whereas the truth is that my style is more the product of my physical limitations. I have twitches and tremors that tend to place hyperrealism firmly outside the scope of my capabilities.

My painting enjoys moderate success, no doubt in part due to my history, which Caitlin, my gallerist and agent, insists I use to my advantage. Her view is that anything positive I can pull from my experience is fair game. I feel uneasy with this approach, as though I am exploiting something vaguely unsavory but then, what do I know. I put aside such sensibilities and queasily play the victim.

"The Victim," sometimes I wonder if that's how Tom sees me.

It's noon. I'm hot and sleep-befuddled. The sheets are twisted and clinging to my skin but the pain in my head has gone. I feel better than I did earlier and can't really recall what was so wrong. I go through to the bathroom and turn on the shower, standing in front of the mirror as I wait for it to run warm. Gray eyes look steadily back at me or at least one does, the other one only pretends. The skin either side is showing the faint beginnings of crow's-feet and what once was smooth is now marked by their tiny patterings. I of all people can hardly lay claim to them as laughter lines. Otherwise my olive skin, courtesy of my father, is pulled tight over high cheekbones and a strong jaw, marred only by the scar showing its puckered edges from beneath my fringe. My hair needs trimming. It's still dark and I keep it long to my shoulders, swept to the side to obscure my scar and distract from my sightless eye. It is a capable face and it frustrates me that I can't always live up to what it offers.

After my shower I dress, pulling on jeans and a white T-shirt. I'm losing weight again. My hip bones stand out hard and knobbly under the skin and my legs are becoming those of a child.

I go down to the kitchen to find Tom has been busy in my absence packing the picnic basket, which is ready on the side.

"Hey, you feeling better? I thought it would be nicer not to bother with a pub if that's okay with you but to have a late lunch in the garden if we can. It should be warm enough, and it might give us a chance to get a feel for the place."

It sounds like a nice idea, so I add a bottle of prosecco from the fridge.

Tom shakes his head. "Really? Given how you were this morning, shouldn't you give that a miss today? I know you've been fine, but we don't want to push things if you're having headaches again."

He moves to take the bottle from my hand and I feel a sudden spurt of irritation, hot and bitter.

"Tom, please don't, I'm not a child," and I place the bottle firmly next to the basket. "If we're going to do this then we should make a day of it." The sun is shining and the idea of a proper picnic under the trees suddenly appeals. I imagine lying next to him on the grass looking up at the leaves, with the fizz and pop of bubbles on my tongue and suddenly I'm inexplicably happy. I don't know why I've been finding this so difficult. Maybe the countryside is just what we need. A house and a garden with perhaps a studio, looking out across fields. I wrap my arms around him and lay my head between his shoulder blades, feeling the heat radiating from his back.

"Let's go and see this place that's got you so excited."

He turns and smiles at me, his eyes crinkling up in that familiar way and I push aside the last vestiges of doubt.

2

MAY 2004

*"But all was false and hollow; though his tongue
dropped manna"*
— Milton, *Paradise Lost,* Book ii

She was just what he'd been waiting for. The first time he'd seen her, booking in at reception, he'd known she was his.

He checked no one was watching and bent forward. Quickly, like a snake, he flicked out his tongue and ran it across the door handle where her hand had been. He was sure he could feel the molecules of her dancing on his tongue. Her DNA mingling with his saliva. He swallowed. Now he owned a little something of her and the thought made him feel stronger, more alive.

He'd watched her this time. He'd seen her lips gently parting to reveal her inner pinkness, all dark and secret. He'd imagined the plump softness of them and the slippery moistness of her mouth against his tongue.

He closed his eyes and still she shimmered, bright against the sooty blackness of his lids. God, she was glorious and the very thought of her was more than he could bear.

He slid from the doorway and into the corridor, shielding his tumescence from prying eyes. He must find out more, who she was and where she lived, and what she did and where she went. His mind ticked like a bomb, ticktock, her time running out.

He'd slipped out and followed her for a while, until she met up with those simpering bitches. Girls with coarse dark hair and shrill voices, with their pushed-up tits and mottled thighs. Not like her. She was golden and perfect, a firefly luring him and pretending not to know it.

She'd made him angry, laughing with them. It cheapened her. It made her lose some of her glow and he needed her in all her shimmering perfection.

He'd stood at the bus stop burning with rage and his civilized veneer had slipped, just for a moment. He'd turned as a woman joined the queue and for a second their eyes had met. He'd felt her instinctively recoil and move away from him, for she'd glimpsed behind his mask and had sensed what he was; she'd felt the thing living deep within him. Oh, if they only knew. His body was a carapace with the real him curled up inside it, looking out at the world from behind the wet bulges of its eyes. He rarely let the mask slip but when it did, when they saw him and he smelled their fear, it was sublime.

He wandered through to reception to look up her details but that old cow was back behind the desk. Maybe later. He fixed his most charming smile in place and strolled over, no harm in a bit of practice. He had learned early on that life was much easier if people liked you. If they trusted you and you were clever, you could make them do whatever you wanted. He'd studied his father with his clients, the way he put them at ease, made them feel comfortable and safe. He'd watched for the facial expressions, the tone of voice and the words that conveyed empathy.

He leaned across the desk. "Afternoon, Mrs. C. Heard you'd been off; you feeling better? You certainly look good today."

Mrs. Kerr looked up from her screen and blushed. "Oh, hello, I didn't realize you were there. I'm fine love, it was just a bit of a cold, that's all. You're sweet to ask though."

She smiled up at him and he caught the faint scent of lavender talcum. He smiled back, gifting her with the full wattage, while inwardly shuddering to imagine what frowsty crevices she'd been dusting. If his mother survived, which was unlikely, she would eventually be like this. Old and ugly and useless and stupid, even more repellent than she was at the moment with her scraggy hairless scalp and her wigs.

"I was just making some tea Mrs. C, do you want one?"

It was his private joke, calling her Mrs. C. She'd once laughed and told him it was Kerr with a "K" and he'd almost said, "Whatever made you think the C was for Kerr you old. . ." but stopped himself just in time.

Thinking about it, perhaps he should call his mother the Big C. God he was funny.

Perhaps this could be his golden girl's consolation; she would never have to get old or ill but could stay young forever.

3

"Houses are like people—some you like and some you don't"
—L. M. Montgomery, *Emily Climbs*

We are nearly there. The countryside rolls endlessly by, a blur of green monotony, and my good intentions of earlier roll away with it. No matter how hard I try, how much I rationalize, my apprehension mounts with each passing mile. Tom is oblivious. I glance sideways to see him smiling to himself, fingers drumming on the wheel to a soundless song and I spitefully imagine something bucolic. Probably involving cows and combine harvesters.

I hadn't realized quite how close we are to the county border. Thorpwood House, if it still exists, is just beyond the hills, no more than a handful of miles away. Thorpwood House, my alma mater, that place where I was last truly me. The landscape feels familiar to me like an echo of the past reverberating with each beat of my heart.

I struggle with traveling, my anxiety increasing the farther we get from home and the greater the distance from the places I know. My therapist has told me it could be my damaged brain becoming overloaded by new stimuli, or it could be post-traumatic stress disorder. A need to feel in control of my environment, to have the security of familiar surroundings and to feel safe. Whatever the reason I must always fight it lest I allow the boundaries of our lives to shrink still further. I have good days and bad but many of the things that others take for granted, like a weekend away or a holiday, are for me a challenge. This is what makes me angry, with myself for allowing it to be so and with my attacker for stealing away that piece of mind. Before him I would do anything, go anywhere without a thought of danger or consequences. The lack of any parental input had allowed me to be reckless, wild even, but not now. The teenage me would roll her eyes in that way she had and cringe with embarrassment at what she became.

My parents were in New York at the time of my attack, attending to one of my father's business interests. They flew back immediately of course and spent the next few weeks and months at my bedside, each as ineffectual as the other in their own way.

My mother was, and still is in her own mind, a budding starlet of the seventies who spent most of her formative years clinging to the hope of fame by the skin of her frosty-pink fingertips. Her main claims to that fickle mistress include a bit part in *The Spy Who Loved Me* and on occasion being at the same parties as such celebrities of the time as Michael York and Susan George. Unfortunately, she wasn't destined for cinematic greatness and by the time she was twenty-four she had met, married and fallen pregnant by my father—not necessarily in that order. At the time of "my accident," as she euphemistically insisted on calling it, she was thirty-eight and while still attractive was more "mumsy" than she cared to acknowledge. My father's wealth allowed her to concentrate her time exclusively on languid inactivity and on holding back the physical ravages of time, both of which she was rapidly making her life's work. Parenthood had never come easily to her; she approached it as a rather tedious part for which she hadn't quite mastered the lines, and I've always felt the idea of a child appealed to her much more than the inconvenient reality. The realization of what she'd done had sunk in almost before my umbilicus was healed and I was bundled off to Thorpwood House as soon as was decent. The long trips my parents took abroad providing both the reason and the conscience salve. My hazy recollections of her in the weeks following the attack involve much dramatic sighing and weeping, interspersed with peevish demands that the nursing staff fetch iced water—for her of course, not me.

As for my poor father, the strain almost broke him. He found the only way he could hold things together was to fuck his secretary hard and often, a cliché that could conveniently be relied upon to help him forget the various misfortunes life placed in his way.

I have always felt ambivalent about my father; on one hand I have craved his love but on the other despised him for his obvious shallowness and belligerent masculinity. He is not an attractive man. Too swarthy and hirsute to meet any traditional requirement for handsomeness but he does have the power money conveys, coupled with a certain lupine quality that some women find alluring. Personally, I find him rather repellent and fail to imagine what young and ostensibly intelligent women found so irresistible that they would succumb to his hairy advances. He did eventually marry this inamorata and went on to produce beautiful twin girls, a replacement for me plus a handy spare, of whom I'm surprisingly quite fond.

On my release from hospital I was transferred initially to a rehab unit and eventually into dear mummy's reluctant care, by which time my father had moved out of the family home. My mother had, in some perverse way, come to blame me for my father's leaving and it began to feel as though I had deliberately gone to the effort of having my skull bashed in just to ruin her life. The fact that I could remember nothing of the incident further frustrated her. It made her view me with frank suspicion as though I had perhaps made the whole thing up as an extreme form of attention seeking. It was a relief to us both when I was deemed well enough to live independently.

I now have little contact with either parent although I do occasionally see my father when I meet up with my half sisters. The passing years have not been kind to him. His graying hair, coupled with the certain guilty shiftiness he exhibits when he sees me, have accentuated his wolfishness such that on the rare occasions when he has visited my home I've been seized by the sudden urge to check he hasn't eaten one of our cats or pissed on the furniture.

My contact with my mother is limited to the occasional stilted telephone call, usually initiated by me and driven more by an urge to irritate her than by any filial affection. My favorite ploy is to feign concern over her drinking habits, always guaranteed to provoke the desired reaction and cheer me up at least a little.

I drag myself back to the present; that's all in the past and I need to let it go. Instead I concentrate on the view from the window and see that finally we've arrived.

We turn into Cleaver's Lane, flanked on one side by fields and the other by dense woodland. The trees arch over the road, unfurling their leaves toward the light. The property is on the right, with rusted gates opening onto a gravel carriageway between the trees. "The Lodge," incongruously painted directly onto the gatepost, removes any element of doubt that we're at our destination.

"It *is* the same house, I'm sure of it," Tom says.

His awestruck tone makes me want to slap him. My bad.

The driveway opens out onto an expanse of neglected lawn and directly in front of us is the house. It's a Victorian villa with red brick elevations beneath a tiled roof. Despite my reservations I have to admit it is an attractive house, mellow and welcoming in the afternoon sun.

A car is parked on the gravel and as we pull up, the agent from Stratton and Keep gets out to greet us. He's a tall thin man with an exceptionally high forehead and comedic teeth. He introduces himself as Kevin Gaines and proceeds to enthusiastically pump Tom's hand all the way to the front door.

"So glad you've made it, hope it wasn't too difficult to find. This really is an absolute gem, been empty for a while but the old boy has finally had to sell up. You're the first to see it and lucky I'd say, as I'm pretty sure it'll be snapped up."

I try to catch Tom's eye but my amusement in the moment is gone as I see the expression on his face. He is spellbound and I start to understand he will stop at nothing to own this place.

Mr. Gaines turns to shake my hand. "You must be Mrs. Dryland, so pleased to meet you."

His hand is cold and clammy against my skin and I resist the urge to pull mine away and rub it frantically against my jeans. There was a time when I would've done, with scant regard for politeness or social nicety, probably shouting "Clammy!" a couple of times for good measure. I've come a long way since then; now I smile and make do with a surreptitious wipe.

"I'm Isabel, Isabel Dryland-Weir."

I have retained my maiden name, in part for professional reasons but also to hold on to my identity. If you lose yourself as I once did, you feel the need to grasp more tightly to the newfound you.

The front door opens onto a narrow entrance hall with dark floor-boards and a faded runner leading up the wide staircase. The earthy smell of mildew and neglect seeps from the walls, mingled with an undertone of wood smoke. For a moment I feel a fleeting sense of déjà vu that passes as quickly as it came.

Two doors open immediately off the hallway. To the left there's a dining room carpeted in a mossy green. There's a fire still laid in the grate as though waiting for the owner's return, the logs now silvered with cobwebs and dust. The walls are papered; striped in burgundy, cream and a dusty verdigris that was probably once gold. The paper is lifting at the edges, curling back to expose the flesh-pink plaster beneath, like a wound.

To the right is a sitting room, which extends into a later addition to the property, giving dual aspect to the garden and grounds. Some furniture remains and faded curtains hang from fringed pelmets. A desiccated houseplant of unknown provenance sits browning on the windowsill, its leaves turned toward the glass as though reaching in desperation for the sunlight and moisture beyond. Its partner, a parched chlorophytum, listlessly dangles its spidery babies over the sill in the vain hope they'll find water. Although it's hard to ignore the melancholy air of neglect, I like the feel of this room and the play of the light through the dual windows. For the first time I glimpse the possibilities of what I could do with a house like this.

Tom is deep in conversation with his new friend Kevin, animatedly discussing renovation options, and I follow them through the dining room into the kitchen. I don't like the kitchen at all. It makes me feel disoriented and trapped. I need air. I go to the back door and fumble with the latch. It won't open.

"Steady on Mrs. Dryland, it's locked. Here, I've got the key."

Gaines unlocks the door and I stumble into the garden. Tom appears not to have noticed my distress. I feel irritated both with myself and with him. I occasionally get panicked in unfamiliar places and though it is another thing that frustrates me, I seem unable to control it. Tom is usually sensitive to this, sometimes annoyingly so, but today he is preoccupied, wrapped up in his desire for this house.

I take several deep breaths and compose myself before returning to the kitchen and its air of oppressiveness and neglect.

Kevin Gaines looks quizzically at me but says nothing, instead continuing his conversation with Tom. The house is apparently owned by a retired clinician, a widower with dementia who now lives in sheltered accommodation. His daughter has power of attorney and it's she who's handling the sale. I switch off, concentrating instead on the view from the window, so many trees and the impression of nothing for miles. It's so unlike home.

Tom is talking to me. "I love it," he says, "we could really put our stamp on it, make it a home. We probably won't get another chance to find anything like this. What do you think Iz?"

I certainly have the urge to stamp on something, but I don't have the heart or the energy to quash his enthusiasm. I say nothing.

We continue our guided tour of the property to the soundtrack of Kevin's sales patter. Downstairs the remaining rooms are pleasant, if unremarkable. There's a study, a larder cum storeroom, a cloakroom and upstairs four "exceptionally spacious" bedrooms and two bathrooms. Above it all is an attic "with options to convert" but to which there's currently no means of access.

Tom desperately wants to see the grounds. There's close to four acres in all, which is mind-blowing compared to where we live now—unless you consider the numerous parks and the communal green space we share with our neighbors. He bounds out the door with such exuberance I half expect Kevin to throw him a stick or a ball.

I have taken against Mr. Gaines and it isn't just the unfortunate dentition. I find him overly chummy and patronizing with Tom and dismissive of me, so I'm glad when he asks if we'd like to "do the outside" on our own.

"I have another viewing to do, so if you're okay on your own I'll just lock up and leave you guys to it."

He self-importantly locks up the house, testing the locks and patting his pockets a few times before making his way to his car. I watch him drive away with some relief. My threshold for irritation can be low.

The "outside" is spectacular, I can't deny it. To think we might actually afford all this. At the rear there is garden laid to lawn, with trees and shrubbery. Weed-strewn flowerbeds and a sundial covered in moss and lichen. There's a vegetable patch and beyond that a paddock and what was once a tennis court. There's also an orchard and woodland—everything so dazzlingly green and overgrown but somehow the better for it. There is a beauty in this place that touches the artist in me, a thousand shades from viridian to chartreuse. But there is also the potential for darkness, for how many would-be attackers could such leafy covert conceal?

I shrug the thought away and despite myself can feel the pull of this place. It's a mixture of attraction and repulsion. We fetch the picnic basket from the car and settle under the trees in the orchard.

Tom is asleep. The drive, the heat and the wine have conspired against him. I'm happy being alone with my thoughts. This garden has the power to lull and soothe and I think I could grow to love it. The air is heavy with the sounds of the budding summer. The sawing of grasshoppers, the drone of bees drunk on nectar, lazily bouncing from flower to flower. I've hardly touched my wine, but still my eyelids begin to droop, the sun a red haze behind them, and sleep steals over me.

When I wake I find the picnic blanket has been wrapped around me and Tom is nowhere to be seen. The afternoon is on the tipping point of evening, the sun dipping below the trees and dew gathering on the grass. There's a chill in the air. I shiver and sit up, wrapping the blanket more tightly around my shoulders. I was having the oddest dream. The memory of it is still there like an itch in my brain but it fades away as quickly as I try to grab hold of it.

I feel lost and for a moment have the irrational feeling that Tom has driven away and left me here. It's unlike him to wander off and leave me alone in a strange place.

The sky is darkening and I look back at the house. The windows glow orange in the setting sun so for a moment it looks as though it's on fire. Its welcome demeanor of earlier has vanished. There's no sign of Tom at all, he must have headed in the other direction through the orchard to the paddock and woods. I leave our picnic stuff and pick my way through the trees, following a trail of recently trodden grass.

The orchard suddenly ends, and I come out into a clearing at the edge of woodland. The air seems heavier here somehow and the sound of birdsong has faded with the approaching dusk.

A building stands in the clearing overshadowed by the backdrop of trees. Pitch-roofed and imposing, it appears to be a workshop. Red brick and tile like the main house. Double wooden doors to the front, their surface bleached and cracked by time. These are barred and tightly padlocked, as is the smaller door to the side, and both look as though it's been many years since either was in use. The arched window is obscured by something on the inside, so I walk round to the back of the building where there's an annex of sorts, also with a window high up beneath a flat roof. I stand on tiptoe to look inside and for a split second a face looks back at me, pale features and a cloud of yellow hair. I involuntarily start and step back, the beginnings of a cry forming in my throat before I realize it's nothing more than my reflection against the blacked-out glass, the blond hair just a trick of the dying light.

At that moment there's a rustling and Tom appears through the trees.

"Hello you," he says. "Sorry I left you for a bit, but you were fast asleep and after this morning's headache I didn't want to wake you up. Don't you think this is amazing?"

He threads his fingers through mine and we look at the workshop. I can feel his excitement like a tangible force. He looks so happy I know I can't deny him this. Yes, it's been a bit tense recently but that's only because of the baby thing. Maybe he's right, maybe we can settle here and things will just happen. I allow myself the fleeting thought of a child, our child, running to us across the lawn. I so want to give him that, for I love this man with all my heart. I'm sure I do.

"Izzy, do you realize this has got its own driveway? A completely separate track off the lane that runs down the side. This would make an unbelievable studio for you if we converted it. I know it's a bit dark with all the trees but we could make one side floor to ceiling glass and add a skylight or something. You could store all your canvases and stuff out here and have an office. It's what you've always said you needed. I know you think you don't want to leave London but just imagine what we could do with this."

He squeezes my hand and smiles at me. "Please, just let me do this for you."

"I know," I say, "it is lovely, but it just feels so, I don't know, sad somehow."

"It won't be once we've finished with it."

He smiles and I note his choice of words. It would seem our moving here has already been decided. Somehow, I don't seem to mind. I know when I'm beaten, and this place has certainly won the first round.

I try to ignore the sense of foreboding that sweeps over me as we make our way back to our picnic spot and onward to the car.

4

JULY 2004

"I did not know what she suffered from, but I
knew that her malady must have been horrible"
—Octave Mirbeau, *Le Calvaire*

H is parents were going away for a few months, doing their bucket list while she was still strong enough.

His mother placed her hand on his arm. He hated being touched unless it was on his terms. He looked pointedly at her clawlike fingers, the nails a faint violet, the papery skin translucent and dry.

"We'll pay the rent on your flat while we're away, so don't worry about that," she said. "It'll just take a weight off our minds knowing you're in the house. I couldn't bear the thought of coming back to find something had happened, not on top of everything else. We would've asked your sister but it's difficult for her with the baby.'

She saw him looking at her hand and two faint spots of color appeared on her cheeks. She rarely touched him, not since he was a boy, and she seldom made eye contact. If she did, her eyes slid quickly away to fix on something just over his shoulder. He suspected she was a little afraid of him, but he never pushed it. He always played the doting son. Occasionally long-suffering or a bit reluctant, because you had to keep it plausible, but generally he was The Good Son. He gritted his teeth and patted her hand, a little bit harder than was necessary, and felt her stiffen at his touch. That'd serve her right putting her diseased paw on him.

"Don't worry about anything, Mum. Of course I'll stay here and look after things. You just go and enjoy yourselves. Look, it really isn't any trouble—it'll actually be nice to be back in the old house again."

He pondered the exciting opportunities this would present. It was remote enough for his purposes but not so remote as to cause him difficulties traveling with her. He needed to be patient and plan things down to the last detail. Unbidden memories of his past mistake surfaced and he quickly pushed them away. He'd been young and reckless back then and hadn't realized his capabilities.

It was time for his most ambitious project to date. He'd been watching her now for long enough to know where she went and when she was alone and had worked out how he would get her into the car without a struggle, willingly even. He didn't want her stressed, he needed her to love him, at least for a while.

While he was lost in these thoughts his mother watched him, her eyes sad beneath heavy lids. She felt entirely disconnected from the son she had borne. When he was a baby and a little boy she'd loved him unreservedly. He'd been her life, but as he got older she sensed something different about him, something that just wasn't right. He'd sometimes been cruel, to insects and occasionally to animals, and although she'd tried to dismiss it as just a phase he was going through, she knew in her heart it was more than that.

As he grew she'd begun to feel uneasy being alone with him, even avoided it as much as she could, and then felt so guilty because surely that was a terrible thing for a mother to feel.

Now that she was approaching what was probably the end of her life, she worried about him more than ever. What could he be capable of, or what might he have done. It was nothing she could put her finger on, and she had no evidence, but despite his charm and his acts of kindness she felt a chill in the air when he was around her. A sense of creeping malevolence.

Richard came in with the coffee. It had been a while since he'd seen his father and in the interim he'd shriveled and aged. His once healthy complexion looked sallow and there were crevices of worry around his eyes. He'd been a big man but his wife's illness had diminished him. He seemed shrunken now and drawn in on himself.

He observed this change in his father with detached interest. He was intrigued to see how one person's illness could make another healthy person look so ill. He knew his father loved his mother and if this was what love did to you he was glad it was a weakness he didn't need or feel. It was pathetic and demonstrated just how far beyond his parents he'd evolved.

His father's hand shook slightly as he passed him the coffee. "Here you are Son, strong no sugar, hope that's still how you take it."

He was tempted to say he now took two sugars just to wind his father up—God, those childhood lectures—but he didn't have time to waste on small pettiness.

"Thanks Dad," he said, "that's fine."

His father perched on the edge of the sofa next to his wife and took her hand.

"Mum and I'll be flying out on the Sunday. It's an early flight so if you want to pop over Saturday for the keys and to say goodbye that'd be nice or if you can't, you can take the keys now."

His father's eyes flickered upward to meet his and there it was. That fleeting look of speculation, of suspicion tinged with dread. Just what was it that his father suspected him of, what was the thing that had lain unspoken between them for all those years? He smiled to himself. He thought he knew but he also knew the old man would never have the guts to voice it. If he hadn't by now then he never would.

"Sorry Dad," he said, "I've got something else to do on Saturday so won't be able to. If it's okay with you I'll say goodbye and take them while I'm here."

A glorious plan was forming, one worthy of his genius. He smiled, feeling so uncharacteristically benevolent that he deigned to hug his mother goodbye. Her bones were frail like a bird's and he wondered for a moment what his father would do if he suddenly crushed her until they splintered like twigs.

5

"Love does not dominate; it cultivates"
—Johann Wolfgang von Goethe

Today we have moved in and the last of our things are being unloaded from the removal van. Our cats, Major and Mina, glare balefully from their box in the hall and I fear my expression mirrors theirs. The Lodge is now our home.

The last few weeks have been difficult. Initially after the viewing I allowed Tom's enthusiasm to infect me—until the old doubts began to creep back in. I loved my old home with its proximity to the gallery and to my few good friends, but this quickly became irrelevant. I have never known Tom to show such disregard for my feelings as he has over the past few weeks. Perhaps he's never wanted anything quite as much as this.

When I come to think about it, he's never really been challenged in all the time we've been together. There's never before been a time when we've disagreed over anything so important, not because I'm passive by nature—far from it—it's more because the boundaries of my life have tended to be so restricted there's been little to take issue over. Maybe with hindsight I should've been more assertive just to maintain my place in things.

It sounds disloyal but I've sometimes suspected Tom thrives on my vulnerability, that it allows him to be in control without being perceived as controlling.

Tom and I first met in 2011 at an open art exhibition. I was showing a collection of winter landscapes, abstract studies in a palette of whites, purples and grays. Tom was early for a meeting and only came in to kill some time. I was taking a break and he found me in the corridor sitting on the stairs. The chatter and the lights were beginning to overload me. There were too many signals to process, so I'd gone in search of a few moments of peace and quiet. I'd also stopped drinking at the time and the chink and fizz of champagne glasses was becoming unbearable.

"God, are these people always that pretentious?" he said, leaning against the wall at the foot of the stairs.

I wasn't in the mood for company so chose to ignore him but he persisted.

"Most of it seems a bit emperor's new clothes to me, unless I'm missing something. I suppose I don't mind the snowy ones, if that's what they're meant to be, at least they're interesting."

Obviously not an art critic. I couldn't help but enjoy a certain short-lived satisfaction before he went on to say, "Bit pricey though. How anyone can ask that for just slapping a bit of paint on a canvas I don't know."

I looked at him properly for the first time. I registered that he was tall and nice looking in an understated sort of way. He had the most striking eyes, a pale brown, almost amber. His suit was well cut, expensive without being ostentatious and he wore nice shoes. I wasn't past noticing such things.

I snapped. "So, I suppose from that you work for nothing doing something worthy for the good of mankind? You must struggle to afford those shoes."

He laughed, "I'm sorry, I must sound a complete prick. I'm actually on my way to a meeting and I'm really not looking forward to it, it's obviously affecting my usually charismatic personality."

I saw him glance with sudden interest at the scar at my temple and the slight mistiness in my left eye.

"Are you Isabel Weir? I was just reading your bio. So, they're your paintings. God, you must think me terribly rude."

I felt the familiar embarrassment at Caitlin's promotional efforts, but he looked so genuinely contrite I couldn't help but smile and soon, against my better judgment, we were chatting as though we'd known each other forever. I'm okay when I'm one to one, it's crowds that get me confused and aphasic. Often what's on the inside feels clever and articulate but what comes out isn't so much.

He eventually asked me if I fancied meeting up for a meal and, although I tended to be wary of new encounters, I said yes, and we went out the following Saturday to a trendy Italian restaurant in Soho. He was amusing in a gentle self-effacing kind of way and seemed genuine. He asked me a lot about what had happened to me and how it affected me and my life, but not in a creepy or gratuitous way. Not like some of the boys at college who only asked me out because they'd heard stories, albeit most of them wildly inaccurate, about what had happened to me—and that I'd sleep with anyone after a few drinks.

The latter had an element of truth and was partly why I'd stopped drinking, that and the fact it was damaging my recovery. I'm not exactly ashamed of anything I did, I look at it objectively and mainly I just feel sorry for the girl I was back then. Most teenagers are learning how to make and break relationships, how to be and how to feel, how to forge the friendships that last into adulthood. I spent my teenage years relearning how to control my limbs and to speak coherently. Finding a way to live in the world again as the new and unimproved me. Yes, by the time I was at college I was sufficiently recovered to function practically but emotionally I was little more than a fourteen-year-old living in a twentysomething's body. That coupled with my residual boundary issues and tendency toward impulsive and unin-hibited behavior was a recipe for disaster. I soon gained a reputation for being a bit "weird." I was lonely, isolated and afraid, and sought any short-lived comfort I could find. To say I slept with every boy at college would be an exaggeration, although I was certainly generous with my carnal favors. Of course, on reflection it may just be that I'm my father's daughter.

Tom and I saw more and more of each other and eventually he knew all there was to know about me. He had a knack of making me open up and talk about myself in a way I hadn't really done before. Nothing ever seemed to faze him. He was kind and understanding and didn't seem to mind if I was having a bad day and couldn't face something we'd planned. He made me feel safe, loved and accepted, so much so that I began to believe there was perhaps a normal future out there for me after all.

The only cloud on the horizon was Maria, my oldest and dearest friend, who seemed distrustful of Tom and fiercely protective of me.

Maria and I met at school when we were seven or eight and soon became inseparable. The minute I clapped eyes on her with her cloud of wild hair and her eyes with their glint of wickedness I knew she'd be a friend for life. Like me she was a full boarder. She'd lost her Italian mother when she was six and a half. Now there was just her and her father. In the words of the self-obsessed and pretentious girls we were back then he "simply adored her" but trying to balance the pressure of work with single parenthood had become increasingly difficult for him so, like me, she ended up spending a great deal of her time at Thorpwood House. We were soulmates, both olive skinned and dark haired and we would spend hours weaving a glittering future for ourselves, one full of glamor and adventure. We just knew we were destined to have lives more exciting and successful than our classmates, which just goes to show how wrong you can be. We'd live a star-spangled life together in New York or Paris, or somewhere equally exotic, with parties, money and men. It didn't happen for either of us but the grounding of my childish dreams was perhaps just a little bit harsher than hers.

Thorpwood House was not entirely the bastion of morality and learning the staff promoted and the parents so readily bought into.

By the time we were fourteen we were already the stuff of teachers' nightmares. Overprivileged and underdisciplined if I'm honest, with a total disregard for authority, all arch looks and smart mouthed comments. Bright and irreverent, we were rapidly becoming rebels, bunking off into the village to buy booze. Even once hitchhiking into the town.

It's funny: objectively I understand I was once that girl but can't imagine how it felt emotionally to be that confident, unfettered and free. I wonder what she would have been had she lived.

Of all my school friends Maria was the one who visited me in hospital, played my favorite music, talked to me for hours about everything and anything she felt might reach my unconscious mind.

"Isabella"—she always used the Italian form of my name—"please, you've got to wake up." Her hand cold and anxious in mine.

Sometimes even now I hear her voice in my dreams and find myself sitting bolt upright, wide awake, expecting to see her troubled face at my bedside.

Maria stoically continued to visit me in hospital and throughout my time in the rehab unit, and I would see her trying not to look shocked or cry as I drooled and twitched and mumbled my way through her visits. I was such good company.

I never returned to Thorpwood House and inevitably our lives took very different paths, but we always stayed in touch, making the effort to meet up as often as we could. By the time I met Tom she was already married to Stuart, an accountant, and was expecting their first baby. When I first told her about Tom she was instantly suspicious of him. Even after they'd met a few times she remained wary and said he seemed a bit too good to be true. Her comments hurt me, and though she would have vehemently denied it, I have always suspected she thought him too good to be with someone like me. I wonder whether she would have felt the same were I not as I am.

Eventually she came around, helped by the fact that Stuart and Tom became friends, and she was matron of honour at our wedding. When I look at the photos and see her with her mass of hair blowing in the breeze, smiling fit to burst, I know she was genuinely happy for me and I can forgive her fierce overprotectiveness. I am sad to leave Maria behind. She has promised we will still see each other as often as before but I know the distance will make things harder for us both.

The last few boxes are done and the removal van is pulling away down the drive. Tom has gone into the village to pick up something for supper. This is it; he has dragged me, not exactly kicking and screaming but with some definite reluctance, into a new chapter of my life. I'm left with the feeling I should have put up more of a fight but it seems I no longer know how to assert myself. Sometimes I feel as though I'm not really here at all.

I shut Major and Mina in the kitchen with a litter tray and some food. They're wild-eyed and restless and Mina starts to make a feral keening noise that's hard to bear. They're indoor cats anyway, because of where we lived, so I'm not sure why they're finding this enforced captivity quite so intolerable.

"Look," I say to them, "this is going to be so much nicer for you, so just put up with it for a week or so and then you can go outside and explore."

They eye me malevolently and I fear our special relationship has been irrevocably damaged. I do have some sympathy with them as I haven't yet dispelled my own aversion to this kitchen. God knows how we're going to eat.

6

"Farewell remorse! All good to me is lost; evil be thou my good"

—Milton, *Paradise Lost*

H e wiped the sweat from his eyes and stopped to catch his breath. Talk about a dead weight. He pulled off his T-shirt and used it to mop the droplets from his face and his chest. He ran his hand down the smooth contours of his body, lingering for a moment on his nipples. He loved his own perfection.

The last roll of insulation was unloaded, the last of the Thermalite blocks stacked. He originally wasn't going to bother with all this but better safe than sorry, particularly when this time he was taking things to fruition. There'd be no mistakes this time.

It had taken ten trips to different DIY outlets to get all he needed. Now it was finally done and it was definitely going to be worth it. He hadn't decided on the space he would need; would he go for functionality or would he consider comfort? It was hardly going to be a hotel suite but he didn't want to be a complete monster—at least not to start with. He pictured a secret boxed-in room, a snug little hideaway just for the two of them. He experienced a tremor of anticipation that was almost sexual.

He took a moment out to remember the girls back at uni. They'd all fancied him. He'd felt their hot hungry gazes, their animalistic longing. Sometimes he'd pick an ugly one just for the hell of it and treat her to his special smile. Sexual but not predatory, masculine but never aggressive. He'd spent a long time studying people, their body language, their expressions, and it had all paid off. He may not be like them, but he knew how they ticked.

He'd been so tempted to try it again, so tempted by the little blondes but he never had. He'd never forgotten though how good it had felt for that one life-changing moment. And now he would feel that again.

The cat was ready in its box. Poor old pussy, but once it had served its purpose he'd let it go. He had no interest in what animals could offer, not anymore.

Funny how things came full circle. His father had taken him to the animal sanctuary once in a misplaced attempt to teach him that "animals have feelings too." He'd seen the kittens mewling and peeing, the baby rabbits, the fledglings with skin like his mother's scalp, but he still couldn't see the point. They were weak and helpless and what could possibly be more worthless than that.

7

*"A photograph is a secret about a secret. The more
it tells you, the less you know"*

—Diane Arbus

I walk from empty room to empty room. In the time since we viewed
the house someone has been working hard. The rooms have been
cleared of furniture, the curtains taken down, the dust and the cobwebs swept away. All that remains are the carpets, softly releasing
their musty scent, and an exquisite writing desk in the sitting room
with a note taped to its glossy surface.

> *Hi, so sorry but we couldn't fit this one in the van and didn't
> want to damage it. I'll pop by either later today or tomorrow
> and collect it if that's okay. Sorry for any inconvenience, Gemma.*

I assume "Gemma" is Mrs. G. Maitland, who handled the sale on
behalf of her father—a Mr. Connor, I've since learned.

I run my hand across the desk's surface. The intricate map of the
walnut veneer is polished to a shine, smooth and cool as glass beneath
my fingertips. I ease open one of the drawers. Inside is a pile of old
photographs and a tiny lacquered box. Intrigued, I take out both
and sit on the floor. The first of the photos is of a wedding, from the
late 1960s from the style of the clothes. The groom, whom I assume
is Mr. Connor, is gazing in wonder at his stunning bride. In Tom's
words he's "batting well above his average." The same couple appear
again and again. On holiday, in the garden, proudly holding a baby

of indeterminate sex and later on with two small children. There's a sturdy little girl and a striking boy, with the family dog sitting at their side. The girl looks awkward and bored and I wonder if this is Gemma. In contrast, the boy is smiling and looking directly into the camera. He is beautiful like his mother but it is the ruddy-faced father who really catches my eye. There is something that feels vaguely familiar about his face that I can't quite put my finger on.

I turn my attention to the box. It's like a Japanese puzzle box and it isn't immediately obvious how it opens. I twist and turn and suddenly it comes apart and several small objects fall out onto the floor. As I reach to pick them up I recoil with horror. They are teeth. Five or six of them, their undersides browned with old blood. I scrabble back from where they've landed and as I do, I see they have no roots. I heave a sigh of relief. They're milk teeth, souvenirs of a beloved child and unsurprisingly not the trophies of a deranged killer. I am ashamed of my foolishness.

I tenderly pick up the teeth and return them to the satin lined box. I'm filled with an inexplicable sadness for the now-dead mother who kept them and for the children I may never have. The tears are a sudden hot surprise against my skin.

There is a knock at the door and I quickly gather up the photos and the box and put them back in the drawer. These are personal things and I feel guilty for the invasion of privacy. I dash the tears away and go through to the hall.

A woman is at the door, aged somewhere in her forties with an open and pleasant face.

"Hi, I'm Gemma, sorry to disturb you but did you see my note? I hope I'm not interrupting but I was sort of passing and thought I'd pick up the desk now and get it out of your way. Oh, and here's a card and a bottle of wine for you, hope you like white."

She smiles and in her face I think I see a memory of the little girl in the photo.

"Oh hi. No, not at all, that's absolutely fine and thank you for the wine, that's so kind of you, it's lovely. Please, come in."

She follows me through to the sitting room and there's a stilted moment of awkwardness where I feel as though it's her home and I'm the interloper.

I hold out my hand. "I'm Isabel. My husband, Tom, has just popped out but I'm sure I can help you get it out to the car. It's so beautiful, is it antique?"

Her handshake is warm and firm. I instantly like her. She has a calm capable manner about her, and I imagine her as maybe a nurse, kind and reassuring to her patients. In reality she's probably an erotic dancer, I never seem to be very good at judging other people.

"Ah thanks, it's for my father, I'm moving it up to Fairview for him. He's got dementia so it's important for him to have familiar things around him, especially things that hold memories, and he always loved my mother's desk."

"I'm sorry," I say, "that must be terribly difficult for you."

"It is pretty awful. Dad and I were close, particularly after my mother died." Her voice cracks and she clears her throat. "Some days he's still there and it's all fine, other times he just seems so lost. I hate it, particularly when he gets agitated about something and I can't help him."

I see her mentally shake herself, as though casting off the thought.

"Anyway, you don't want to hear about such depressing stuff when you've just moved into a new home." She looks directly into my face and smiles. "I really hope you'll be happy here. It was a wonderful place to grow up."

I'm still intrigued by the children in the photo so ask, "Was it just you or do you have brothers and sisters?"

Instantly a shadow crosses her face. She hesitates for just a second too long. "No, there's just me," she says.

I sense sadness and the hint of things unsaid. I wonder if I've inadvertently touched upon some family tragedy. My next words are carefully chosen to steer the subject away.

"We've obviously not had chance to meet anyone yet but do you know any of the neighbors, are they nice?"

She seems relieved at the change of topic.

"I don't really know them as it's been years since I lived here, and Dad tended to keep himself to himself latterly. To be honest he became a bit of a recluse when my mother got ill and he was even worse after she died. I think there's a young couple in Stour's Lane though—that's the one that runs down the side of here—they might be grateful for some new friends. My husband met the wife when we were clearing out the house. He said she seemed really nice. If you cut through the orchard and out by the old coach house you're in the lane. Their house is about half a mile along on the left."

"Oh, so that's what it is," I say. "I'd seen the building when we came for a look round and was thinking of converting it into a studio. I'll probably spend a lot of time alone there so it's nice to at least know there're some people nearby."

She looks slightly curious at this but doesn't comment.

"It's been locked up for as long as I can remember," she tells me. "My father used it as a workshop for a while, way back when we were kids. Then when my mother got ill he lost interest in things. No one's been down there for years. I didn't even think to check what's in there. It's probably full of old rubbish."

I tell her not to worry, we'll clear it out at some point and if we find anything valuable I'll let her know.

I offer her coffee as a courtesy, which she politely declines, and together we carry the desk out to her car. Luckily it's not too heavy and I can manage despite the weakness I have in my right arm. We agree to exchange mobile numbers just in case I have any queries, and I promise to text her if we find anything useful in the coach house.

I watch her drive away and return to the house. As I move to close the front door I have the fleeting sensation of breath at the back of my neck. I turn on a spike of panic but of course there's no one there.

8

AUGUST 2004

*"Innocence is a splendid thing, only it has the
misfortune not to keep very well and to be easily
misled"*

—Immanuel Kant

Rachel clipped her blonde hair back behind her ears and breathed in the sweet smell of meadow hay. She banged the lid firmly down on the bin of rabbit pellets and checked there were no strays on the floor. Mrs. Watson had seen rats and they didn't want them at the feed. Everything had to be stored, sealed or swept away. A single pellet, a grain of corn and you'd never, ever hear the end of it. Rachel closed her eyes; she loved the smell of the store. It had the same effect on her as freshly baked bread or newly mown grass. A warm comforting smell. She would miss all this when the summer was over.

Liam came into the storeroom and dumped a sack of carrots in the doorway. His lean frame momentarily blocked the slant of weak sunlight coming in through the door, casting a pool of dark shadow.

"Where do you want these, Rach? If you need 'em lifting you'd best give me a shout, they weigh a ton."

She liked Liam. Even though he'd only been helping at the sanctuary for a short while and was older than most of the others, she already counted him as a friend. Despite his age he didn't talk down to her and he was fun to work with. She could fancy him a bit if she thought about it but it wasn't really worth the effort. He was way too old for her. It was also a tiny bit odd that he was there. She suspected community service or something if she was honest.

"It's okay Liam, just dump them by the hay. Mrs. Watson's going to reorganize everything anyway because apparently we've got rats again."

Liam set down the sack and leaned against the doorpost watching her.

"You nearly finished, cause we could walk back into town together if you like?"

She was a pretty girl and she had a way about her that was older than her years. Innocent but not. He sometimes had to remind himself she was only sixteen or maybe seventeen. Pity, if she was just a few years older he might've given it a go.

"No, I'm staying on for a bit but there's no need for you to wait, I'm okay walking back on my own. I won't be much longer anyway. I've got to finish the rabbits and do their waters, then I'm pretty much done."

Rachel didn't mind walking home alone, she was usually finished well before it was dark in the summer and most of the journey was through the estate. It was only the first stretch past the industrial units that she didn't much like. Recently it'd started to creep her out, giving her the feeling that someone was watching.

He had picked his position carefully, just at the point where he was out of the view of any houses but not far enough around the bend that he could be seen from the other end. The units were deserted as was usual at this time, the car parks windswept and desolate. He'd already checked for CCTV and had watched for security guards. Most of the units were empty now anyway, so he was pretty confident he was safe.

He was hopeful about this evening. It needed to be soon as the cat was flagging and he didn't want to have to go to the trouble of finding another one. Last night there'd been some fucker with her so he'd driven on by, but tonight he had a good feeling. There was a tightness in his groin that was quite pleasurable. He'd put the finishing touches on his hideaway—or perhaps on reflection he'd call it his Sanctuary, always good to know irony wasn't dead—everything was ready. It just needed her. It was hungry for her like he was, yearning and keening and howling for her in the night. He released a shuddering breath and let his hand stray to his crotch where he eased down the straining zip. He slipped eager fingers into the musky warmth but then thought better of it. The last thing he needed was to be pulled in for pulling one off. Regretfully he returned his thoughts to the other job in hand.

It was about time. He pulled the car over at a careless angle, leaving the engine running—it mustn't look contrived. He opened the boot and reached into the holdall. The bag with the cloth went in his pocket and he pulled out the cat by its scruff. Its sides were heaving and its fur was flecked with blood. It was a feisty little bastard. It'd scratched and clawed at him, bitten his hand and screamed like a bitch when he'd broken its leg. Even now it looked like it'd try a bid for freedom if it got a chance, three legs or not. He had a grudging respect for it and hoped his girl showed the same kind of spirit. He fancied a bit of spice.

Rachel walked quickly. The rabbits had taken longer than she'd thought and she was already late. Evening was drawing in and the sun was no more than a pink bloom on the horizon, the color leaching from the sky. She was annoyed with herself. She'd forgotten to charge her phone that morning, otherwise she'd have phoned her dad for a lift.

She noticed a car up ahead, half on the curb with the door open. There was a man kneeling in front of it cradling something small in his arms. Oh God, it was a cat. It looked like he'd run it over. She saw him stand and look helplessly up and down the empty road and without even thinking she broke into a run. Swiftly she passed the hunched gray units and the deserted yards. As she reached his side she saw it was a small tortoiseshell, with the pearly white of bone protruding from the matted fur of its leg.

"It just ran out from the units straight in front of me," he said. "I couldn't do anything, it went right under the wheels, I think I've killed it."

He slid the shutters down on his soul and turned his eyes toward her. She saw his hands were trembling. He was flushed and looked as though he was on the point of tears.

"Oh God, this is awful, what the fuck am I going to do. I don't know whose it is but I can't just leave it here to die. Do you know if there's a vet anywhere nearby?"

Rachel looked at the cat; it was such a sorry little thing. Its eyes were glazing over and it lay all limp in his arms. She felt sick and as if she just might cry too.

'There's one off the high street, down the side by Marks and Spencer, I think." She hesitated for a moment, wondering what she should do. "I don't even know if they'd be open now."

He smiled at her gratefully. He had such a nice face, such lovely eyes. She couldn't help noticing how fit he was and felt herself blush as he looked at her.

"I know I shouldn't even ask," he said, with just the right hint of hesitation, "but do you think you could come and hold him? I don't think I can do it and drive as well."

He saw the flicker of doubt cross her face, so quickly backtracked. He didn't want to seem too pushy and scare her away.

"No, don't worry, of course you can't, it was silly to ask you. I understand, it's fine, I'll manage somehow. I'll just put him on the back seat."

Old childhood warnings flashed through Rachel's mind, "Don't talk to strangers," "Never get into anyone's car," and here was both a stranger and a car.

But another bolder voice said "Oh come on, what are the chances that some random psycho just happens to run over a cat right in front of you?"

She didn't know it at the time but this was the only decision in her short life that would ever really matter. The one where the scales hung in the balance. On one side her future, on the other something else entirely.

How could she not help? She wanted to be a vet, or at least a veterinary nurse if her grades weren't good enough. After all it was why she volunteered at Mrs. Watson's. She took a deep breath and the scales tipped, the unlucky dice fell.

"No, it's fine, really. 'Course I'll help. I'll just sit in the back with him. Have you got a blanket or anything?"

She opened the back door and slid in.

"Actually, you can just put him on my lap if you like, he'll be fine."

He had to stop himself from laughing. What a piece of piss. It couldn't have gone better if he'd planned it. Oh, wait a minute, he had, right down to the last glorious detail.

She smiled at him and held out her arms for the cat, and in the confines of the car he could see her shimmering. Her energy blazed like a halo, crackling and sparking from her hair. He quickly took the plastic bag from his pocket and pressed the pad against her face, covering her nose and mouth. He felt the chloroform cold against his hand. If anyone came along now he was royally fucked, even he couldn't talk his way out of this one.

The cat saw its chance and slipped away unnoticed—at least someone might escape with their life.

Rachel's eyes went wide with panic, the pupils flaring and dilating as the adrenaline flooded her system. Her feet drummed helplessly against the floor as she strained against him, trying in vain to free herself from his grip. She felt her lip split against her teeth and her mouth pooled with her own hot blood.

He watched as her eyes slowly dimmed and lost their luster. He counted. He'd researched this well. He needed her at stage three, unconscious and physically incapable. Too long and she'd hit stage five, paralysis of the chest muscles, asphyxia and death. Game over player one, before he'd even played.

He leaned forward, his lips soft against her ear, "Got you," he said, and as her consciousness surrendered the last thing she felt was his tongue, burrowing, and the fumbling of his fingers against her breast.

9

"The worst loneliness is not to be comfortable with yourself"

—Mark Twain

The weeks have rolled by and life at The Lodge is falling into a pattern, one where Tom is happy and I am not. This is the house he's always dreamed of but I find myself torn between loving and hating it. It unsettles me. I have tried so hard to find happiness here and have occasionally glimpsed its sunny upturned face, catching me unawares pottering in the garden or planning out the color scheme for a room. Trouble is I can't sustain it. I seem unable to find peace.

I am trying to make a home. I'm gathering photos and planning my mood boards for each room but my enthusiasm falls too readily away. I start the day full of ideas, my palette a subtle mix of misty grays and heritage greens. I picture the rooms as an eclectic mix of traditional and contemporary; our favorite things from our London home seamlessly inserted into the tranquil space of a Victorian drawing room. No matter how much I focus, I find I lose my thread and slip into apathy. We will have an interior designer eventually but I need them to have a sense of my taste. To translate my vision into reality, not inflict me with theirs.

We are lucky. My father put money in trust for me until I was twenty-one—just in case I ended up wearing all my clothes at once while I howled at strangers in the street. This cushion has allowed me to pursue my art and has supplemented Tom's income so we can do all the things we want to do just that little bit more easily. It has also

served another purpose, of course. It is the balm, the emollient my
father rubs into his conscience to salve the wound of his guilt. And
yes, I am aware that I'm a hypocrite.

Tom leaves early each morning for his job in the city—investment
funds, how dull—so I spend my days alone. Too much solitude seems
not to be good for me. I was alone for much of my day in London but
not lonely like this. No sounds from the street, no people going about
their daily lives. Nothing. When we're both here the air feels lighter
somehow, the atmosphere lifts. When it's just me it changes. It seems
to clot and thicken until I'm wading through treacle, its ticky tendrils
dragging at my limbs. The weather hasn't helped. The summer has
been long and sultry, which has added to my lassitude.

I am still troubled by a kind of déjà vu. It will come upon me
unexpectedly, the sense that I've been here before. I'll walk into a
room, or more specifically go into the kitchen or come through the
front door, and the familiarity of it all hits me with the quality of
a childhood memory. Or like the recollection of a dream. To start
with it was fleeting—a blink and it was gone—but recently it's
solidifying. It's becoming more pronounced and it troubles me. It's
not something I've experienced before and it seems irrational, not
linked to my injury or to anything that makes any sense. I know I
haven't been here before but the feeling persists. When it comes over
me it feels so real; so real that the other day I found myself standing
in the driveway looking up at the house, concentrating on its every
detail. I then closed my eyes and tried to summon up a memory of
actually coming here, of walking up the drive and knocking on the
door. That way madness lies.

I haven't said anything to Tom. In part because I don't want to
worry him but also because I don't think I can bear the oversolicitous
concern it will bring. He will try to wrap me in kindness, to cosset
me in a way that reduces me to a child. I don't want that anymore.

I'm also struggling to sleep. This has always been problematic for me—common in my situation—but now it's worse. My nights are haunted by dreams, prophetic and terror laden. I've taken to dreaming of my attacker, something I haven't done in years. In these fevered nightmares he's a dark figure behind me, his hands grasping and clawing at my hair. As I turn and am about to see his face, I wake trembling and sweating, my heart thundering in my chest. Recently I've had to get up to clear my head and to allow the tingling aftermath of panic to subside. I walk the rooms—not the kitchen obviously—in the moonlight and listen to the house breathing. I swear it does. A sibilant sigh on the edge of silence.

My dream has always been the same, the same scenario over and over. It was every night in the early days. Every time I closed my eyes, until the very thought of sleep was enough to send me spiraling into dread. I have no memory of those events, they mean nothing to me, unless there's something buried deep that only sleep sets free.

I can remember the morning of my attack with complete clarity. The halls of Thorpwood House vibrating with the pent-up energy of girls soon to be released for the summer. The summer of 1994. The dentist was paying his annual visit to the school that day and groups of us were periodically called from our form room to sick bay where he would slide his slippery-gloved fingers over our gums and probe us for cavities, all under the vengeful gaze of Matron as chaperone. The fees the parents of the privileged few paid to Thorpwood House took care not only of our educational needs but also of such tiresome parental duties as dental checks and vaccinations. Each year we were subject to these unwelcome attentions. The dentist, with his face like a boiled ham, would no doubt have been high on my list of likely assailants had he not at the time been avidly peering into the mouth of some unfortunate girl.

I had lost a bracelet, and once my teeth were pronounced present and correct, I slipped away to the sports pavilion in case I'd lost it during games. I was feeling resentful and angry that day. Resentful toward the girls whose parents would be taking them away for the summer, to loving homes and sun-kissed beaches. Angry at the fact that I would be spending my summer at the school—a fate usually reserved for the "overseas girls."

I can remember walking past the tennis courts under the dark shade of the yew hedging and back out into the shimmering glare of the morning sunshine. Then there is nothing. No sense of impending danger. No leering stranger luring me with promises of sweeties or the chance to stroke his puppy dog. No searing pain, just a void in my existence like the suspension of time.

Despite various reports of suspicious vehicles, no perpetrator of the crime was ever found. It remains the great unsolved mystery of my life. The breaking and the making of me.

For a while my story captured the attention of the press. The heady combination of teenage victim, exclusive school and "frenzied" attacker proving irresistible. I couldn't think it at the time, mainly because I couldn't think much of anything, but I have since wondered if he, for I really can't imagine a she, read my name, saw my childhood photo and absorbed the details of me. Whether he took pleasure in his handiwork or feared me for what I might know or say. In my darker moments I have wondered if he hovers at the edges of my life watching me still. It's odd to think that all this time he's been out there, living his life in parallel with what he left me of mine.

I had hoped Tom was unaware of my nocturnal wanderings. He's not. Last night as I slipped back under the quilt he reached and stroked my hair, gently soothing me back to sleep. My dream was different this time but no less unsettling. A flaxen-haired girl was under the trees trying to give me a key. Again and again she tried to give it to me, pressing it into my palm. Each time it dropped into the grass. It kept falling through my fingers no matter how hard I tried to keep hold of it. It was so vivid that when I think of it even now I can still feel its pressure in my hand and the sense of loss. It's as though I was on the brink of something important and now it's lost to me.

Tom looked at me strangely this morning and I sense a conversation coming on. Luckily it won't be today, not when there are things to do. He met our neighbors last week and has invited them to dinner. It might've been nice if he'd perhaps spoken to me first. They're coming tomorrow and now I must do what I can with the dining room and prepare the menu. I must make an effort to get things right in the hope they'll be friends.

The dining room is shabby despite Tom having stuck down the loose wallpaper and replaced the hideous wooden chandelier with a simple shade. There are no curtains and we're not really set for entertaining yet. I've ordered yards of ivory muslin off the internet and I drape this around the window to hide the rail and artfully knot it in swathes at the corners. It hangs at the sides like curtains, bunched and gathered on the floor. It's a bit theatrical but in the absence of anything else it'll have to do.

Thankfully it'll be dark when we eat. We're stepping into autumn now and the evenings are drawing in. I'll light the room with candles and tea lights, which I've placed on every available surface, the mantelpiece, the windowsill, the shelves either side of the fireplace and in the grate itself.

Our light beech table and chairs look so out of place here. I've covered the table with an ivory damask tablecloth, a wedding present from someone, which helps. It's too big for the table and hangs nearly to the floor. Tomorrow I'll add a jug of roses from the garden, those big full-blown rosettes. I stand back and survey my handiwork. It may be a tad Miss Havisham but with the candles lit and the table laid it'll do.

10

"Cover her face; mine eyes dazzle. She died young"
—John Webster, *The Duchess of Malfi*

He turned to look in the back seat. He wasn't happy. Already she was starting to let him down and after all the time and love he'd spent on her. He'd been careful to cover her with the rug to keep her safe from prying eyes. Now, somehow, her arm was dangling in the footwell, her face exposed. She looked ugly, not like his golden girl at all. Her lids were swollen and had slightly parted to reveal a rind of white. Sightless and disturbing. He shuddered. Her face was slack, and a thin strand of drool hung from her lips. This was not what he wanted. He needed her coruscating life force lustrous and glittering, not this dead meat. He felt a spark of anger. He'd have to make her pay but for the moment he had to concentrate on getting her safely stowed away.

He dragged her out of the car. God she was heavy, much heavier than she looked. Was this another of her tricks? Would he peel back her layers and find a mass of jellied fat?

He half carried, half dragged her to the door. She'd lost a trainer and her heel scuffed in the dirt. She was making him sweat and not in the good way he enjoyed so much. He all but threw her onto the floor, her face grazing against the concrete. Her eyelids fluttered and opened, she was pulling herself back, floating at the edges of consciousness.

"No you fucking don't," he said, reaching for the chloroform pad.

He wasn't sure how long he could keep her under or what the effect might be but he certainly didn't need her waking up now. Not until she was safe and secure. Tucked away where no one would hear her scream.

He looked around the storeroom at the boxes and clutter. No one would even know the room was there unless they were looking for it and no one would; nobody came here anymore. It was virtually his space to do with whatever he liked. The accumulation of old crap that'd built up over the years masked the true dimensions so, unless you measured, you'd never realize what he'd done. If anyone found it in the future it might take some explaining—except he had that eventuality covered as well. He was certainly inventive if nothing else. Another of his manifold talents.

He moved the precautionary stack of empty boxes and slid the panel of board to the side to reveal the hidden door. He admired his handiwork; two layers of plywood and some insulation and there it was, both sturdy and soundproof. He'd even remembered a vent at the top to allow in some air. He didn't want her snuffed out like a candle. Any snuffing to be done was down to him.

The boxed-in space beyond the door was only a couple of feet or so in depth but it ran the width of the storeroom. It was perfect for his needs. He'd even added a pillow and a blanket—nice touches. He needed to be comfortable if she fancied a cuddle. He'd worked hard on this, over three weeks it had all taken him; he'd never been one to cut corners, particularly on a project that promised such rewards.

He slid into the space and laid her down with her head on the pillow. He unzipped her jeans and rolled them up. She certainly wouldn't be needing those anymore. He ran his finger experimentally down the inside of her thigh. This was better, her skin was warm and soft as velvet. God this was going to be good, but he mustn't rush things. He'd leave her for a while; let her equilibrate to her new surroundings and start to shine.

He was sure as he'd pushed the door closed, that she'd started to twinkle. A gentle phosphorescence that would lighten his darkness for a while.

11

"I drink to separate my body from my soul"
—Oscar Wilde

I must get ready. Our guests will be here soon. I pull on dark jeans, straight and tight, and a top I've always liked. It's silky and slouching, revealing my collarbones and shoulders. I've not been eating well and am probably too thin but I like how I look in this. Long-limbed and lean. My face is another matter. The lack of sleep has taken its toll and there are purple shadows under my eyes. I reach for the Dermablend to cover my scar and dab a little under each eye as well. I need makeup tonight. Tom doesn't like me with makeup, he says it makes me look tough. Tonight I need tough. For some reason I feel nervous and out of sorts. I apply eyeliner, bold and dark, and roll mascara onto my lashes. A sweep of bronzer across my cheekbones, dark lip gloss and I'm ready. I wind my hair into a careless knot and secure it with a comb, loose strands framing my face. I add the necklace Tom bought me for my thirty-fifth birthday, a cascade of hammered silver, and stand back to survey the damage. The woman looking back at me has a sharp edginess far removed from my everyday self.

I go down to the dining room. The table's laid and the roses are soft and blowsy, already shedding petals like giant confetti. I've kept things simple for the meal. Asparagus, poached egg and hollandaise to start, Stilton-crusted fillet steak with a port wine sauce and then a lemon torte. The torte and the sauces I made yesterday so thankfully I won't need to spend too much time in the kitchen tonight.

Our neighbors Madeline and Joe have just arrived. I can hear Tom in the hall and make my way through to greet them.

"Hi," I say, "I'm Isabel." I smile and add, "Izzy to my friends."

Joe air-kisses somewhere west and east of my cheeks.

"Izzy, hi, Joe and this is Madeline."

He's tall and slightly overweight with light brown hair and a pleasant face—apart from the slightly predatory glint in his eye. He takes my hand and lingers over it for just a fraction too long.

I turn to Madeline. She is tiny, a waif with tumbling Titian curls. Her face is devoid of makeup bar a dusting of gold at the edges of her eyes. She has milk-white skin with a sprinkle of freckles across a tilted nose and a surprisingly full-lipped mouth. She turns to me and smiles slightly, revealing tiny even teeth, vaguely translucent like grains of Arborio. I knew I should've done risotto. Her eyes are the color of the sea, each, I note, with its own shard of ice.

"Isabel," she says and extends a chilly hand, every nail a perfect pearly oval.

My hands with their blunt-cut nails look mannish in comparison. She has dressed up for the occasion in a shimmering sheath of a dress that clings to every curve. I had felt happy with how I looked but now I feel gangling and wrong, my features painted on like a babushka doll.

The evening is unseasonably warm and we've arranged drinks in the garden before dinner. Tom has bought lanterns and fairy lights which give the terrace a magical glow. My nervousness has increased now they're here and I find myself shivering despite the evening's warmth. I down my first glass of prosecco with unseemly haste. Tom looks pointedly at my glass, his eyebrows waggling like errant caterpillars. I choose to misunderstand and chirp, "Top-up, anyone?" proceeding to refill my glass well beyond the level of good manners. I need the wine to kick in to take off the edge. In fact, I wish I could flip back my head like the Pez sweet dispensers we had as children and decant the whole bloody bottle down my throat.

Dinner is shaping up to be a disaster. Not because of the food—the poached eggs were perfect, the hollandaise smooth and creamy—because we have split into two factions. Madeline is talking exclusively to Tom and I am left with Joe. Not that he isn't a nice man, I'm sure he's lovely but there's something overly intense about him that makes me feel slightly uncomfortable.

I quickly learn he's a research scientist in the food industry and a nutritional expert with every fiber (Ha!) of his being. I now know all there is to know about complex carbohydrates, low GI, soluble fiber and more. I try to steer the conversation away by asking him about his holiday. Instead he neatly segues into the health benefits of cold-pressed Mediterranean olive oil. I fear the boredom will become too much for me and I'll lose consciousness, plunging head-first into my food or toppling to the floor. I give Tom my "help me" face but he doesn't notice.

I find myself watching Madeline instead. She has a way of looking up at Tom from under her eyelashes which looks coquettish although it may just be a mannerism, the consequence of being so short. She's hanging on his every word and I register a twinge of jealousy—where did that come from?

Maybe it's because there were girls like her at college. Ethereal help-less creatures on the surface but shot through with tempered steel. All wide-eyed sweetness around men, who flock to protect them; ruthless with girls who they see as competitors.

I'm aware I'm drinking too much. I feel unmoored and slightly wired, my filters are slipping. The window is disturbing me too. I don't like the shimmering reflection of the candles against the growing darkness outside. I wish we had proper curtains. I feel too exposed, as though there's a watcher out there. Again and again my eyes are drawn to it. The flickering lights catch at the corners of my vision giving the illusion of movement, or a face beyond the glass. My heart thumps in my chest and I feel frightened. I don't like it at all. The tension in me is building and threatening to spiral out of control.

I go through to the kitchen to prepare the steaks. Tom makes no move to help. I sear the first three and place them in the oven. I can hear Tom's voice from the dining room and the answering tinkle of Madeline's laughter. I look at his steak. It's exactly two centimetres thick and blue, that's how he has to have his fillet or fill-*ay* as he insists on calling it. Why can't he come out here and help cook the damn thing himself. In a sudden fit of spite, I pick it up and hurl it at the wall. It lands with a splat and hangs there for a stunned moment before sliding down the tiles, leaving a bloody trail. I realize I am very, very drunk.

I become aware of someone else in the room and turn to see Joe. I didn't hear him come in and now he's right behind me, so close that we're almost touching.

"I wondered if you needed any. . ."

His voice tails away and together we watch the steak complete its descent. I look at his shocked face and begin to laugh. High pitched drunken laughter that feels as though it'll never stop.

I say the first thing that comes into my head, "Tenderizing," which sets off fresh peals of laughter. This isn't good.

"Tom's," I hastily add, lest he thinks all the food has been hurled indiscriminately around the kitchen.

He scuttles back to the dining room, all offers of help forgotten, and I retrieve Tom's steak. It looks vaguely gritty so I'll have to wash it. Another Tom cardinal sin, "never wash steak, it removes some of the juices." Oh well, I give it a quick rinse and slap it in the pan before adding it to the others. I stagger to the fridge for the Stilton and the port wine sauce and somehow get the whole thing finished, plated and out to the table.

Joe avoids my eye and Tom senses a shift in the atmosphere and tries to draw us both back into the conversation.

"Izzy's an artist," he says, "if you ever want to commission something for your home, she'd love to be involved."

Oh please! I'm sure I've just snorted derisively and rolled my eyes heavenward. Madeline looks across at me and flaps her little hands together like a performing seal.

"Oh, how exciting! I thought I detected an artistic temperament."

She looks expectantly across the table at me as though daring me to seize my steak knife and saw my own ear off à la Van Gogh. I don't deign to answer.

The rest of the meal passes in an uneventful blur until the cheese course. Joe has resumed his discourse on nutrition, and I've been polishing off the Sauternes.

Suddenly I lurch to my feet, knocking my wine over in the process and announce, "For fuck's sake, enough of the healthy nutrition, I think it's time for some saturated fats," before fetching the cheeseboard. I bang it down hard in the centre of the table to a stunned silence. A lone grape rolls to the edge of the board, desperate to escape. I think the evening's over.

They've gone. We're sitting in the wreckage of the dining room, me doggedly finishing the last of the wine, Tom staring into space. I know I've messed up, possibly big time, but he should share at least some of the blame.

Tom looks across at me and sighs wearily, here it comes. "Izzy, why did you have to do that?"

"Do what?" As if I don't know. I manage the slightly confused air of the wrongly accused. "Sorry, but I don't know what. . ."

He interrupts me, a hint of anger entering his voice. "You know exactly what, behaving—I don't know—drunk and belligerent. They were nice people and you were just rude and hostile and frankly embarrassing. You've been odd ever since we moved here. I actually think you need to talk to someone, get this sorted out."

I glare at him with exactly the drunken belligerence he's refer-ring to.

"Talk to someone? What the hell's that supposed to mean? Talk to someone like I'm talking to you now or talk to someone while I'm lying on a couch? If that's what you mean just say it."

He sighs once more.

"Okay, if you need me to spell it out for you. I love you and I'm worried about you. This move seems to have really got under your skin and I think you need help. You're all on edge, jumping and twitching at everything like a frightened rabbit, wandering about in the night."

I ignore the last bit, "Help? I needed help this evening but oh no, you were more interested in Madeline."

As soon as the words are out I wish I hadn't said them. Now I've made myself sound jealous and petulant. Some sober part of me registers that I'm just projecting my anxieties about a baby onto him, which isn't fair. I want to make amends but he looks so angry that my apology catches in my throat.

"Now you're just being childish. I just was being sociable and friendly, something you seem to have forgotten how to do. The way you're being is making things really difficult for both of us."

He has a pained long-suffering expression that winds me up. He never rows, never raises his voice. Instead he does what he's doing now; talks to me very calmly as though I'm a child, or worse. Tonight it just makes me want to pick a fight with him. I adopt a jeering and antagonistic tone.

"Oh please, difficult for both of us? What's difficult for you? You're never fucking here."

"Listen. . ."

"No, you listen, you wanted this place, but you can't wait to get out. I'm on my own here, day in, day out. Don't you get it? I'm fucking lonely, not that you give a shit."

He looks at me with an expression I haven't seen before and says, "Hello, one of us has to work if you hadn't noticed, earn some real money . . ."

Hmm, Daddy's allowance seems to be conveniently forgotten. I open my mouth to remind him of that little fact but before I can he continues, ". . . and maybe if you weren't so hostile you'd make new friends. Now you're finally away from Maria I'd hoped you'd move on."

For a moment I'm too stunned to reply. Where did that come from?

"What's Maria got to do with anything? I know you've never much liked her but you needn't think you're dictating who I can and can't be friends with."

He's wrestled the first sparks of anger back under control.

"It's not about liking or dictating," he says calmly. "Your friendship with her is, I don't know, so rear window. She's the past, you and me we're the future. You know I only want us to be happy."

He reaches for my hand but I can't do this. I can't think clearly enough to articulate what I want to say. Instead I resort to "Fuck you," which is always an argument lost, and I go to bed.

I lie here in the dark and run through the events of the evening in a drunken asynchronous blur. I don't know what's wrong with me. I feel strung out and anxious, apprehensive like I'm waiting for something to happen.

Tom and I don't do this. We never really row. We never go to bed not talking, all angry and resentful. We love each other; we're two sides of the same coin but this house seems to be spinning us out of kilter.

12

"What lies before us? Horrible thoughts arise in my heart"
— C. S. Lewis, *The Last Battle*

When Rachel awoke she thought for a single fleeting moment that she was in her bed at home. In her room, with her books, her perfume bottles and the contents of her makeup bag strewn across the dressing table.

She must be ill. She ached all over, her foot throbbed and her head felt as though she'd been hit or maybe shaken, her brain bounced back and forth against her skull. She slowly realized she had no idea where she was and as her senses gradually returned, with them came the dawning realization that something was terribly, terribly wrong. She tried to gather her thoughts. Her head hurt so much she couldn't think.

She was sure her eyes were open so why couldn't she see? There was nothing, just blindness, velvet-black and complete. She held her hand up to her face and blinked but there was no faint light to adjust to, nothing to fire her rods and cones back to life.

Her mouth was drug dry, her tongue furred and firmly Velcroed to its roof. She tried to swallow to clear the sickly sweet taste of chemicals that filled her head and the bile that rose in the back of her throat.

The memory of what had happened crashed through her. Wave after wave of paralyzing panic pulsed and crawled from her scalp to the tips of her toes. Her heart pounded as though it would burst from her chest and she felt the hot sting of urine. In her terror she scrambled to sit up. Her elbows were pressed against rough walls on either side. She was in a space no wider than she was. The air was wrong. It was too heavy and still. She was in a box. She was buried alive.

The scream rose in her throat and shattered the silence. Again and again until her lungs burned and her throat was raw, but there was no one to hear.

He sat calmly and quietly. He needed to collect himself, to still his thoughts. To still his knee that jumped and jigged with a life of its own.

What he needed was a chill pill, a nice little calmative to take the edge off, to iron out his kinks—well perhaps not all of them. His mother was bound to have been given something; a "mother's little helper" to smooth out her rough times and help her sleep.

His parents' room still gave him the same frisson of excitement as it had as a child. A forbidden territory, the place of secret moans and sighs. Of creaking springs and muffled whispers overheard by the unseen listener on the stairs. Much of his childhood had been spent in dark corners, hiding, watching. Sometimes in the night he'd stood by their bed and watched them sleep. His mother's hair across the pillow, shimmering in the moonlight like spilled honey. Their soft exhalations, the flutter of their eyelids and their mouths falling gently open. Their vulnerability stirred an emotion in him even as a child. Something slithering and nameless that both thrilled and repulsed him.

He looked through his mother's drawers, in both senses of the word, and found what he sought, placing the two yellow pills on his tongue.

He looked at his parents' bed and idly wondered if they still fucked. He laughed out loud at the thought of his father fumbling under her nightdress in the dark. Getting it while he still could. He pulled back the covers, slipped between their sheets and closed his eyes.

13

"Did I do anything last night that suggested I was sane?"

—Terry Pratchett, *Going Postal*

I have acquiesced and have agreed to go and see Dr. Stedman, my erstwhile therapist and companion on my journey toward recovery (sorry, Doctor, "improvement").

The Sunday morning after the fateful dinner party was one of tears and self-recrimination on both sides. Mainly mine. I awoke sweaty and nauseated. I'd been sick in the night and my mouth was dry and sour, my chest twisting with that hateful mix of guilt and shame that inevitably follows drunkenness, at least for me. The moment I saw Tom I burst into tears. I didn't want to but I felt so ill my resistance was gone. All my previous belligerence burned out in the night.

"I'm so, so sorry," I said, "I don't know what happened. For some reason I felt all on edge and then I started drinking and it all sort of fell apart. I feel so embarrassed. God, I'm sorry."

He wrapped his arms around me and pulled me close.

"Hey, shush, it's fine. It doesn't matter. So what, you got drunk, we've all done it. And I'm sorry for bringing up about Maria, it didn't mean anything, I was just angry with you and being spiteful."

He gently pushed my hair back and looked into my eyes.

"It was partly my fault anyway. I shouldn't have just invited them and put that extra pressure on you, I'm sorry."

Then he added, "It doesn't take away from the fact that I'm worried about you though."

He held my hands in his and I finally told him everything; the feelings of déjà vu, the dreams, the trouble I've had sleeping and eventually we agreed I'd talk it through with Dr Stedman, just to see what he thought. Tom always believes he knows what's best for me. This time he may be right.

We spent the rest of the day together, back to our old companionable selves. The pleasure of having Tom at home soothed my soul, my previous irritation soon forgotten. The only thing that gnawed at the edges of my contentment was the roses. They had been so beautiful the day before. Now they'd been destroyed in the night. A deer, a muntjac or something, had come into the garden and torn the bushes apart. Great wrecked blooms were scattered like tissues across the lawn, each broken head a little grief of its own. Luckily nothing else seemed to have been touched.

So here I am today, in the waiting room for nutjobs. Already I feel irritated and wish I hadn't come. I'm not like these people, at least not anymore. Opposite me there's a man with his mother. A man with the face of a child, wide-eyed and guileless. An angry scar puckering the side of his head where the hair has ceased to grow. I feel ashamed of my thoughts, there but for the grace and all that.

Another woman nearby is staring at me and suddenly without provocation she shouts, "Whore!"

Hmm, perhaps she knows me.

This is rapidly followed by "Aardvark" and "Windmill," which tend to resonate less. She looks contrite and mouths "Tourette's."

I nod understandingly, we each have our quirks.

I'm called through to the consulting room where I sit down in the armchair—no couches for Anton—and relax into its beguiling softness. It's a trick chair this one, you sit on its lap like a ventriloquist's dummy and it makes you talk. I realize my palms are sweaty and my pulse has quickened.

Anton Stedman is black, which for some reason came as a surprise when I first met him. His name conjured up a whiskery old man, with gold-rimmed glasses. Instead he was black and beautiful. Of indeterminate age, his skin is still smooth and unlined, a deep ebony with a texture like velvet. In the earlier days, when I reached the point where I could no longer focus on his voice or absorb his words, I would zone out and imagine running my fingers across his cheek to feel its dusky softness. His hair is cropped short, tight and wiry against his scalp. He's older now and a hint of gray is beginning to bristle at his temples, but he still has the capacity to turn heads. He has beautiful hands, long fingered and filbert nailed. The backs are smooth and brown, the palms a creamy pink. They're his Neapolitan ice cream hands. He dresses like a country squire, all dapper tweeds and polished brogues. Today he's wearing cords and a mustard moleskin waistcoat with a tweed jacket and a pocket square ablaze with color. Today he is autumn. If I were a portraitist I would paint this man.

Seeing him after so long makes me want to cry. I want to bury my face against his chest, breathe in his tweedy safeness and bask in the comfort he exudes.

Definition of transference: *a redirection of feelings for a significant person, usually a mother* (although not in my case), *toward the therapist.* Maybe I should run now.

"Isabel," he says, his voice gentle, "it's been a long time. How are you?"

I clear my throat and we begin.

Well, usually I love the soothing quality of his voice, the slight sibilance of his *S*'s like sea over sand. Today it's no more than the hiss of hot air escaping. To sum up his professional view I could be dippy, screwy, loco, or even squirrelly nuts.

He has gently raised the specter of psychiatric comorbidity in traumatic brain injury. A rare (let's hang on to that thought) condition where, after a period of latency that may last several years or even decades, the subject—that's me, folks—develops a delayed pseudo psychosis that may manifest as hallucinatory experiences and feelings of hostility and aggression, sometimes exacerbated by alcohol misuse. I knew I shouldn't have mentioned the dinner party. Rare, he admits, but particularly associated with frontal lobe injuries such as mine. He offers me something he thinks might help. A little risperidone maybe or perhaps a snifter of olanzapine. I think not.

Oh, Anton, Anton, really you disappoint me. I have a nasty suspicion you sense a paper coming on, a nice little mention in *BJPsych* perhaps. I thank him for his time and no, I don't think I'll be coming back.

I leave the office and step out into the rain-lashed street. I'm a little stunned at what I've heard and will not countenance it, not even for a moment. I don't want medication, the very thought of it scares me. I've been down that road, the dry mouth, the muddled thoughts, all creativity stifled. I know myself. I've lived like this for twenty years and yes, there may be something wrong, something playing at the edges of my consciousness, but no, not that.

14

"Fear is static that prevents me from hearing myself"

—Samuel Butler

Rachel had learned something new, not that it would ever be any use to her now.

Panic cannot be sustained, and terror relents. The brain protects itself. It doesn't allow itself to frazzle and fry in a flood of chemicals, neurons bursting their sheaths and synapses burning to ash. Neither does adrenaline pump interminably until the heart explodes. Instead, panic and terror rise hand in hand, swelling until you think you'll die. Until you wish you would to make it stop. And then they subside, leaving you weak and shaking, giving you a chance to gather your wits and your breath before it starts all over again.

In such a lull she had taken stock of her surroundings. She was in a long narrow space. Tall enough to stand if her legs would allow, long enough to lie down and then some. It was pitch-black. There was no window, no source of light, but she no longer thought she was buried because there seemed to be the faintest of breezes coming from somewhere. The walls felt rough and gritty, perhaps breeze block or brick, but one of the longer sides seemed to be made of rough wood, with a panel which she was sure was a doorway. If this was the case, she was unlikely to be underground, which gave her a fleeting sense of relief. There was also a pillow and a blanket and a bucket, although it was a bit late for that now. Her jeans had been taken without her knowing and her knickers were cold and damp. She was desperately hot and dehydrated. She needed to drink. If there was a door perhaps someone would come, but then this made her think of her captor and released a new wave of terror. What did he want from her? Was she going to die?

She tried to calm her thoughts. If he wanted to rape her she would let him. She wouldn't resist or struggle, she would do whatever she had to in order to survive. At least it wouldn't be her first time; she wouldn't have given him that. If she got out of here she wouldn't have to think of him every time someone touched her in the future. She knew from her biology lessons that skin sloughs and sheds, continually renewing. She would focus on that. The skin he touched now would be shed and gone, even the moist epithelium of her innermost places. In a month, in a year, there would be nothing of her that he'd touched. She'd be renewed. As long as she didn't let him into her head she could shed him like so much old skin.

She heard a faint noise and with it came a surge of hope; maybe someone was outside, someone who could help her.

She screamed, "Help, help me, I'm in here . . ." then froze in terror as she heard the scrape of the door opening. This was no savior.

He pushed into her space carrying a work light, and slid the door closed behind him. For a fleeting moment she saw her surroundings. As she'd thought it was a tiny room made of gray blocks, their surfaces riven with swirls. She crouched in the corner and closed her eyes. Like a small animal facing a predator she squeezed her lids shut. If she couldn't see him maybe he wouldn't see her.

She heard him move until he was so close she could smell him. Expensive aftershave, light citrus and herbs, underlaid with a tang of excited sweat that made her blood freeze.

He lifted her chin with a finger and softly sang, ". . . One, two, three . . ."

All thoughts gone, other than the desire to live, she found herself sobbing, "Please don't hurt me, please don't hurt me," over and over like a mantra.

This was what he needed, this felt so powerful and right.

He played the beam of light onto her face and watched the fear rippling across her features as he hummed.

". . . four, five, six . . ."

She was going to help him get his kicks.

Terror clouded her mind and at first the tune meant nothing to her. Then, with dawning horror, came the realization that these were lyrics from one of her favorite songs of all time, Jet's "Are You Gonna Be My Girl." The song she'd been playing all summer.

She bit back a scream as he lay down next to her. His warm body pressed against hers in the small space. He smoothed the hair back from her face and softly whispered, "You're so sweet . . ."

He sighed as he felt her trembling. It would be so sad to watch her shimmer slowly fading, but then beauty never lasts.

He was so gentle that just for a moment Rachel dared to hope that he wouldn't hurt her after all. Then she felt his fingers, hard and insistent, grinding at the tender parts where her legs met.

15

"She lacks the power of conversation but not the power of speech"

—George Bernard Shaw

My visit to Anton Stedman, the purveyor of snake oil, has had a result. Perhaps not the one anticipated but nonetheless a positive outcome—or an affirmative influence, to use his terminology. I suspect that was his intention all along, to goad me into finding my own solution, to prove him wrong. I should've thought of that before. Sneaky old Anton, he knows too well my resistance to medication, and how loath I am to let my damage "win."

Our conversation has focused me, driven me to find some way to occupy my time and my mind. One thing I do know, without the benefit of Anton's opinion, is that people like me can more easily slide into inertia and depression. Motivation diminishes, serotonin levels start to fall and before you know it you've fallen too far. Your star has dropped from the firmament and into the abyss.

Since we've been here I've hardly worked. I've tried to paint but my uneasiness, the edge of panic I sometimes have in my chest, renders me incapable of making art. My brushes sit untouched, my canvases gather dust. Instead I've decided to start clearing the coach house. I'll make it into a space where I can work; the painting will come when it's ready.

I've told Tom little about my visit to Anton, just that I saw him as promised and we talked things through. He was persistent, asking me how it went, and I found myself wary, not wishing to tell him too much. I find myself doing that more often, backing away from telling him how I feel.

If I'm honest I don't want to tell him what Dr. Stedman said as he will immediately pounce upon it. He's one of those people who like to have a reason for things, something tangible he can understand. Before I know it we'll be off to the clinic together, I'll be coming away with pills I don't want or need and end up passing my days in chemically induced passivity.

There, now I've said it. I sound disloyal and not a little paranoid but it's the truth. If I thought it would be otherwise—that he'd be indignant on my behalf and that we'd laugh it off together—then of course I'd tell him. The truth is I can't be sure of him anymore.

I'm beginning to realize some aspects of my life are regressing. When I first met Tom I was living in London, making an almost living from my art. Traveling to and from galleries and exhibitions and living my life. It may have been a guarded and solitary little life but it was mine and I was independent. Now I am not so much.

Maybe at first it was a relief to have the comfort of Dryland beneath my feet, to hand over the rudder of my existence and let another steer the course our lives would take. Now it's an annoyance. I have no doubt Tom loves me, as I do him, but he's sometimes so protective of me that he disempowers me.

I make my way through the orchard to the coach house, retracing my steps of so many weeks ago. It's the first time I've been down here since we moved in and the air has the same quality I remember from before. An expectant stillness, a muffling as though a giant bell jar has been lowered over the coach house and the woods, cutting out the sounds from the world outside. The trees are beginning to turn; their greens and golds are muted and a wind ruffles their higher branches, dislodging the first leaf fall. The night has brought more rain and the lane is damp and puddle strewn, with the last vestiges of a morning mist hanging over the grassy verge. The sky looms gray and heavy, although there is a hint of a break in the clouds, a promise that the sun will eventually come through.

I look up at the building. It's obvious now that it's a coach house, with the height and breadth of the doors to the front and the window in the crook of the apex. There is no way I'll be able to open the front doors. They're secured with chains and a wooden bar, the padlock pitted with rust and its shackle welded by time and the elements into a permanent upturned U. I walk round the side of the building where there's the smaller door, also padlocked but perhaps more promising in that this side of the building is more sheltered. It's less exposed to the wind and rain. The door is partially obscured by brambles, which I push back to reveal a small hasp and staple with a keyhole beneath. I've come prepared. Along with the bunch of old keys that came with the house I've also brought turpentine and artist's oil medium to use as lubricant. It would've been easier to ask Tom to do this for me but I needed this to be mine, at least to start with. Almost like a secret.

The padlock is old-fashioned with a plate over the keyhole, and once I free this I find the lock beneath is clean and dry. I add a drop of oil and slowly work my way through the smaller keys. I'm hampered by my tremor but eventually there's a satisfying click and the shackle falls open.

The door itself is less accommodating and it's many minutes before the key turns and the door can finally be opened. As I turn the knob and start to push, the brambles suddenly spring back, embedding their thorns in the skin of my forearm. I instinctively snatch my arm away and as I do, bright beads of blood spring red to the surface like a warning.

I push the door wide and step into the gloom of the interior. The space is vast, the roof higher than I expected, as though there had once been a loft space above. The air has a mouse-whiskered mustiness and the culprits make themselves known through their soft scuttlings away from the light. A plank of watery sunlight suddenly slants through the small window above the doors. It teems and sparkles with the motes of dust disturbed by my intruder's feet. As my eyes adjust, I see that the roof is high and vaulted, crisscrossed by beams and hung with swathes of dusty cobwebs like Spanish moss. I stand quietly and breathe in the silence; no déjà vu, no flash of memory, just a quiet calm like first snowfall. There's something about the height and the beams that reminds me of our old apartment. I think at last I've found a place I truly love.

The arched window by the door where I came in is obscured by some boards and sheets of ply, which I push to one side to let in more light. As I do, I notice there's a light switch by the door, round brown Bakelite from a bygone era. Someone at some point has run power down here. I flip the nipple more in hope than anticipation. Nothing happens—it was too much to wish for—but at least there must be conduit for wiring from the main house, which means we won't be starting entirely from scratch.

The space is not as cluttered as I'd feared. Around the walls there are boxes, old furniture and odd shapes looming in the half light, draped with dust sheets and sacking. It's nothing that couldn't be tackled with a bit of help. The roof seems sound, no obvious gaps in the tiles and, although the bricks are blackened and grimy in places, I think the building would be useable as it is until we can get the proper work done. It'll need complete clearing and industrial cleaning to get rid of the cobwebs and dust, but with the windows cleaned and the doors wide open I could work here in the daylight. If I could get Tom to help get the front doors open to let in air and light, I could then work my way through the boxes.

Halfway along the side wall I notice there's another door, which must lead to the little annex. I carefully pick my way to the back and try the handle. It's firmly locked. None of the keys seem to fit so there must be some more somewhere back at the house. That'll have to keep for another day; right now I need time on the internet to look for rubbish removal and industrial cleaning services.

For the first time since we moved here I feel genuine enthusiasm for something.

I carefully lock the door behind me and turn to see a figure standing in the driveway. My sympathetic nervous system is anything but, and instead sends me into an instant spiral of fright. The involuntary adrenaline surge rushes through me, fight or flight, even though I can immediately see it's a woman in her mid- to late sixties. Quick threat assessment and I decide that even I could tackle this one if need be. She actually looks more startled than I do.

"'Ello, I didn't mean to scare you or nothing," she says apologetically, "but I've been waiting to catch you for weeks. I'm Mrs. Arthur," and she extends a hesitant hand.

She's shorter than me with graying hair pulled back under a head-scarf. Her raincoat is a dull brown, tightly belted around an ample waistline. With her wide little feet in sensible flats and her bag and umbrella over her arm, she's a throwback to the 1960s. Two beady eyes nestle like brown currants in the soft dough of her face. She reminds me of a little brown bird. A sparrow maybe, bright-eyed and inquisitive.

"Hi, I'm Isabel," I tentatively reply, unsure whether her name should mean something to me. Before I can say anything else, she launches into her mission.

"Jill, call me Jill," she says, "I've been wanting to catch you, see if you need any help. I do a bit of cleaning up at Stour Cottage, nothing 'eavy mind you, just a bit of dusting, 'oovering, ironing and such like. I was waiting to see who'd moved in, see if they needed my services." She pulls in a lungful of air before continuing.

"I used to do a bit for the Connors way back. Lovely couple they were. Me and my Bill was both patients of 'is, lovely man, shame 'ow 'e's gone. She were lovely too, sad though mind you, and so young when she went. She'd been ill before, back when those kiddies were small, sad for them but sad for 'im too, 'e was never the same after she went. My Bill done a bit of gardening for them a while back after young Alan left. Don't need a bit of gardening do you? My Bill's not as young as 'e was but 'e's still handy with the mower and shears. Since 'e retired there's more time so 'e'd be glad to take on another." She pauses for another much-needed breath.

After the calm of the coach house my head reels from the onslaught. The thought of someone coming in for a couple of hours cleaning really appeals, as much for the company as anything else, but if this is how she always is I don't think I could cope with the stream of consciousness. I suppress the urge to just tell her to stop talking; I know I mustn't say things like that anymore, it's not polite.

She misreads my expression—that's a refreshing change—and bristles slightly.

"If it's references you want I'm sure Mrs. Armstrong would be 'appy to do one and my rates are very reasonable, eight pounds per hour, you won't find better or many who's willing to come all the way out 'ere."

"No!" I reply, much too sharply then try to backtrack a bit, "I was just wondering if we really need anyone. I'll have to talk to Tom but maybe a couple of hours a week. We'll see."

She beams at me. "What about the garden? As I was saying Bill could manage a few hours too, get it all tidied up for the winter."

God, the woman's like a steamroller. "Um, let me have a think about it and a chat to Tom."

I'm beginning to feel uncomfortable so need to get rid of her and get back to the house. "Tell you what, have you got a phone number I can take? Then we can contact you if we need to."

She rummages in her bag and produces a preprinted card which she eagerly presses into my hand.

"What about a reference? Do you want me to speak to 'er?"

She tilts her head in the direction of Madeline and Joe's and I realize I don't actually know, or more likely remember, their surname.

"Is Mrs. Armstrong Madeline?" I ask, "Madeline and Joe?"

"Yes, that's 'er," she says, "if she's not too busy I'm sure she'll do you one."

"No, no, it's fine. It's just that I've met them but didn't know that was their name, that's all."

She smiles a tight little smile. "Yes, that's them. 'E's a lovely man. She's a different kettle of fish though, cold, leads 'im a merry dance I reckon."

I don't want to stand here and gossip about Madeline and Joe. I really need to see them at some point and make amends but dread the thought of going round there with my big wedge of humble pie, even though I promised Tom I would.

Her chatter, the speed and cadence of her voice, is making my anxiety bubble and I want her to leave. Then it suddenly strikes me that she mentioned "kiddies" living here, children plural, not child. Much as I'd like to get rid of her I recall the boy in the photograph and curiosity gets the better of me.

"So, you knew the family that lived here quite well then?" I inquire in a tone of studied nonchalance that rings false even to my own ears. I'm still not good at this kind of interaction. I often lack subtlety or misread the signs.

"Oh yes, they were a lovely family, well per'aps not the boy so much, but the girl was a sweetie. Now what was 'er name? Gillian? No, I'd remember if it was the same as me. Jenny? No . . ."

"Gemma," I quickly provide before she can run through every vaguely possible name she can think of.

"That's it, little Gemma. She was lovely. I didn't take to 'im though, gave me the creeps if I'm honest. The mother doted on 'im, poor thing, but the things I heard from Mrs. Harris."

My head is starting to spin. Despite this I can't help myself so ask, "Who's Mrs. Harris?"

"She's my friend. I told you, 'er Alan used to do odd jobs for them, bit of gardening and that. Soft mind but a good boy. 'E—what was 'is name? Anyway, 'e used to bully 'im something wicked, so I 'eard. Don't know what 'appened but Mrs. Harris said Alan came 'ome one day scared 'alf to death, wouldn't go back.

Never been the same since, not that 'e was ever right to start with mind."

I'm starting to doubt the wisdom of anyone ever employing Mrs. Arthur or indeed "her Bill."

I should know better but still I persist. I'm intrigued by the boy in the photo and the evasiveness I sensed in Gemma. I wonder if he died.

"I've met Gemma," I say, "but not the son, is he still local?"

Anyone else might wonder at my interest; not Mrs. Arthur. She moves closer to me, the consummate gossip, and lowers her voice conspiratorially.

"I don't know the details mind you but 'e used to work with 'is father at the practice. I 'eard there was a family falling out or something after the mother died and 'e went abroad. Last Bill 'eard, 'e was doing well for 'imself, that sort always does, running a company in the States I think."

I wonder at this. I'm certain Gemma said there was only her and I don't understand why she would take the trouble to lie.

I extricate myself from the garrulous Mrs. Arthur by assuring her that I'll be in touch if we need her services and slowly wend my way back to the house. I find myself more interested than I would normally be, intrigued by the family who lived here before. It's as though I hope in some way that they hold the key to the house's atmosphere, its emanations and the effect it seems to have on me.

I stand and regard it from across the lawn. Its windows blankly reflect the gray of the sky back at me, coldly hostile.

16

SEPTEMBER 2004

"To die will be an awfully big adventure"
—J. M. Barrie, *Peter Pan*

She knew it was over. For a while she'd hung on by her fingertips to a gossamer thread of hope that he'd tire of her, that he'd let her go. Really she should've known from the start it was over. Denial had sustained her for a while but that didn't work anymore. Nothing worked anymore.

She had moved beyond terror, beyond pain, she was now nothing more than a burning nub of consciousness and hate, an animal trapped and dying. If she could, if she had the strength, she would fly at him; she would tear out his throat with her teeth and claw the eyes from his skull.

Whether it was the lack of food—she hadn't eaten for days—or the periodic drugging, she felt detached. It was as though she'd already left and was floating above her body, looking down from the stars. One eye was swollen shut, not that it mattered anymore, there was nothing to see. Only him. Her legs were streaked with blood, her earlobe torn where he'd gnawed and bitten, the blood caked hard on her face. Her body was broken but not her soul.

Every night—or was it day? She had no sense of time—she sent her thoughts flying out across the treetops, screaming, "I'm here, I'm here." She would squeeze her eyes tight shut and will herself back to her home, to her parents. Please God, don't let them die not knowing what happened to her or where she went. Don't let them think she ran away and left them. Sometimes for a moment she thought she saw them, there against the blackness. Her mother quietly crying in the kitchen, her father staring blankly at the television, his face aged with the creases and furrows of loss.

In her bid for someone, somewhere to know where she went, she had scored her initials into the stone with the only tool she could find. Over and over in the dark she had scraped and scored but he'd seen what she'd done and had gouged at the wall and at her, until there was almost nothing left. Still, he hadn't got everything; he hadn't seen what else she would leave, not yet. She hoped she'd remembered the order of it but her mind sometimes wandered and lost its way. Sometimes she struggled to remember who she had been, and why.

He was outside, she was sure of it. She couldn't hear him, she could sense him. She could do that now. She could almost smell him. She sent a torrent of hate through the wall, spitting and burning like acid.

He opened the door and she could see his silhouette dark against the soft glow of the light outside. He had a bottle in his hand and a towel on his arm—like a waiter, she thought and fought the irrational urge to laugh.

He spoke to her softly, three words, "Time to go."

Sometimes he didn't speak. Sometimes there was only silence and pain, silence broken only by her muffled screams. Sometimes he sang to her, which was worse somehow. Songs from the charts that she'd never get to hear again. Today he was talking.

He poked her with his foot. "Come on, ticktock."

She had nothing to lose, not now. She pulled back cracked lips, revealing the gap where a tooth had been.

"Fuck you," she said, and sensed rather than saw the incredulity flood his face.

He lunged and the towel was suddenly against her face, and he was pouring and pouring. The sickly sweetness ran into her nostrils.

It filled her mouth and her eyes. The cold streamed into her hair and her ears, burning the bites and gouges. She had no strength left to fight and her hands flapped and flailed helplessly against him as he pinned her down. She gasped and choked as her chest flooded with ice and she felt her heart skip and slow as her lungs struggled for breath.

The pain exploded and then she could fly. As weightless as air she slipped his grasp. Lights crackled and sparkled behind her lids like fireworks, and the person she was and the person she could've been began to slip and fade away. Time rippled and folded in on itself, revealing possibilities that would never now be. Before the final pin-prick of light went out, she glimpsed for a moment the husband she would never love, the children she would never know—and then she found peace.

He observed her dispassionately, what a mess. It really had been time for her to go. She'd been so beautiful and fun while she'd lasted; shame she hadn't had the stamina. Like his mother she'd allowed her beauty to rot.

Her eye was open. He tentatively touched the wetness of an eyeball—no reflex. He'd seen the vet do that when they put old Buster down. Only difference was, the vet didn't fully appreciate the transcendent beauty of the moment in the way that he did.

17

"Nothing in this world is hidden forever"
—Wilkie Collins, *No Name*

We've done all we can with clearing the coach house. I worked my way through the boxes and found nothing of interest or value, just boxes and boxes of endless detritus accumulated over the years. Things broken and never repaired, things obsolete but still working, things that "might come in useful one day." All of it destined for the dump. It made me feel sad to think that one day someone would go through the refuse of Tom's and my life discarding things without a thought. Perhaps no children to say, "Oh, look this used to be Dad's," or "Remember when Mum got these?" Sometimes I acutely feel the loss of the children I've never had. I feel the bitterness giving me my lemon soul.

The waste container and the big items were taken away yesterday and today the commercial cleaning company is here to sandblast and steam away the years of cobwebs and dirt.

We eventually found the key to the annex. It's a workshop complete with workbench and vise, and a dusty tool collection dangling from the wall. According to Tom some of these are quite specialized and in good condition so I'm waiting to hear if Gemma wants them. Otherwise it's eBay. We've left the annex alone for the moment. It's just as cluttered but much cleaner than the rest of the building, and with a lower roof so we can deal with it ourselves once it's cleared.

Today I've driven into the village for the first time since we've been here. It was painful to realize how isolated I'd become. There's been nowhere to go and I've gone nowhere. For the sake of my sanity it couldn't continue so I've insisted on getting a car. There was no need for one in London; here my shiny black VW Golf is an essential. It's new to me and I love it. Regardless of how many "careful owners" have already had their hands on it, to me it's mine. Tom doesn't really like me driving, he's afraid my concentration will lapse and I'll have an accident, but I have my license and I'm legal so he's had to accept it. I also rejected the cars he found for me. It's my money I reminded him—a little too snarkily perhaps—and I'll have what I want. Driving might be more difficult for me than for most but that doesn't mean I want a geriatric's car. Thanks, Tom, but no thanks.

I have an even greater challenge facing me next week. Caitlin's been in contact. Someone has been inquiring about me at the gallery and is "desperate" to meet me. He's a potential client who wants to talk to me about a commission, two large pieces for the reception area of his new offices. It's familiar territory for me as I used to do big canvases that we hired out to companies for their boardrooms and reception areas. It was quite lucrative for us and gave them a way of refreshing their space without too much outlay; tranquil to dramatic at the turn of a canvas. They all eventually got sold off but maybe now I've got the space I could do some again.

This client insists on meeting me so I'm traveling back to London next week. Although I know I have to do it, the thought of a train journey and taxi fills me with anxiety. I could hear the impatience in Caitlin's voice on the phone, "No one's heard so much as a peep out of you for ages. What've you been doing? Working, I hope. We were beginning to wonder if you'd died." No Caitlin, not yet although some days it's felt like it.

The village itself came as a shock in that I realized I'd been here before. I remember Maria and I caught the bus here from Thorpwood House on one of our clandestine trips. It scares me to think the school could be that close. I wonder if Tom knew that when he first found The Lodge.

Half of me wants to find out if it still exists, the other half shies and skitters away from even thinking of it. There's something unbearable about the idea of it still being there. The sun still slanting across the same playing fields, the same morning mist hanging over the trees. Even some of the same staff stalking the corridors, older perhaps but no wiser. A new generation of girls with their dreams and secrets, prowling the dorms and playing hockey on the pitches so near to where my life was rudely interrupted. Daring each other to run through the trees where I was found—me, the ghoul of Thorpwood.

Although so many of my memories are lost or obfuscated, for some reason I can still picture my school with utter clarity. Clear and bright as though seen through a lens. It's like it's frozen in time, that place where the person I was meant to be lost her life. It makes me shudder even to remember it and I hope it's gone. Sold off and replaced with a new housing estate, its memories and echoes forever erased.

The village has changed little except for some expansion at its edges and is rather quaint. It's still a village in the true sense, in that it hasn't yet been swallowed up by the nearby town with its industrial sprawl that's gradually eating up the countryside. There's a main street if you could call it that, flanked by small shops and an eclectic mix of houses. Some red brick Victorian like The Lodge, others thatched brick and flint from an earlier time. It even has a village green with an algae crusted pond fringed by bulrushes, its surface like carpet, and two pubs, one of which is thatched and inviting. In the height of summer it would be a lovely place to come.

I've walked from one end to the other and have found the obligatory shopping center with its Co-op and its chemists, and now I'm tired. The slight drag in my step has become more pronounced.

I met Madeline on my travels. I was walking along the main street so lost in my memories that I almost missed her. I nearly bumped into a man coming in the other direction, and when I glanced up to apologize, there behind him was Madeline. Seeing her was lucky. It means I won't have to make another trip to Stour Cottage. I walked there the other day after some sustained and wearisome nagging from Tom but thankfully no one was in.

Stour Cottage itself was a bit of a surprise in that its name is a touch of whimsy. I had envisioned a chocolate-box cottage, all whitewashed walls and bullseye glass, dog roses round the door. Instead I found something more like a Hof Haus, built of timber and glass with a hard-angled starkness. It was set well back from the road on a plot of land that must once have formed part of The Lodge.

In the cold light of day and with a clear head I found Madeline to be more ordinary and while not exactly friendly, she did seem more approachable than the night of the dinner. She accepted my, I have to admit, rather grudging apology with good grace, saying, "Please don't worry, it's absolutely fine, I quite understand. Tom told me you'd had some problems."

Well thank you for that Tom. I was going to pass it off as an unfortunate case of too much wine; he's made me look like the loony next door. More to the point he hasn't mentioned speaking to Madeline. I hadn't realized he'd seen either of them since that unfortunate night.

As she turned to walk away I couldn't help noticing the mark on her neck, purple like a bruise—or maybe a love bite. Someone must still be having some spontaneity in the bedroom.

On my way back I decide to stop off at the coach house to see how things are progressing. It looks as though the contractors have finished and the front doors stand wide open to air out the space and clear the residual dampness.

I get out of the car and stand in the clearing, which still holds its air of gentle quietude. Someone has lit a bonfire not too far away and the air is redolent with the scent of wood smoke.

The coach house is spotless, with the beauty of the brickwork and beams revealed for the first time in many decades. It has the airy feel of a barn conversion and would make a living space if we wanted to convert it. Come to think about it I'd feel a lot happier living here than in the main house.

As I stand and look at the building I notice something odd. The dimensions of the annex outside appear bigger than the inside of the workshop. It's difficult to tell with the brambles and bushes encroaching but I'm almost sure the window inside is much nearer to the back wall than it looks to be from out here. Despite my tiredness I have to find out. I step inside and am immediately beguiled by the lofty tranquility of the place. Whatever we do with it we must retain its essence somehow.

I go through to the workshop and as I thought, the little window is much closer to the rear wall. I pace it out to be sure and run my hands over the back wall, tapping to see if there's a space behind. It doesn't sound hollow and feels sturdy enough although it's difficult to tell as it's covered by a sheet of board, which is drilled with small holes and covered with the hooks that held Mr. Connor's tool collection.

I go back outside and try to pace out the distance from the window to the edge of the building. It's difficult as it's partly obscured by brambles. That's strange. There is a difference, as if there's a space of some sort beyond the inner wall. Tom will be home soon and I'll ask him to help me move the board to see what's behind. I'm sure there's a simple explanation and I could look myself but for some reason it unsettles me. Suddenly I want to go back to the house.

It may be my imagination, but the quality of the air seems to have changed. It's become charged and expectant, waiting. The back of my neck prickles with the sensation that I'm being watched by hidden eyes, and the leaves on the bushes shiver and tremble as though someone has just brushed past them. I quickly get back in the car and drive the short distance round to the front of the house. I'm cold and tired and need something to drink.

The house is cool and silent and hostile again today. I unload my shopping from the car and go through the hall to the kitchen, dumping the bags on the table on my way to the sink. I'm desperate for a coffee. My leg aches and I lean my weight against the sink as I wait for the kettle to fill. The hard edge pressing into my hip feels like a memory and there's a hint of wood smoke in the air as if it's followed me in from the garden.

Suddenly someone speaks behind me, his voice hate laden and vicious.

A single word, "Bitch!"

Immediately time slips and folds and I'm here but I'm not. This is real but it isn't. I feel myself pressed to the floor, rough hands in my hair tearing my head back. Me too terrified to scream.

On some level I register that this isn't happening. I'm by the sink alone, clutching its edges, my knuckles white with tension. A storm blows through my head and then there's nothing.

When I come to I'm on the floor. I'm terrified but I'm not hurt. I take a moment to understand I'm alone, that there's no one here and there never was. I slowly gather my fractured thoughts and take stock. It wasn't a seizure, there was no taste of burning rubber, no clonic jerking, and thankfully the contents of my bladder are still safely stowed where they should be. I don't feel thirsty or sick or any of the other things I associate with fitting. I think I just fainted.

I'm afraid to stand just yet so I crawl through to the stairs and up to bed. I need to sleep, to suspend my existence and not be in the world for a while.

I wake before Tom is home and find I'm surprisingly calm. I'm warm and drowsy and wobbly with relief, bathed in the kind of detached calmness that follows a shock. I lie here trying to make sense of what happened, because that was more than déjà vu, much more. I still don't believe that I'm ill. I won't believe Dr. Stedman's theories, plausible though he made them sound. There was a clarity to what I experienced that felt real, as though I'd fallen through a rip in time and found a glimpse of my past. I'm afraid, terribly afraid, by what's happening to me. I won't deny it but I'm not saying anything yet. I feel something prising its way open in my mind and for now I'll let it be.

18

SEPTEMBER 2004

"And he beholds the moon; like a rounded fragment of ice"
—Gustave Flaubert, *The Temptation of St. Antony*

He tamped down the last of the soil and scuffed the dead leaves and bracken back over the spot where she lay. As he stepped back to observe his handiwork, the clouds parted to reveal the full moon. It hung like a giant pearl that transformed the scene into a tableau of shimmering loveliness. He tilted his face to the man in the moon and savored the symbolism of it. He had been mildly irritated with himself for not thinking this bit through as well as he should've. Now, as the moon's beam soothed him, he realized he had nothing to fear. No one was likely to dig here among the trees, not for decades, if ever.

He'd been glad of the cover of darkness, not just for the gift of concealment it gave but because it softened and hid her. He didn't like to think of how she'd looked at the end. He preferred to remember how she was at the start; pink and golden and perfect—until he'd sucked the life from her.

He picked up the shovel, the pick and the flashlight and made his way back to the house. Tomorrow he'd take care of the rest of it. Now he needed to sleep.

He stood in the doorway and surveyed her little space. It seemed so quiet and lonely now she'd gone.

He flared his nostrils. He could still smell her. That animal ripeness she'd come to develop, overlaid now with a tang of blood and a whiff of chloroform. Her face suddenly flickered unbidden into his mind and he recalled the sheer hatred in her voice. He'd felt the venom in those two last words, "Fuck you." Ungrateful little bitch. He pushed the unwelcome thought away.

He slid wide the door and switched on the work light. He had to get all this cleared away, which seemed such a shame while she still scented the air so nicely. He sighed as he gathered up the crumpled blanket and pillow. No use crying over spilled milk.

The light picked out a scrap of blue, shining in the corner of the room. Her panties. He picked them up and crumpled them into his pocket; those he would keep for later.

He took the bundle of bedding out into the autumn sunshine where the bonfire was already burning brightly. He pressed the pillow to his face and breathed deeply for one last time before dousing it all with petrol and adding it to the fire. It caught with a sudden roar, blazing quickly to a veil of ash as the last essence of her made its escape into the world. He added her jeans and trainers and stood back to watch as the rubber melted and burned and the denim flared. He had counted the eyelets, the rivets and zips and would come back for those later. Better safe than sorry.

He donned the gloves and surgical mask and went back to the storeroom. Most of the blood that she'd shed had been on the blanket, or his tongue had lapped up its briny trail—but he needed to be sure. He scanned the floor for dark spots and stains, covering each with sodium hydroxide. It may not entirely do the job but it would degrade any lurking DNA enough to make things difficult. A quick rinse over with hot water and a bleach-based detergent, the addition of a few well-chosen props and it'd be job well done. He was bored with this now the fun was over. He wanted time to "reflect."

◦∞◦

Later, he stood in his parents' bedroom, naked before the long mirror. He liked to do that, to watch himself stand to attention. He pressed her panties to his face. The memory of removing them made him shiver. Her skin had been like velvet, her kitty like a mouse's ear. He grasped himself with the scrap of blue silk and began to stroke.

19

"And the supreme mystery . . . was simply this:
here was one room; there another"
                                    —Virginia Woolf,
                                         Mrs. Dalloway

W e're out in the coach house again. Tom has reluctantly agreed to
help me explore behind the tool board. I can see he's irritated.
It's hard to miss. He wears his irritation like a cloak, flapping it in my
face at every opportunity, great dark wafts of impatience. He doesn't
understand why I need to know or even why I care.

We've pulled forward the workbench to reveal the two sheets of
board fixed fast to the wall.

"Honestly Izzy, I don't get you sometimes. Why are we having to
do this today? You know there's not going to be anything behind here,
or if there is it'll be, oh I don't know, a generator room or something
equally impressive."

I can't answer that. I just don't like things unexplained. The thought
of secret spaces and hidden hidey-holes makes my flesh crawl.

"It won't take us long. If there's nothing there then fine, I'll leave it,
but it just doesn't make sense. Tom, it's not just a few inches, it looks
like there's a couple of feet difference."

He sighs—he does that a lot lately—and begins to unscrew the
boards from the wall behind. There are two, both firmly attached
with screws around the edges and down the middle. Each one causes
him to emit a fresh sigh—at this rate he'll end up on the floor gasping

for air. My mind throws up the image of a landed fish, flapping and squirming, rubber lipped with red gills heaving.

Eventually the first board comes free and we move it to the side. Behind there appears to be a wooden partition wall. Concealed behind the second sheet there's a door of sorts, fastened flush with two recessed bolts. I am vindicated and allow myself a small whoop of triumph. Tom is visibly surprised but I can't revel in my small victory as I'm beginning to feel inexplicably anxious at what might lie beyond. I notice there's a vent in the door, which troubles me more. Why is it there and more to the point, why was it all so carefully hidden?

With some effort Tom pulls back the bolts and begins to open the door. As he does a waft of stale air escapes the space like a silent scream. I am suddenly filled with presentiment and dread which makes my soul recoil. I feel it flattening itself against the ridges of my spine. There is fear in this place, I can smell it.

I realize I've gasped aloud as though the air's been knocked out of me and Tom turns to look at me.

"What on earth's wrong now? You've gone white as a sheet."

"I don't know," I reply, "there's something not right with this place."

"Oh, for God's sake Izzy, will you stop this. There's nothing sinister about it, look."

He slides back the door to reveal a small room, if you could call it that. It's built of gray blocks and contained within the original structure. The floor is concrete, and the space is empty bar four or five metal containers of various sizes, their surfaces eroded and pitted with rust. Tom reaches in and kicks at one and we hear the hollow slosh of liquid inside. He tries to open it but the lid is welded tight, which prompts a second kick of frustration. Where did all this anger come from?

"Wait here," he says, "I'll need to fetch pliers or something to grip it with," and he leaves me alone staring into the small space.

My initial dread has subsided but still I'm uneasy. There's a tang of fear in the air and I'm filled with the same sense of sadness I felt the first time we ever came here.

∞

When my head was being scanned with such remarkable frequency that I almost set up home in an MRI scanner, I can remember overhearing something about claustrophobic patients and fear. That if a patient panics in the scanner room some staff believe there's an increased likelihood the next one will panic as well. It's as if a pheromone is released into the air that signals fear from one to the other. That's how this room feels to me, as though someone else's fear has stained the air.

Tom's coming back with some pliers. His face is all pinched and peevish, his forehead puckered like a walnut. He never used to look at me like this. What happened to all that kindness? That solicitude and love for my vulnerability? Somewhere along the line we seem to have gone off plan. He's always had something vaguely untouchable about him, the sense of emotions held in check, but now I feel an unbridgeable distance is growing between us. One that was never there before. Sometimes I think a baby would set everything right, other times I fear we'd just be papering over the cracks.

"Right, let's see what we've got."

He turns the pliers and the lid opens with a hiss.

He inhales sharply. Petrol, he says.

He opens the next to find the same and a third contains solvent of some kind.

"There, it's a flammables store," he snaps, the impatience evident in his voice. "Are you satisfied now? No torture chamber or walled up victim?"

I don't like his tone.

"But why was it hidden," I persist. "I'm sorry but it's odd it being hidden behind boards all secured like that."

"I don't know and I don't really care. It was probably for safety or something, or to keep children out. They probably kept lots of stuff in here at one time because the walls have been reinforced if you notice. You're going to have to stop this, Izzy. All this looking for danger where there is none, always worrying. It's just a flammables store, nothing else. I'll take the cans to the dump and get the walls ripped out, then will you be happy?"

Looks like we're done here. I accept what he's saying but it still feels wrong to me, the way it was hidden. I've noticed there are scratches and gouges in the blocks of the wall and I absently run my fingertips over them. They're deep and have been made with some force, over and over again. I feel a cold zipper of fear run up my spine.

20

JULY 2017

"It's a thing to see when a boy comes home"
—John Steinbeck, *The Grapes of Wrath*

I t was strange to be back in England after all these years. The hotel
he'd booked had been fine for the night but not what he was used to,
not anymore. The country seemed all so small, so drab and provincial
after the States. Even Heathrow had lost the edge-of-the-world glamor
he remembered from his childhood. God he was glad he got out when
he did, for more reasons than he cared to think about.

His parents had been so disappointed when he didn't follow in his
father's footsteps. They were almost ashamed that he'd opted to be
technical and not clinical. Childish though it was, he wished they
could see him now. His company's pioneering work in tissue regenera-
tion, bone allografts and implants had made him a small fortune, more
than it ever would have in the UK, where they lacked the American
pursuit of perfection.

The States also offered so much more for a man of his predilec-
tions and money. Here he'd spiraled out of control. At risk of ram-
paging like the madman he wasn't, all his inner demons bursting
forth. He'd had no choice but to get away. The more extreme reaches
of the BDSM scene in the US at least gave him an outlet of sorts.
Strictly top of course and not for the squeamish and so what if he
didn't always hear the safe word the first time of asking. Or if he got

a bit "overenthusiastic" sometimes. It helped keep his urges at bay. It stilled the dark fantasies that beat their wings in the cavern of his skull. Trouble was he found it all so sanitized, so consensual that it wasn't sensual.

He'd been tempted for a while by America's secret spaces. When he'd acquired his cabin on the lake he'd allowed himself to fantasize about the opportunities it presented. It was only ever fantasy; he never acted on those thoughts. Not anymore. He wouldn't deny he craved the thrill of another girl but he'd learned to keep his urges in check. He had too much to lose now.

It was the thought of what he could lose that had brought him back. His sister would've been happy—no, let's not pretend—his sister would've preferred to do the documents electronically. As he would have, until he saw that name on the papers she'd sent him. He could still taste the fear he'd felt when he read it.

He'd followed that name on and off in the early years, first on MySpace, then Facebook and Twitter, but there'd never been anything to cause him alarm. Only her commercial page and that didn't warrant his attention. Eventually he'd stopped looking, safe in the knowledge his past wouldn't find him. And now here it was.

He thought about his sister. God, it was over a decade since he'd seen her. He wondered, would that glint of fear and dislike still peep from her irises? It made him want to push his thumbs into them. She'd always been a stony little Gem, what she needed was someone to grind down her sharp edges. If he thought about it, what she really needed was someone just like him.

He watched her cross the foyer with that same brisk walk, confident and capable. No greeting, just a curt tilt of her head to indicate the lifts. Together they waited for the doors to open.

"No hello for the little bro then?" he asked.

Something about her still made him feel childish and antagonistic. He could almost sense himself regressing just looking at her and it made him hate her more.

"Let's not make this more difficult than it has to be, let's just sign the documents and go. I still don't understand why the hell you insisted on coming all this way, there was really no need. It would've been far easier for everyone if you'd stayed away."

She looked at him with sudden concern. "I take it you're not intending to see him while you're here?"

He looked at the stubborn jut of her jaw, her body pressed into the far corner of the elevator, as far away from him as she could get. He deliberately reached out his hand toward her and watched her flinch.

"Why, is he asking for me? Return of the prodigal and all that?"

"No, and it's best you don't. It'll only upset him and he doesn't need that."

"Tempting though that prospect is, I've decided I'll give it a miss, thanks all the same."

Before she had chance to retort the lift opened at the fourth floor and they stepped out into the carpeted plushness of Balfour and Roe, Solicitors LLP.

The girl behind the desk was a neat little thing, fair hair pulled back into a tight chignon. There was a time when he'd have liked to get to know her and loosen her up a bit. Make her all sparkly and pliant.

She gave him a coolly professional smile.

"Please take a seat, Mr. Balfour will be with you shortly."

She indicated the leather tub sofa and chairs where another client was already seated, all weak chinned and anxious. He took the sofa, careful to make room for his sister, and smiled to himself as she pointedly chose a chair. So, they had old Balfour. If he remembered correctly he'd been one of the old man's bridge cronies. He stretched his legs before crossing them, resting his ankle across the opposite knee in a pelvic display of dominance. He glared at the man opposite who quickly looked away.

God he was bored already. If it wasn't for that bitch he wouldn't have had to bother with all this. He was tempted to just walk away. With a bit of luck he could be back on the 21.30 out of Heathrow, with a pretty little stewardess and free-flow champagne all the way. He knew he couldn't. This was too much of a coincidence. He had to find out what she was up to.

Mr. Balfour came down the corridor toward them. He'd aged. Father Time had robbed his face of its definition, the once-strong jaw was now jowly and slack, and his full head of hair reduced to a dandelion clock. His eyes were still as sharp though. He extended a puffy hand, the back speckled like a bloated hen's egg.

"Hello Mrs. Maitland, sir. I'm so sorry about your father, such a fine mind, exceptional bridge player. Please do come through."

Introductions over, they got down to the business in hand. He liked how old Balfour seemed to address everything to him despite the fact that the old bastard had given her the authority. He was obviously a man after his own heart.

Mr. Balfour slid the papers across the desk. He skimmed them briefly for form's sake but really he just wanted to sign and get the hell out of there. He needed time to consider his next steps.

As his eyes scanned the document her name leaped out at him and he registered the same jolt he'd felt when he'd first seen it. It had taken him some moments to recognize the tightness in his chest and the twisting in his stomach as fear. For a fleeting moment he'd felt the shadow of the boy he'd been back then, the boy he'd suppressed for years.

He'd never experienced emotions like other people and when he was younger it had bothered him; the fact they could feel things in a way that he couldn't. It had driven him to do things, try things, anything to make himself feel. It was then he discovered the pleasure to be had from inflicting pain. Nothing compared to the feeling of power it gave him, or the ultimate joy in taking a life.

He wasn't a stupid man; he knew exactly what he was but had learned to manage his darkness. He'd had to, if he was to have a life.

"Sir, are you all right?'

He looked up to see Mr. Balfour leaning toward him across the desk, his face creased with concern.

He arranged his features into a semblance of filial sorrow while his mind whirred and ticked.

"I'm sorry, this has just brought it all home to me, that's all. Poor father."

The thought of her in that house enraged him. She was responsible for what he was, and for the thing that happened after. She'd shown him what he could be and what he could feel, and then she'd cheated him. He didn't know what she was planning but he wouldn't let her destroy him. He'd destroy her first.

His sister couldn't know, no one could know that he'd be staying around for a while.

Somewhere deep within him, the boy he'd once been slowly opened his eyes.

21

"In a well-balanced, reasoning mind there is no
such thing as an intuition'"
—Agatha Christie, *The A.B.C. Murders*

There's a storm in my head, a tempest of swirling thoughts. I can't get the hidden space out of my mind and I'm afraid I'm starting to obsess again. This happens sometimes. My thoughts lock on to something and won't let go and whatever it happens to be runs like an endless dialogue at the back of my mind. It's like a word or a song on the brain, only worse.

I've been back there several times now and the whole thing bothers me even more. Tom ripped out the partition and we found it was double skinned and packed tight with insulation. I get what he said about flammables and the risk of explosion or fire but to me it seemed too much like soundproofing.

I'm disturbed by those marks on the wall as well. I've looked at them again and one in particular makes me uneasy. It's as though something was written there, something scratched into the blocks and then scored out. Most have been obliterated but with this one there's the faint impression of letters. One I can't make out, the other is a C or a G. I'm sure it's the work of a human hand and not some random damage.

Maybe Tom's correct, as usual, and I'm making a fuss about nothing. Seeing danger where there is none—little old nutso me. I don't know, it just doesn't feel right. It's another itch in my brain to go with the others. I can't make it go away. I won't, or rather I can't, talk to Tom about it for he has no patience with me anymore.

I made the mistake of asking him about his conversation with Madeline. It'd nagged at me, the fact that they'd met and the way she seemed to speak of him with such familiarity. He acted so defensively when I asked that if I didn't know him better I'd suspect him of infidelity. He squirmed and excused and told me he'd meant to tell me but with all the other things he had going on it was so unimportant it completely slipped his mind.

Apparently, he bumped into her by chance and they went for a coffee. He thought it best that he broach the subject of my "behavior" seeing as how I'd been so reluctant to do it. Did he honestly think I'd jump at the chance of being sent round to their home like a naughty child?

She seemed a bit low, he thought, which was why they ended up going for coffee. She felt compelled to pour her little heart out and Tom did a spot of comforting—that was after he'd aired my mental capacity issues of course. She's having a tough time of it apparently. Joe's aggressive and difficult to live with and she's feeling a little afraid of him. Really? He seemed mildly predatory but I didn't sense aggression from him when we met. I suddenly remember the mark on Madeline's neck and then I wonder. They don't all wear wifebeaters or have "love" and "hate" tattooed on their knuckles. That would make things too easy for us. I may not warm to her but it's sad if it's true.

While we're on the subject of Tom, he took the opportunity to tell me again that I've changed in the months since we came here. That may be true but if it is, he's changed too. Once so attentive and loving, now he's distracted and distant. Sometimes even when he's here he's absent.

I've come to the coach house again today. Now the partition is down I need to sweep up some of the debris and dust before it pollutes the main building. I've opened the little side window to let in some air and have tied a scarf tight over my face. The insulation was probably fiberglass and I don't want to breathe any in. I picture the tiny spikes of it piercing my lungs like spears.

I ignore the frisson of fear that I feel and start at the back of the room, sweeping around where the containers had stood. The floor is fairly clean apart from a few dark spots where something has spilt. It looks like dark paint but it comes away too easily when I scratch at it with my nail. It crumbles to dust, leaving a smudge on my skin like a bruise.

As I sweep, my eye catches on something glittering in the crack where the floor meets the wall. It's a hair clip tightly wedged in the gap. I prise it out and see that it's pretty and distinctive. A small cluster of marcasites, glossy and metallic in a flower design, set on a simple hair slide. It feels surprisingly cold to my palm. It's rather beautiful, dainty and vintage, so it's a shame that it's so broken. The setting is bent, and part of the clip has been snapped clean away. I discard it into my sweepings and continue across the floor before scooping everything into a black bag to take up to the bins. Finally, I mop the small floor to remove any traces of petrol or spillages and watch as the soapy water pools and settles into the dips and cracks.

Just as I'm finishing my phone rings. It's a slightly frosty Caitlin wanting to know what I'm doing about the prospective client. The reception is bad out here so I leave everything where it is and go up to the house to take her call.

I've arranged to go up and meet him next week. I was meant to go before but cried off after my fainting episode with the excuse that I was unwell. It appears he's quite persistent and has been back in again and again. It isn't fair to keep him waiting when he's so keen, particularly when it's potentially such a good commission. We're not so well off that I can let that go. I've made a definite date and will keep it this time. I've had no further "episodes" and am feeling more confident than I have in a while. Even though so much has been troubling and inexplicable, I've felt more focused since we've begun work on my coach house.

I need to meet this client for no other reason than Caitlin wants him out of her hair. He apparently keeps ringing her and is getting on her nerves. But then again, all men tend to do that to Cait—the hardened misandrist.

I notice the light on the answering machine is blinking. Three messages on the landline, probably all from Caitlin. She's been trying to get hold of me "on and off all day" but I'd better just check.

The first is Caitlin, "Hey Izzy, could you pick up the phone babe and give me a ring please, today if poss. Thanks."

The second is Caitlin, impatient this time.

"Hi, it's me again, where are you? I really need to speak to you about this commission. Give us a call when you get this."

The third is a wrong number or at least I assume so, although they wait on the line in silence for a while before hanging up. I can just about hear the quiet hiss of their breathing, in and out. They don't speak. I wish people wouldn't do that, it's the second or third one in the last couple of weeks and its beginning to feel slightly sinister. I really don't like it. At least say "Hello," or "Sorry, wrong number"; it's only polite.

I delete all three and make my way back through the unkempt orchard. I must speak to Tom about getting someone in to do the garden. He loves the house but the land is proving a bit of a challenge. Bar mowing the lawn and trimming back the hedges immediate to the house, he's hardly had time to get out here and it's rapidly turning back into wilderness. I may give Bill Arthur a ring if I can find the card his wife gave me. Let's hope he's a little more taciturn than she is.

The floor in the annex is nearly dry, just a few piebald patches where the water has pooled in the various dips and cracks. There's a hazy map of Italy by my bucket, nestling in its sea of concrete. Sicily is fading slowly away and little Elba's all but gone.

As I gather up the black bags I take one final look around and suddenly notice some scratches that look strangely like writing. They're on the floor by the corner wall, near where the hair clip was wedged. They're so small that the marks would hardly be visible if they weren't highlighted by the dampness that's drizzled into the grooves. It's made the wet stand out dark against the dry. It looks like numbers with the letters "HEL" scratched into the floor. I kneel to have a closer look and see the ten digits are uneven and hastily done. I run my fingers slowly across them and feel the muscle of my heart contract. I don't know what this means but it makes me feel more than ever that something is wrong.

The face of. Mr. Connor from the photo comes unbidden into my mind and I feel fingers of uneasiness creep up my back. I wonder if he is somehow part of this mystery.

I need to trust myself. I may not act or function entirely like other people, I may sometimes lack the social graces, but some of my instincts I feel I can trust. I may not read people well but I can read places. I tune in to their atmospheres and quiet emanations. It's as though a part of my brain has compensated for what's missing elsewhere. Every instinct tells me something bad has happened here. Tom would say that's nonsense and he's probably right but I do need to think about this and consider what to do.

22

"By slow, thoughtful watching, you can gain much"

—Ernest Vincent Wright, *Gadsby*

It was definitely her, no doubt about it. He'd recognize that face anywhere, even after all these years.

He should've dealt with things when he had the chance but back then he was too young and afraid. Afraid of being caught, thrilled by the feelings she'd released in him. Seeing her again awakened something dark. He felt it stirring and he needed to be careful. He could feel an undercurrent of rage gaining momentum and he mustn't let it fracture the tight control he'd worked so hard to gain.

He'd hidden in the trees at the edge of the orchard earlier that evening and had watched from a distance. He'd seen her tipping the wine down her throat all so happy and flirty. Didn't she realize? She had no right to be there, no right at all.

Now he stood by the dining room window outside the circle of light and he watched her. The curve of her throat with its jangle of silver, the boniness of her arms all sinew and skin. He shuddered at her darkness. She had no shine or glimmer, no sparkle or glitter. It was no wonder that afterward he'd only wanted his golden girls. She sucked the light from the very room and dimmed the candles as she passed. She did nothing for him and had nothing he wanted, not anymore. This would be purely self-preservation. But despite his best intentions he closed his eyes and let himself savor the thought of killing her, let it calm his mind.

He'd seen her earlier, there at the window, hanging her rags like a shroud. He'd willed her to fall from the chair, for him to hear the scream and the happy snap of her neck but she hadn't. No gash of red. No pearly iridescent bone. No, she'd continued to defy the gods, clinging to life with her tenacious, bony fingers.

He stepped closer and for a moment her eyes flickered toward the glass and widened as though with fear. Could she sense he was there? Did she feel her future out there in the darkness, plotting and planning and spreading its wings? He liked the thought of that. The idea that his power and presence could flow through the glass and still touch her.

He looked at the table. A jug of white roses was there in the centre, a blizzard of blooms. He realized with a thumping heart just what they were—the Winchester Cathedral, his father's pride and his mother's joy. He felt his control waver and the hate washed over him; of all people she shouldn't have them.

While they dined in the light he was there in the blackness unleashing his rage, slashing and wrecking and breaking the bushes until no blossom was left. He ground a final blowsy head with his heel and unzipped his fly, releasing a hot stream of urine onto the bushes. He pissed on the leaves and the flower heads, venting his fury. There, let the dirty bitch touch them now.

He crouched in the shadows and watched her descend into drunkenness. He saw her hurl bloody meat in the kitchen and row with her husband. Her mouth a black hole in her face as she shouted. Now that had his interest. Maybe that was his way back inside her head again. Could he really stand to get that close to her, the ugly, ugly bitch? To think he'd once thought that she'd shown him the shape of his life.

23

"Whatever our souls are made of, his and mine are the same"

—Emily Brontë, *Wuthering Heights*

I'm on my way to London to meet my prospective client. His name's Matthew Weston and he's arranged to meet me at the gallery. Usually for commissions like this I like to see where the canvas will hang, to understand the dimensions of the space and the way the light will fall. This won't be possible today as his office is apparently "all a bit of a building site," which is why he's suggested we meet at the gallery.

Tom has dropped me at the local station to catch the link train into town. He wasn't happy about me going alone but I convinced him that I'm fine. I can manage this, honestly. Let's hope I'm right. The dryness of my tongue and the way it's cowering against the roof of my mouth makes me doubtful.

The village train station is rather sweet. It's red brick and wood, complete with a fretwork canopy over the platform and hanging baskets. These are disconsolately trailing the last remnants of summer but must once have looked lovely in bloom. The whole place is like something from a bygone age and I half expect to see a stationmaster with a handlebar moustache and peaked cap come striding toward me. Perhaps Peter and Bobbie from the *Railway Children*, in flat cap and pinafore running across the footbridge above the tracks.

The connecting train is nearly empty, which is good. I sit and look out of the window as we chug our way toward the nearby town. The fields and hills pass by my window and I wonder if we're near Thorp-wood. On a clear day you could hear the sing-song horn of the trains from the school, the sound carrying on the wind as they approached the crossing. I hurriedly push the thought away, putting it back in its box and tamping down the lid. Today could be stressful enough without adding to it by waking the ghosts of the past.

We soon arrive at the main line station and I take a few deep breaths before leaving the safety of my carriage. I put on my iPod to block out extraneous sounds as I need to concentrate on the destination boards, the platform numbers and times. My iPod helps me. I play white noise rather than music as it cuts out the sounds without adding a new distraction. It helps me focus.

I find where I need to be and settle to wait for the London train. The platform is busy. Luckily I find a space on a bench and close my eyes. It's difficult to explain to someone who's never experienced it but if too many stimuli come at me at once, I lose my ability to focus on any one thing. It all becomes a jarring cacophony of sound and flashes of color, and I lose my understanding of things.

The train when it arrives is more crowded than I'd hoped. I manage to find the seat of last resort next to a woman of distressingly ample proportions. I squeeze in next to her bulk and sit quietly with my eyes closed and my head resting against the coolness of the window. This is when I know I seem a bit odd. Occasionally at times like this a kind stranger will ask me if I'm okay and I resist the urge to say, "No, and I never will be." Instead I smile and reassure them I'm fine, concerned that I'm concerning them.

I concentrate on my breathing and allow my pulse to slow, letting the journey slip by as if from a distance.

London is as it always is. I love my capital city and being here makes me realize how much I miss it. My heart feels it's coming home.

The black cab pulls into Frith Street and stops outside the gallery. I'm early but Caitlin is there to meet me, I can see her through the frame of the window. It seems a lifetime since I was last here. The street is still the same eclectic mix of restaurants and wine bars, tattoo parlors and coffee shops, with their tables and chairs cluttering the pavement. It's all still buzzing with people despite the chill in the air. I breathe in the scent of it. The clash of coffee and exhaust fumes, the aromas of India and the Mediterranean, all colliding in the familiar scent of my lost home.

I go into the gallery and Caitlin throws her arms around me, crushing me to her in her usual flamboyant style. Being hugged by her is a bit like being mauled by a friendly Doberman. All hard muscle and underlying menace. She holds me at arm's length and surveys my face.

"God girl, what've you been doing? You look like fucking death. You need to come back home right now, this country life doesn't suit you at all."

"Hey Cait," I reply, slightly ruffled by her honesty, "love you too."

Caitlin is a walking stereotype. Her black hair is topped by long unstructured layers with a close-clipped undercut at the sides, complete with razor lines. She's had another piercing since I last saw her. A septum ring, which makes her look like a mildly angry bullock. Best not mention that. She holds my hands and I see there's new ink as well, a rainbow on the inside of her wrist.

She's irreverent and sometimes abrupt to the point of rudeness and I love her. She makes me feel more normal somehow, as though I'm the foil for her craziness. I've always been drawn to people like her and, although physically they couldn't be more different, there's an echo of Maria about her.

"Where is he then, Cait? If he's that desperate to meet me I'd have expected him to be here already."

"He'll be here in a bit. He's been a right pain in the arse ringing me every couple of days."

She scowls at me so aggressively, as if it's my fault, that I can't help laughing.

She laughs too and adds, "He's a bit of all right to look at though".

I raise my eyebrows at this, and she gives me a sideways look. "What? It doesn't mean anything. I can still appreciate an attractive man. Same as you looking at a pretty girl doesn't mean you're gay."

She curls her tongue under and waggles its stud at me lasciviously, "Although if you change your mind it's not too late."

I ignore this. It's been a long time since Cait could get a reaction out of me, and anyway she kissed me once when we were both drunk and it didn't float either boat.

Her forthright manner and belligerent sexuality belie the person she is inside. Behind the façade lies one of the sweetest, most caring people I know and once she's decided she likes you she'll move heaven and earth for you. Most men I know are terrified of her or, like Tom, pretend to find her vaguely distasteful when really I know they're intrigued. It's unfair. If they set aside their prejudices and took the time to get to know her, they'd realize her worth. She knows her business inside out and has the most amazing eye. The pieces she has in her gallery are special and those of us she represents are privileged indeed.

Matthew Weston still hasn't arrived, so we opt to go for a coffee in Bar Italia. God, it feels just like old times.

He's arrived while we were having coffee and is sat with his back to the door, deep in conversation with Lauren, Caitlin's assistant. She's pushing her blonde hair back from her face and laughing at something he's just said.

He turns as we come in and suddenly it's as though I'm fourteen again and seeing a boy I fancy. I feel a blush burning my cheeks and find myself suddenly overwhelmed by a feeling of gawky awkwardness. The attraction is real and instant and takes me completely by surprise.

He's slightly taller and broader than Tom, dark haired with dark eyes and the whitest teeth, set in a lightly tanned face. One of his front teeth has a small chip and he runs his tongue across it in an unconscious gesture. My brain takes in everything about him. He's wearing a checked Black Fleece shirt—I know that because I looked at the exact same one for Tom last Christmas—with blue jeans, Chelsea boots and a Bell and Ross watch on his wrist.

His handshake is warm and firm and as his hand touches mine I have the sensation that I know him. Not in the sense of having met him before but like I understand him, who he is, and how he sees the world.

I become aware that I'm still holding his hand. Caitlin is looking at me oddly and I feel as though the air in the gallery is humming around me. I struggle to regain my composure and with some semblance of professionalism we sit down to discuss the commission. As I tap notes into my laptop I see that my hands are trembling.

I'm meeting Maria for lunch and I feel shaken if not a little stirred. Matthew Weston was lovely, perhaps a little too lovely and I'm disturbed by how he made me feel; as if the distance between our souls was no more than a hair's breadth.

As an artist you need to connect with your clients, particularly when it's a private commission. You can't just paint what you feel. You have to translate their vague ideas into exactly what they didn't know they'd always wanted. You have to bring the picture in their mind's eye out into the world. Matthew Weston had seen my work and told me it "touched something in him." I felt I could paint this man's life without him ever having to utter a word.

I've accepted his commission. It excites me and makes me feel some of my old enthusiasm for my work. But I must be careful. I love Tom and he loves me. Just because we're going through a rough patch I mustn't forget what we have and allow myself to be tempted by this feeling of attraction. Not once have I been unfaithful to Tom, not even in thought let alone deed, but for a fleeting moment I imagined it was my tongue gently caressing the chip in Matthew Weston's tooth. He's dangerous although he doesn't know it and I must be on my guard.

J. Sheekey's is busy and Maria's already here. She stands up and waves frantically as I come in and I join her at the table by the window. It's been three or four months since we last met up and it's good to see her. She looks tired but otherwise she's the same old Maria.

"Isabella, God it's been so long. I'm so sorry I haven't got out to see you yet, but it's been impossible with Harry and the baby. It's been nonstop."

She pushes her tangle of hair back from her face and I see the violet shadows bruising the tender skin beneath her eyes.

"I never realized having two would be so hard otherwise I never would've done it. I'm dead on my feet, it's relentless. Bottles and nappies, shit, pee and puke. Harry's decided he hates preschool as well, so there's tears and tantrums every morning. I think I'm going mad. God it's good to just get away from them for a few hours. Whatever you do don't . . ."

She suddenly stops and looks contrite. "Oh Bella, I'm so sorry."

I put my hand on her arm and reassure her. I've told her again and again it's okay. I like hearing about her children, I'm fine with it—although it's not strictly true. There's a growing pebble of want in my chest for a hot little hand in mine and a voice saying "Mummy." I don't tell her that though. It's the only thing that's a barrier between us and I'd hate her to feel she has to guard her words with me, or that I'd think her insensitive.

She changes the subject a little too quickly. "What about you Bella, come on you must have loads of news. How's the new house coming on?"

I don't really know where to start so find myself for once giving her a banal and polite response.

"It's lovely. Loads to do inside though and the garden's huge. Tom absolutely loves it."

She cocks her head to one side and looks at me. She can always tell when I'm holding something back.

"And what aren't you telling me? What about you, are you okay? You don't look very happy, is it Tom?"

She puts down her wine glass and watches me with concern. Her tuna tartare is momentarily forgotten. Even after so long she's still worried that one day Tom will let me down. For once I wonder if she's right.

"No I'm fine, honestly, it's just . . ." and I tell her about the house, how I find its atmosphere odd, and about the hidden space in the coach house. When I speak of it, the familiar feeling of apprehension surfaces and my food swells and sticks in my throat.

Unlike Tom she's intrigued by it all and agrees it seems unusual. She also knows my history better than most and is concerned it's preying on my mind.

"God Bella, it does seem a bit odd. It's probably nothing but I can see why it'd creep you out. I don't know how you could find out. What about the people who used to live there? Isn't there someone you could ask about it just to put your mind at rest?"

I hadn't thought of that. I've texted Gemma about the tools but haven't heard back. I could maybe ring her about those and just drop it into the conversation somehow. Perhaps then I could put it out of my mind.

The rest of our lunch is like old times, catching up on each other's news, sharing the gossip about mutual friends—who's divorced and who's seeing who. I tell her about my new commission and plans for my studio; she tells me what's happening with her children and with Stuart's job. It's so good to have some company. Someone to talk to for a while who treats me like me.

After lunch we stroll round to Covent Garden together for my cab back to Paddington. I find our goodbye so emotionally charged I feel a hint of desperation and have an overwhelming urge to cling to her leg like Harry does and beg her to take me home with her. Somehow, I don't think Stuart would approve.

As my taxi pulls away there's a finality about our parting that leaves me bereft, all shipwrecked and adrift.

I text Tom from the train and when we pull in he's waiting for me. He smiles when he sees me, a smile that lights up his amber eyes and warms my heart. He kisses me hello with his old affection and I feel a swell of relief and love for him, all thoughts of Matthew Weston pushed from my mind.

The new distance growing between Tom and me and the rush of attraction I'd felt toward Matthew were things I didn't share with Maria. I'm glad. It would've been disloyal.

24

"It is serpent nature to lie motionless for its prey"
—Catherine Cooper Hopley,
Snakes: Curiosities and
Wonders of Serpent life

He'd positioned himself at a point where he could see her but where there was little chance she'd see him. It was always an advantage to know your territory and this he still knew like the back of his hand.

He was aware on some level that it was dangerous for him, being there. In his new life he had control. He had built a careful construct that allowed him to function, to live and to work, hidden in plain sight. In this place the memories were too strong; memories that called to his past self and weakened his resolve. Being there disturbed his equilibrium and made him conflicted.

He should just enjoy the irony of *her* being *there* but too much was her fault. If that day, so long ago, had ended differently then he would never have known. He would never have been aware just how blunted his emotions were, or what it took for him to truly feel. He would never have had to run away from what he'd done and spend his life denying himself the one thing that made him alive. She deserved to die; for daring to be in his house and for what she'd done to him.

He would kill her. She owed him that—once he'd satisfied his curiosity as to what she was doing there and what she perhaps remembered.

He'd need to be careful. It may have been the best part of a decade or more but there were still people who would remember him. He'd changed his appearance as much as he could and time had conveniently done the rest but someone with his striking good looks was bound to stick in the mind like a honeyed burr. As long as he didn't come into close contact with anyone from his old life he was safe.

Last time he'd quietly stalked his prey, staying under her radar. She'd sparkled and shimmered through her short little life blissfully unaware of the clock ticking. This was a slightly different game. Now he felt the urge to punish. He hadn't thought it all through yet, such spontaneity was strange to him, but he'd wait to see where she led him. So far it had been no more than along the garden path, where he'd waited and watched. He was sure she'd sensed him for he'd seen her pause like a frightened deer, all but testing the air with her nostrils flaring.

For all those years he'd denied his true nature, surely now he could allow himself one last indulgence. Yes, he needed to finally be rid of her but he hadn't entirely forgotten how good it felt to cause a creature fear and pain.

He'd started gently with the random phone calls. No heavy breathing, let's not be crass, instead he'd relied on silent menace. Something he could do so well. He was enjoying the effect, subtle as it was. He loved hearing the change in her voice from disinterest, through irritation to now just a hint of fear. He'd felt the tremble in her voice, the husky tone of her, and had been surprised to find a pleasurable straining at his fly. Now that was unexpected.

It provided a diversion while he learned her movements and habits and weighed up the opportunities for his gentle insertion into her life. He was thinking art. He needed to use what was there to get himself in and art was his opening. A picture painted in blood.

Annoyingly he'd lost track of her in the village earlier and he'd had no choice but to come back and wait. She'd eventually returned. She'd stood for a while looking up at the coach house before disappearing inside. He'd noticed with interest and not inconsiderable pleasure that her leg seemed to be dragging. He hoped it hurt her.

It had bothered him at first, the fact that they appeared to be renovating the coach house, but he'd recovered his equanimity soon enough. He'd reminded himself of the careful planning and covering of his tracks and had felt a renewed hatred toward her. A loathing just at her being there and for making him doubt himself.

He registered he was getting cold now and the light was failing. He pushed himself away from the trunk he'd been leaning against and slipped silently away between the trees. He was gone before he could notice Isabel come out of the coach house and begin pacing out the length of the annex wall.

25

"Your theory is crazy but it's not crazy enough to be true"

—Niels Bohr

Her phone is ringing, about to go to voicemail. I don't really want to leave a message as that way I can't easily ask her anything.

Suddenly she picks up, "Hello?"

"Oh, hi Gemma, it's Isabel, you know, from The Lodge? Really sorry to ring you but I hadn't heard back about the tools so wasn't sure what you wanted us to do with them."

"God, I'm sorry, I'd completely forgotten. To be honest with you I don't know if we can really be bothered with them. Are there very many or what?"

Here's my opening. "There were some in the workbench drawers but most were hung on the tool board in front of the storeroom door. We've boxed them all up."

There's a short pause. "Storeroom?" A note of puzzlement in her voice.

"Yes, you know, the little space behind the back wall? There was nothing much in there by the way, just some containers of petrol and stuff."

She sounds genuinely confused, "I don't know where you mean, I never even knew there was anything behind there. Must be something Dad put in when we were kids."

There it is again, the "*we.*" I wasn't mistaken.

"Anyway, about the tools, I don't think we'll need them. You can do whatever you want, either keep them or get rid of them, it's up to you.

If you put them on eBay you might even get something for them." She laughs and goes on, "You deserve some reward for having to clear out the coach house. I still feel bad about that, we really should've done it before you moved in."

I thank her and ring off, promising I'll try not to bother her again.

Well, I think that confirms it. She didn't know about the space behind the wall, which is odd. If it was something innocent, why didn't she know it was there? This means I'm no further forward. I'll just have to try to stop brooding on it.

It's easier said than done and now I'm down here again, pulled by the thread that seems to connect me to this place. I just needed one last look, one last chance to dispel how I feel and to try to make sense of it. Tom has already contacted a local builder to knock out the walls and dispose of everything and soon it'll all be gone. The builder's going to put in a partition to split the main coach house in two. I'll have the front half with the side entrance and window, plus the double doors at the front. I'll need to do something about the light but it'll be a much better space to work in.

I've brought some paper with me this time. I press it against the marks on the wall and gently shade across it with a pencil. It transfers the images from the wall to the paper, like a brass rubbing. Just in case. I do the same with the numbers on the floor and sit there for a while trying to imagine who could've made them and why.

The writing doesn't look like a child's. I suppose it could be but why would they do it. Why would someone take the trouble to scratch a message—if that's what it is—into the floor? Maybe it's part of a child's game, no more than a coded message once left for a friend. It just seems too deliberate somehow and the force with which the marks on the blocks have been made belies the suggestion of a child's hand.

I look at the numbers again, ten random digits and the letters "HEL." The number doesn't seem to make sense as a phone number, not even a mobile or toll-free number. "HEL" doesn't make any sense either. Was it a name? "Helen" or "Hello" or even "Help me"? I shudder at the thought of the last, the goosebumps bristling along my arms.

I fold the pages and put them in my pocket. The marks on the wall look clearer on paper and there's definitely something more than just random scratches. A letter C or a G stands out distinctly. I need to show this to someone.

I know I'm going to really, really regret this. I've driven into the town. I'm considering going to the police station to tell them about the room and see what they make of the marks and the numbers. I haven't decided yet as I could just end up looking stupid or neurotic or just plain mad, still, I feel the need to do something.

I haven't said anything to Tom as we seem a bit closer at the moment and I don't want to spoil things. He's been so solicitous and loving toward me, almost as though he feels guilty and is trying to make up for his previous moods. I know what he'd say if I mentioned this to him—probably the same thing as Anton would, although he'd be running after me with a syringe and a straitjacket.

Particularly as it happened again yesterday, not quite the same as before but still disturbing and strange. This time I was coming through the front door when I felt a breath on my neck. It was like someone gently blowing and ruffling the hairs at my nape. So strong was the feeling of someone behind me I turned, fully expecting to see someone there, Tom perhaps, home early to surprise me. There was no one but as I turned back to the hall a thought came unbidden into my head. Bell-clear like a voice, my voice, "I should never have come." I had the same feeling of slippage in time and then it passed in a moment.

I'm not given to fanciful imaginings, or at least I didn't use to be. Now one has stealthily crept into my mind, insinuating itself into my thoughts. What if these aren't my memories. What if I'm somehow channeling the resonance of something that happened here in the past—like a haunting?

I've walked round the town for a bit. There's a very good art supply shop, Carter's, which I must remember. They're looking for someone to teach an art class, which could be just what I need. A chance to meet people and occupy my time. I'm now hovering outside the police station looking furtive and shifty and probably criminal all at the same time. I take a deep breath and go in. If I don't do it now I never will and then I know I'll only regret it.

There's a civilian support worker behind the desk. She's a pudding-faced girl with permanently surprised eyebrows and an unfortunate mound of cleavage, doughy and uninviting. I try not to look. She stops what's she's doing with an air of deep suffering as though I've interrupted her in the middle of something monumental. I see her slide her phone out of sight.

"Can I help you?" She asks in a tone that suggests she'll do anything but, and her astonished eyebrows arch skyward in indignation.

"Um, yes, I'd like to speak to someone please. It's about. . ." I hesitate. What is it about really? Nothing more than a half-formed idea or a hunch.

I find I've fixated on the speckling of blackheads across her shiny nose.

She looks impatient.

"Are you here to report a crime? A theft? Have you lost something or been hurt?"

"No, I mean yes, I might be."

God, how do I manage to make myself sound so stupid when I'm not.

I start again, "I need to speak to someone about something that might be important or at least something they should know about. Just in case it's relevant to anything. I'm not really sure."

She looks as though she's fighting and losing an inner battle not to roll her eyes heavenward and officiously she tells me to wait. She has an expression that needs a good slap. I fight back the urge to suggest that if she'd wanted to be a police officer she should've tried harder at school. She goes to a telephone at the back of reception. I can't hear the conversation but imagine something from a bad eighties cop show, "Hello, Guv? There's a woman out 'ere wants a word but doesn't know what it's about. Think we've got a right one 'ere sir."

She comes back and huffily asks me to take a seat; apparently someone will be with me soon.

I glance surreptitiously at the others waiting with me and try to decide—hardened criminal or hapless victim? It's impossible to tell.

There's a bedraggled-looking youth with angry spots and a tattooed neck, looking sullenly at the floor. Hmm, let's not be prejudiced but "Perp" beside his name I think.

An older woman is sat next to him wearing both a headscarf and a hat, her lips moving in a silent dialogue. Looks like I'll need another category for the mentally impaired. There's just me and her in that group for the moment.

Before my little game can continue the girl behind the desk comes over and I'm taken through into an interview room. It's small and airless with a table, three chairs and no window. The walls are painted the color of despair. I take the single chair, I think that's the idea, although I'm tempted by one of the pair. They seem more reassuring somehow—like there's safety in numbers.

Soon I'm joined by two officers; a spiky, ferret-faced woman with dirty blonde hair pulled back in a ponytail and a stocky, balding man. They introduce themselves as DCs Arnold and Pickett and sit down opposite me across the table. She, DC Arnold, is sharp-eyed and alert. He has a "no one at home" expression which must be endlessly comforting to the criminal fraternity.

They ask me for my name and I hesitate for a moment. Mrs. Dryland-Weir sounds snooty and for some reason I think it will alienate them. Mrs. Weir would be a lie, so I settle for, "Mrs. Dryland, Isabel Dryland."

I realize I've taken marginally too long to answer and they exchange a look. Good start. Now I've made it look as though I have difficulty remembering my own name.

"Right Mrs. Dryland, I understand you've got something you'd like to tell us."

I take a deep breath and start at the beginning with how we first found the space.

They watch me as I talk and I start to feel increasingly uncomfortable. The longer I go on the more fanciful and ridiculous my story sounds. I notice she has stopped writing part way through and is now tapping the pen against her teeth in a staccato rhythm that sets mine on edge. DC Pickett has the long arms of the law crossed at his chest and would find it challenging to look less interested than he does at present.

My discomfort ramps up a notch as I realize they're not taking me seriously at all. I begin to stumble over my words, becoming increasingly aphasic. I have the sudden thought that they might ask me to write something down and I feel the sweat prickle against my scalp. It's not that I'm illiterate or anything, far from it, but I have difficulty with the orientation of certain words and letters. I'm fine typing or texting but when I physically write things, I find letters and words reverse themselves like images in a mirror.

I know why their scrutiny is unnerving me so. It's reminiscent of the time after my attack when I was deemed sufficiently lucid to be interviewed. The police officers assigned to my case would watch me with the same unblinking intensity, as though willing me to remember. They would fire endless questions at me; what did I do, where did I go? Did I see, hear, smell, taste, touch, sense or feel anything? Anything Isabel, anything at all? "Come on Isabel, we need you to focus, we need you to help us."

I would sit mute with my father at my side urging me to remember. My mother looking pained and probably wondering if her hair looked all right or if the officers found her attractive. I would end up feeling sick and guilty, as if I had failed a test or had somehow let them all down.

Sitting here is making me feel like that child again and I wish I hadn't come.

I get to the end of my story and there's a moment's silence before the questioning starts. They don't quite understand why I'm here; what was it exactly that made me so suspicious that I felt I needed to talk to them? Is there anything I'm not telling them? Any concrete evidence that's led me to think a crime's been committed?

The mention of concrete reminds me of the numbers on the floor. I'd become so flustered I'd forgotten to mention them. I take the pages from my bag. They barely take the trouble to look but I notice that ferret-face does at least jot them down on the interview pad alongside my half-recorded words. She hands the papers back to me and I stow them away in my pocket.

DC Pickett then asks if anyone else shares my suspicions and even goes as far as to ask if I've spoken to my husband and if so, what does he think? Really? Are we back in the 1900s? I should perhaps tell him my husband doesn't think I should have the vote and that Mrs. Pankhurst deserves to be hanged.

I realize with dawning horror that I've said this aloud and now they're looking at me with a hint of hostility.

"I didn't mean any offense, Mrs. Dryland. We're only trying to ascertain if there's anything here to concern us. We wouldn't want to waste our time."

It's obvious they're not really interested and I suspect they've dismissed me as a rather silly woman with an overactive imagination and not enough to occupy her time. Of course that could be true. They patiently put forward a number of plausible explanations, similar to the ones Tom's used in fact, and reassure me that they'll be in touch should it become relevant to any ongoing investigation. They're not good at hiding their impatience. Although they tell me I'm welcome to come in and see them again should I think of anything else, I suspect their definition of welcome is a little different to mine.

I thank them for their time and take my leave. It went about as well as I'd feared, and I'm left feeling foolish and vaguely dissatisfied. There is nothing else I can think of to do.

26

*"I gave him my heart, and he took it and pinched
it to death; and flung it back to me"*
—Emily Brontë, *Wuthering Heights*

The wind battles hard and salty off the sea and the air has a lucent quality that sets the granite cliffs in stark relief against the sky. Tom and I walk hand in hand along the sand, our feet leaving their memories imprinted for a moment at the water's edge. I look out across the white-capped waves to where Gull Rock sits dark and brooding, ringed with a wheel and swoop of gulls and spun with spindrift. This is happiness—or it should be.

We're at Trebarwith on the North Cornwall coast while our kitchen is being transformed. Gone are the dated units and the tiles with their carrots and pepper pots, to be replaced with ivory laminate and cool steel, the granite floor an echo of the cliffs above us.

I love the Mill House Inn nestling in the dip of its wooded valley, and our room with its whitewashed walls and dark beams. The tiny window opens onto a wall of lichen-crusted granite, clustered with ferns and sea campion. In the mornings I lie here before Tom is awake and listen to the soothing plink and trickle of the water draining from the hillside. I feel clear-headed and calm. There are no nightmares here or nighttime wanderings, no feelings of panic or misplaced déjà vu.

I would normally find a trip such as this a challenge and the strangeness of the place with its unfamiliar surroundings would be a threat to my very peace of mind. Instead I feel relieved. Relieved to be away from home and also reassured for I have proved Dr. Stedman wrong. Surely if I was unwell, as he suggested, I would take my symptoms with me. I would not watch The Lodge receding in the rearview mirror and feel my fears left behind, safely confined within its walls.

Tom and I have spent welcome time together. We have gone for walks and had lingering lunches of potted crab and ploughmen's in dark paneled inns, with the scent of wood smoke in the air and the ceilings netted with glass floats that reflect the light in its rainbow colors. Together we have slowly rediscovered at least some of our pleasure in each other's company.

We have talked. Tom has acknowledged his absence, the long hours he's away and his air of preoccupation or distraction when he's home. He says it's his work. The deal he has going through and what's happening with the markets is occupying his mind to the exclusion of all else.

I have told him that I've been afraid. Afraid that it's me on his mind and not in a good way. He cupped my face in his hands at this and told me he loved me. He promised he would never leave me for he knows how much I need him. Needless to say, my heart hardly quivered with boundless joy at that pronouncement. Of course, I was glad to hear he still loves me but it would perhaps have been better to hear that *he* needs *me*, even just a little. Instead his words made me feel like a burden, his responsibility rather than his joyful choice. I hate myself for this new insecurity. The fear that he will tire of me and my idiosyncrasies, that he'll no longer find my oddness endearing and will move on.

Despite his words all is not well for he's disinclined to touch me. He'll hold hands, as he is now, or smooth the hair back from my eyes, but it's in bed I sense his reluctance. Twice this week I've felt it. The first time it was no more than a slight half-heartedness. The feeling he was going through the motions while his mind thrust elsewhere. The second time I'm sure he feigned sleep.

I came through from the shower and slipped naked between the sheets. Tom was turned away from me, so I slid my arm around him and molded myself against the contours of his body, feeling his skin warm against mine. He didn't stir or turn toward me. I slid my hand down to find him, expecting his response hard against my palm. Instead there was nothing. His breathing—and everything else—stayed soft and even. Too even. Tom doesn't know how he sounds in his sleep. He doesn't hear the snuffles and pauses in his breath or the tiny snorts and mutterings that punctuate his dreams. Never have I known him to sleep so calmly and so quietly. He laid there, knees tucked up like the coyest bride, faking slumber.

I thought at first he was teasing me. I went to laugh and tickle him but something stopped me. Instead I lay there for a moment and listened to him breathing—such regularity, never a break or stutter in his inhalations—before I turned away. I am hurt and confused for the bed is one place where I never doubt myself; after all, practice makes perfect.

Part of the reason for this break was to get away from the house, to help relax me in the hope that "things might happen." I'd hoped I might go home with a tiny Cornish baby seeded inside me. That looks unlikely now.

We stroll back from the beach and up the wooded valley toward the Mill. After lunch we will start the long drive home and I am filled with apprehension. I must try to view our return as a fresh start or a new beginning and perhaps I'll feel happier.

We're having lunch and already I feel we're losing ground. Tom is withdrawing back into himself, his thoughts turned elsewhere. I'm losing patience. I've given him every chance to tell me what's wrong and have even been willing to take the blame upon myself, to acknowledge my part in things. If he won't tell me what the problem is then I can do nothing to help put it right.

I've lost my appetite for lunch. My salmon lies pink and flaccid on my plate and I can't bear the thought of it in my mouth. I'll make do with some bread and a glass of wine. Maybe a drink will allow me to sleep through the long tedium of the journey home.

I glance up from my plate and catch Tom looking at me with the strangest expression on his face; an inexplicable sadness or regret.

A chill runs through me. "What?" I ask. "What is it?"

His expression changes in an instant. "What do you mean, 'What?' It's nothing."

"You were looking at me so strangely, what's wrong?"

"Oh Izzy," he says, "everything's not about you, I was just miles away. I'm sorry," and he reaches across the table to touch my hand.

I'm worried about him. There's obviously something but he can't or won't share it with me.

The journey has taken over four hours but finally we pull into the driveway of The Lodge. I watch Tom's face light up at the sight of the house, with its mellow brick and pleasing proportions. I tend to forget how much he loves it, how much it means to him, and feel guilty about my own ambivalence. I wish I could love it too. I wish I could fall into its warm embrace and think, "This is home."

It's nearly dark but in the sweep of the headlights I can see how tired the gardens look. Wind-strewn leaves are scattered across the lawns and dead foliage litters the borders. I must find Bill Arthur's number. He can at least restore some order out of the chaos to see us through the winter.

The new kitchen is everything we'd hoped for. I smile as Tom runs his hands across the shiny surfaces with a reverence he usually reserves for a new car. The previous air of oppressiveness and neglect has gone, as has the strange familiarity that so troubled me. It's light, airy and modern and at last feels as though it's mine. If we can achieve the same with the rest of the house, then perhaps I can make a home here after all.

I see there's a small cardboard box on one of the units. It contains a selection of random objects, all dusty and furred with cobwebs. There's a collection of pens and a small notebook. A hand mirror and a couple of unopened letters. I pick up one and look at the postmark; it's from 2015. This must be stuff the fitters found under the old units but didn't feel they could just throw away.

I open the little notebook. It's a diary from the year before last, the important dates marked with a spidery hand. I flick through the pages and see the first Tuesday of the month was bridge night—at least until May. After that, Tuesday evenings have been scored through with surprising force until the word "bridge" has been all but obliterated. I also see the handwriting has deteriorated as the months have passed and odd words and phrases have begun to appear. "Remember the kettle," "my armchair is by the window" and later, "R Connor is me." I realize with sadness that I'm seeing the evidence of a deteriorating mind. A slow and irrevocable loss of self. I turn toward the end with a morbid fascination and witness his worsening condition. The poor man has written of men hiding in the curtains and, over and over again, "Did the boy do it." I quickly close it and discard both the book and the remaining contents of the box into my shiny new bin. Its lid closes with a gentle hiss and I push all thoughts of Mr. Connor and his diary from my head.

Tom goes to fetch our bags from the car. I navigate the darkened hallway and go into the sitting room. All is quiet. It never ceases to surprise me, the lack of sounds. No cars, no distant sirens, just the silent blanket of the countryside, only punctuated by the bark of a muntjac or the shriek of prey fulfilling its purpose.

I still recall the feeling I had of being watched during our dinner with Madeline and Joe. It always stops me from turning on any lights until the curtains are drawn. I glance at the blank window and for a second there's a face, white and stricken, looking back at me. Before the scream can burst from my throat I realize it's the play of the moonlight against the glass, nothing more. I must stop this. I close my eyes and breathe deeply, in and out. I try to still the feeling of panic gathering at my mind's edge. I long for the noise of the city, to be anywhere other than here. Tonight, I will dream again, I know it. As I pull the curtains tight I sense sleep's dark portent closing in.

Tomorrow I must occupy myself, so I'll start work on Matthew's sketches and preliminaries. I've had some ideas while we were away, inspired by the savage beauty of the Cornish coast. By its muted colors, and the quality of the light on water.

The thought of seeing him again gives me a sudden shiver of antici-pation and I use it to push away my fear.

27

"We are always paid for our suspicion by finding what we suspect"

—Henry David Thoreau

I can't find the card given to me by Mrs. Arthur anywhere. It must've got thrown away. I'm beginning to think I have no choice but to ask Madeline for the number, it'll be easier than trying to find someone else to do the garden.

It's cold today so I pull on my Barbour and scarf—see, I'm becoming quite the country wife—and set off for Stour Cottage. It's only a short walk before I reach the drive and their house standing stark in the trees. When I came before these were still in full leaf, which softened the harsh lines and sharp angles of the house. Now the leaves have almost gone, and it stands brittle and glittering against the clawed branches. Its glass walls reflect the lane back at me, blank and uninviting. It's a modern-day witch's house in the woods, with the sparkle of steel and glass instead of sugared gingerbread.

There is no gate, instead the crushed slate drive opens straight onto the lane. I self-consciously crunch my way to the door. Regrettably Madeline is at home, not Joe, and she opens it with a look of expectation on her face. She's dressed impeccably in a loose silk shirt and dark leggings; her mist of red-gold hair swept up in a scarf and a shimmer of gloss on her lips. I can't help but notice she's braless as there's a hint of nipple against the fine fabric. Do people really go to that much effort when they're home alone? I must take notes. Her face falls for a moment and then she greets me, all mouth-smiles and spite-eyes.

"Oh, hi Isabel, sorry, I thought it was someone else."

That was obvious.

"Hi Madeline, I'm sorry to bother you but I wondered if you could let me have Mrs. Arthur's number, I understand she cleans for you. She'd given me a card but I seem to have lost it."

She moves to the side and grudgingly beckons me in. "Please, you'll have to come in for a minute. I'll need to look for it."

I follow her into a large atrium, to call it a hall would be a disservice. The glass stretches floor to ceiling, the entire height of the house. The interior walls are white, and a floating staircase rises to a landing edged with more glass.

It's a breathtaking space and despite her animosity I can't help saying, "My God, this is amazing, it's like something off *Grand Designs.*"

She softens slightly and smiles, "I know, we love it. Joe's got an architect friend who works with a German company. He designed it, it's a one-off."

She offers me coffee, the consummate hostess—unlike some. I decline. I don't feel comfortable enough in her company to prolong the encounter. I sit down in an open-plan area that leads off the kitchen and wait while she finds the Arthurs' number. While I wait I look around, it really is a spectacular house.

I notice there's a scarf draped over one of the steel-backed stools. It's a striped Paul Smith. That's funny, Tom has one just like it.

Madeline returns with a piece of paper which she hands to me.

"There's the number. She really is very good. She talks a lot but if you make sure to choke her off right from the start she soon gets the message."

She notices me looking at the scarf and gathers it up from the chair, casually folding it and holding it to her chest.

"Thanks, that's great. It's her husband we want to get hold of actually, for the garden."

The defensive way she's holding the scarf is making me wonder, is it Tom's? His has a small hole in the corner where he caught it and I'm suddenly itching to check. Bar wrestling it from her arms—which I suppose I could do but it might prove awkward—there's no way I can.

I can't help myself, out it blurts, "Tom has a scarf like that."

It sounds hostile and accusatory rather than a statement of fact. We look at each other for a moment and I'm sure there's a challenge in her cool green eyes.

"And so has Joe," she says quietly.

There's a heartbeat of real awkwardness, prickly and intense, before I say, "Anyway, I'd best be going, thanks for the number."

She looks back at me.

"Perhaps you had," she says and turns toward the door, a trail of permafrost in her wake.

If it is Tom's scarf that means he's been here for some reason and not mentioned it. It could of course be a coincidence but a small and nasty seed of doubt has been planted. It's already sprouting roots. I must look for Tom's when I get home.

I've looked everywhere. I've turned out every fucking drawer and cupboard and it isn't here. What started as a mild niggle has now escalated into full-blown suspicion. I know he's worn it recently. I've seen it on him but now it's nowhere in the house. I feel sick. Please not that. Please don't let him be seeing Madeline behind my back.

It's late and he's still not home. He's always working late nowadays. Isn't that the usual excuse? Is my husband that much of a cliché? I suddenly feel an unfamiliar jolt of sympathy for my mother. Is this how she lived her life; always wondering where my father was and where he'd been, and what he was really doing? Desperately trying to stay slim and young and attractive for fear he'd leave her for a firmer buttock. All to no avail. For a moment I can taste her bitterness in my own throat.

I sit in the dark kitchen, my nice new kitchen, and wait for him to come home. There's no dinner. Fuck dinner. I need him to tell me what's going on. I'm wound like a coiled spring. Waiting.

I hear his key in the door and the thud of him dropping his bag in the hall. He comes through into the kitchen.

"Shit, it's been a hell of a day . . ." He stops in confusion. "What are you doing? Why are you sitting here in the dark? What's wrong?"

I go to speak as he flicks on the light. He's wearing it. It's round his neck, the ends tucked neatly into the collar of his coat. My relief is almost overwhelming and I feel the prickle of tears behind my lids.

"Izzy, what's wrong? What is it?"

I step toward him and put my arms around him burying my face in the wool of his coat.

"It's nothing," I say softly, "nothing at all. I'm just glad you're home that's all, it was getting so late."

He holds me at arm's length and looks into my eyes.

"Are you sure you're not having another bad day? You'd tell me if there was anything wrong—promise?"

I keep my own counsel and say nothing. I feel weak and foolish and pathetic. This is not me. Not me. Not me.

I make omelette and salad and we eat it on the sofa in front of the television, me nestled in the crook of his arm.

Later we go to bed and this time he makes everything all right for a while. But just before I fall asleep a treacherous thought worms into my mind; what if he went there before he came home and she warned him?

28

*"What seest thou else in the dark backward and
abysm of time?"*
—William Shakespeare, *The Tempest*

Bill Arthur is a lovely man. He's tall and wiry and his lived-in face of laughter lines and happy crinkles seems younger than his years suggest. He's one of those lucky men to whom the years are kind and he remains attractive despite his advancing age. In his Levi's, striped shirt and gilet he looks fit and I imagine he can still turn ladies' heads when he so chooses. He's sprightly and quick with a twinkle of mischief in his eye that belies his taciturnity. He says so little I worry that marriage to Mrs. Arthur has robbed him of the power of speech.

I have been working and although I'm happy with what I've produced, I find my concentration lapses more quickly than it did before we moved. Unwelcome thoughts creep in and drive me in search of diversion and distraction. My thoughts drift unbidden to Madeline. I've casually mentioned her or Joe in conversation and there's been no hint of evasiveness or any fleeting look of guilt shadowing Tom's golden eyes. There's been nothing more to feed my suspicion but still it remains a ravenous maw. Waiting. I haven't resorted to furtive spying or checking the messages on his phone. I'm not that creature yet—although there is still time.

I haven't started using the coach house, even though the partition is finished and the walls of the secret space have been magicked away. The power is going in next week and the annex is plastered and painted ready to make me an office or a storeroom. I'm pleased with how it's going but I need more light before I can really use it, so for the moment I work in the house.

When I find I need distraction I seek out Mr. Arthur, or Bill as he insists I call him, and distract him from his work as well. I trail after him like a bored child as he goes about his raking and his pruning. With a bit of coaxing he'll talk, and I find him pleasant company. He has a gentle wit and is a source of local knowledge which he'll share without adding his wife's light peppering of malice and opinion.

I have found out that Mr. and Mrs. Connor had two children, Gemma and Grant, and that Mrs. Connor died over a decade ago. Now I know for sure that Gemma lied to me about her brother and I wonder why.

Bill's told me that he worked for the Connors years ago, doing the garden at weekends, but it became too much for him what with his day job as well. He'd originally only stepped in to help after Alan Harris left but somehow ended up committed. I smiled to myself at this, imagining his wife volunteering the poor man's services to all and sundry with little regard for his leisure time.

I'm turning into a gossip myself. I want to find out more about Grant Connor and about the unfortunate Alan Harris. I'm on my way to find Bill with the pretext of a coffee. It's amazing what true loneliness can do to you.

I find him cutting back the roses, his hands encased in leather gauntlets against the thorns.

"Hi Bill, how's it going?"

"Better for seeing you with the coffee," he says and we sit down, side by side on the garden bench that's quietly rusting at the edge of the lawn. We're becoming two old codgers together. Soon he'll be taking me for a pint and a game of darts.

I launch straight in. "Bill, you mentioned Alan Harris the other day and so did your wife when I met her. I know I'm just being nosy but I'm intrigued. What happened there? Your wife made it sound as if there was some sort of incident."

Bill gives me a sideways look but clears his throat and smoothes back his hair. Oh good, that's usually the sign he's got a story.

"The Harrises are a sad little family, got problems. My Jill used to be friendly with the mother, Ivy Harris, way back and she got to hear a lot about the boy and what'd happened, passed it all on to me whether I wanted to hear it or not. You've met my Jill, so you know how she likes to share."

He twinkles at me and we exchange a conspiratorial look.

"Anyway, little Alan Harris had a difficult birth and I don't know the medical term for it, but he wasn't quite right. Jill reckoned he'd been starved of oxygen or something, made him a bit slow. I know you're not supposed to say that anymore and I don't mean anything by it but it's the best way to describe how he was.

"The father was a bit of a bastard by all accounts and when they found out the boy had problems he cleared off. Ivy always made excuses for him, said he couldn't cope but to me it seemed a rotten and heartless thing to do. Anyway, there was just her and the boy and she doted on him. Always did her best for him, tried to make him as normal like as she could. She wouldn't send him to a special school or anything, so he went to the school in the village and then on to the local comprehensive. It wasn't fair on him really. He couldn't cope, always in special needs and bullied a lot by some of the others. I always felt sorry for the lad."

He stops and gazes into the distance, remembering.

"Eventually he stopped going and I think the authorities got involved but I don't know the details. Mr. Connor, who I always found a kind enough bloke, eventually offered him a gardening job here, just helping out and doing a few odd jobs. He did a lot of it himself; he was practical enough and always found the time despite his practice, but Alan was a useful pair of hands to have around."

He pauses for a sip of his coffee.

"So what happened? Why did he suddenly stop coming?"

Bill resumes his story, "Well Jill reckoned it was down to the boy, Grant. He was a strange lad if you ask me, something of the darkness about him." He laughs at that. "God, listen to me, I sound a right old woman—no offense."

Oh Bill, Bill, ageism and sexism all in one sentence. I make an exception and let it pass to hear the end of his story.

"Anyway, according to what Jill heard from Mrs. Harris, Grant used to torment him something wicked. Alan was a few years older but couldn't stand up for himself, not to one like Grant. It started off as a bit of teasing apparently but then got increasingly out of hand and nasty until the boy was proper afraid of him. Mrs. Harris tried to speak to the mother about it once but it didn't do any good. Mrs. Connor was a lovely woman but she seemed blind where that boy was concerned. She doted on him and he could do no wrong in her eyes. She said she'd speak to him but she was sure it was nothing more than a bit of high spirits, no harm meant. High spirits! Grant was old enough to know better and she knew it, picking on a poor lad like Alan. Only saving grace was that he was away at boarding school latterly, so Alan only had to endure him over the summer."

The more I hear about Grant Connor the less I like, and I feel sorry for poor Alan. I of all people understand what it's like to be different.

"Anyway, it was sometime around the mid-nineties, ninety-four or five I think. Something happened over the summer. According to Jill—this is all secondhand mind you—Alan came home halfway through the day rambling and crying with his face all cut and pee down his trousers. His mother couldn't get any sense out of him. He kept babbling something about a girl and how he didn't do it and that they were all going to die if he told. It was awful apparently; the boy was terrified out of his wits. Mrs. Harris was going round there to see what'd happened to upset him so much but Alan got right hysterical. She told Jill he was in a dreadful state, screaming and crying, slapping his own head over and over, kept saying he mustn't tell. The mother put him to bed and called the doctor but I don't know what the upshot was. Alan didn't hardly speak for nearly a month apparently, according to Jill, worried the mother half to death, and he never went back to the Connors'. I don't think she ever found out what'd triggered it and nothing ever came of it. It wouldn't, you see. People like Ivy Harris can't deal with the likes of the Connors. Too in awe of them. And her past didn't help. Alan was more withdrawn than ever after that. I don't think he works now, still lives in the village with his mother. Same flat, one of the council ones in Bluebell round behind the church."

Bill reaches the end of his story. It's the longest I've heard him talk since he's been coming here. We sit quietly for a moment, both no doubt wondering what happened to scare poor Alan so. I feel uneasy and shiver despite my warm fleece. It's the mention of a girl that disturbs me and for some reason makes me think of the coach house. I'm amazed that Mrs. Harris didn't pursue things; I'm sure I would if it was a child of mine. I'd have gone to the police or at the very least I'd have gone round there to find out what happened. Perhaps she was afraid. Afraid he'd be blamed for something or worse, be taken away from her. Bill's right, some people are disempowered through no fault of their own.

I must leave Bill to finish his work and get back to mine. Before I go I remember something.

"Bill, can you keep an eye out for Mina? She didn't come in last night which is strange; she never stays out overnight."

I can hear the phone ringing in the house but I don't rush. It'll only be a wrong number again. It's happening more and more, either they just ring off or they leave a silent message. Last time there was music playing in the background. An old record, The Smiths I think it was, "This Charming Man" which spooked me more than it should have. There was something that set my teeth on edge and left me feeling out of sorts. I don't know who keeps ringing and there's no ring back number so I can't find out.

29

"What greater gift than the love of a cat"
—Charles Dickens

'm troubled. The nightmares have returned since we've been home and twice now I've imagined a face at the window. The second time I was alone in the kitchen and I had that same odd sensation of a fleeting memory. I'm losing the equanimity I found at Trebarwith, it's slipping through my fingers like sand. The familiar nub of anxiety is back. It sits in a hard lump behind my sternum waiting to spread and grow. I'm just so glad that I'm not here alone at the moment. I don't think I could stand it. I'm glad of the chatter and noise from the decorators and bathroom fitters as they go about their work.

The things Bill told me about Alan Harris seem to have wedged in the folds of my brain. His words are feeding my unrest, particularly the mention he made of a girl. I think I understand why she troubles me so; she feels somehow linked to the hair clip I found in the coach house. Its shiny petals sparkle in my mind's eye, accusingly, like an unanswered question. Gemma knew nothing about the storeroom so who did the hair clip belong to and how did it get there? I wish I'd not been so quick to dismiss the clip and throw it away.

I'm better when I'm away from here. I lose the haunted feeling I so often have of being watched. That sensation of hidden eyes following my every move and burning into my skin. My anxiety fades as the distance grows so I find excuses to be out of the house. I'm driving into the town today to pick up some varnish and to let the Carters know how well the course is going. As well as Carter's art shop, Paul and Leanne Carter run evening art classes and have enlisted my services for "Intermediate Acrylics." I'm enjoying it but can't help wondering which prodigious talent got to teach "Advanced." Tom thought I'd find it too challenging but it's done the opposite, it's helped me feel more rooted here. I get to meet people like me. People who speak my language of color and form.

While I'm there I could call on the Harrises. Part of me knows that I shouldn't, that it's an odd thing to do in anyone's book but odd's never stopped me before. I just need to know. The spikes of their fear will have been smoothed by the passage of time, so perhaps they'll talk to me. Perhaps they'll tell me what, if anything, happened back then.

I've found their address thanks to Bill, Twenty-Four Bluebell Court. Eat your heart out Nancy Drew.

Bluebell Court is ill-named. I doubt a bluebell ever graced these concrete courtyards, or winked like lapis lazuli amid the gray. It is a depressing place. It leaches the color from the sky and deadens my soul. I feel slightly panicked. I can't tell if it's the place that's doing it or the thought of what I'm about to do.

The block where Ivy Harris lives is one of four. Built of dark brick and concrete, it's streaked and stained by pollution and the elements. Although it's only four stories high, it's overbearing, hunched over its communal garden of cheery dogshit and litter. Luckily number twenty-four is on the second floor so I don't need to consider the lift with its graffiti-covered doors that yell entrapment. The stairwell I use instead is concrete and steel. It's gently fragranced with the uplifting scent of the urine that's crystallizing in its dark corners. I so don't want to touch the handrail. I didn't know such places existed in towns like this; I assumed they were the preserve of the inner cities, all sunk in deprivation.

I reach the second-floor landing where there's a row of doors, each a depressing clone of its neighbor. As I look for number twenty-four

I become aware I'm being watched and turn to see two small boys observing me. "They're scrawny and guarded, squeezed into younger children's clothes."

I knock and wait. Eventually I hear the sounds of a bolt pulling back and the turn of the lock, and I come face to pinched face with Ivy Harris. She's a steel wire of a woman, rake thin and somewhere in her early sixties. Her hair is dyed a harsh black and badly cut. The roots are a silver skunk streak across her scalp. She eyes me suspiciously and draws in the skin of her cheeks, emphasizing her smoker's kiss. She folds her arms in the universal gesture of defense and waits for me to state my business. I was expecting this to be difficult, but now I've seen her I realize just how difficult it's likely to be.

I start tentatively, "Hello, my name's Isabel. I wonder if I could speak to Alan if he's in?"

I was hardly anticipating an effusive welcome, but her stark response throws me for a moment.

"Why? What do you want with him?"

Gosh, someone even less versed in the social graces than me. I suspect she would sniff out dissemblance so I decide to be at least half-honest.

"I've recently moved into The Lodge and I know Alan used to do gardening and odd jobs there and I was wondering if he could help explain something that's been worrying me."

"Why? He don't know nothing about The Lodge, he hasn't been there for years. He hated the place so why have you come here bothering him?"

"Please, Mrs. Harris. I'm not going to bother him, it's just Jill Arthur said he might speak to me." That's the less honest bit.

At the mention of Mrs. Arthur's name she relents slightly.

"If you knows Jill you'd better come in then but I'm not promising anything mind, and don't you go upsetting him."

She closes the door behind me and for some inexplicable reason she pulls the bolt across. I suspect it's only habit—God, I'd bolt myself in too if I had to live here—but I immediately feel myself starting to panic and struggle to calm my breathing.

"Please," I say, randomly.

She looks at me rather oddly as though she can sense my desperation.

"Please, could I just speak to your son for a moment?"

She relents but with the stark warning, "Remember, I won't have you upset him mind, he's not well.'

She moves away from the door and points me through to a living room. It's cluttered with newspapers and piles of washing, all redolent with the smell of ashtray. Her sleeve falls back to reveal an arm marked with the scars of ancient needle tracks.

Ah, IV Harris. That must be the past Bill alluded to.

"Alan! There's a woman 'ere wants to have a chat with you or something. You okay to talk to her or shall I tell her to go?"

There's no answer. Instead a mountain of a man lumbers into the room, his thighs straining against his jogging bottoms and his feet spilling over crushed slippers. He looks to be in his early forties, although it's difficult to tell, and has a thin scar running from the edge of his left eye and down his cheek. He looks at me warily and as his eyes meet mine I experience the feeling that I've seen him before. The jolt of fear almost sends me running to escape. I know it's irrational so force myself to steadily meet his gaze. I try not to think of the bolted door.

"Hi Alan," I say, keeping my voice low and steady, "my name's Izzy and I live at The Lodge. Is it okay if I ask you a few things?"

His eyes are like glittering slits in raw pastry. Watchful.

"What, what you want?" he says.

I notice at the mention of The Lodge he moves across the room to be slightly nearer to his mother.

I'm nervous now and don't really know what to say or where to begin, so I start gently.

"I've not been happy since I've been there," I smile at him encouragingly, "and it's getting worse."

I don't know that I want to go into detail about my dreams or the space behind the wall. I can feel Mrs. Harris's eyes upon me so I need to tread carefully.

"Jill Arthur, your mum's friend, mentioned something that happened back when you worked there and I wondered if it would help me understand something I've found."

I fizzle out a bit and nobody speaks.

I clear my throat nervously. Here goes. "Jill Arthur said there was something about a girl there and that whatever happened upset you a bit?"

Immediately his eyes fly open and I can see the fear in them, still alive and well. He physically recoils, wobbling back from me like a startled mollusc, almost as though I'd struck him.

His mother's voice is strident and angry. "He don't know anything about any girl, he never did. What are you saying?"

"I'm not accusing him of anything. I just wanted to know if he ever saw a girl there or knew anything about the room in the coach house."

Alan has started moving again, edging ever closer to his mother. His eyes flicker nervously toward hers. She puts his arm around him and looks at me accusingly while he stares at the floor. He starts a low humming, with his hands pressed to his ears. My panic shrieks and spirals along with his.

His mother seems reluctant to let him go but she leads him to a chair, her eyes blazing at me. He leans into her like a child but lets her release him so she can usher me to the door. Her hand is hard and bony on my arm.

"I warned you not to upset him. I suggest you clear off and don't you be coming back 'ere, poking around into things that don't concern you. The Connors were nothing but trouble, that's all. Nothing but trouble, scaring the wits out of my boy. He's a good gentle boy and he never done nothing, you hear. Don't you let that lot be saying different."

As she tries to bundle me out I turn back to Alan and our eyes lock for a moment.

"Alan, I'm so, so sorry, I didn't mean to upset you. I'm sorry."

His next words are so quiet I hardly catch them but they make my blood freeze.

"She looked just like you."

I call out to him in desperation, "Alan, please, what did you mean?"

It's too late. He's shuffling away down the hall and his mother is pushing the door closed behind me with a string of expletives.

"Go on, fuck off, get the hell out of here."

I all but run down the landing, my chest rising and falling with the raggedness of my breath. I didn't mishear him, he definitely said, "She looked just like you." Who did and when, and why did I feel so afraid of him?

The two boys are still on the landing, laughing at me now and pointing.

I turn angrily and shout at them, "Fuck off you little shits, before I smack you one!"

Perhaps on reflection I could fit in here after all.

All I can hear in my head is "She looked just like you." I remember what Bill said about nineteen ninety-four or five and I'm starting to wonder if there's really something that links my past to The Lodge. Dr. Stedman is wrong. Tom's wrong. It's time for me to make Tom listen and believe me. He needs to take me seriously for once and help me unravel it all. They need to speak to Alan Harris. Someone official needs to find out what he knows. Someone needs to listen to me about the room. I need this house to unlock its secrets and set me free.

Tom is late again. I've made dinner and I'm waiting for him to come home. Once we've eaten we need to talk. He can't brush this off as me "having a bad day" or being "upset and confused" by the move. Not anymore. He has to hear me out.

While I'm waiting I need to look for Mina again. I've called and I've called; I've banged dishes and put out food by the door but there's no sign at all. Tom says cats wander off, which they do, and he's told me reassuring tales of ones that reappear after years on the run. But not Mina. Both she and Major are house cats. They never went out at all back in London, so I hardly imagine her straying far. It's horrid out, dark and raining; she'll be cold and wet. I must try and find her.

I really don't want to go outside alone in the dark but I can't just leave her if she's out there somewhere, lost and afraid. I turn on the outside lights to flood the lawn with as much brightness as I can. I'll try to venture out as far as I'm able.

I fetch a jacket and torch and tentatively go out to the garden calling her name. I'm afraid she's lying hurt somewhere. I shine the torch into the flower beds and under the shrubbery. The shadows make everything sinister and threatening and I fight the urge to run back in the house. I notice there're footprints in the freshly dug soil by the window. It's as if someone has been standing there looking in. There's only Bill Arthur and I really can't imagine "my Bill" spying and lurking under our windows or standing in a bed he's just dug. I can't think about that now. I'm spooked enough already.

My torch beam picks out a flash of white by the sundial and I feel the first prickle of dread slowing my limbs. I don't want to look. As I draw closer, I see a tiny body there in the dirt. Mina. Her fur is all matted and wet and her little limbs are stretched out as though she's in flight.

Somewhere I register a low keening sound and I realize it's me; my throat with a will of its own is signaling my grief.

I gather her up in my arms, weak with fear. She's unmarked bar a smearing of dark soil but her head lolls unnaturally off to one side. Her eyes are glassy and blank. Someone has killed her, they've broken her neck.

I fall to my knees in the wet grass and curl my body over hers. She is my baby and she's hurt. Someone has done this to her.

I stay there gently cradling her in my arms as the rain lashes and swirls. My mind has closed down for a while. It's gone somewhere safe.

I can hear Tom calling my name, loud and urgent, but I can't answer.

"Izzy, Isabel, where are you?"

I am spotlit in his torchlight. I hear feet pounding across the wet lawn.

"Oh God, Izzy, what are you doing? Why are all the lights on?"

He sees Mina's bedraggled body in my arms and stops, shocked.

"My God, what's happened, what have you done?"

My grief gives way to rage and I scream at him, "What have *I* done? You did this, this is your fault."

"Izzy, what are you talking about? I haven't done anything, what on earth do you mean? Come in, please, you're freezing cold and soaked to the skin. Tell me what's happened. Talk to me."

He tries to pull me to my feet and I lash out at him. Fighting him, arms flailing, as the wind and rain seethes around us.

"You did this. You made us come to this fucking place and now someone has killed her. It's all your fault."

I feel the grief and defeat wash over me pushing my anger aside. This place hates us, I can feel it.

30

"It is not a lack of love, but a lack of friendship
that makes unhappy marriages"
—Friedrich Nietzsche

Tom and I are at breakfast. I feel sad and ill. My head's pounding and my throat's razor-blade sore. My cat is dead. Never again will she curl up with me on the bed or wake me with the rasp of her tongue on my arm. Major sits at my side bereft, he misses his troop of one. He'll be a house cat now, like it or not. I can't risk losing him too.

I'm so very sad but more than anything I'm angry because I know someone did this deliberately. I'm sure they did. I can feel the sharp malice of it. Tom has talked of foxes and badgers and spelled out to me all the possible hazards of the countryside; I remain unconvinced. She was not there yesterday morning. I know it. Her body was unmarked and had been laid out too deliberately. There for me to find. I have explained all this to him. How her body wasn't there and then it was, about the footprints in the flower bed, the precision of her positioning. Right there where I'd see her. I feel prickly and feverish just thinking of it.

I have again voiced my feelings about the secret space. I have told Tom about Gemma and the fact she had no knowledge it was there. I have told him of the hair clip and the numbers I found, and even that I went to the police. I have also told him about the memories I've had and what Bill Arthur told me, and most importantly of all, those words Alan Harris spoke. He's now looking at me across the table. Looking at me as though I'm mad.

"Isabel, what the fuck? Are you mad?'

Told you so. I hate the fact that he'd use that expression, to me of all people.

I say nothing. For once Tom's control has failed him, he's certainly not mister calm now.

"You're telling me you went to the police about this. Dear God, I can't believe they didn't lock you up for wasting their time. You're actually telling me you sat there and told them this shit? I'm sorry to sound angry with you but . . . I've asked you to get help, I've begged you almost, but you won't listen. You do realize this is all nonsense. You can't go on like this, it's madness."

I'm surprised by how measured my voice is as I answer him. It seems I'm the calm one this time.

"Okay, so what's your explanation then? Let's start with the room. You say it's a 'petrol store,' why? Why would someone need to store petrol in the kind of volume that needs its own store? There's a garage five minutes away in the village for God's sake. And what about the numbers on the floor and the hair clip? Doesn't that worry you at all?"

"Frankly no, it doesn't. The whole place was full of junk. A hair clip could've easily got kicked in there or maybe it was one of his wife's and fell out of her hair. I don't know but Christ, does it matter? You've put together a whole load of random things and built a story round them. I don't know what to say to you anymore, I don't get why you're doing this."

He pauses for breath. "You say Gemma didn't know about it as though that's proof of something but it's not. Her dad could've built it when she was a kid or after she left home or something. He would hardly have bothered to tell her about it. The fact she didn't know it was there means absolutely nothing."

I want to say, "Them, it was them actually. She had a brother but she lied." I don't bother. It's hardly relevant anyway. His explanations make me sound foolish, they're all so measured and potentially plausible.

"What about Mina then? You can hardly explain that away. You know I've been looking for her for days. I tell you her body wasn't there in the morning and then it was and what about the footprints under the window? I don't think they were there before either." I feel the start of tears at the mention of her name.

"You 'don't think.' That's about right Izzy, you don't seem to think anymore. I don't know what's wrong with you. You're imagining things that aren't there and just making shit up. You're worrying me to death. Look, it's sad about Mina, I'm sad too, 'course I am, but she's been got by an animal. These things happen. As for the footprints, they were probably made by Bill poking his bloody nose. I've a good mind to sack him anyway, filling your head up with a load of gossip."

I think I'm beginning to hate Tom.

"Tom, why don't you believe me? There is something here. Something happened with Alan Harris way back when, that scared the fucking hell out of him. He freaked me out today. As clear as day he said, 'She looked just like you.' It was around ninety-four and she looked like me, Tom, like me. And there was something about him that scared me. That's got to mean something. With the feelings I've had that I've been here before, how do you explain all that?"

I watch the anger slowly leave his face.

"Oh Izzy," he sighs. "I know what you went through. I understand more than anyone how much it bothers you that you don't know what happened but really, this is such nonsense. You go and see some poor woman and her half-daft son and start asking them about something from twenty-odd years ago. He could've said anything. Would you've believed him if he said she looked like Julia Roberts? No, but because he said she looked like you you've latched on to it. You were there in front of him and you've said how disturbed he was, that's probably why he said it. And of course he scared you; the state you're in at the moment you're afraid of everything. Just stop and think about this logically. Just because something bad happened to you in the past it doesn't mean everything has to be sinister. There aren't secrets and dangers lurking round every corner, really there aren't."

I suddenly remember the phone calls, the silent messages.

"Someone's been phoning the house as well. It didn't bother me at first, I thought it was just a wrong number but it keeps happening. They leave silent messages and play music."

His control slips again, "For God's sake Izzy, stop this! It'll be an automatic dialing system, someone trying to sell insurance or double glazing or something. Those systems dial numbers automatically and if someone picks up before there's an agent available they just ring off."

I've heard breathing and they wait there for a while but there's no point in telling him that.

I'd wanted something from him. I'd wanted him just to believe me and to help me. I'm beginning to realize he only sees my damage. He can't trust my judgment or my mind. How can he love someone he thinks is that incomplete and more to the point how can I love him?

"I'm sorry, Tom. I'm obviously wasting my time here. I'd hoped you might believe me, that you'd help me find the truth, if it's out there to be found. I'm not saying my version of things is necessarily right, it could all be nonsense like you say but don't you think it might be worth exploring? Finding out one way or the other?"

He takes my hands but I pull away.

"Let go of me. You hold my hands or cup my face but it doesn't mean anything. You take no notice at all of what I say or think. Just stop, it doesn't work anymore."

He sighs, with all the world-weariness he can muster, and says, "I want to help you Izzy, I do. I love you and I'm worried about you, I don't understand what's happening to you . . ."

"Nothing is happening to me, for fuck's sake, you can't just . . ."

"Stop it! Enough! You need to go and see Dr. Stedman again and this time I'm coming with you. It's not that I disbelieve you, I really think you believe what you're telling me but baby, it's ridiculous. You're letting what happened to you distort how you see the world.

You're confusing what's real and what's not. I would never have suggested we move here if I'd known how much it was going to upset you. I can't bear seeing you like this. I thought you'd be happy here, that you'd like the quiet of the countryside, not this."

I feel anger bubbling under the surface about to erupt and I fight to keep control.

"You really think this is just me upset by moving house? That I'm so mentally fragile that I can't cope? Don't you get it Tom, it doesn't work like that. Yes, I know some things are hard for me. I understand that. I manage it. I know how to live inside my own head. I managed before you came along and I'd manage again."

My last words shock me, they sound like a threat.

I am so hurt. I'd had doubts about us for a while and it appears I was right. He doesn't love the real me, the person I am inside. He loves my damage, my weakness, the dependency he thinks I have on him.

He doesn't like me wearing makeup as it "masks my vulnerability." He doesn't like me to drive in case I "lose concentration." He doesn't like me coming back too late from my art class—as though I'm a child. When I think about it, he's always suggesting I might not cope. Always sowing that seed of doubt before I even try.

"We have a problem Tom Dryland, but it's not me, it's you. You need to think about how you see me and what you want from this relationship. We are not going to see Dr. Stedman, understand? If you don't believe me and won't help, then fine, but just think long and hard about where this leaves us, okay?"

My throat is so sore I can hardly speak and I feel as though I'm burning up. I won't go back to bed though. I won't let him see me as weak.

We look at each other across the table, the air shimmering and crackling with hostility. I wonder, how did we get to this?

31

"Cats are a mysterious kind of folk"
—Sir Walter Scott

He was bored with the watching. It was beneath him to be lurking in lanes or skulking in the shrubbery. A man of his talents needed to be more creative in his cruelty. More Promethean in his persecution. He could of course just finish her off and discard her but he was beginning to enjoy this nice new game.

He'd watched her petting and fussing over those cats like the frigid old spinster she ought to be and he'd pondered life's wondrous symmetry. He liked the sense of hidden patterns, of fractals spinning in the helix shell. A divine plan for his eyes only.

He knew all about cats. He knew what they were. His mind was filled with words and signs and arcane knowledge and he knew everything. Cats: revered by the ancient Egyptians as the goddess Bast, Celtic guardians of the Otherworld and Norse companions of the goddess Freya. Devious little creatures, little shape-shifters through the centuries. He'd never liked the way they looked at him, all jade-eyed and knowing, like they could see into the recess where his soul should be.

This little one had come dainty pawed into his clutches with not so much as a whisker's twitch, lured by a sardine on a string. So much for guardians against evil or goddesses of protection, and nine lives would soon be debunked.

He liked the feel of it, the rightness of it, a cat playing its part again, albeit a minor role this time. He absentmindedly stroked its fur and felt its soft vibrations beneath his palm. Worthless, stupid thing.

It calmed him though. He needed to be calm after today and where he'd seen her go. If he closed his eyes it took him back to his childhood and a simpler time; a time when this was all he needed, a creature's fate in his hands. Now he needed so much more and could feel the pressure building. He was losing control. Coming back home had done something to him. He could feel the strands of the man he'd chosen to be slowly unraveling.

He had to try and contain things for the moment though, pick his time. For now pussy could take the edge off his hunger. She was so wonderfully soft it was a shame he couldn't keep just a piece. A little piece of pussy-pelt as a reminder of a job well done. He'd never been one for souvenirs though, not since that first time. Too bleeding obvious, too formulaic, too expected of him, and he was nothing like they expected. Although come to think of it, pussy pelt in all its connotations had a certain ring to it. Shame he hadn't thought of it before.

He snapped himself out of his reverie. It was time. As a boy he'd liked to be inventive over a death, even a small one. It was only respectful to extract the maximum out of a life when it's taken, but now it was time to be subtle. He had to cause the bitch pain while not giving anything away. It couldn't look too deliberate; it had to be a message for her alone.

He'd considered wringing its neck like a chicken. He'd enjoyed watching his father do that enough times but a cat was a bit chunkier and he wasn't sure he could get the necessary grip. He wished he still had access to the lab. A little chloroform would've made things so much easier.

He settled on chinning it like a rabbit. He wrapped his fingers round its neck in an "okay" gesture, although he hated to tell it but there was absolutely nothing okay about it. Nothing at all. He then grabbed its back legs and pulled, while simultaneously pulling its chin up to bend its back in a whipping motion. It was a struggle but he soon heard the satisfying pop of its little vertebrae. He gave it a few good tugs for good measure; if he was lucky he might get a good tug out of it later too.

It was dark and it was wet. He perched on tiptoe and watched her through the rain-splattered window. She looked troubled, poor poppet. If only she knew, her troubles were really just starting.

32

"The earth laughs in flowers"
　　　　　　　　—Ralph Waldo Emerson

Tom is trying to burn me. There's a pit of fire and he's pinning me down. I try to cry out but my mouth won't work, my lips are all cracked and dry. My tongue is huge. It's filling my mouth and I'm choking.

I'm wet, burning wet. My hair's streaming blood and someone has hold of it pulling me back. It hurts. My head hurts.

I can hear sawing. They're walling me in. The saw is rasping and grating, in and out in time with my breath. I can't breathe. There's something on my chest. It's a cat but it's dead. I think I'm crying.

I hear voices. I try to sit up but hands press me back. There's bitterness, cold on my tongue, and a pain in my arm. I'm gone.

I have been ill. Very ill apparently, with a fever and infection that turned into pneumonia. I should've gone to hospital but Tom wouldn't let me go. He thinks it's his fault I was ill so he needed to look after me here at home. Doing his penance and I should be touched—bad choice of words perhaps. I find that I'm not.

I lie in the darkened bedroom and gather up my thoughts. They're scattered and far-flung, cowering wide-eyed in the corners of my mind. I'm over the worst but my head's still a maelstrom of febrile dreams and confusion. I struggle to remember what was real and what was not.

I realize there are flowers in the room and the most wonderful bouquet sits by my bed. Dusty green-pink roses and white ranunculus, hypericum and sea thistle and seeded eucalyptus. I reach for the envelope that sits unopened. They're from Matthew. I'd e-mailed him with some preliminary sketches and photos, and suggested we should meet to go through them, to see if they met his brief. Caitlin must've told him I was ill. I remember delaying our last meeting through "illness." He'll think me a sickly creature indeed, all vaporous fits and fainting.

The card is simple, adorned only with a single eucalyptus sprig that looks hand-painted. Tasteful.

> *Dear Isabel*
>
> *Caitlin told me you were ill and I had to let you know that you're in my thoughts—perhaps more than you should be.*
>
> *The ideas you sent across are wonderful. I knew when we met that you would understand what I wanted even better than I do myself. Please let me know when you're well enough to meet up and perhaps I'll come out to you to save you making the long trip. Don't think that's too much of a kindness or in any way an inconvenience as I'd actually love to see where you work!*
>
> *Do take care and get well soon. Matthew x*

I reach out a hand and touch the softness of a petal. They are beautiful. I love the subtly muted colors and gentle fragrance of the roses. He knew exactly what I'd like and the words in his card conjure up his image and the sound of his voice. I like to think I'm in his thoughts.

⌣

There are other flowers in the room. A vase of white lilies sit by the window, their funeral scent competing with Matthew's bouquet. The long-stemmed anthers have dropped pollen onto my new gray carpet, making a stain like bile. I don't like them at all. They're coffin flowers for the dead, all lifeless waxy perfection.

I try getting out of bed to move them but as I stand up my legs turn to water and my head spins. They'll have to wait for Tom.

Later when I wake Tom is sitting by the bed. He has Matthew's card in his hand. When he sees I'm awake he hastily returns it to the bedside table where it belongs. He looks vaguely guilty and suddenly I feel sorry for him. I stretch out my hand to him.

"Hey."

He takes my hand in his and this time I don't pull away.

"Oh Izzy," he says, "I've been so worried about you. I'm so sorry."

I'm not sure what he's sorry for; it's not his fault I was ill.

"Why are you sorry silly, you didn't make me ill."

I try to smile but my lips are cracked and dry. I must look a sight.

"I know but I've thought about what you said and you're right. I made us come here and everything's gone wrong, so it is my fault. I'm meant to look after you."

Please Tom, after all I said don't you get it? It isn't your job to look after me. We should be partners, equals. I don't say this, he looks so tired.

Instead I ask, "Who are the lilies from?"

"Madeline dropped them round. She's visited a couple of times to check how you are. She's been really concerned, which is sweet considering what she's going through."

I imagine her in my house with Tom, all silk shirts and pert nipples, while I've been up here in bed. It doesn't sit well with me and I feel a little of my kindness seeping away.

"What is she going through?" I ask and I hear the arch tone to my voice despite my best intentions.

"Joe has moved out. Remember I told you they were having problems, well apparently he's left. I don't think it's permanent, more a trial separation to see if they're better apart."

I don't say anything other than "That's sad," but a little part of me finds it a bit unusual that Joe's the one who's gone. I thought he was the would-be abuser and I thought the abused usually fled. I remember the scarf and fleetingly wonder how long ago it was that he left. I don't want her lilies in the room.

"Tom, please could you take the lilies down with you when you go. I don't like the smell and they're spoiling the carpet."

He looks at me and suddenly asks, "Who is Matthew?"

"My friend," I reply, "you know, like Madeline is yours."

He looks like I've slapped him and I regret saying it. He's not a bad person and neither am I, so I mustn't act like one.

"I'm sorry," I say, "that was petty. He's not a friend as such, he's the commission I told you about. I'm doing some pieces for his office, that's all."

Despite where we are there's still love here. There has to be. I turn his hand over and trace my fingers across his palm.

"Don't worry," I whisper, "we'll work it out."

33

"I can resist everything except temptation"
—Oscar Wilde

It's hard for Tom and me to find our way back. There've been no more arguments—our last one shook us both—but our truce is uneasy. We skirt and sidle around each other like fencers without the thrust and parry, all cautious words, carefully chosen. No sex just now. I can't think about it at the moment.

All I can think about is what happened to Mina. I'm filled with a mixture of sadness and fear and it's haunting me. I know Tom was probably right, that a fox or a badger caught her and killed her; a swift bite and a twist to her neck, and she'd gone. Still, I can't rid the thought that someone was here with their face at our window watching. Watching me feed her and stroke her and love her. Waiting to kill her. I can't feel safe here anymore.

The decorators have finished the bedrooms and the bathrooms are nearly done. I'm going to be alone here for a while and the thought fills me with dread. Bill is still doing the gardens—no, Tom didn't sack him—but he won't be here every day. I'll be here alone with the creeping malevolence I feel at every turn.

I've moved my work out to the coach house. Everything's gone from the house, all my canvases and paints, all my sketchbooks and scribblings have found their new home. There's power out to it now and while the light's not ideal, I need the space for Matthew's canvases, which arrived last week. They're virginal, white and enormous, a story not yet written. Working soothes me, the feel of my brush in my hand, the colors of my paints singing to me, it quietens my soul.

I'm pleased that the trees are almost bare; it means no one can hide unseen in the foliage, watching me. The front doors stay bolted and barred and I'm glad of them now. The thought of the glass that we'd planned sends prickles of fear down my spine. I can't be so exposed.

I'm meeting with Matthew today and I feel slightly shivery and sick at the prospect. I'm frightened by how I feel about him and by how much I want to see him again. He's been too often in my thoughts and now I'm fully recovered, it's time for us to meet. I know it's foolish but I've read and reread his words and wondered at the suggestion that he feels it too; that connection, that thread that pulls invisibly between us.

I've decided it'll be better for us to meet in the coach house instead of the house. It feels too intimate somehow to have the reality of him here in my home.

Another reason for my decision to move out to the studio before it's completely ready is that we need the room in the house for my sisters. They've finished their foundation course and were intending to live back at home until their degree starts—Drama and Performing Arts—now they can't. Apparently there's trouble in paradise. They've begged me to let them come and stay for a while as they need to get away. Daddy has dallied—now there's a surprise—and unlike his current secretary, his wife isn't taking it lying down. My poor father once again has found himself caught between his cock and a hard place. Someone should tell him a definition of insanity is doing the same thing over and over again and expecting a different outcome.

It's a while since I last saw Amy and Zoe, my Midwich Cuckoo sisters. They bear little resemblance to either parent and most certainly not to my father. They're blue-eyed with white-blonde hair, all long limbed and Nordic. I'm looking forward to seeing them again and selfishly not just for their own sake. They'll be much needed company for a while and hopefully their presence will ease some of the tension that still crackles between Tom and me.

I walk through the orchard to the coach house. For a second I think there's a figure there in the trees but it's a trick of the light. I blink and it's gone. The anticipation of seeing Matthew again trills through me and distracts my mind from my fears. A part of me knows this is dangerous, that I risk throwing my marriage away on a whim, but a little hard part of me doesn't seem to care. Not anymore. Tom is not who I thought he was, or who I wanted him to be, and he has his secrets too. I know it. I can feel them teeming under his surface like eels.

The day is cold and diamond bright, the leaves rustle frost dried beneath my feet, all crisp with promise. I feel the static in the air, electrifying my sweater and making my scar tingle. I'm Frankenstein's monster coming alive.

Matthew is already there. He's standing in the cold, waiting, his figure perfectly framed by the backdrop of trees. He hasn't seen me yet and stands with his hands thrust deep in his pockets, his breath a swirling mystery about his head. His expression is unguarded, and a small secretive smile plays at his lips. He hears the snap of a twig and looks up at me and the smile breaks out in full; a real and wonderful pleasure at the sight of me. God, it's been so long since anyone looked at me that way.

"Isabel, at last. I was beginning to think the fates were conspiring and we'd never get to meet again."

He offers his hand and I take it. It's hot and dry from his pocket. He's like fire and ice and he melts me. The static lifts my hair and draws it toward him. I try not to follow.

I unlock the doors to my studio—let's call it that now—all fingers and thumbs and we go inside. The inside is warm but he brings a hint of frost in with him, clinging to his coat, cold and hoary. I turn to him all warm and whore-y and he smiles.

"I've been so looking forward to this," he says and there's something in his expression that makes me think it's me he's been waiting to see and not just my art.

I undo my portfolio and start to show him my sketches. There are wild cliffs and teeming oceans hidden within the lines and swirls. My plan is to work two pieces. The first a monochrome, on board not canvas, with granite cliffs and gray skies, teeming seas and spume. All worked without color but instead with texture, impasto and sgraffito. The other will be on canvas. The same subject matter in color this time. The greens and blues of the ocean and sky, the purples and grays of the heather and the rock. I'm excited as I show him the preliminary canvases of how I want it to be, and I'm aware I'm talking too fast and waving my arms. All jazz hands. He stays silent, letting me lay out my wares.

I come to a stop and wait expectantly. I can feel his eyes on me, watching, but can't see his expression. God, I hope he likes it.

"This is amazing," he says, and my heart starts to beat again.

"I'd seen your paintings before and thought they were wonderful, they're so complex and powerful I knew I had to have one." He pauses for a moment then softly adds, "And your picture was there in your profile and I liked your face too. You looked like someone I wanted to know."

I turn and he smiles at me.

"And now I do."

He's taken off his coat, releasing the scent of his aftershave. It's fresh and clean like new-mown grass or sheets blowing in the breeze. It's him and his smell in my space and I want him. The tension in the few feet between us is real and unmistakable and I know he feels it too.

I can't help myself; I take a step toward him and lay my hand against the warmth of his chest. It's impulsive and wrong and it's crossing a line but I do it anyway. In that moment I know I'm right. He does feel it too. I can feel his heart racing beneath my palm, in time with mine. He looks at me long and hard, serious now. He cups my chin in his hand and tilts my face upward and time slows. My heart plucks its strings to a tune that's as old as time and I'm falling.

As his lips reach for mine I suddenly stop. What am I doing? Tom, I love Tom, this is wrong.

"I'm sorry," I say, "this is wrong. This isn't a good idea. I'm sorry, I made a mistake," and I gently push him away. I can't so carelessly hurt and wound someone I love. I'm not built that way.

There's a second of awkwardness, a charged silence before I speak again. "That was my fault, I'm sorry. Please, can we just forget it ever happened?"

"Forget what?" he says and smiles. "We're fine, nothing happened at all."

We fight our way past the moment and talk of the commission again. His enthusiasm is real and infectious, and I tell myself we'll work well together—that and nothing more. He's so interested in what I do and how I work. He looks round my studio and office, opening doors and cupboards and asking me questions with a boyish exuberance I can't help but find endearing.

All my old sketchbooks are out on the side and he starts to look through them, studying each one intently until he finds something that makes him smile. I squirm with embarrassment when I see what it is; an abortive attempt at self portrait with lots and lots of mini-me's peeping out from the pages. None of them are quite right. Usually I'm comfortable with my work but not this. When I go to grab the book he won't relinquish it. Instead he holds it high above his head, before tearing out a page and carefully folding it into his pocket. When I ask him why he tells me he just wants to remember my face. The thought makes me shiver, the thought of him somewhere alone gazing into my eyes.

I know I should tell this man I can't accept his commission, that I can't see him again, but I won't. I feel I should run from him but I won't. I'm playing with fire.

34

"Father is rather vulgar, my dear. The word
Papa, besides, gives a pretty form to the lips"
—Charles Dickens, *Little Dorrit*

Amy and Zoe have arrived. I hear the crunch of tires on the gravel and go to the door to meet them. My father's BMW 5 Series sits low and silvery on the drive, a slinking car that matches the man.

I was going to pick up my sisters from the station but my father decided he would drive them. He wants to see me apparently, which in itself is strange. It's been over a year since we last cast eyes on each other and I don't think either has missed the contact. Even stranger is the fact that for once I'm looking forward to seeing him.

Tom is less enthusiastic. He has little time for my parents and has always felt indignant toward them on my behalf, or at least he did. For some reason he particularly dislikes my father, a feeling that's amply reciprocated.

Things between Tom and me are slightly better, maybe. I've tried harder than before, spurred on by my feelings of guilt over Matthew and what so nearly happened. I've avoided the list of unmentionable things: that's secret spaces, Alan Harris, Mina and Madeline. Instead I've shown enthusiasm about the house and interest in his work. We're making progress but still he sometimes seems withdrawn. So very distant I need a telescope to really see him.

The fact that I haven't spoken about these things doesn't mean I've changed what I think. It doesn't mean I've relinquished my desire for the truth about this place. Just that for the moment I've decided to keep my own counsel while I gather what's left of my courage and think what to do. It's obvious Alan Harris won't talk to me again so I need a different plan. I can't live here feeling like this.

The doors of the car open and the twins tumble out, all golden haired and alabaster limbed. They look so young. Like a single organism they run to the door and I'm enfolded in the tangle of their dual embrace. They're all kisses and laughter and lightness and they blow through me like fresh air. I'd forgotten their energy and exuberance; the sheer life of them.

"Izzy, God . . ."

". . . it's been so long. Thanks . . ."

". . . for letting us come."

"It's been so awful, you've no idea . . ."

". . . You wouldn't believe the things they've said to each other . . ."

"It's been totally . . ."

". . . out of control."

I'd also forgotten the unnerving way they have of finishing each other's sentences and talking in unison. I pity the men that try to marry them, they'll never prise them apart.

"Shush, he's coming."

I turn to greet the paterfamilias and am shocked to see the old man who's making his way up the drive. The years have caught my father in a sudden and savage ambush. The weight has fallen away from him; his previous virility has been stripped away to leave an aging lycanthrope, red-eyed and whiskery. His hair has turned to silver and his face looks sunken with yellow, rheumy eyes. A lifetime of dissipation and excess has wreaked its havoc and I feel suddenly saddened at the evidence of his mortality.

We greet each other awkwardly. I've never known what to call my father. "Dad" implies a closeness we've never had, "father" a formality

I don't feel, and the others, the "papas," the "daddies" and the "pops" sound just plain stupid so I tend to settle for his name.

"Hello Tony."

I hold out my arms to soften the blow because he always looks so hurt. But really, what does the man expect? He who never read a story, tied a shoelace or brushed a single hair. I always feel the urge to sniffle, "It isn't my fault. I was there, you were the one who wasn't." I never do.

"Isabel, darling, hello."

We hug stiffly. For a man who obviously has no issues with physical contact he's always awkward with me. He bobs and parries, never knowing quite where to put himself. Maybe that's the problem, maybe it's platonic contact he struggles with. God, let's hope he doesn't forget himself.

Tom comes up behind me, compelled by courtesy. He'd hoped they'd arrive midweek so he could be spared the contact but no such luck.

"Tony."

"Tom."

They each suppress the urge to wrestle the other to the ground and instead make do with an overly violent handshake. I watch, waiting to see which one cracks first and shouts "Mercy." Disappointingly it doesn't come to that. The macho posturing over, we go into the house.

Tom takes the twins for a tour of the garden—anything to get away—and I'm left alone with my father. The silence stretches out awkwardly and I steal a look at him. He looks tired and unhappy and for a fleeting moment I want to hug him before I remember who he is. I remember how I felt waiting for Tom the day I couldn't find the scarf and I harden my heart. He put my mother through that over and over again through the years of their marriage. I never expected to be on her side over anything but I'm older now and wiser.

"So," I say, "this is unlike you to put yourself out and come all this way personally. If you didn't want them to take the train you could've sent a car. Is there something wrong?"

He doesn't answer and we stand quietly by the window. Despite Bill Arthur's best efforts the garden looks wintery and forlorn and I find myself thinking it's a shame that the twins aren't seeing it at its best. Despite how unhappy I've felt since we've been here I can't deny how beautiful the place can be. I still feel that strange ambivalence, that attraction and repulsion.

My father suddenly turns to me. "Are you happy, Isabel?'

The question throws me utterly and I don't know how to answer. We don't have the kind of relationship where I can tell him my troubles. I just shrug and it's my turn to avoid an answer.

"Don't ever just settle, Isabel. Don't do something just because you think you have to, you'll never be happy, not really."

I wonder what he's referring to. Marriage to my mother? Leaving her?

He continues, "I've always loved you, you do know that, don't you? Things were hard for me when you were young. Building up the business, and . . . things with your mother."

Not all that was hard father, from what I've heard. I wonder where this conversation is going.

"There's a lot I regret, a lot I'd do differently if I had my time over."

This is so unlike him it's starting to worry me.

I ask him again, "Is there something wrong?"

"I just wanted to see you that's all. It's been so long and I'm not getting any younger."

I'm tempted to tell him I can see that. Instead I stay silent and wait.

"I need to slow down. I've had some tests and they're a bit concerned, it's nothing to worry about, not really, but it does make you take stock."

I feel a sudden surge of concern that borders on grief and it catches me unawares. It's unexpected and overwhelming. He sees my face and a wry expression flits across his, a solitary whiskery eyebrow raises. It's an expression I remember from my childhood and it sends me flying back to a time when he was the world to me. When all I wanted was his affection.

He smiles, "Don't look like that, I'm not dead yet. I just thought it'd be nice to see you and see your new home, just to check everything's going okay." He adds, almost as an afterthought, "I've always felt bad about what happened to you and that I wasn't there when I should've been. I want to know you're happy now, that's all. If you need anything, anything at all, just let me know."

Dear God, he says it now, after all these years. The hurt has long healed and a hard little part of me, the scar that it left, thinks "too little, too late." I'm too stunned to speak and there's nothing to say.

"Don't spend your life like I have, always chasing after something. If you find happiness, grab it and hold on to it, there's nothing more important in this life, believe me."

Well actually, Father, there is. There's love and there's kindness, there's thinking about those who love you and considering their feelings too. I say none of this as I know there's no point and that in his way he's trying to set things right. Best let sleeping dogs lie.

After my father's left I think about his words, so out of character and unlike the man. Where does my happiness lie? Is it here with Tom or elsewhere, waiting in pastures new? It's strange that my father should speak of such things at a time when we're all adrift.

35

"Lift not the painted veil . . ."
—Percy Bysshe Shelley, "Sonnet"

Having the twins here has shifted the atmosphere and changed the feel of my home. Their presence has forced Tom and me to sweep our differences out of sight, at least for the moment, and during the week when he's away I now find I'm seldom alone.

Occasionally they'll borrow my car and go off somewhere together but mainly they're here. They'll tire of Facebook, or reading, or daytime TV and come flitting through the orchard like sunlight to watch me work. At first I found it distracting. I could feel them hovering, their eyes following my every brushstroke. Mostly though, I've been glad to have them around. They've made me less nervous, less afraid.

Things that would have troubled me and preyed on my mind, I've instead been able to rationalize and set aside. For instance, there was a man in the lane the other day, just standing there for a moment looking straight at my studio. The hood on his sweatshirt was up and shading his face from view. I think it could've been Joe. I went to raise my hand in greeting but before I could he'd gone, vanished into thin air or so it seemed. Once this would've sent me scurrying back to the house awash with fear. Now I was able to dismiss it as no more than a curious walker and carry on with my work, the twins a comforting presence at my side.

I've given them canvases to try out their talents and to my delight have found a real difference between them. One that's stayed hidden beneath their uniformity for twenty years. Amy, bless her, has no eye for color, no sense of shape or perspective. Zoe certainly has. She has a raw talent that's showing its face, primitive and unformed but there nonetheless. I like the idea that my sister has talent. The idea that just maybe mine came from my father, and not from my mother as all have assumed—her in particular. I've always been irritated that she who showed so little interest claimed my talent for her own. The only time I've ever heard pride in her voice is over "my daughter, the artist, but of course she gets it from me." Perhaps not, Mother, perhaps not.

This newly discovered skill has brought disharmony. There's an unheard-of spark of discord crackling between the mirror images. Zoe wants to sit in on my art class, Amy does not, so tonight Zoe alone has joined my little group.

We meet every week in the hall of the primary school. It's parquet floored and plimsoll scented and warmed by fat Victorian radiators, rounded and smoothed by their decades of paint. It's high ceilinged and brightly lit so suits us well.

My class is a disparate bunch of mixed ages and varying abilities. There's Moira, mild and midfifties who has diligently completed "beginners" and is now earnestly plodding her way with me. She's a diligent worker but her pictures are wooden. Although I'd never, ever tell her that. She tries so hard.

Then there's John, Mr. "I've sold a few." In his forties and a triumph of arrogance over ability if ever there was one. If I'm honest I don't much warm to John. He argues with me about technique, all pinch-faced and insistent. Once I'd have told him exactly how it was but I'm a good polite girl now. I gently explain why he's wrong, as he invariably is, and then I ignore him.

Walter is eighty-five and mainly here for the company. He's painted all his life and I imagine the walls of his home alive with flowers and landscapes; row upon row of trees like cabbages, with the greens used straight from the tube. Walter is a nice man, soft and plump like a jolly Santa, chattering away.

Unlike the mannered Laurence who's long-fingered and effete. He's all chichi cravats and long dark coats of studied elegance. Moira watches him with moist-eyed longing—she's a divorcee I suspect. I find him sinister. He's dark and vampiric, as is his art.

Then there's the lovely Daniel. Daniel's a bit of an enigma and difficult to age. At least in his midthirties I'd have to say, maybe more. Smooth-skinned and crop-haired, he's an attractive man. Mr. Trendy but Understated. He's very earnest about his work and I feel his dark eyes following my every move, him hanging on every word. He has some talent but he's another one who needs to loosen up a bit, his art is too tight and feels repressed.

My husband and wife team are Colin and Lorna. Matching jumpers, forty going on sixty, they want to set up an eBay shop and leave the "rat race." I want to tell them it's not that easy, darlings, so don't give up the day jobs just yet.

Lastly there's Mark, my favorite. A nice, unassuming man, from Seattle I think he said, with real talent. He's told me he wanted to study art but his parents pushed him into engineering. A real shame as I think he could've made it, and with the wind behind him he just still might.

And tonight of course there's Zoe.

This is my little group and I've grown rather fond of them in the short time we've been together. Contrary to Tom's prediction I haven't found it particularly stressful or too difficult. Yes, there've been occasions when I've lost my way or stumbled over my words but somehow it doesn't seem to matter. There's a joy in sharing something I love and my class are slightly in awe of me. To them I'm the real deal so they don't care if I'm slightly odd; my flakiness adds to the illusion of artiness.

It's slightly harder with Zoe here. I find performing in front of someone I know makes me feel vulnerable. It's as if she'll know if

I'm nervous or if I make a mistake and will judge me more harshly. Foolish, I know.

I've got them working on light, shade and tone and have set up a still life. It's an old teaching technique; I've painted the objects with white emulsion and have set them against a white backdrop, lit from the side. They're to produce a single-color study using the shifts in light and tone to create a three-dimensional image. Textbook stuff and not the most exciting but these are things they need to understand, regardless of style and technique.

I watch them as they work. Moira's tongue is out again, her concentration almost tangible as she tightly and carefully dabs. Her brow furrows with the effort.

Walter is working and chatting to Daniel. I can't hear the words but his lips are moving, and I can see it's distracting. Daniel's too polite, too reserved to say anything.

Laurence has stopped working and is watching Zoe from under hooded lids. Hmm, time for me to move among them to see how they're doing and offer advice. I enjoy this bit. There's the surprise of unexpected work well done or the satisfaction at seeing real improvement.

Most have done a reasonable approximation of what I'd asked, apart from Walter who's rather missed the point and produced a two-dimensional picture in black and white.

I walk behind Laurence's easel and am surprised to see he's abandoned the exercise I gave them and has instead done an alla prima picture of Zoe. It disturbs me; her skin is too pale and her hair is a bright yellow-gold cloud of wild brush strokes, fluttered with leaves. He's painted her eyes closed and has somehow managed to make her appear not asleep but dead. He turns and smiles at me and I notice his teeth are snow white and even, his eyeteeth long and sharp.

"What do you think?" he says, "Pity I'm no good at eyes."

His picture has unnerved me. Why has he painted her like that, with those pale perfect features devoid of life?

I raise my voice slightly. "Leave her alone, she's my sister."

Two spots of pink appear on his cheeks and he says, rather shocked, "Sorry, I didn't mean to upset anyone. It's just a sketch, that's all. I'm sorry if you don't like it."

I go to snatch the picture from his easel, but he grabs my wrist. His long fingers dig into the skin.

It's my turn to be shocked and I say, more loudly than I intended, "What the hell do you think you're doing. Let go, you're hurting me."

He releases my hand as though it's burned him and for a moment our eyes meet. For a split second I glimpse a look of real menace, which is quickly replaced with an expression of confusion and embarrassment. It's so fleeting that I wonder if I imagined it. I notice the others have stopped working and Daniel is watching us, poised as though to intervene. Zoe appears at my side and I realize I'm shaking.

"Hey, Izzy, it's okay. I don't mind—really."

She smiles at Laurence, defusing the moment, and says, "I like it actually, it's kind of weird. Can I have it?"

He smiles back, his discomfiture fading as he unclips the sheet of paper. He hands it to her with a theatrical flourish.

"Course you can, here. I'm glad someone likes it."

I can feel the eyes of the class on me and manage to squeeze out a smile too. "I'm sorry Laurence, I just get a bit big sisterish and over-protective sometimes. I didn't mean to snap at you like that."

"And I'm sorry I grabbed you," he says. "It was just kind of instinctive. I didn't mean to hurt you."

Once everyone's settled back down Mark comes over to check I'm okay.

He speaks quietly so the others can't hear, "Hey, let me have a look at that," and takes my wrist in his hand, gently rubbing at the two red marks from Laurence's fingers. "You'll have a bruise there tomorrow," he says and looks so concerned that I feel the prickle of stupid tears.

The class is over. We've cleared away but a few of them are lingering behind, chatting. Zoe comes over to me and I can see from her face that she wants something.

"Izzy, they're going to the pub for a quick drink. I know we've got to get back, but can we go—please?"

I have no real reason to say no and I feel I need to make amends for earlier. I'm sure I embarrassed her, so I agree to go, and our little band sets off for The Swan. John's disappeared, Walter doesn't like pubs, and Lorna and Colin had to get home for the dogs, so there's Moira, Laurence, Daniel, Mark, Zoe and me. I'm kind of glad Laurence has decided to come as I feel bad about leaping down his throat like I did. I wouldn't want it to damage the harmony of the group. I hope he stays away from Zoe though, he's much too old for her and there's something that feels out of kilter about him.

I don't think I really need to worry as I notice Zoe's walking with Daniel, his dark head bent to her blonde. Moira's finally got close to Laurence—no accounting for taste—and I'm left to walk with Mark, which pleases us both. I tuck my arm through his and we walk in companionable silence to The Swan. He's such a genuinely warm man.

36

"It serves me right for putting all my eggs in one bastard"

—Dorothy Parker

The twins have been with us for three weeks now. They'll probably stay for a while longer, until they need to go home for Christmas. They've given Tony and Sandra time to sort things out so hopefully all will have been smoothed over by the time they get back. On one hand I dread them going; on the other I want them to leave because I too need to sort things out—with Tom. The progress we'd made seems to have stalled and we can't go on like this.

Zoe has continued to come along to my art class and has started seeing Daniel. Amy was resentful at first although they've both been in relationships before—if you could call them that. She seems to be getting over it now and has at last stopped trailing around like a lost soul, all drooping and disconsolate. I suspect she assumes it'll all be over once they get back to London. Sadly I fear she may be right. I feel a bit sorry for Daniel. He has a certain intensity about him, and I suspect he's more serious about the relationship than the twin in question is as I often hear her giggling about him with Amy. There appear to be no secrets between these two, absolutely none.

I was worried he was too old for her. I know they're twenty but there's something about the twins that seems younger and almost childlike sometimes. It's as though they've spent so long cocooned in their own secret world that some aspects of life have floated by, leaving them innocents. For some reason I think of the tale of the Babes in the Wood and Laurence's picture of Zoe unfurls unbidden in my mind. I shiver despite the warmth of the kitchen.

According to Zoe, Daniel's only twenty-nine, which really surprises me as I had him several years north of that, closer to my age in fact or even slightly older. He's smooth skinned and very pretty, if a man can be described like that, but he has creases by his eyes and an air of maturity that belies his youth. He's often at the house now and I tend to view him as a peer rather than my junior.

Amy, who seems privy to every detail no matter how intimate, tells me she's looked on Facebook. He doesn't seem to have been on there for very long. She's established that he's an architect and that he's been working in South Africa, or was it South America, for the last couple of years. That would explain both the onset of wrinkles and the studied neatness of his art. Also the hint of an accent I sometimes detect. He seems a quiet, pleasant man who's kind to Zoe and tolerant of her intrusive twin. I fear his heart may soon be broken.

We're at the breakfast table. Amy and Zoe have their heads together whispering about something and Tom has just left for work. I was treated to the most perfunctory of kisses, a cool dry peck. A brief rasp of his lip skin against my cheek for appearance's sake and no more. I'm scared for us.

I was intending to take the day off from working and we were planning to go into town for some early Christmas shopping. Now I can feel the beginnings of a headache so may leave them to go it alone. I've slept better since they've been here, which has helped with my headaches but not today. I still sometimes dream and wake in the night confused and disoriented. Nowhere near as often though, and not with the spine-tingling terror of before. The easing of my anxiety during the day seems to have helped me to relax more at night.

Amy suddenly lets out a shriek of laughter. "God, Zoe, he didn't!" and they dissolve in fits of giggles.

"Are you two talking about Daniel again? I feel sorry for the poor boy, he's so lovely to Zoe and you two are horrible."

They exchange a look and Amy smirks, "What do you mean 'poor boy'? There's nothing of the boy about him."

"All man for sure," Zoe adds and they're off again.

"You two are disgusting and anyway Amy, how would you know?"

A sudden thought crosses my mind. "You haven't like, both . . ." I tail off embarrassed. I don't know that I really want to say what I was thinking or hear the answer. It sounds too sordid. But they are identical in every respect even down to the tiny matching tattoos on each slender ankle.

Zoe looks indignant, "No, not with Daniel, we wouldn't," she retorts. "I really like him actually. And anyway, we haven't, he says he wants to take things slowly."

Amy laughs. "What she means is he doesn't fancy her. Hey, Zo, maybe he's gay."

I ignore Amy; I'm more focused on Zoe's last comment, "What does that mean, 'Not with Daniel'? You mean like you have in the past with other ones?'

I'm looking at them with real interest now, interest tinged with horror. There was me thinking they were innocents. They're both looking vaguely sheepish.

"What, like both of you at once? Oh my God that's sick."

It's their turn to look horrified now.

"Not at the same time, God no. That'd be like incest or something."

"No, we've just shared sometimes. Not with anyone we've really liked but . . ."

"Don't look like that Izzy. No one's been hurt or anything, they haven't even known. It's just been a bit of fun."

Amy adds, "We've compared notes, it's like research. Human Biology," and once again they're rolling about with laughter.

I have no idea whether to believe them or not. A little part of me suspects they have both slept with the same unwitting men and that worries me. I want to tell them it's dangerous, they'll hurt someone or get hurt themselves, playing with people like that. I don't, it's not my place.

By the time we're ready my headache has worsened. There's the throbbing and pulsing behind my blind eye that's telling me it won't go unless I take something and go to sleep. I don't want to miss our shopping trip or lunch but I know I must. I give Amy my car keys and sadly watch from the door as they drive away.

The silence of the house wraps itself round me like a blanket. I've never known anywhere that can do silence as well as this place. It's thick and smooth and seems to slow time and make everything languorous and heavy. I drag myself upstairs, pop two pills and climb into bed. They help with the pain and make me sleep. I can't bear the thought of lying here with my head pounding, listening to the silence and waiting; waiting for the sound of an intruder or a voice calling me in my head. Instead I sleep.

When I wake the bedroom is cold. The calming dove grays and soft pinks that we chose for our room instead feel frigid and drab. My head no longer hurts but is muzzy and thick and my mouth is dry from the tablets. I look at the clock. Its red-eyed glare informs me it's only two o'clock. I have ages before the twins return or Tom gets home. It's not a day for Bill either, he's not coming as often now so it's me on my own yet again.

I lie on my back and look at the ceiling. I can feel the heavy thump of my heart in my chest and the awareness of it makes me feel anxious. The codeine is making me jittery. I need to get up.

I go downstairs and flick on the TV. It's yet another program about treasure lurking undiscovered in attics, priceless art and rare porcelain. There was no such luck with ours; just cobwebs and carapaces, bat droppings and dust. Birds rotted to feather and bone. I can't settle.

There's that silent feeling of expectancy vibrating the atoms of the air as though the house and I are waiting. I can't stand this feeling with its undercurrent of malice. I'll have to go to my studio instead. Even if I don't work on Matthew's commission I can at least potter and tidy. I always feel calmer there.

I've done all I can do. My heart's not really in it today and if I try to work when I feel like this it'll all go wrong. The unrest will flow down my fingers and onto the canvas, leaving taint where it touches.

I must also talk to the twins for I'm sure someone's been in my studio since I was last here. Things have been moved and the door to the annex was open. I'm positive it was closed when I left. It's not that I mind them coming down here but I'd like them to at least let me know. It's vaguely unsettling to think that someone has been here going through my things. Two of my brushes are on the floor and as I bend to pick them up I see one has been snapped in two and a splinter from its shaft spitefully pierces my thumb. I'm confused as to how it got broken like that and I feel a ripple of unease at the sudden sight of my blood.

I walk slowly back to the house. The trees in the orchard need pruning before the spring, sometime from November to March according to Bill. He was going to give me the number of someone who'd do them as it's too much for him on his own. I must remember to remind him.

The days are so short now that it's already getting dark. I hurry back across the lawn. I stop. The light's on in the kitchen and it wasn't when I left. I know it wasn't, it was still light. I don't know what to do. I cross the grass cautiously staying out of the light from the window, until I can see.

It's Tom. The one day I wasn't meant to be here and he's managed to get away early. Once I would've been glad and run straight in to greet him, now I hesitate, unsure of my welcome.

As I watch I see his lips are moving, he's talking and it dawns on me that there must be someone in there with him. Madeline suddenly drifts into view and places her hand on his chest. It's a gesture so reminiscent of me touching Matthew that I feel the guilty heat of it in my palm. Part of me wants to run away, not to face what I think I'm seeing. Instead I slink to the wall by the window and wait. Out of sight and so obviously out of mind. My heart is in my mouth, I can feel its pumping tubes and valves beating in my throat. I want to be sick but I listen, my traitorous ears are craning and straining.

"Madeline, please, we can't go on doing this."

"But, Tom darling, I need you. You know I do, every bit as much as she does. And you know how good we are together, don't let her get in the way of that."

I watch Madeline step into him and reach up to place her hand on his cheek. I imagine her nipples softly pressing against his skin. I will be sick. My heart pounds and my legs feel too weak to bear me up. Still I watch. I will see his betrayal played out in front of my eyes.

"This is tearing me apart. I can't do this to her. She needs me and I still care for her despite everything. She's so sad and disturbed it breaks my heart. She knows something's wrong. I know she does."

Madeline sighs. "Then let's take what we have for the moment, we'll work something out. Darling you deserve so much more, you need something for you. Come back to mine like I asked, it's so lonely now Joe's gone."

She gives a theatrical shudder and I feel my hatred like the blade of a knife.

"I can still hardly bear to mention his name, it was so awful. Please come back for a while, we've got ages before she'll expect you back."

She tilts her face upward and he dips his head to meet hers. Her tiny teeth catch at his lower lip, in a gesture both sensual and tender, and I look away. I slide down the wall and crouch in the soil. So we're over.

I wait until I hear the crunch of his tires on the gravel before going inside, inside where the memory of her perfume hangs in the air like poison.

There was a time, early in my recovery, when I didn't know my own face. When I would look in the mirror and see, not a stranger exactly but someone disconnected from the me I felt inside. It's like that now. I stand in our bedroom in front of the mirror and see looking back at me a sunken-eyed woman. She's all hollowed out.

There was also a time when I struggled to recognize my emotions; was I anxious or happy, angry or sad? Or times when I felt things I couldn't describe, feelings outside my emotional repertoire, feelings that had no name. It's like that now.

I'm sad and I'm angry, bereft and relieved but all from a distance. I'm shutting down.

I look at our bed and imagine them lying there coiled and entwined. The door in my mind peeps open, the bile rises. I rip the sheets from the mattress. I won't lie where she may have lain, with her hair on my pillow like seaweed. I won't. I can't believe he's done this to us. Yes, we've had our problems but I thought we were working things through. I thought we still had something worth fighting for.

I go to the cupboard to fetch the clean sheets and there on the dresser is the watch I bought Tom for his birthday. A present I chose with such love and care. I pick up my hairbrush and pound at its glass, over and over until the crystal shatters. Over and over until its face, like mine, is all twisted and bent, its tiny hands raised in surrender. I sweep the pieces into his drawer, the broken mainspring of my heart among his socks and underwear—and then the tears come.

37

*"One for sorrow, two for mirth, three for a funeral
and four for birth"*

—Anonymous

've had to learn over the years to not be so compulsive. To pause
and to check before blurting, to stop and to think before acting. I've
worked hard to hide my quirks and eccentricities behind a veneer of
normality, whatever that may be. Now I wonder, when did I become
quite so self-contained, so in control?

My well of tears eventually ran dry but a boulder still sits in my
chest. A tight, hard knot of anger and hurt. I quiver and thrum with
the force of it.

I know things haven't exactly been easy since we came here. Maybe
the cracks in our fabric had begun to show long before she came along,
but did he really have to throw it all away? Did he have to walk,
without a thought, into her cool embrace and demolish everything
we'd built together for a pair of cold green eyes? For a cloud of red-
gold hair? Did he have to answer her siren call?

Yesterday, by the time the twins returned, I'd wrapped myself in
the tattered shreds of my composure and bound my wounds. Yes,
my eyes were red and my mood black but nothing that couldn't be
blamed on a headache. Nothing to set their alarm bells clanging.
They're so focused on their own little universe that the rest of us
orbit them in a blur, outside their sphere of interest. Ironic really
that they fled the scene of one adulterous crime only to lift the

tape and enter another. This time with me as the sorry chalk mark on the floor.

Before Tom came home I went to bed, full of murderous intent. I couldn't trust myself to look at him. He'll find out soon enough that I was here and that I saw. Time will tell, quite literally.

I slept in another room last night. Clean sheets or not, I couldn't bear the thought of his hot limbs close to mine. His skin, slick with her moistness, touching mine.

I dreamed again, worse than before, a violent visceral terror of a dream and woke drenched in the dread of it. I must've screamed for he was there, his hand hard on my mouth like a memory, his words soft in my ear, "Shush, Izzy, shush, you'll wake the twins." He slid between the sheets and made love to me that felt like hate. Full of pity, hard and final like a goodbye. I clung to him, and let the self-loathing fuel my rage.

This morning I'm bruised and bereft. I have the stink of him on my skin as a reminder. He wasn't here when I awoke but I can hear him now, showering and dressing for work. I imagine his white-faced horror now he knows that I know. I wait but he goes downstairs without a word and I hear the clunk of the front door. No stomach for breakfast then.

I lie here for a while and let my thoughts ebb and flow, examining the dirty wash of them. A part of me wants to run away; to ring Maria and beg to stay, sobbing and wailing on her shoulder. I won't. Love her though I do, I couldn't bear her sympathy tinged, despite her best intentions, with a whiff of "I told you so." I've had my fill of pity. I may be a lip-puckering mouthful of bitterness but I'm not a victim, not inside.

I must get up. Amy and Zoe will be down soon. I go through to our bedroom. Tom's drawer is upturned on the duvet, a mess of socks and underpants. Everything is strewn with watch parts, wheels and pinions and slivers of crystal. A new pack of underpants lies opened on the floor but you weren't so lucky with the socks, were you Tom. I wonder if your conscience is pricked by those shards and splinters.

His wardrobe is open as are the drawers and I see the small suitcase has gone. So, he has taken the coward's course and run. I have misjudged his incorruptibility, his sense of honor. It seems he has tumbled from his lofty moral promontory to slide into the soft valley of her thighs.

I laugh out loud, a slightly wild and manic laugh, surprising myself that some separate part of me can wax so lyrical in my head at a time like this. I'm mildly shocked to realize I feel relieved. Relieved that I won't have to face him for the moment. Relieved that I know what was wrong. So often he reassured me that all was fine and that I was wrong, that I began to doubt myself. Was the frigid distance and his abstraction a work of my imagining? Was I the one so out of kilter? It would seem not.

I stand in the wasteland of our bedroom and wonder what to do; what comes next. I feel the thoughts begin to shout and clamor, overloading and confusing me, and I begin to slide. I close my eyes and slow my breathing to calm my mind. My inner Scarlett speaks to me, "I can't think about this now, I'll go crazy if I do. I'll think about it tomorrow."

I need to compartmentalize. A trick I've learned to contain and manage the things that would overwhelm me. I open the box in my mind; I lift its smooth and lacquered lid and push this thing inside. I'll wait until I can think more clearly, until I can face it.

I dress with trembling fingers. I hear the twins downstairs now, getting breakfast. I fumble with my jeans. My tremor seems worse this morning and I'm all flutter-fingered and rubber-thumbed.

A sudden shriek pierces the air followed by the sound of something smashing.

I run down the stairs, shirt undone, to see Amy stood at the front door, a pool of milk and broken glass at her feet. She's looking in shock at something just out of my line of sight. A horror I can't yet see. A single word forms in my mind—Major. I pull the door wide and see a magpie dead on the step, a mangled chessboard of a bird. One for sorrow, how fitting.

My relief, so hot on the heels of fear, makes me sharp. "Amy, for God's sake, it's only a bird."

She looks at me, petulant at my tone and mutters, "I'm not Amy, I'm Zoe."

My temper flares. "Whoever the fuck you are there was no need to scream like that, scaring the shit out of everyone."

I see the swell of tears threaten her lower lashes and immediately I'm contrite. "I'm sorry Zoe, I didn't mean to shout at you, but you scared me yelling like that. Jesus."

I put my hand on her arm and realize she's shaking, she's genuinely scared.

"Hey, it's okay, it's just a bird."

"Take it away," she says in a small voice, "take it away, they're unlucky."

I want to tell her that bird's already flown.

I reach to pick up the small body and as I do its head lolls and flops and I feel a cold stickiness against my palm. I see the red of blood and the white of its tiny vertebrae peeping from the downy plumage and my throat catches. Its neck has been broken; worse, it's almost been wrenched in two. I drop it in horror and instinctively back away. It's my turn now to be afraid and I'm seized by the impulse to run back indoors and bolt the door. First Mina, now this. Once could've been bad luck, an animal as Tom so nearly convinced me. Surely not twice.

I realize Zoe is staring at me strangely, so I send her to fetch a spade while I fight to control my rising panic. I won't run away, and I won't throw the poor thing in the bin; it'll have a Christian burial near where we put Mina but not too close, I wouldn't want the birdy scent of it to disturb her slumber.

While I wait I steel myself to pick it up and look at the broken creature in my hand. Close up it's beautiful, even in death. Its plumage is a glossy black, shimmering with metallic shades of violet and green. *Pica pica*, considered the most intelligent of animals. Able to recognize its own image in a mirror and I know how challenging that can be. Monogamous, Tom should note, it mates for life and I scan the branches for its grieving mate. One for sorrow, it's all alone like me.

I notice with a sudden start that there's a distant figure at the end of the drive, standing in Cleaver's Lane half hidden by the tall gatepost. From the height and the build it could be the hooded man I saw before, the one watching my studio. The one I thought was Joe. I think of the mark on Madeline's neck. If it is Joe, what's he doing here, what does he want with me?

Without stopping to think, I shout, "Hey," and start down the drive, the bird still clutched in my hands, my shirt flapping. I've no idea what I'm intending but I do it anyway. Any action is preferable to just standing and waiting for the next bad thing to happen.

He turns and walks briskly away and by the time I reach the gates he's gone from sight. He must surely have run, around the corner and into Stour's Lane.

It's too early for walkers and he was definitely watching us, thinking himself safely hidden from view. I'm afraid. Has Joe found out about Madeline and Tom and is this a message to us? I wonder now at the magpie's significance.

One mystery resolves itself, another forms. The twins and I are alone here now, are we safe?

Zoe returns with Amy and a shovel and together we commit the tiny harbinger of doom to the earth. Each clang of the spade a death knell to my peace of mind. When we're done I go to tread down the soil. I lift my foot and stamp, once, twice, and then I can't stop. Over and over I pound my foot into the dirt. Over and over until I register Amy's worried voice bringing me back.

38

"He does little himself. He only plans"
—Arthur Conan Doyle,
The Memoirs of Sherlock Holmes

He was feeling restless. He'd had to change hotels and hire cars twice already because he couldn't stay anywhere long enough to risk arousing curiosity or becoming a fixture. The manager of the last place had become too interested, watching him with her dozy doe-eyes. Making sure he had an extra egg at breakfast, offering him her wet-yoked ova on a plate. It was the price you paid for being him and it was such a cross to bear. He'd toyed with the idea of giving her what she wanted, plus a little bit extra she wasn't expecting, but it was just too risky. And anyway, she'd leaned in a bit too close to him the other morning and he was sure he'd seen a moustache. What the fuck was he meant to do with that.

He was creeping ever closer to her. He was in, up to the hilt if he so chose but he needed more. He needed her to understand before she died exactly what she'd done. She'd helped create him. She'd made the monster. He'd had to live with the consequences; she'd have to die from them.

He'd fleetingly considered dispatching her husband, breaking her heart as a starter for ten. But he'd been watching the prick for a while now and he was doing a fine job of that all on his own. He'd find another way to break her heart.

He didn't fear discovery anymore. Yes, she'd been poking around and speaking to people she shouldn't but otherwise she was going about her little life like a hamster in a wheel. She remembered nothing; he was sure of it.

Any danger was melting away, even his Sanctuary had gone now. The walls stripped out, all plastered and new and any evidence, not that he'd left any, had been swept clean away. He could breathe more easily. There was just her now and the game.

This place was eroding him, he could feel it. It was stripping him back to his basest self, all the old compulsions jostling to the fore. It was frightening and it was liberating. He'd even begun to see the shimmering emanating from those white-gold girls. Like his Rachel. He ran his tongue slowly across the wet membrane of his lips and savored the memory of her.

He couldn't let them slip through his fingers. They'd be a bonus play, two for the price of one. She was purely business but those would be his pleasure.

Deep in the core of him the boy he'd awoken smiled to himself; that's better, now they'd both get something out of this trip.

39

"Let no stranger intrude here, no invader trespass"
—John Marsden, *The Dead of Night*

'm bearing up. What a strange expression that is but apparently it's what I'm doing. I'm bearing up the grievous weight of Tom's betrayal and abandonment. I had a text from him—such bravery—his lily-livered words flickering and whispering from the screen.

> *Isabel*—oh so formal now
> *Thing's aren't how they seem. I just need some time to think.*
> *I'm at a hotel, not anywhere else. I'm sorry.*
> *Tom*

I read this brief missive with cold dispassion.

If anyone had told me a year ago that I would find myself where I am today I wouldn't have believed I could survive, but here I am. I haven't withered and died on the vine, not yet. Somehow the knowing, bad though it is, is better than the doubt and a little part of me feels this was inevitable. I'm no longer the person I was back when we first met. Tom has struggled with that fact—and I have struggled with his struggling. I blame his mother—don't we always—for I think her special brand of love, with its mixture of neediness and control, has shaped his sense of the world and his understanding of what love is.

Eventually we must talk and try to unravel this tangled mess. Not now. If I try to think about the future there's a roller-coaster dip in my stomach and a shiver through my chest. I can't face it yet.

Last night I didn't dream. Mainly because I lay awake, listening, thinking, waiting. The dull thud in my chest marked the minutes, ticking away each hour and pumping the adrenaline through my limbs. Today I'm drained. My hair's lank and there's smudged indigo dusting my eyes, every year of my life writ large.

Amy and Zoe have asked why Tom isn't here and I found myself giving them some lame story of a crisis at work. I can't face telling them yet. I'm not sure why it should but it feels like I've failed somehow.

My negative energy is polluting the air and affecting everyone's mood. This morning they drooped and sighed until I lost patience and told them to do something, go somewhere. Take the car and go out. I needed them gone for a while; at the moment I need to be alone to find space to think.

Zoe eventually rang Daniel and now he's taken them both for lunch. He's so thoughtful and intense, so different from the twins with their brand of audacious boldness born of privilege, that it's odd to see the three of them together. He's always appeared to me to be reserved rather than shy but Bill Arthur was here when he turned up today and I was surprised to see how he avoided him. I can only assume he's different when there's just him and Zoe for I can't imagine her attracted by such diffidence. He is an attractive man though so maybe that makes up for it. There's a look of Keanu Reeves about him; fine featured with those fathomless eyes that you can almost feel grazing your skin when he looks at you.

Now they've gone I find myself paralyzed by ennui. I'm just sitting in my studio, too listless even to think. The atmosphere around the coach house adds to my lethargy, that heavy-aired stillness. I run my hands over the arm of the sofa and feel every ridge and bobble of the fabric. It's the old sofa from our flat and I feel a wave of nostalgia at the memory of us buying it. God we were so excited. We'd just moved in and every purchase, every eggcup, towel and spoon was an adventure. We were an adventure. Every fingertip's touch, each eyelash, every mole or freckle a discovery and a wonder. I realize that in my mind we're already over, Tom and me. I fear there's no coming back from this.

I'm startled from my reverie by the sound of footsteps outside. The first thought that flashes into my mind is that I'm here alone. No one would even hear me scream. I know the door's locked; it always is. Still I feel a prickle of fear. I never work with the doors unlocked now, the place feels too isolated and remote. Even though I'm happy here, I know bad things can happen.

I freeze and listen. The footsteps have stopped by the doors at the front and my eyes flick upward to check that the bolts are across. I hear someone tentatively trying the doors and see the slight strain of the wood inward. The bolts hold. The footsteps move away from the door and toward the edge of the building. Quickly, without a sound, I move to crouch behind the sofa. If whoever it is goes to the door at the side they could look in at the window and see me if I stay where I am. Thank God I haven't yet put on the lights to give away my presence. The footsteps continue round to the side door and from my hiding place I see the handle slowly turn, followed by the sound of knocking and a voice tentatively calling, "Hello?"

This gives me some reassurance as it seems so courteous and safe somehow but I'm still not moving, even though the voice, a man's voice, seems vaguely familiar. I hear him go to the window and stop. There's a moment's silence and I imagine him, face pressed to the glass, looking in, scanning the space inside for signs of life. I shrink down as far as I can, hopefully out of sight.

The mirror I use to check the perspective of my work is on the bench and I pray I'm not betrayed by its silvery surface. The mortar and pestle for grinding pigment sit benignly by it. The marble pestle has the hint of a weapon about it and for a moment I imagine it a cudgel, breaking bone. I picture its shiny surface wet and red with blood, stuck with gobbets of gray and tufts of dark hair. My hair. I fight to still the rising panic.

I manage to stay unseen and hear the eventual sound of his retreat, followed by the distant slam of a car door and the sound of an engine starting. My teeth are chattering with fright. I unlock the door and run outside, gasping for air. I find myself dry-heaving into the grass so great was my terror.

I hadn't considered it before but with no front-facing windows, other than in the annex, there's no way of seeing who might be approaching. Even with the new windows I'm having fitted to let in the north light, I still won't be able to see the driveway. If I'm staying here, which now I doubt, I'll need a security camera.

I'm so shaken I just sit in the damp grass. Everything overwhelms me, and I cry. I hate myself for how weak I've become. I hardly ever used to cry, what's the point. Now it seems I leak tears like a tap.

I feel better afterward but I can't paint today. I was expecting too much of myself to think that I could. I'd hoped it might help to distract me and calm my thoughts. Painting is so much a part of me that it becomes instinctive and I find I lose myself in the stark order of monochrome or the vibrancy of color.

Matthew's commission is nearly finished so soon he'll be committed to memory. It's funny but I don't feel the same excitement as before at the thought of him. I wonder, was the attraction I felt something real or was it just my reaction to Tom's remoteness? Was my sense of the impending loss of him driving me to imagine comfort and longing elsewhere? Whatever the case I'll keep my distance. I won't rebound or seek revenge. I won't compound Tom's sin with one of my own.

I walk slowly back through the apple orchard, lost in these worthy thoughts. Windfalls lie brown and white-speckled, softly rotting among the leaves and the vinegary scent of their decay seems symbolic somehow. Much promised but gone to molder.

I'm startled by the sound of Bill Arthur's voice calling my name, "Isabel, Isabel, I'm glad I've caught you."

I turn and see him walking toward me, coming up fast on my blind side with a piece of crumpled paper in his hand. A spurt of adrenaline makes me aware of just how much my mystery visitor has disturbed me.

Bill looks pleased with himself this morning and despite the bleakness of my mood a faint smile finds its way to my lips. He approaches, waving the piece of paper.

"I found it, the number for Steve Turnbull." I must look blank as he adds, "You know, the tree man."

I don't have the heart or the inclination to tell him we probably won't need him now, so thank him anyway and take the crumpled sheet from his hand.

I look at the number in some confusion.

"Sorry, I jotted it down in a bit of a hurry. You'll have to change the dialing code, that's the old one from way back. It's been a long time since we've used him but I don't think he's moved."

I realize I can't talk to him. My nerves are stretched like piano wire and I just want to lock myself away, to hunker down with my fear. I manage a watery smile and rudely leave him standing there in the orchard.

The house is quiet and my thoughts feel enormous in all this stillness. A surge of pure loneliness runs through me like a chill stream. It's cold and clear with nothing reflected back bar my own thoughts. I feel a stirring of panic that this could be my life from now on, solitary and silent. My mind spirals ahead to a future where I'm old and strange, withered and whiskery, shuffling through sterile rooms. No lover to keep my oddness in check.

I have to eat. I go through to the kitchen to make a sandwich and instead pour myself a glass of wine, a large one. I think I'll opt for a downward spiral into alcoholism as a happy alternative. I'll be kind to myself and curl up on the sofa with my wine and watch a movie; perhaps an afternoon tearjerker where I can wallow in someone else's misery.

I go upstairs to change out of my jeans and am unprepared for the hollow sound of my footsteps, the echoing squeak and creak of the stairs. I've spent a lot of time alone in this house but never have I felt quite so lonely.

I'd thought I would cope when the twins go home, for go they will, eventually. I thought I could stay here, bravely defiant. Now I'm not sure I can. Maybe I'll go back to London with them when they leave.

I kick off my jeans and the piece of paper Bill gave me flutters from my pocket to the floor. The numbers in his spidery hand look up at me with a jolt of familiarity, their pattern resonating with me in a way I can't explain. I reach to pick it up and as I do it comes to me: the annex; it's reminiscent of the numbers etched there on the floor.

Despite myself my interest's piqued and I riffle through my bedside drawer for the copy I made but it isn't there. Then I remember, I took it with me to the police station. Unbidden the memory of that visit comes back to me ripe with my humiliation. I remember their exchange of glances and the way they spoke to me, so coolly patronizing and dismissive.

I find the pages furtively crumpled in the pocket of my coat. I smooth them out and examine the marks and numbers alongside those on the sheet from Bill. The scratches and gouges still give me the same familiar flicker of unrest. There's mystery here and pain, I'm sure of it. I feel its echo as I look at the marks and in my mind's eye I can see the scrabbling of the frantic fingers that made them. I shrug the image away and instead concentrate on the numbers. I was right. They start with almost the same pattern of digits, no more than a single number the difference between them. This cannot be coincidence; my number is a phone number after all. My heart quickens at the thought that the answer could be no more than a call away.

Regardless of all that has recently happened and how anxious and unsettled I feel, I'm still compelled to solve the mystery of this place. There's an urgency to it now for if Tom and I are truly over, then we'll sell the house and I'll never know what haunts me or what may have happened here.

With shaking fingers I dial the number, replacing the first four digits with the local code. I wait as the line clicks and whirrs into silence. Nothing. I sit back disappointed and compare the numbers again. Bill's number has a missing digit, a one immediately following the leading zero. I try replacing the first five digits of my number instead. Now I seem to be a digit short. I take the copy to the light and there, in the dusty graphite of my rubbing, is the slightest shadow of a number three. I'd missed it before but it's there, faint but unmistakeable.

This time the line connects and somewhere in a distant home the phone is ringing. I slam down the receiver before anyone can answer and the reality of what this could mean hits me like a physical blow. It leaves me breathless.

I must think how to solve this. I need to know who the number belongs to, or more likely belonged, for it must be many years since unknown fingers scratched those numbers in the floor. I recall the hair clip, bent and broken, and imagine those same fingers, urgently prising and scraping with their makeshift tool.

I make a resolution, sitting here on my bed, a promise that I will find you, if you exist, and set you free.

I'll start with when. I go to the PC and Google "dialing code changes UK," more in hope than anticipation. The search engine starts its magic, trawling the ether for intelligent life. Wikipedia answers the call with PhONEday and the Big Number Change and I learn that new codes have been issued over the years, most recently in the early 2000s—well over a decade ago.

40

"Memory is the treasury and guardian of all things"
—Cicero

Another message from Tom:

Izzy, We need to talk, can I come over?
Tom

I delete it without replying; no is the answer, I'm not ready for you yet.

I'm feeling strangely elated today. I'm fizzing and popping and can't keep my hands still. I was thinking during yesterday's art class and I believe I may have a plan. Rather than facing Tom, I think I'll visit Mr. Connor. I know it's wrong, that I shouldn't bother a sick old man but I need to gather more answers. Although if my suspicions have any substance at all, there's the real possibility that he isn't just a sick old man. He could be something far more sinister. I need to be careful. I have to find out about the storeroom, when was it built and why, but I also have to keep in mind that I could be delving somewhere dark and dangerous.

I suddenly remember the diary the kitchen fitters found and the words that were scrawled there, over and over again. "The boy did it" or something like that. It may mean nothing at all; most of what was written in those later pages was no more than the ramblings of a failing mind but it might be significant. He may know something. This strengthens my resolve and gives me some slim justification for what I'm going to do.

I know I'm still obsessed. The thoughts running endlessly, round and round at the back of my mind, thoughts that won't stop until I solve the mystery I've created. Thoughts that are easier to face at the moment than facing what's happened to Tom and me.

I couldn't remember where Gemma had said her father was living so I went on the internet again. The name Fairview leapt out at me as soon as I saw it and there on the website was a picture of tranquil lawns and shady oaks, and a country house lit with the lambent light of twilight years.

I'm here. I get out of the car and make my way across the car park. I've brought shortbread as a sweetener. All old people like shortbread, surely. I suddenly hope he still has his teeth.

The building itself has a pleasing symmetry. Tall windows evenly spaced beneath lichened gray stone lintels, its porticoed doorway a wide and welcoming portal to the afterlife.

The reception desk is in what was once the hallway and an imposing stone staircase sweeps upward, richly carpeted with a wide runner and gleaming stair rods. The handrail of the elegant bannister is burnished to a shine by the caress of a thousand palms and I almost hear the gentle glide of a gloved hand and the swish of taffeta.

In contrast the reception desk is manned by a stern-faced and heavy-jawed matron. Steely haired and clad in nurses' tunic and trousers. She regards me steadily over the majestic bolster of her breasts. I clear my throat nervously and hesitate for a moment. I realize I don't know if he's Mr. Connor or Dr. Connor. I'd kind of assumed he was a doctor but now I come to think of it I don't remember anyone ever referring to him that way. I decide to settle for mister.

"Hello, I've come to see Mr. Connor?"

My voice holds no entitlement, instead there's an upward lilt that implies a question as though I'm perhaps asking her permission.

"Have you visited us before?" she asks, reaching for the visitors' book and pen.

"No," I reply, "this is my first time."

Book and pen make a strategic retreat.

"And what is your relationship to Mr. Connor?" she asks, in a tone that to my guilty ears sounds dangerously like suspicion. "Friend or family?"

Friend or foe would perhaps have been more appropriate in the circumstances.

I offer an ingratiating smile and try to look harmless.

"Friend," I say, and then qualify with, "of Gemma, his daughter, we were at school together." I smile—winningly I hope—and add, "We've actually just moved into his old home, so I was hoping to have a chat with him about it. Gemma said he'd love that, if he's up to it."

I clamp my mouth shut. I almost forgot the first rule of fabrication, to keep it simple. I resist the urge to blurt a full and faux life history. To tell her how close I was to Gemma, how well I knew her father and of course her mother too and how terribly sad it all is. Phew.

It appears that mention of Gemma's name is sufficient reassurance as book and pen are slid back across the desk with the request that I please sign in.

The name I write is not quite my own, "I Weir" lends a certain ambiguity—just in case.

She presses an unseen buzzer beneath the desk and a fresh-faced girl appears through double doors. Together we make our way along the corridor, my feet sinking into the deep plush of the carpet with silent, deceitful stealth.

We pass a well-stocked library, a dining room and an airy sitting room. The latter is inhabited by high-backed chairs, mainly bereft of occupants. A wide-screen TV plays quietly on its own in the corner, amusing itself with a tactless display of advertisements for wills, stair-lifts and funeral plans, all designed to remind the residents of their decrepitude or imminent demise. The room is quiet bar the disjointed mumble of a lone voice and the clack of knitting needles. The walls are a soothing eggshell blue adorned with Monet prints and soft landscapes, blurred and misty as though already viewed from beyond the veil. I look for an oven to put my head in.

Eventually we reach a set of security doors and swipe through into a newer wing which has less the feel of a good hotel and more that of a hospital. The plush carpeting and soothing pastels continue but here the air has a taint of humanity, an undertone of mothballs and musty secretions. All the scents of old age.

We stop outside a white door marked number eighteen and my companion gently knocks before going in.

I wait furtively in the corridor and hear her say, in a voice that's overly loud and cheery, "Hello, Mr. Connor, look who's come to see you, isn't that nice."

He obviously doesn't agree as her enthusiasm is met with a resounding silence. She beckons me in regardless.

Mr. Connor is sitting in a high-backed chair by his bed. A honey-comb blanket, soft blue like a baby's, is draped over his knees. He doesn't look up as we come in, instead he stares steadily into a world we cannot see, the film reel of his past flickering for his eyes only. I look at his face and try to remember the face of the man I saw in the photos, the man whose face I seemed to know. There's no remnant of him here but I still experience a slight jolt. Not quite recognition but almost.

The person in front of me is aged beyond his years, the skin of his face hanging in slack folds the color of a mild cheese, a Wensleydale perhaps. I can see he was once a big man from the heft of his shoulders and the hard jut of his jaw but all is shrunken and collapsing in. His mouth works in silent rumination. His soft unfocused eyes are milky and moist, windows to a soul that's already packing its bags.

He looks harmless, not at all like a man who'd construct a cell, locked up and hidden from the world. He doesn't look like a man capable of imprisonment and evil. Then again, who knows what scenes of violence or what dark memories might sustain him. Who knows what he might know. I suppress a shudder.

He's smartly dressed in a crisp check shirt and Aran cardigan. His trousers are pressed and razor-creased and his feet neatly clad in corduroy slippers. He's not at all the shuffling and disheveled man of my imagining.

His hands disturb me. They're large and gnarled with knuckles swollen like oak apples. His fingers are pluck, plucking endlessly at the blanket on his lap. I watch them, mesmerized, and feel an answering twitch in my own fingers. A memory from the time soon after my attack when my fingers worked with a will of their own.

I pull myself back to the present as the nurse speaks to him again.

"Mr. Connor, hello."

Pluck, pluck, pluck.

"Mr. Connor, you've got a visitor."

She turns to me and says sotto voce, "I don't think you've visited before, have you? He's often much better than this, particularly in the mornings, but isn't having a good day today. Just make sure you sit where he can see you okay and speak slowly and calmly. He's been more confused on and off lately so try to stick to one thing at a time otherwise he sometimes can't follow and gets frustrated. Oh, and try not to question him too much. It's threatening for them and makes them feel they're being interrogated."

She adds as an afterthought, "Did you say you were family?"

"No," I answer, "I know his daughter, Gemma."

She turns back to Mr. Connor, "This lady's a friend of Gemma's, isn't that lovely. I'll leave the two of you to have a nice chat."

She pulls up the visitor's chair close to his knees, too close I feel, and leaves us alone.

I edge the chair back and sit down clutching the packet of short-bread like a weapon. I look at the man in front of me and have no idea where to start. If I don't tread carefully I could get into all sorts of trouble and fleetingly wonder if visiting a vulnerable adult under false pretenses is actually considered a crime.

Before I came I had a plan, to say I knew Gemma from school and that I'd been to their house way back when. I'd concoct some tale of playing in the coach house, of going into the storeroom when we knew we shouldn't. I realize now that I'm here that this won't work at all. I have no idea what school she went to or whether she boarded like me; for all I know she never brought friends to the house or was home tutored or they lived abroad for a while. The possibilities and pitfalls are endless. For my naive ploy to have worked he would have to be so far lost in dementia as to make my visit pointless anyway.

I recall Gemma telling me, no more than a handful of months ago, that often he was, to use her words, "still there" so this may not be so easy. I'll have to tread cautiously and play it by ear, watching him for signs of evasiveness or guilt.

"Hello Mr. Connor, I've brought you some biscuits, I hope you like shortbread."

I tentatively hold out the pack but he makes no move to take them so I place them on the coverlet of the bed.

I try again. "My name's Isabel, I'm a friend of Gemma's."

At the mention of his daughter's name he looks at me properly for the first time and I feel a spark of contact flow between us. His eyes meet mine and it's hard to explain but I get the sensation that he's there but he's not, as though he's regarding me from behind thick glass.

Encouraged, I continue, settling on a kind of half-truth as a way in.

"I was talking to Gemma about your old house, it's so lovely there."

He continues to look at me intently as though he's trying to place me, delving into the vaults of his memory bank. It may be my imagination but there's something unsettling and vaguely sinister about his gaze; it's too probing and intense and I shift uneasily in my chair.

"I don't know you," he says. "Who did you say you were?"

So much for tales of childhood pranks, of sunny afternoons running through his orchard to the coach house. I'm lost now as to where to go with this so settle on honesty, at least to start with. I throw caution to the wind. After all, even if he is guilty of something he can't harm anyone now.

"We've bought The Lodge, me and my husband, and Gemma was telling us a bit about it, all about the gardens and the coach house."

With sudden panic I wonder if he knows his house has been sold, God, I hope I haven't upset him.

I watch him carefully for any sign of shock or any reaction at the mention of the coach house but there's nothing, not a flicker.

Instead he asks, "How is she?"

I presume he's talking about Gemma so tell him, "She's fine," then add disingenuously, "Will she be coming to see you today?"

I have a ripple of fear that she'll suddenly appear and catch me red-handed. That would be difficult to explain.

He looks mildly panicked, his eyes scanning the room as though the answer's hidden there.

"Why, is it Tuesday?" he asks. "She always comes Tuesdays."

Reassured I answer, "No, it's Thursday today." Thankfully.

He appears to gather himself and I begin for the first time to really get the sense that there's another person here in the room with me. His eyes lose their vacant look and he focuses on me properly. I'm surprised by the keen intelligence that's now apparent in his gaze but then I remember he used to be a clinician of some kind. I must be on my guard for he may be well versed in detecting half-truths and lies.

"It's such a beautiful old house. My husband loves it, we both do. We can't believe how lucky we were, it coming onto the market just when we were looking to move."

I swear, as I say it I can feel my nose growing.

"I hope you don't mind me coming to see you but we wanted to find out a bit more about its history and wondered if you'd be able to help. Gemma said your family lived there for years so we thought you might know when it was built and who was living there before."

He looks at me with no trace of his previous distraction.

"That's very flattering," he says, "but I'm not sure how much I can tell you. We bought it back in the early seventies and it was over a century old then. Built in 1870, architecturally very much of its time. Typical features of the Gothic revival with its porch and bay windows."

He settles in his chair and I notice his hands have stopped their restless twitching.

"Of course, most houses around that time were slate roofed but they tended to use more tile around here because of the Marston clay pits. Availability of local tiles you see. From what I understand it was originally built as a vicarage but that's about all I can tell you. If you really want to know its history you could probably find out more from the National Archives."

He stops and I watch him begin to slip away, his mind struggling to stay engaged.

"It was home," he finally says. "Eleanor and I bought it back in seventy-two and it was a hundred years old then. Built in 1870 I think."

A wistful look crosses his face and I see him drifting backward.

"How is she?" he asks.

For a horrified moment I think he's talking about Eleanor, who I assume is his late wife. I have a ghastly image of him dissolving in grief all over again at the news of her death.

I hesitate for a little too long and he impatiently repeats, "Well, how is she?"

It's no good, I have to ask, "Who?"

"Gemma, of course, is she coming today?"

I suspect we may turn this circle a few times before my visit is over.

"No, she comes Tuesdays doesn't she and it's Thursday today." I need to gently steer him back on track.

"Do you remember the old coach house?" I ask. "We're fitting it out so I can use it as a studio. I'm an artist, well a painter at least, and it's where I'll be working."

I give a small self-deprecating smile and in response I see a flicker of irritation, so he is still with me.

"Of course I can remember it," he snaps, "I'm not senile yet you know."

"We've had to take out all your workbenches I'm afraid and knock through into the fuel store. It's made it so much bigger though." I smile, watching him intently. "It's been turned into my office so we've put it to good use."

He's regarding me steadily with just a hint of confusion. No guilt or evasiveness, no suspicion, nothing. I'm not really getting anything from him so perhaps I need to be more direct.

"It was quite a job knocking out those inner walls, you certainly made it to last." I laugh nervously. "We were wondering what on earth you kept in there."

He begins to look more confused and mildly distressed.

"I can't remember," he says. "I can't remember a fuel store. I don't know what you're talking about. Why are you here?"

His eyes have the same panicked look as they did earlier, and he looks round the room in confusion.

"I didn't use the workshop much, too far from the house and then there was Eleanor . . ."

He trails off and I see the start of tears welling in his old eyes.

I quickly change the subject, trying a different tack.

"I've got Bill Arthur doing the gardens again. He was telling me all about when he used to work for you, back when Alan Harris left, do you remember Alan?"

"Alan's a good boy. Always does what he's asked. Shame he doesn't want to come any more. I need to have a word with that mother of his, find out what's going on with him."

I notice the slip into the present tense and fear I'm losing him completely. This could be my only opportunity.

"Why did he stop coming; do you have any idea what happened?"

So much for not interrogating him. I may as well just grab the lamp by his bed, tie him to the chair and shine the light in his eyes. Perhaps club him with the shortbread for good measure.

He looks at me this time with frank suspicion.

"Who did you say you were?"

"I'm Isabel, a friend of Gemma's." I go for a preemptive strike, "She's fine, she says hello and she'll be over on Tuesday."

I clear my throat and try again, "Bill said Alan seemed very upset . . ." My turn to trail off this time and wait.

"He doesn't get along with Grant. Grant can be a bit much sometimes, what with his teasing. No harm in him, not really, but Alan's always been wary of him. I don't really know what happened, some silly falling-out I expect. Alan can be so sensitive sometimes but then I suppose things are difficult for him."

He hesitates and looks worried.

"There's no harm in him, not Grant. Never, not Grant, he wouldn't."

I have the feeling I may be getting somewhere.

"Wasn't there something about a girl?"

The transformation is sudden and startling. Mr. Connor leans forward in his chair, stabbing his finger toward my face in a gesture that's angry and intimidating.

"What are you saying? What girl? No one said anything about a girl."

He struggles to get to his feet, slipping and sliding on the handy wipe-clean surface of his chair. I stand too, frightened by the sudden change in his manner, his sudden anger. My chair crashes to the floor and he pushes me with surprising strength, hard against the wall. He crowds his face in close to mine, the spittle flying from his lips to my cheek, all hint of his previous distance and distractedness gone.

"Why are you talking about a girl? He wasn't even there I tell you; he didn't do anything. Even if he was, he wouldn't have done it. Never."

I'm shocked and try to push him away as nursing staff come rushing into the room, summoned by the commotion.

"He was at home all the time, he wasn't there," he shouts as the staff try to calm him and lead him back to his chair, "you can't say he was."

They try to quiet him, but he's agitated and distressed.

"Hush, Richard, it's all right."

One of them turns to me accusingly. "What did you say to him? I've never known him like this, so upset."

"Nothing," I reply, "nothing at all. We were just chatting about his old home."

I'm shaken and the shock of it brings the first hot sting of yet more tears. I just wasn't expecting him to turn so quickly from passivity to rage.

"I'd better go. I'm sorry if I've upset him, I didn't mean to."

I can't stay here to explain, I'm genuinely scared and need to get away. I quickly slip out the door while they're otherwise occupied and make my way back along the corridor, into reception and away.

I'm too shaken to drive so sit in the car park for a while trying to make sense of what just happened. The weather has changed for the worse and the rain beats against the car, streaking the windows like tears. I can hardly believe it; one minute he was a harmless old man, the next he all but attacked me. I don't understand what triggered it. I'd swear he knew nothing about the storeroom, unless he's a very good actor, but something upset him. It wasn't the talk of the coach house or even Alan Harris, instead it seemed to be the mention of a girl that set everything in motion. He was angry, there's no doubt about that and there was fear in his eyes too, fear of accusation or blame but from whom? I realize I didn't ever get the chance to ask him about the words in the diary.

41

"I was infatuated once with a foolish, besotted affection"
—Anne Brontë, *The Tenant of Wildfell Hall*

The weather hasn't improved. The rain lashes against the house and the windows run like rivers. It's dark and depressing and there is no sanctuary here. I have tipped from a place of vague fears and flights of fancy into full-blown anxiety. I can't calm my heartbeat, which flutters like a bird in my chest, or stop the clammy coldness of my palms. I don't know what to do.

My encounter with Mr. Connor has compounded all my fears and brought me close to breaking point. I of all people can't bear the thought of physical violence and had he the strength and the means he would surely have done me harm. I know I brought it on myself for visiting him in the way that I did but that doesn't make it any easier to bear.

When I got back from seeing him I couldn't stop shaking or still the violent chattering of my teeth; so I did something I try not to do, which was to use alcohol as self-medication. First, I checked the house and closed all the curtains—tightly, no stray chink for a spying eye or white-faced apparition—then sat in the kitchen and drank three glasses of gin. Straight down like water, no ice, no tonic, just pure alcohol to take the edge off. Ever since I've been strung out and wired, barely in control.

I've tried so hard to make myself believe there isn't any real and present danger. That belief has gone now. Even when faced with

Mina's death a part of me wanted to accept Tom's version of things. That an animal had killed her and dragged her body to where she lay; that the footprints in the flowerbed were Bill's, not snooping but looking for me maybe.

I had almost convinced myself that the magpie was just a coincidence. A bird that flew into the glass, confused and disoriented. Now my visit to Fairview has left me confused and disoriented, and made everything seem more sinister and frightening. I'm afraid I've stumbled into something real. I shiver when I think of my silent caller, that unknown someone softly breathing his malice down the line.

Nights now hold new terrors. The slightest sound, real or imagined, sends me spiraling up from sleep to full alertness. Listening, with the blood pounding in my ears. Last night I slept fully clothed, propped up on a mound of pillows in readiness to leap from the bed should the need arise. They won't catch me lying down, wallowing helplessly in my bed like a beetle on its back.

There is no point in taking my fears back to the police. They've dismissed me once with not so much as a raised eyebrow or spark of interest and I have nothing much fresh to tempt them. Just a dead cat, a dead bird, a mad old man and an unknown visitor to my studio, who did nothing more sinister than politely knock.

Over and over I've played out my visit to Mr. Connor in my mind. More and more I think the girl holds the key. Something happened to a girl here. What and when, and at whose hand, remains the mystery. Mr. Connor seemed afraid, desperately afraid that someone would be wrongly accused but I can't believe he'd be so angry and impassioned in defense of Alan Harris. Was Alan the boy in that diary from so long ago, or was it Grant?

I wish Tom was here if only for the comfort of his presence in the night. I've been tempted to text him, my fingers like olive branches tap-tapping at the keys, but I can't. The image of Madeline on tippy-toes, his head dipped to meet her parted lips, is burned on my retinas, a memory yet to be erased.

I've gone, wild-eyed, to Stour cottage twice now, intending to confront her. Both times there's been no one there. I may not wish to speak to Tom but I can deal with that pert-faced bitch. No need to be civilized now, no need to watch my boundaries anymore. A line has been crossed and this time not by me. I need the confrontation, I crave it, as though it will release the pent-up tension; so far I've been denied.

I need to work, I need the distraction but I'm scared to go to the coach house. I'm afraid of being alone there since my stranger came a-knocking. Even though Zoe eventually told me it was her and Daniel who'd been in my studio while I was out—he apparently wanted to see where I work—I still feel a hostile presence, like a violation.

This morning I spent almost an hour in the bath. I'm afraid to shower. Who knows what sounds might hide in the rush of running water, what footsteps might go unheard. I let the heat from the water soak into me but it didn't help. It didn't melt the tension in my limbs or wash away my sense of foreboding. I paced the kitchen, agitated, unable to settle and my breakfast wound itself into a choking bolus in my throat.

The twins have again asked me what's going on for even they can't fail to notice Tom's prolonged absence or to feel the pinging tension that quivers in my wake. I've had no choice but to tell them that things between Tom and me "aren't good," master of understatement that I am. I've omitted the sordid details but have told them enough to end the thinly veiled questioning and the searching sideways looks. They're genuinely upset for me and have tried so hard to offer comfort and support. Sadly, the reality of our relationship is that it's too distant, the age gap too great for them to really help. It's not their fault, it's just how things are and it's better if they just carry on being their own sweet version of normal. I'd hate for things to get awkward or for them to feel they had to leave. God, anything but that right now. I know they have to go home soon and the thought of being here alone is more than I can bear. I need to find somewhere to rent, somewhere ready for when they go.

Of course, I haven't told them of the fears that really plague me. That burden for the moment is mine alone.

I'm startled by a sudden knocking at the door. For a moment I stand frozen with indecision, to open it or not. The twins haven't heard over the volume of their music, which removes any option of pretense that no one's home. Normally loud noise would confuse and befuddle me. Nowadays I welcome the mind-numbing volume. It burns up my brain with sound and stops me thinking.

I wait and the knocking comes again, louder and more insistent this time as whoever it is tries to make themselves heard. It looks like I have no choice but to face whoever's there. For a moment I shock myself with the fleeting and unbidden thought that I might arm myself with a knife from the kitchen, slipped inside my sleeve with deadly intent.

Instead I unlock my phone, tap in the emergency number and place it in my pocket, my finger gently placed on the dial button, ready to press should the need arise. I take a deep breath and make my way down the hallway through air that feels charged with threat. The door stands solidly giving nothing away.

I open it with a bold defiance I don't feel and there on the step is Joe. A thinner, wetter, grayer Joe looking apprehensive and lost with his soft brown hair plastered to his head. I fight the urge to slam the door closed in his face and stand poised, ready for any sudden move.

"Hello Joe," I say, warily watching him. I'm coiled for flight or fight with my fingertip twitching in my pocket. "What do you want?"

My voice sounds hard and accusatory.

He drags his eyes up from contemplation of his soaking shoes and I'm shocked by the look of desolation I see there.

"Isabel, hi." He stops and looks utterly bewildered as though he has no idea why he's here. I watch as he visibly gathers himself.

"I'm sorry for disturbing you, for just turning up like this but I really do need to talk to you."

His awkwardness and embarrassment are almost tangible, and I notice how crumpled and mildly dishevelled he looks. He's lost weight. Gone is the smugly nourished man of our last encounter, replaced by a figure gaunt and drawn. It really doesn't suit him.

"Please Isabel, can I come in, just for a moment?"

Amy Winehouse screams "no, no, no," but it would seem I have no choice except to let him in. I haven't forgotten the mark on Madeline's neck or the things Tom told me, but now he's here in front of me I find it hard to believe him capable of violence. The twins are here anyway so I'm hardly alone.

I reluctantly step back from the door to let him in and he disconsolately trails after me to the kitchen where he perches damply on one of the stools. The elephant in the room settles its gray bulk next to him.

I place my phone carefully on the side, still within arm's reach, and buy myself some time by offering him coffee. As I pass him the steaming mug I note his hands are trembling, the nails gnawed to the quick. Oh Joe, I can't believe there's much nutritional content to be had there.

The hot coffee with its surge of caffeine seems to unlock something inside him and although I've said nothing to prompt it, he suddenly blurts out an apology.

"Isabel, I'm so, so sorry for what's happened, please tell me you're okay."

I'm surprised by this and unsure what it is that he's apologizing for. Beating Madeline until she fled into the arms of my husband perhaps? I realize I feel hostility toward him. It's as though he is somehow to blame, as though he didn't try hard enough to keep her happy. I want to hurt him.

"You're sorry? I don't get it Joe. I'm not quite sure what it is that you're sorry for, unless of course your wife running off with my husband is somehow your fault because it's certainly not mine."

At least I hope it's not. I hope the fault line in my brain is not to blame. I feel the anger bubbling beneath the surface and get a sudden spiteful urge to punish him, which I know is irrational. He's not responsible for Tom's actions.

He clears his throat nervously, "I didn't know what to do. I recognized the signs but there was nothing I could do to stop it. I should have tried to warn you or something but I didn't know how. I didn't know what to say. I just hoped I was wrong, that I was imagining things because of before but once I realized what had happened and that Tom had gone I felt awful. I've been to your studio a couple of times to try and catch you. I just felt I had to come and see you to . . ." He pauses for a moment. "Oh I don't know, check you were all right I suppose, try and explain things."

He turns haunted eyes toward me. "I just feel so responsible."

I'm the one trembling now, afraid of what he's going to say.

"I don't understand Joe, what are you saying? How can you be responsible for this? If you've done something to cause this, if this is somehow your fault I need to know, I need to understand what you're telling me." I pause. "Did you hurt her?"

He looks genuinely shocked. "Of course I didn't, why would you say that? I'd never hurt anyone, let alone her. I'm responsible because I knew what was happening, it's not the first time. She's done it before, more than once. It's what she does."

He pauses as though reluctant to say more.

"It's like she gets bored with life or needs to prove something to herself—or to me. It's partly why we moved out here, it was supposed to be a fresh start, reaffirm our relationship. I even paid to have the house designed and built for her hoping it would keep her happy."

He laughs a bitter self-mocking little laugh before continuing. "If it's anything like before though, it won't last. She'll tire of him soon and it'll all be over."

He says this as though I should be glad at the knowledge I'll get the faithless shit back when she's done. I'd started to set aside my anger and feel sorry for him but not now.

My voice drips sarcasm, "Oh well, that makes everything fine then. Thank you so much for taking the trouble to come round and let me know. What a relief. I feel so much better for this little chat."

"Isabel, please, that's not what I meant. Look, I just want you to know that there'll be a chance, a chance for you to try and mend things if you want to. It doesn't mean anything to her. It'll all blow over."

I feel the threatening burn of more tears, tears of anger and frustration more than grief.

"How can you say that? How can someone break up a marriage like she's done and it not mean something? Of course it means something, she's ruined everything." I correct myself, "They've ruined everything."

He doesn't understand. I don't think Tom and I can ever be the same after this. I don't see how this can heal and mend. I drag my arm across my eyes and look at the broken man that sits in front of me. He looks so wretched I can't help but feel sorry for him and reach out my hand to touch his arm. He seems so different from the man I met at our dinner party.

"How can you do it?" I ask. "How do you forgive someone and take them back after something like this?"

All his pain is in the answer, "Because I love her," and he breaks down into wrenching sobs.

I realize this visit is for him and never was for me; that it's a chance for him to pour out his heart to someone he thinks will understand.

Once he's recovered we sit and talk and I learn of the painful merry-go-round, the circle of betrayal, remorse and forgiveness that is his and Madeline's marriage. He tells me she's his life, that he never in his wildest dreams imagined someone as dull as him would ever find someone like her. I resist telling him it would probably been so much better for him if he hadn't. I know I'm only hearing one side of things but to my ears his words ring true. The confident man I met before was a sham. She's destroyed whatever self-esteem he had and eroded all belief in his own worth. She's lied about his violence. He's a nice man, a hurt man, and I was wrong to be afraid of him. I feel vaguely ashamed that I considered him even for a moment to be capable of murdering Mina or of leaving dead magpies at my door.

Once he's gone I stand at the sink and rinse out the French press, watching the grounds swirl down the plughole—my grounds for divorce.

I'm glad Joe came. He's made me realize I must resolve things one way or another between Tom and me and face the future. Whatever it may hold. I still believe there's no way back from this but we will see.

As I stand there I register another emotion behind my anger, relief. Relief that Joe told me it was he who came to my studio. Despite all that's happened, behind all the hurt, there's a shred of hope that my studio can now feel safe again.

I still don't understand why Mr. Connor reacted to my words in the way that he did; just maybe there's nothing to understand. Perhaps it was no more than a symptom of the sad disease that's eating at his mind. I don't know. It felt so real though, his anger was somehow so present and true. And there's his diary. Those words must have meant something to him when he wrote them.

Maybe there isn't any danger here but that's not how it feels. I'm so confused. I feel as though something evil is traveling toward me, gathering momentum as it comes. I close my eyes and try to let my tension ease and ebb away.

42

"Love looks not with the eyes but with the mind,
and therefore is winged Cupid painted blind"
—William Shakespeare,
A Midsummer Night's Dream

Matthew's commission is finished. The couriers came to package and case the canvases for delivery to Catlin's gallery last week. One I was happy with, the other perhaps not so much for I found something jarring about it. A discordance as though the turmoil of my mood had transmitted itself through my fingers to the canvas, leaving a hint of unhappiness concealed in the curl of a wave or hidden in a rift in the rock.

Normally I would've been at the gallery to meet the client. Not this time. I couldn't face it, or rather him. I could hear the confusion in Cait's voice when I asked her to handle things for me but for once she didn't challenge. She didn't tell me how unprofessional it was or how much it could damage my reputation—as if I actually have one—or all the other things I already knew. I wonder, did she sense that something else lay behind my words, as she didn't question me at all other than to ask, "Are you all right?"

The truth is I don't know what I was most scared of; seeing Matthew and feeling the burning attraction of before, or perhaps not feeling it. Whatever the reason I felt the need to stay away and now I'm left with a sense of loss, as if I've let something wonderful slip from my grasp. That could just be wishful thinking on my part for we've had no more direct contact since his visit here, only emailed images and updates that were warmly professional. Nothing more.

It shames me to admit it but my days feel almost more empty and desolate now than they did when Tom first left me. Maybe it's the combination of his leaving and my project ending that gives me this sense that I'm in limbo, waiting.

The twins have gone out for the day—again. They're becoming so bored with life here. I've spent the morning clearing up and rearranging the studio for whatever comes next. I'm dressed for the task in old jeans ripped at the knee and a discarded T-shirt of Tom's, which I've knotted at my hip. It was freshly laundered so it doesn't carry the smell of him. I couldn't bear that. My hair started the day caught up in a scarf. Now loose strands have escaped and are tucked behind my ears, leaving my scar on full display.

It's a clear day, bright and warm for the time of year. I've worked with the door and windows open to let in the air. Since knowing my visitor was Joe this spot has once again become my place of quiet solitude. I'm still fixated, I still have a real and unsettling puzzle to solve but it's lost its sense of immediate threat.

My mood has lifted once again in that strange unpredictable rollercoaster of emotions that's part of who I am. I hated it at first, those mood swings that sent me from excitement or joy one moment to devastation the next. It's improved over the years, my keel has become more even but still I shift more quickly than most from despair to happiness, from anxiety to gay abandon. Today I am abandoned in more ways than one.

Even as I'm thinking these thoughts I hear the crunch of gravel and with it comes the familiar lurch in my chest. I go to the door expecting to see Bill or maybe even Tom, since I ignored his last text. Instead it's Matthew. I hold my breath and watch him.

Matthew walking toward my studio, Matthew caught in winter sunlight, Matthew with that same tentative smile playing at his lips.

He's wearing jeans and a tweed jacket—I've always had a weakness for tweed—and despite all my resolve, the sight of him makes my heart sing.

He stops a few feet from the door and looks at me. I sense that he's nervous.

Neither of us speaks. For the moment we're the same people we've always been, nothing has changed. All I need to do is greet him with calm detachment, warmly but perhaps with a hint of polite confusion—whatever is he doing here—and nothing need happen. We'll discuss the paintings, I'll hope he likes them, he'll insist that he does, a polite handshake, a goodbye and he'll be gone. Nothing need happen at all.

"Isabel . . ." he finally says.

It's only my name but it's enough.

I let my eyes meet his. Now I'm almost lost.

"You shouldn't be here," I say and my voice sounds soft and hoarse in the silence.

"I know," he says and he takes a small step toward me, his leap of faith.

The heat of his lips against mine ends all my doubts and resolutions. I have never felt so sure and certain about anything in my life. I reach my arms up around his neck and mold my body into his. A little part of me registers that I must look a sight, all disheveled and grubby from working but I don't care. We stand in the driveway and kiss, here in the open where anyone could see us but I don't care.

I take his hand, leading him into the studio. I push the door closed behind us and he turns, gently pressing me back against the door. I'm pinned by his hips and he runs his hands up my bare arms before cupping my face in a way that could remind me of Tom. Luckily, there's something different in his touch, it's less proprietorial somehow. Not once does he touch my scar or so much as look at it, instead his eyes are fixed on mine and I'm trapped like a moth in the light of his gaze. He pulls the scarf from my hair and bends to kiss me again with an urgency that matches my own and I slide my tongue along the ridge of his teeth until it finds that tiny chip at last.

I feel the pull of my old impulsiveness, that shuddering, reckless excitement as my boundaries and inhibitions fall away. It's been so long since I've let myself feel like this. My fingers find the button of his jeans and I see his eyes snap open with surprise. This time it's he who pulls away.

"Are you sure about this?" he whispers.

I could still stop this. I could continue my pretense that I don't want this. In answer I press my lips against his and slide my fingers between the buttons of his shirt to feel the silky heat of his skin.

He lifts me up and I curl my legs around him as we all but fall on my old sofa. It lets out a soft gasp of disgust as we land. Spoilsport, I won't let it ruin things.

He unknots my T-shirt and his hands are on my skin bringing me alive. He dips his head and his lips graze the skin of my stomach and I'm lost.

We make love there on the sofa, our bodies each finding the rhythm of the other as though we've done this a thousand times before. The sofa's small and cramped and spiteful on our skin. It doesn't matter. We laugh and we kiss and I feel at last as if some missing part of me has found its way home.

When it's over and we're lying in each other's arms I feel a fleeting dread that maybe that was it. That now we've given it free rein the attraction will be spent and we'll be strangers again. I still find it hard to believe I can feel this way about someone I've met no more than a handful of times. Then he turns to look at me and I know, without any doubt, that he feels the same.

He smoothes the hair back from my face.

"I tried to stay away, I know you're married and this is wrong. . ."

I take his hand and press his palm to my lips. He doesn't need to say anything. I understand him completely because I've felt the same irresistible pull. Like I've known him and loved him before, perhaps in another lifetime if I believed in things like that.

This has made everything so much more complicated, still I'm glad. My father's words come into my mind, his warning not to settle, to take happiness where you find it. Oh, I've certainly done that and now we'll see where it leads. There's no going back from this and I can hear the spit and crackle of my bridges burning.

Matthew is looking at me with such tenderness, his fingers tracing the line of my jaw and the curve of my lips. I need to be honest with him. He'll know from Caitlin's promotional efforts that something dreadful happened to me in the past. I need him to understand what he's getting into.

I open my mouth to speak, "There are things you need to know about me . . ."

He places his fingers gently across my lips.

"Shush," he says, "I don't need to know anything. I don't care what you may've done or what might have happened to you. I don't need you to tell me all the things you think are wrong about you. I don't care. To me you're perfect as you are. You don't need to lay yourself bare or tell me your secrets. I want to unwrap you like a gift, to get to know you little by little while you do the same with me. All I know is we're meant to be together."

No one, not even Tom, has ever spoken to me that way before. Not had doubts or concerns because of what happened to me, not needed to know the sordid details or how it affected my life—or might affect theirs. It's a breath of fresh air and I'm grateful.

"One thing you do need to know is my marriage is over, Tom's left me," I tell him, and then hastily add in case he misunderstands, "That's not what this is about, please don't think that's why this happened."

He smiles at that. "It never would've crossed my mind. I know you feel the same way as me. I've seen it in your eyes."

I have to know so ask him, "What about you, have you got someone in your life?"

I hold my breath. I can't bear to hear there's a wife somewhere, or worse that there are children.

"There was someone for a while but she died," he says. "We married young, we had fun and it was good for a while but we were starting to, not exactly drift apart, more like grow out of each other. We'd started to want different things from life. We weren't exactly fighting or anything like that but there was a lot of tension. Then there was the accident and it was all over."

I feel sad for him but recognize within myself a distasteful little stab of relief, which shames me. I hold his hand more tightly and do both him and her the courtesy of not asking anything more.

"Don't look like that. It was sad but it was all such a long time ago now. I'm glad for the time we had but I've sometimes wondered how much longer we would've lasted. She wasn't happy anymore and if I'm honest neither was I. The only thing I'm relieved about is that there weren't any children. That would've made everything so much worse."

I feel the familiar pain at the mention and picture the pretty dark-haired babies he'd never have with me.

He misreads my expression. "I don't mean I don't like children, it's just it would've been so hard for them whichever way things went. Losing their mother or, if that hadn't happened, the upset of divorce which I'm sure would've come eventually."

I have to torture myself with the question. "Did you want children?"

He hesitates for a moment before answering.

"Not back then I didn't, we weren't ready, and I don't really think about it now to be honest. If it happened with the right person, that'd be great but if it didn't I wouldn't care too much. Anyway, what's with the third degree?"

I shut up and kiss him again. Let's not spoil things before they've even really started.

He kisses me back and I know this is where I want to be, cocooned from the world forever.

All too soon we're gathering our clothes from the floor and reassembling some sense of normality. I coil up my hair and hold it while Matthew hunts for my scarf down the side of the sofa. He holds it up triumphantly and I see his cheeks are flushed. He's lost the tentative smile and gentle hesitation of earlier. I can feel the energy coming off him. He's charged and elated and his eyes shine with something that puzzles me for a moment for it looks surprisingly like victory. Men are so strange sometimes.

He twirls me round to bind my hair with the scarf and as he does he blows gently on the back of my neck. For a moment the magic is shattered by a skewer of fear and a fleeting memory. I spin round startled but he gathers me into his arms, oblivious to my panic and kisses it clean away.

43

"I would always rather be happy than dignified"
—Charlotte Brontë, *Jane Eyre*

I'm allowing myself to be me. I've set aside my checks and balances and am fizzing with a wildness that makes me want to laugh and sing and shout from the rooftops. It's not madness, just the madness of love.

I'm in control; it's not like before when I ran the frenzied gauntlet of manic productivity, sex fueled and alcohol steeped. When I didn't eat or sleep and when those that loved me, Cait and Maria, watched me self-destruct. Their faces creased with helpless concern while they waited. Waited to pick up the pieces from the fall that would surely come—and come it did. Two years before I found Tom the abyss found me. It opened its maw and consumed me. For two whole months I was gone, shut down, lost to the world. I avoided hospitalization only because my father, God bless Daddy, arranged for someone to look after me. To check I was fed and clothed and not wallowing in my own filth, while Dr. Stedman coaxed and cajoled and medicated me back from blackest depression. No, I'm not going there again.

This is joyfulness. The joy of finding someone who loves me for who I am. Unlike Tom who deigned to love me despite who I am and what I've done, Matthew loves me regardless.

Last week we went to a Christmas fair—not in the village, Matthew wanted to go somewhere much further afield—and I knew magic. We rode on the reindeer carousel like children, something Tom would never have done, too foolish and undignified. We ate bockwurst for lunch, out of waxed paper. Spicy and hot. Dripping with butter and onions, all washed down with mulled wine like fire in our throats and I loved it—and him! We had pretzels rich with cinnamon, dusted with sugar like snow that I kissed from his lips, and when I told him I wanted to make love to him there behind the market stalls he pressed his hot mouth to my ear and called me crazy. I am. I'm crazy for him and the life he breathes into me.

He bought me a bauble crafted by hand. A shimmering, golden-haired angel. She was plump like a cherub with gossamer wings and I cradled her in my palm like a secret. She looked so like a tiny perfect child that my eyelids stung with unshed tears and my heart ached. I wished I could blow on her and make her real. A Christmas gift of the baby I'm afraid I'll never have.

I know this is fantasy and can't last forever; nothing is this perfect but for the moment I'll seize what we have with both hands and hold it to my heart.

I want to open myself up to him, to tell him the things that have happened, the things that I've felt since I've been at The Lodge. I want to tell him all of it, those things that Tom dismissed as foolishness and which made him so scornful and angry. I want him to be my ally, to help me unravel the secrets and find the truth.

I'm afraid he'll look at me as though I'm a fool, or worse, that I'll see pity in his eyes and watch them cool. If I do speak it'll be a test, a make-or-break for us. If he passes I'll know he's for real, that this is for real and that I can trust him with my heart but not yet. It's too soon. When I feel the urge to open my mouth and let it all pour forth, I stop and clamp my teeth tight on my words, swallowing them back.

Being with Matthew for even this short time has underscored the fact that Tom and I are over. No matter what happens with him and Madeline I can't go back. I can't trust him anymore. I can't live the life he wants for me. Not now I've glimpsed what life can be. I need to stop hiding from the truth. I need closure both with Tom and with this house and all its secrets.

The house is finished. It may not have the final stamp, the personal touches that make a house a home, but it is finished—sadly in more ways than one. The rooms are all decorated, the carpets laid and curtains hung. Each room cool and elegant in shades of "Mizzle" or "Dimity" or bathed in "Borrowed Light." Every name redolent of calmness and grace, suited to its history and tradition. For someone it'll be the home of their dreams. Who knows where the future lies but for me it isn't here.

The twins have gone home. They'd become tired of the countryside; those two aren't suited to rural life, they need the thrum and buzz of the city to survive—as do I. Their leaving has been a mixed blessing. On one hand it's given me the opportunity to see Matthew without awkward questions or furtive deceit, on the other it means I'm here alone. I don't know why I didn't want them to know about him. I suppose it seemed too soon or perhaps I was afraid that bringing him out into the light would shatter the magic and he'd turn to dust. Whatever the reason, I didn't tell.

I'm trying not to dwell too much on being alone, after all even when Tom was here I spent most of my days in my own poor company. It's the nights I find unbearable. Even though I've tried to convince myself that there's no danger I'm still afraid of the feel of the place and the dreams it stirs. We have a security alarm now so I know I'm physically safe but that doesn't dispel the dangers in my head. I imagine waking to its frenzied shrieking and knowing that the past has finally come for me.

I have to remind myself, I need to be strong if I'm to start my life all over again—a third time lucky. I need to be more self-reliant. I can't be who I was, not exactly. I try to remember this in the dead of night when the noises start; the creaking and settling of ancient timbers, the plink-plink of the pipes cooling and the noises at the window. One particular night the panes rattled and tapped with a click-clicking like the pecking of birds or the rattle of tiny stones. I laid there in the dark imagining the tap of bony fingers, like the death that almost took me, until I was compelled to look. I stood frozen at the window, expecting God knows what. There seemed to be nothing there, just the lawn bathed in moonlight.

I don't know how, or why, I do this. How I stay here alone, night after night. I seem bound to this place against my will until I uncover its secrets. I'm like the heroine in a bad movie, the lady detective venturing into the house alone. No gun, no backup, let's not even put on the lights—as the audience shouts "No, don't do it!" I feel I'm just waiting for something bad to happen.

The only nights I haven't been afraid are the ones when Matthew has stayed. When he's walked through my home as if he lives here and I could pretend it was true. When we've lain together in the cool of the guest room, his skin warm beneath my touch and his scent on my sheets. He's taken to the house as though it's his, he seems to know its every corner better than I do.

Maybe I should get a dog. Not something I've ever considered before but needs must when the devil drives. It would have to be big. Not huge like a Newfoundland, equally not a poodle or some tiny lapdog. I need something alert and dependable, strong but not too fierce. My brain throws up the sudden image of a Rottweiler, with dark evil eyes and slathering jaws. Perhaps not.

There's an animal sanctuary near the edge of town, maybe they'll have a rescue dog. Kind-eyed and loyal that could sleep at the foot of my bed and come with me to the studio. Be my early warning system. The more I think about it the more I like the thought. I don't know what Major would think but I'm sure we could work something out.

I console myself with the fact this solitude is not for long as I'll be spending Christmas with my father's family. He's invited me before, back before Tom, but I always declined so eventually the invites stopped. It wasn't so much that I didn't want to spend time with him and the girls, it was Sandra. I don't know the woman and my memories, those that I have, are of a brittle blonde, kitten heeled and clawed, pert busted and busy. In skirts a shade too short and tight, the fabric straining over rounded buttocks, ripe for my father's patting.

Now I'm being unfair—why as women do we always like to blame the woman?

I'd hoped I'd see Matthew over Christmas, but he's told me he'll be away seeing relatives. There was a hint of evasiveness, defensiveness even, when I asked him his plans so I didn't press. It was the first small blot on our near horizon. I won't let it trouble me. I know I'm sometimes too impetuous, not seeing when I'm too full-on, so must guard against it.

I also wonder how Daniel is coping now that Zoe's gone. I couldn't make sense of their relationship, one minute they seemed so close, other times they were almost like strangers.

I'd also noticed a change in Zoe, before she left. She'd become much quieter, almost withdrawn sometimes. I'd often catch her staring at nothing, lost in introspection. Amy had noticed it too; I'd see her watching her twin with a ripple of worry on her brow.

Daniel brought a takeaway round on their last evening. It was a kind of farewell dinner although I know they intend to stay in touch. It's funny, I found Daniel difficult to engage with at first but he's grown on me. That evening in particular he was charming and amusing and, although I've not really noticed it before, he has the most dazzling smile. He's such an attractive man when he smiles, he should gift us with it more often.

We stuffed ourselves with wontons and chicken satay, chow mein and crispy duck, all washed down with a dry white wine he'd chilled until it was almost viscous. Afterward the twins played Scrabble while Daniel and I washed up. We're easy in each other's company now and we worked together in a companionable silence that once would have felt awkward.

I was dying to know if he was intending to continue seeing Zoe so decided to ask him outright.

"Um," I hesitated, not really knowing how to introduce the subject, "do you think you'll be seeing Zoe over the holidays at all? You've spent so much time together while she's been here, won't it be a bit odd not seeing each other?"

He smiled and passed me a plate to dry, our hands briefly touching.

"I 'spect so, if I get the chance. I don't know what I'm doing yet but if I get up to London then yeah, definitely. Even if I don't manage over Christmas I'll get up there after. Sometime in the new year."

He cocked his head and looked at me with those unfathomable eyes of his.

"She's important to me, more than I think she knows, so I'm not going to let her escape that easily."

He reached out and brushed away some suds that had somehow made their way onto my cheek. He let his hand linger there for a moment and looked earnestly into my eyes.

"Don't look so worried Izzy, we're okay. I'll probably see my sister and her family over Christmas and then catch up with Zo in the New Year. You never know, you and me might even end up being family."

"I'm sorry to pry," I said, "that's not how I meant it. I'm only asking because I don't want to see her get hurt, that's all. You know me, I'm not very good at subtle."

He laughed at that.

"It's okay, you don't need to get all big sisterish on me, I'm not going to hurt anybody. Promise."

He flashed that smile again.

"I've got a big surprise for her actually but she'll have to wait until after Christmas to get it."

I tried to cajole him into telling me what it was but he wouldn't have it. He just kept pressing his finger to his lips and telling me it was his secret.

This made me think of Matthew and his evasiveness over his Christmas plans. I felt a flicker of worry. Everyone and everywhere seem to have secrets.

44

"After such knowledge what forgiveness?"
—George Eliot, *Gerontion*

'm all packed and ready to leave—thank God. Major has gone to the cattery and the dog—yes, I've got one now—is waiting patiently by the door, his ears cocked in expectation.

I couldn't be here on my own. I couldn't survive without sleep, so in the end I went to the sanctuary, just to see. Mrs. Watson, the old lady that runs it, didn't have anything suitable, only a sad little Yorkie, shorn of her tresses and looking forlorn. I nearly weakened, she looked so sad but I hardened my heart. She wasn't what I needed. Mrs. Watson eventually directed me to a dog rescue and there I found him, looking oddly optimistic despite the bareness of his cell. His coat was shiny and his eyes bright, his face marred only by the ridge of scars across his nose, evidence of past hardship.

I like the fact that he was damaged—not that he'd suffered, obviously, just that his face was scarred. It meant he suited me. Our eyes met through the bars and I knew. I've never owned a dog before—my childhood wasn't tailored for pets—but there I was. I found myself lead in hand, armed with biscuits and tins of tripe, a dog bed and a rubber bone. Both my heart and my purse felt lighter.

Major has had a major readjustment. Not given to retreat, he marshaled his forces at first and hissed and spat. Hugo—that's what I've called him—just looked confused. I do hope that's not his default when faced with threat. Eventually a truce was called. I placed their bowls together and they ate, side by side, each occasionally pausing to eye the other with frank suspicion. Day by day it's improving so I'm cautiously optimistic.

Day by day I'm improving too; just his presence at the foot of my bed helps me to sleep at least a little. His gentle breathing and the knowledge there's another soul there, next to mine.

I don't think he's a man's dog though. The first time he met Matthew every muscle tensed and there was a low rumble in his throat. A wariness there I'd not seen before. He's slowly and gradually relenting. At worst he ignores him and at best he'll let him pat his head or stroke the soft fur beneath his ears. Another readjustment.

He's coming with me today—Hugo, that is, not Matthew—and the twins sounded mildly horrified on the phone.

"A dog?" Amy said. I could almost hear her nose wrinkling in disgust. "Won't it smell?"

"No," I reassured her, "*he* won't. He's company for me now you've gone and it's too soon to put him back in kennels."

They'll get over it when they see him, I'm sure.

I think I've remembered to turn everything off, I've checked the windows and locked the doors. The only thing I haven't been able to do is find my car keys. I haven't driven for a week or so but I know they've got to be here somewhere. I'll have to take the spare for now.

I smile to myself, standing here in the hall with my case all packed. A bitter little smile. Tom would never trust me to do things like this. He'd say I'd forget to pack any pants, or I'd leave the iron on and burn the place down. He'd take charge; checking my case and making me wait in the lobby while he locked up the flat. I wonder now at my own helplessness. Maybe it was easier just to comply or more likely that I mistook control for caring, enduring love.

Thinking of Tom reminds me, before I set the alarm I have one last thing I must do, I must telephone him. I have put this off for far too long and it's not fair on either him or me.

I press his number with trembling fingers, the thought of finally talking to him makes me feel nervous and strange. The call connects and it's no more than two rings before he picks up. It's as if he's been poised all this time, mobile in hand, waiting for my call. The sound of his voice is still a jolt to my heart. I feel defibrillated.

"Hello, Izzy? Thank God."

Oh Tom, for what I wonder.

"I've been praying you'd ring. Oh God, Izzy I've . . ."

It sounds as though he's found religion. I interrupt. We can't do this over the phone. I need to sit down with him face to face and talk things through properly and calmly.

"Tom, we need to talk. This has gone on long enough. We need to sort this mess out but not now. I can't talk to you over the phone like this."

"Izzy please, just let me come home. I can make it up to you, I promise."

Let him come home? I fight the urge to point out that he was the one who left; he's talking as if I banished him. Wherever he is sounds hollow and echoing and I have an image of Madeline's vaulted hallway, all blank walls and glass. I realize I don't want to know where he's living or whether they're together although from the sound of it I would think not.

Annoyingly it's as though he reads my mind.

"Izzy, I'm at Steve's, I just want to come home, it was all a mistake. Please listen, it didn't mean anything. I'm so, so sorry, I never meant to hurt you. I don't know what happened."

Really, well I do. You ran off with somebody else, that's what happened. So, he's not with Madeline now then but with Steve, his old friend from uni.

"Tom, I've already said, I'm not doing this over the phone. It's your house too so you can come home whenever you like but I won't be here Christmas week. I'm going to my father's and coming back after New Year's."

There's a moment's silence and the sadness washes over me. This should've been our first Christmas in our new home, a time of love and happiness. Despite everything he's done I still feel regret at thought of a Christmas without him and find myself wondering what he'll be doing or where he'll go. I harden my marshmallow heart. There's always his mother's, she'll love that.

He sounds hurt. "I'd hoped we could be together over Christmas. I've got time off . . . I've bought you something, a present. . ."

His voice is so hesitant. There's none of his usual confidence and it brings a lump to my throat. No, I won't cry anymore. The time for tears has passed and does he really think a present will make everything all right?

"I'm sorry Tom but it's not that simple. You can't expect to just come back as though nothing has happened. Things have changed, I'm sorry. Look, we're really not doing this over the phone. I'm back on the Wednesday after Christmas, we can talk then."

"Izzy, I'd hoped we could use the time over Christmas to talk, to try and make things right. Please Izzy, don't do this, don't leave me to the mercies of my mother."

He's trying to make a joke of it but I can hear the pain in his voice. I can hardly trust mine.

"I'm sorry Tom, I've got to go. Just text me and let me know what you're doing and we'll talk in the new year."

I hesitate, I can hardly wish him a Merry Christmas but it all seems so callous somehow. Christmas makes everything so much harder, so pathos laden and tragic.

He senses my hesitation, "Izzy, wait . . ."

I ring off before he upsets me or wears me down and I picture him standing there with his phone dead in his hand.

God, that was so much harder than I thought it would be. I do still care about him but it doesn't change anything. It breaks my heart that we've ended up like this. Broken.

꙰

I take one last look around the hall. The house is already taking on that feeling of emptiness. It's gathering that sensation you get when you return from a holiday, that feeling that you've been away for years. I swear it smells musty already. An oppressive silence wraps itself around me and I shiver; after all this time it can still give me the creeps.

I set the alarm and make my way out to the car, locking the door carefully behind me. I'm going to drive to Richmond, the farthest I've ever driven on my own. I'm not fazed, this is the new, new me.

I go to unlock the Golf and as I do I notice the driver's door is slightly ajar; that's odd, I'm sure I locked it properly the last time I used it. The interior light is the faintest of glows and I experience a stab of anxiety at the thought that the battery might be flat. I push Hugo into the back and hold my breath as the engine grinds one, two, three laborious turns before firing into life. I almost weep with relief. If it'd been flat I wouldn't have known what to do. I don't know where Tom keeps the charger or even if we have one, and on Christmas Eve there'd be no one I could ring.

I put my case in the boot, my newfound confidence dented for a moment. Maybe Tom is right and I can't be trusted. Maybe I will never be the "executive of my own life," to use Dr. Stedman's term. Perhaps I'm destined more for middle management. I mentally shake myself; no, I won't fail so easily.

I get in the car and drive slowly away, leaving The Lodge a brooding presence behind me. No tree lights twinkling in those windows, no cheery wreath at my door.

45

"I have felt the wind on the wing of madness"
—Charles Baudelaire

He lay back on the bed and stretched the muscles of his lean frame. He linked his hands behind his head and stared at the ceiling. Dear God, he'd touched her. His skin crawling against hers. She'd looked at him with that cold gray eye alight with life and trust, all so soon to be snuffed. He had her though and at last he had his plan. He just needed to book the second hire car and get the timing right.

He needed a break. Thank God he could now be alone for a while. The watching was easy, it was the being around her that hurt. The intensity of it all. Keeping the carapace closed and his shutters down. All the fucking time. Sometimes he wanted to lash out or bite her, to feel the soft give of her flesh beneath his teeth. It was all he could do to still his breathing and hush his mind.

He wasn't happy. It was all starting to get under his skin and that wasn't right. He wanted to get under their skin—both figuratively and literally—not the other way round. He was just too involved and that wasn't how he worked. He liked his own company, his own inner world, not this interaction. Not this level of sticky human contact. He wasn't sleeping and could feel the strain of it stretching him thin. My God, all the kissing, the caring and the just being human, how do they *do* that? He couldn't survive in their world.

He was starting to be careless and that wasn't like him at all. He wondered, could he be ill? For the first time he questioned the wisdom of what he was doing, and the effect it seemed to be having on him.

The other night he'd found himself at the stroke of midnight, stood there in the garden just watching the house. He'd thrown a handful of tiny stones at her window, just for the hot dark hell of it. Then he'd seen her, silhouetted in the moonlight. The white disk of her face and the black pits of her eyes. For a fleeting moment he'd thought his mother was back from the grave and had run terrified into the trees, the branches tearing and ripping at him as he fled. That wasn't right; that wasn't him.

He shrugged the memory away for it disturbed him still. He needed to calm himself with the thought of the joys and the pleasures to come. He took the crumpled picture from his pocket, the one that he'd stolen, and began to scrape at the place where those eyes would be. Over and over, until the paper was torn and scarred. She was like a delicious itch that he mustn't scratch, not yet.

Once Christmas was over he'd strike. When the January dead-zone took its toll on the weak and depressed, he'd strike. Poor Izzy Weir, brain damaged and deserted, no wonder she couldn't cope. Guilt-racked husband and distraught sisters huddled at the wintery graveside, he could see it all. And when it was over, when the sod had settled over her, he'd come back to comfort the golden twins. He'd take them one by one, those little gilt-y innocents, into his warm embrace.

He pressed his face into the pillow and throbbed and swelled with the thought of it.

46

"Secrets are generally terrible. Beauty is not hidden"
—L. M. Montgomery, *Emily Climbs*

Christmas is well and truly over. January unfurls flat and gray, laden with uncertainty.

Matthew and I aren't seeing each other for the moment. He's giving me distance and space to sort out my life. He held my hands that last time and told me he'd respect my decision, that he wouldn't contact me. Instead he would wait and if no word came he'd know my answer.

Tom came home. When I opened the door to find him there I was surprised by the surge of affection that flowed despite everything. He wrapped his arms around me and for a moment I wavered. He's been my life for so long it's hard to imagine him out of it forever. Then I told him and I watched as the incredulity unfolded across his face, the disbelief that anyone other than him could ever want me. I found myself hating him after all.

At first he didn't believe me. He'd thought I'd be waiting. That all he had to do was explain and beg forgiveness and it'd all be all right, that we'd go back to how we were before. Him in control and me gratefully compliant. He's explained it was foolishness, meaningless. Nothing more than a fleeting infatuation borne out of unhappiness, on my part that is, that was driving a wedge between us. Note the hint of blame, which really didn't help. He's realized once again that it's me he loves—hurrah—and it always has been. Now we can put all this behind us and start again.

No Tom, I don't want you anymore.

I know I'm hurting him but I must be true to myself. I've thought long and hard and my mind, what's left of it, is made up. If we'd had a child it might be different, we'd owe it to them to try. All we have is his betrayal and his sense of entitlement and I need more than that.

To add insult to injury he even took exception to my dog.

"Really Izzy?" he said. "Was that sensible when we've just had the place decorated?"

No Tom, probably not but it's not your decision anymore.

I don't wish him unhappiness, I hope he finds the right person to love and that she loves him back. He just needs to understand that person's not me, not anymore.

We're trying to be civilized while we sort things out; living in the same house but not together. I've decamped to the guest suite with its memories of Matthew while Tom has the marital bed, or should it be the martial bed now? We maintain a polite civility. It's hard. I catch him watching me in unguarded moments with an expression I've not seen before. It's as though he doesn't know me anymore. Perhaps he never did.

If we can bear to, we'll hold out until the spring to sell the house. Tom, always the consummate businessman, wants to split off the coach house with a plot of land and sell it separately to "maximise our investment." He's contacted planners and the local authority, all coolly professional, to start the ball rolling. Sometimes I suspect he just thinks he's calling my bluff.

I've no idea what I'll do. When I try to think of the future there's a blank wall of blackness, not unlike my memories of the past. Blackness behind and in front and I'm trapped here in limbo. For now, I have no choice but to take things day by day and let fate unfold.

I don't know what happened with Tom and Madeline. Whether he experienced an epiphany—after all it was the right time of year—or

whether she tired of him as Joe said she would. I haven't asked and
he hasn't said and to be truthful I don't care. One day I might wonder
but not now.

We seem for the moment to have come full circle; me here, Tom
working late, and the house closing around me. I hate January at the
best of times but now its bleakness threatens to swamp me. I have no
projects at the moment, so my only distraction is teaching my class.
Tom has his work to occupy his time and his plans to break up and
sell off our home—perversely now that it's almost lost I'm starting to
think of it like that. I have nothing except Matthew and, much as I
want him, I can't have him yet. I need to focus. I need to close this
chapter of my life so even if it kills me I'm going to uncover the secrets
of this house before the sale board goes up. I can't bear the thought of
walking away with more unanswered questions and another mystery
in my life.

I can't go back to see Mr. Connor, even if I wanted to. Fairview
eventually informed Gemma of my visit and she phoned me, her voice
quivering with anger. We'll skip the sordid details but suffice to say
I'm in no doubt of the consequences should I pitch up there again.
Instead I'm going to try the phone number. If it leads nowhere so be
it but I have to try.

I tap in 141; I don't want anyone ringing back. I carefully key in
the numbers and wait. I hear the tone of a phone ringing in that same
distant home but no one picks up. I experience a mixture of disappointment and relief and am about to ring off when a man's voice
comes on the line. An answer-phone recorded message.

*"You're through to the Graingers. There's no one available to come to the
phone at the moment so please leave us a message."*

I ring off, fairly buzzing with excitement. The gods have smiled and
I have a name without ever having to speak to anyone. I remember

the gouges and scratches on the wall and the mark that looked like a letter C or a G. G for Grainger perhaps? A shiver runs through me and I sit back on the bed, heart racing.

I know it's a long shot, but I wake up the PC and type "Grainger" into Google. That alone won't be enough so I add the name of the village as a start. A list comes up but there's nothing here to catch my interest. I trawl through parish council information, village news and then many, many different Graingers. They're all out there on Facebook and LinkedIn, all trustingly tweeting their innermost secrets to the ether. I've always been wary of social media, too afraid of someone out there, someone watching me.

I try again, this time adding the name of the other nearby village, Marston. Again nothing, just the same random Graingers and information about Marston and its historic clay pits. I hesitate for a moment over one site but it's for a city of the same name in Missouri with a J. Grainger, MD. I attempt the town name instead but still there's nothing.

My eyes and neck are beginning to ache. I can't think where else to go with this. As a last resort, and feeling rather furtive and foolish, even though I'm in the privacy of my own home, I type in "missing persons." This is what I've wanted to do all along but for some reason didn't dare to try. The Missing Persons Bureau UK comes up and I click onto their unidentified case search. It's the wrong thing. It's all about unidentified bodies that remain unclaimed and I close it quickly, shutting my eyes against the grainy photos of those poor lost souls.

I'll try "missing person UK Grainger" and then if that doesn't work I'll have to think again. I tap it in, more in hope than any real expectation, and diligently work my way through every entry.

Suddenly there it is, in an old newspaper archive. My heart stops. Rachel Grainger, aged seventeen, went missing from the town where I go each week to teach my course; Rachel Grainger, who disappeared in the late summer of 2004. It doesn't say what happened to her or if she was ever found.

My mouth has gone dry and I feel sick at the thought that Rachel Grainger might've ended her days locked in that tiny space in what's now my studio office. Unbidden, a dream I once had comes into my head, of a golden-haired girl in the orchard trying to press something into my hand and I remember the desperate insistence in her eyes. The goosebumps roil and ripple up my arms and I feel my scalp prickle and contract. I take a deep breath. I know I'm letting my imagination run away with me; I need to find out more.

The library is warm and silent, the air fragranced with the unmistakable scent of books. It's reminiscent of the library at Thorpwood although it lacks the wood paneling and sense of history. It has the same muffled silence, thick with the hum of brain-waves and punctuated only by the occasional stifled cough or mumbled sorry. I go to the desk and explain to the librarian that I'm interested in seeing local newspapers from the summer and autumn of 2004. She raises her eyebrows questioningly at this and informs me that that far back they'll probably be on fiche. I look confused and she explains.

"Microfiche. We've only digitized from about 2005 onwards."

I still look blank and she smiles.

"Come on. It'll be an education for you. We used to archive everything that way," and she leads me through to a side room off the main reading area.

It's a cool air-conditioned room with a bank of filing cabinets and two ancient-looking machines with screens and an array of knobs and trays. She explains the process for finding the various newspapers I might want, and how to insert the microfiche sheets into the reader for viewing. She tells me to shout if I need anything—perhaps not the best advice in a library—and leaves me to work my way through the papers from 2004, edition by edition.

To save time I choose the local *Herald* as the most likely for it seems to be the longest running and the one most widely subscribed. I decide to start at the end of September and work backward. It's a laborious process and my eyes soon burn from the zooming in and out and scanning across each page, column by column.

After almost two hours I find what I've been looking for, a second-page article from late August giving an update on the recent disappearance of a local girl. She's one Rachel Grainger who failed to return home from her summer job at the local animal sanctuary. It would appear that despite extensive police investigation and an initial suspect no progress has been made in establishing what may have happened to Rachel or her current whereabouts.

I work backward and two weeks earlier I find the front-page headline detailing her disappearance. Rachel Grainger of Elvesham Road, aged seventeen, who smiles out at me from a grainy photograph. She has blonde hair and a pretty, lively face, and I'm glad to note she strikes no chord of memory with the girl in my dream. That would be too weird to even contemplate. I scan the article and learn that a local man, Liam Smith, was taken in for questioning but subsequently released, and that Rachel's family are convinced she has come to harm. The article describes a happy girl from a loving family, the unlikeliest of runaways.

My palms are damp, leaving small beads of frightened sweat quivering on the reader's knobs despite the coolness of the room.

I go back to September, looking more carefully this time. There on page six is a brief update informing those still interested that no further progress has been made in establishing Rachel's whereabouts. The family and police fear the worst, as do I.

Over subsequent editions the updates become less and less frequent until Rachel eventually shifts away from the public spotlight.

Now I know what I'm looking for I move to the digital records. Barring the occasional reference in relation to other cases, or annual appeals by her family, there's no record of either a body or her safe return. Other than the appeals, which are suffused with her family's desperation, the space dedicated to Rachel, and her place in the paper's pecking order, dwindles as the years pass. Eventually she's languishing near to the sports pages along with the local fetes and footnotes. I watch as she fades from the minds of all but those who loved her. It would appear poor Rachel has no resting place and remains consigned to the cold case freezer.

I'm unsure what to do now. For the first time I have real information but don't know what to do with it. I want to speak to the Graingers but don't know how. Once I would have told Tom. I would've relished telling him, "See, I was right," and even he would have to listen and help me now. I can't do that anymore, and anyway I don't want to.

I'm tempted to ring Matthew. It feels so long since we were last together and I miss him so. The more I think about it, the more it feels the right thing to do. I need to know if he believes in me.

47

"When I saw you I fell in love, and you smiled
because you knew"

—Arrigo Boito

I met Matthew for lunch in the end. I drove out to a big old coaching inn he wanted to go to, somewhere I'd never been before. It was a lovely old-fashioned place, softly lit, with low-beamed ceilings and log fires crackling in the restaurant and bars.

He was there before me and I watched him from across the dining room when I arrived. I saw him scanning the room with that quiet watchfulness he has. It gives the impression he takes everything in, missing nothing. He seemed to sense my arrival and looked straight at me across the heads of the diners, a sudden grin lighting up his face. He stood up to greet me and my heart gave that familiar flip as his lips grazed mine.

We had a simple lunch of pizza and salad. Afterward we took our drinks through to the snug and found a quiet corner with a big old leather chesterfield piled high with cushions.

Curled up in that warm corner I spoke to him of my conversation with Tom, of the decision we'd come to and the fact that my marriage was over. He put his arm around me and pulled me close, telling me he'd never doubted me and him, not even for a moment.

I told him of our decision to sell the house in the spring and then, finally, about the coach house and the hidden room. I told him about the numbers scratched in the floor and about Rachel Grainger, and my need to know what had happened. That one thing I had to do before I left that place forever.

His wide brown eyes never left my face and not once did he look at me skeptically or question my judgment. Instead his gaze was one of anticipation.

I didn't mention Alan Harris or Mr. Connor, or what may have happened back in the nineties. That all still troubles me because the date doesn't fit with Rachel Grainger's disappearance. I'd really hoped it would, that the two things would come together to dispel what Alan Harris said to me.

I didn't tell him of my dreams either, or my feelings of déjà vu—I don't want to overload him with too much of my madness, not yet.

When I'd finished he looked thoughtful before asking me what I intended to do. The only thing he questioned was my decision to try and talk to the Graingers. He felt I should probably go to the police instead, and should take at least a day or two to think it over and plan what I wanted to say. He carefully suggested that it may just be coincidence, although he conceded he couldn't really see how, and that I should perhaps be cautious and talk to no one for the moment, just in case.

When he realized I was serious about first speaking to the Graingers he said he'd come with me. He wanted to drive me there and give me some moral support but I don't need him to. I stood my ground even though I could tell he wasn't happy. This is something I need to do for myself.

When it was finally time to go we stood in the windswept car park neither wanting to let the other go. He reached down and took my hands in his and I traced the veins on the back of his hand and the network of small scratches on his wrist.

"Look at your hands," I said. "How on earth did you manage to get them so scratched?"

For a second I caught that same look of evasiveness as he pulled his hands away and examined the network of nicks and scratches.

"They do look at bit of a mess," he said and smiled at me. "But first I was wrestling with a Christmas tree and then they got me cutting some really evil holly. Suppose I should've worn gloves but you never think of it until it's too late."

He paused and pulled me close to him. "I think I just need you to look after me."

I wondered again where he'd spent his Christmas.

"You never did tell me what you did for Christmas in the end. You got to see your family then?" I asked.

There was a moment's hesitation, a beat too long before he answered.

"Yeah, I did, it was great to see them."

There was a finality to the way he said it that stopped me asking more and for some strange reason I was left with the impression he wasn't quite telling me the truth.

Matthew doesn't understand. I have to speak to the Graingers before I go to the police again. I need to be sure there's no other link between Rachel and my home, no innocent explanation that I don't know about.

This morning after Tom had left for work I phoned their number again, half hoping no one would pick up. After a few rings a woman answered, her voice soft and pleasant.

"Hello?"

I've decided I must be open with them but I need to tread carefully. I can't blunder and blurt like I usually do, saying the wrong thing at the wrong time and in the wrong way. I've thought long and hard about what I want to say. I've even got a script.

"Hello, may I speak to Mrs. Grainger please?"

"Speaking?"

There's an inquiring upward inflection in her voice.

"My name's Isabel, Isabel Dryland-Weir. You don't know me but I was wondering if there was any chance I could come and see you. I need to speak to you about something if you'll let me. I know this might sound a bit odd but it's something that could be important."

Already there's a note of suspicion. "What do you mean? Come and speak to me, about what?"

I find myself starting to falter. I must stay on script. "I don't want to upset you or anything but I think I might have some information about your daughter."

Her tone hardens immediately.

"My daughter? Who is this? Who am I speaking to? If you're from the magazine again, I've told you before I'm not interested in talking to anyone. Who are you?"

The speed accelerates and her questions fire thick and fast giving me no chance to answer. The humming starts in my head, my script blurring before my eyes and before I can help myself I blurt.

"I think may have found out what happened to her."

There's silence. It seems to last forever. I can sense the percussive jangle of her nerves, her surge of adrenaline and the struggle between anger and hope.

"Hello?"

I think she's there but there's more silence until she asks, "Who did you say you were?"

The soft Mrs. Grainger is almost back, I can hear a hint of her in the background. Now I can get back on script.

"I'm Isabel, I'm not anybody. I just want to talk to you if I can. It may turn out to be nothing but I do need to talk to you, just in case."

"So, you're not ringing about the article and you're certainly not the police, so who are you? What have you found out? What do you know about Rachel?"

Her voice cracks on her daughter's name and I take a deep breath to calm myself.

"I need to be honest with you, I don't know. I've found something that might be relevant, or it might not. That's why I need to talk to you, to find out, but not over the phone."

I wait. I think I know what's going on inside her head. If the glimmer of hope I've given her is enough then I know she'll let me come. Any hope of finding the truth is better than none at all. There's nothing worse than not knowing; I can tell her that if she'll let me.

I find myself pleading, "Please, can I just come and see you, that's all."

Hope wins out. She's still suspicious—who wouldn't be—but it's overruled by the need to know.

"What do you think you know? Just tell me."

"I'm sorry, I can't do this over the phone, it's too difficult to explain. Please can I come to your house?"

There's a long silence and I resist the almost overwhelming urge to just tell her and get it over with.

"If you really think you might know something, then yes, I suppose you can. But if you're making this up. . ." She hesitates then adds with more certainty, "Yes, when could you come?"

Now she's made up her mind the pitch of her voice has risen again with a note of expectation and I'm afraid. What if this is all nothing but foolishness and I raise the poor woman's hopes for nothing? What if I am nothing more than what Tom says I am?

"I can come tomorrow if you like, if you can give me your address but please don't get your hopes up too much, just in case I'm wrong."

She gives me the number, 24 Elvesham Road and I agree to see her at three-thirty tomorrow afternoon.

I sit for a while, with the phone still cradled in my ice-cold hands.

48

"Nothing remained but loneliness and grief . . ."
—Louisa May Alcott, *Little Women*

I slept really well last night. No dreams, no sudden waking drenched in my own sweat, all disoriented and afraid. I feel focused, as though my quest is coming to an end. I've never thought of it like that before, as a quest, but looking back that's how it feels. Ever since I've been here I've been searching for something.

I need to be credible and sober—in both meanings of the word—so I've dressed carefully for my visit to the Graingers and made sure I've removed any lingering hint of last evening's wine.

Elvesham Road is on an older estate to the west of the town, a suburb of bay-fronted semis from the 1950s, the houses lined up in ordered, tree-fringed rows. I locate number 24, which is identical to its neighbors. It has a gravel and concrete driveway leading to a garage at the rear, and a neat lawn edged by wintry shrubs. These are tidily pruned and sit waiting for the spring.

I park at the curb and wait. There's a stretch of grass between the road and the pavement, and outside the Graingers' this too is neatly cropped and litter free. I'm a few minutes early so I sit in the car for a while to gather my thoughts. I study the Graingers' house. It's red brick and half rendered, with the downstairs windows carefully screened from prying eyes by lacy nets. These hang in the evenest of folds. I have the feeling I'm being watched and detect the faintest movement, a ripple in the snowy curtains at the bay. I get out of the car and carefully lock it. As I do, I glimpse a silver-gray car that looks vaguely familiar. It's slowly turning into a nearby road, almost at a crawl.

The door of the house is glossy burgundy with a high window of frosted glass and a gleaming brass knocker. Both this and the matching bell are polished to a shine. There's a neatness about this place that's too controlled; as though the owners feel that a single slip, a fingerprint on the letterbox or a leaf out of place, and their whole world would descend into chaos. Control contains the unthinkable.

I knock twice, decisively but not too loudly, and wait. The air seems to hang with a sense of expectancy. I hear footsteps and the door opens to reveal a woman in her mid- to late fifties in jeans and a cream polo neck. Her soft gray-brown hair is cut in a bob that frames a heart-shaped face. I can see that once she was pretty but now her features are careworn and pinched with loss. Her eyes meet mine and I see her desperation writ large. Her every muscle is tensed in expectation. I hold out my hand.

"Mrs. Grainger, hello, I'm Isabel. We spoke on the phone yesterday. Thank you so much for letting me come."

She takes my hand in both of hers. Her fingers are adrenaline iced, and she holds on as though she'll never let me go. She suddenly realizes what she's doing and drops my hand as though it's burned her.

"Thank you for coming, please—come in."

I follow her into a foyer and through into an immaculate hallway where the same sense of order continues. Every surface is spotless, not a speck of dust or a fingerprint. The mirror sparkles and even the waxy jade plant on the hall table is leaf-shined and perfect.

She leads me through into a sitting room where two cream sofas eye each other across a dusty-pink rug and a coffee table. The table is centered so exactly, so equidistant from each sofa and so neatly aligned with the pattern on the rug that I'm sure she must have measured it.

The only thing disturbing the order is a single high-backed chair by the fireplace. This is occupied by a diminutive woman of such advanced age that she's become androgynous, her gender only apparent from her clothes. She has a flat little button-nosed face with age-speckled skin that hangs in reptilian folds. Thin white wisps of hair are spun like sugar over a hen's-egg scalp. She doesn't look up when we come in, instead she continues to look at the magazine on her lap.

Mrs. Grainger gestures toward the sofa in an indication that I should sit and introduces the older woman as her mother-in-law. The older Mrs. Grainger continues to ignore me to her daughter-in-law's obvious discomfit.

"Please excuse Mum, she's getting a bit hard of hearing . . ."

The old lady's head snaps round, the skin at her neck quivering like a startled turtle. She fixes me with a look of frank suspicion before addressing her daughter-in-law.

"Excuse me! I hear what I want to hear. What I don't understand is why you've let her come here. I thought you'd given up on all that nonsense."

She indicates me with a curt jerk of her head.

"Mum, please, let's just hear what she's got to say. It can't hurt."

She turns to me. "I'm sorry, it's just that we've had so many upsets over the years. Less so now but we used to get people turning up saying they knew what'd happened to Rachel or claiming they'd seen her."

She gives me a tight bitter little smile.

"We've even had mediums claiming to have messages from her or signs they'd been given in dreams. It was so upsetting for us. It was after the press got hold of everything and they were almost as bad."

I hastily reassure her. "It's fine, really, really I understand."

I shouldn't have said that. I shouldn't have claimed to understand. I have no idea what they've been through.

Mrs. Grainger doesn't seem to notice and asks if I want a coffee. I get the sense she's stalling. That she's desperate to find out why I'm here but also afraid to hear what I might say.

While she's gone I sit in a tense silence with Mrs. Grainger senior. Small talk has no place here. I allow the silence to swell and grow until it fills the room. It's punctuated only by the steady tick-ticking of the clock, which I try to focus on to calm my nerves. The old lady pointedly ignores me and sits leafing through her *People's Friend*. Each page briskly turning with a snap of hostility.

Mrs. Grainger junior reappears with coffee in fine white china mugs, and sits on the other sofa, directly facing me. She clasps her hands around her knees as if to contain their trembling.

I clear my throat. I'm unsure about this. I don't know how they'll react and I could quickly find myself out of my depth. Maybe I should've gone straight to the police instead or at least waited like Matthew suggested. Both pairs of eyes are now fixed on me so I have no choice but to begin.

"This might all mean nothing, so if it doesn't I'm sorry. I had to speak to you just in case. We've um, recently moved house, last year actually, and we've um, been having some work done."

I pause and notice Mrs Grainger's knuckles have whitened where her hands are tightening their grip on her knees.

"We found . . ."

I hesitate again. I don't know how to word this. I don't want to make it sound too awful. I don't want to conjure the image of something terrible, something too frightening and tragic to contemplate. That's not why I'm here.

"I found your telephone number . . ."

I stall again. I don't want to say it was scored into the floor. I don't want to mention the letters screaming "Help."

Mrs. Grainger leans forward across the coffee table, her eyes locked on mine.

"What do you mean you found our telephone number, where?"

"It was in the old coach house on our property. There was a store-room, it was empty bar some old cans and stuff, but I found your phone number written there . . ."

She takes a deep breath. "Where? Tell me."

It would seem I have no choice. I bring the page out of my bag, the rubbing I took of the numbers scratched into the floor. I pass it across the coffee table and watch the confusion cloud her face.

"I don't understand, what is this?"

I speak softly as though that could in any way lessen the blow. "It was scratched on the floor."

Mrs. Grainger doesn't speak but regards me with a kind of horror as her worst fears begin to unfurl before her eyes. She lets out a small sob and gently traces each number with a shaking finger, her eyes bright with panic.

I quickly plough on before she can ask me for any more details.

"I've been to the police about it once already, because the room worried me, it all somehow didn't feel right but that was before I found out it was your number. They weren't really interested but I'm going to go back. I just needed to be sure there wasn't some innocent explanation. Something I hadn't thought of."

Mrs. Grainger has begun to cry quietly, making no move to wipe away the tears welling in her eyes. She holds the crumpled papers to her heart as though searching for some connection or reaching for the essence of her daughter. I can almost feel her pain like a physical thing, that aching pressure in her chest, and I feel an answering prickling behind my eyelids.

"Would Rachel . . ." I flinch at using her daughter's name. "Would your daughter ever have been to my house in the past? Is there any way she could've visited or something? It's The Lodge in Cleaver's Lane, halfway between Marston and Charbury."

She looks at me blankly, "Where?"

"The Lodge, it used to be the old vicarage, in Cleaver's Lane. Is there any reason at all why she might have been there?"

She shakes her head.

"No, I don't think so, we don't know anybody out that way. No, there's no way she could've been there, not without us knowing. I don't understand."

She looks toward her mother-in-law as though for confirmation and the old lady gets up, slowly and painfully, and comes to sit next to her daughter-in-law. Her earlier hostility remains and she holds out her hand to snatch the page, her crabbed fingers grabbing at the paper.

Mrs. Grainger starts to speak, her voice little more than a whisper. "You don't know what it's like, the not knowing."

Oh but I do. Not the same but different.

"She was our life, her Dad and me."

She takes her mother-in-law's hand. "And her Gran, she was her angel."

She smiles distantly and I let her speak. I suspect it's been a long time since she last talked of this and I sense the catharsis of it.

"She was the apple of her dad's eye, just a wonderful, lovely girl. She was perfect in every way. I know everyone says that about their children but she really was. She was so funny and bright. We were so proud of her. She was going to be a vet, it was all she'd ever dreamed of, ever since she was a little girl."

Her eyes cloud. "That was why she was at the animal sanctuary. She was doing voluntary work with the animals, she loved it. She was coming home from there when . . . if only we'd known . . ."

She fixes me with a slightly aggressive look.

"She didn't run away. She wouldn't ever have done anything like that so don't even think it."

I want to say I'm not, but I let her continue.

"She was happy, we all were. The police tried to make her into something she wasn't, asking if she had any problems and did we fight. Did she have a boyfriend we didn't know about, could she have gotten into drugs? I know they have to ask but it wasn't like that. There was just the three of us, we were happy, she was happy."

The old lady puts her arm around her daughter-in-law's shoulder and addresses me for the first time.

"It destroyed them," she says. "It destroyed all of us and it killed my son."

I must look confused for Mrs. Grainger junior explains, "Geoffrey, my husband, he died four months ago. A heart attack. He never got over losing Rachel, none of us did. He was never the same after."

"I'm sorry," I say, "I didn't realize, the answering machine . . ."

She interrupts me, "I can't delete him, it's all I have left of him now, sometimes it helps just to hear his voice."

She starts to cry for real.

"I feel so guilty. Sometimes I can't remember Rachel's voice at all. I've forgotten how my little girl sounded. I've let her voice get lost. How on earth could I do that?"

I can hardly bear this. It's impossible to sit here and not be moved by their grief. I too feel guilty all over again in case this means nothing and I've opened old wounds for no reason at all.

The old lady has been examining the sheet of paper and turns to me with eyes full of suspicion.

"How can we believe this? How do we know you're telling the truth? This could be anything."

"I swear to you I'm telling the truth. Why would I ever make up something like this?"

She snorts derisively. "Oh, you'd be surprised what people will do for a bit of attention, for their few minutes of fame."

She turns to her daughter-in-law. "See, it's always the same. Nothing but upset ever comes out of this, I don't know why you insist on seeing these people. Every time it's the same, you never listen."

Mrs. Grainger continues as though no one hasspoken. "Geoff was never the same afterwards. He was obsessed by that Smith boy, he was sure he had something to do with it, we all were."

I remember the mention of a Liam Smith in one of the newspapers but it didn't give any details. As if on cue Mrs. Grainger continues, her voice alive with barely suppressed rage.

"They never should've had him working at the sanctuary. He'd been in some sort of trouble and was there doing community service or something. They should never have allowed it, not someone like him. He used to hang around Rachel and we found out afterwards that he'd walked her home a few times, just the two of them. They took him in for questioning right from the start but said there was no evidence. He had an alibi apparently, or so they said. Geoff was convinced he'd had something to do with it. He couldn't let it go, kept trying to make him admit it and ended up with an injunction served against him. It wasn't like Geoff at all but we were desperate. The whole family moved away in the end. They couldn't stay around here, what with everyone knowing what he'd done."

She pauses for breath and I see that her tears have stopped. Her anger at Liam Smith, even after all these years, is giving her strength.

The two women clutch each other and the mother-in-law asks me, "So what are you going to do now? You can't just leave us with this," and she aggressively waves the page from my notebook, all but thrusting it in my face.

She turns to her daughter-in-law. "You need to get on and ring that liaison officer straight away, she's still around. Tell her, she'll know what to do."

"I'm not going to leave it," I tell them, "I was always going to the police but I needed to be sure they'd believe me. I needed to talk to you first. I'll go there straight from here, I promise you."

Mrs. Grainger speaks again, "I just need to know what happened to her, that's all. I just need Rachel back. It's the not knowing that hurts, I can't bear the thought of it sometimes."

There's nothing I can say. There's nothing that will ease her pain until she knows—one way or the other. I promise again to take what I've found to the police and I stand up to leave. I've caused these people enough hurt. My head feels as though it'll burst if I don't get away from here.

Mrs. Grainger stands up too and goes to the mantelpiece where there's a gallery of photos spanning her daughter's short life, from bouncing baby to bright-eyed teenager. While she's doing this the grandmother grudgingly apologizes.

"I'm sorry if I seemed rude earlier but you need to understand it's just been so hard on us all, people pitching up here with false hope and their crackpot ideas. Geoffrey had no truck with it but she used to listen to them all, and it nearly broke her. Even after all this time we still get them. Either it's them or it's a magazine looking for an article when they've got nothing better to print."

She reaches out a gnarled hand and grips my arm with surprising strength.

She fixes me with the strangest look and says, "Don't you be another one. If you think you know what happened to her, you find her. I know you can, you've felt her."

The hairs on the back of my neck stand to attention and I move to pull my arm away from her grip. The intensity of her gaze disturbs me.

Mrs. Grainger is holding a silver-framed photo, which she reverently passes to me. The love shines out of her eyes and for a moment she's beautiful.

"This is our Rachel."

I reach out to take it and the metal of the frame feels cold against my palm despite the temperature of the room. A golden-haired girl with a pretty open face stares straight at the camera giving the impression she's looking right at me. She has beautiful blue eyes, wide and bright, and clear skin with a dusting of freckles across her nose.

Her shining hair is held back with a clip. A clip shaped like a small sparkling daisy.

I realize I've made a noise, an odd winded sound and both women stare at me.

"What, what is it?"

Mrs Grainger's anxious face is too close to mine and my head starts to buzz and hum. I think I'm going to be sick and fight to control my breathing. I can't tell them, I can't. I need to go to the police with this.

"It's nothing, I'm fine, really. It was just strange seeing her face, that's all. She was—is beautiful."

My finger reaches out before I can stop it and rests on the hair clip. In my mind I can feel the coldness of the silver and the hard edge of the marcasites; tarnished but unmistakable.

"That was my grandmother's," she says. "Rachel was wearing it the day she went missing."

49

*"The world is indeed full of peril, and in it there
are many dark places"*

—J. R. R. Tolkien,
The Fellowship of the Ring

I catch the start of the rush hour going back into town and sit in the slow-moving traffic going over what I've just learned. I have no feeling of elation, no sense of vindication, just an overwhelming sadness. Everyone likes to be proved right but not over something like this. I feel a certain distaste at how I've made this all about me; about me finding the answers, about me finding my peace of mind when really it's about someone else entirely. It's about a girl called Rachel who it would seem ended her days locked in a tiny room in our coach house. It's her story not mine. The tragedy of it both petrifies me and makes me sick to my stomach. I imagine her utter desperation and fear, there alone in the darkness. Lost and terror-stricken.

There are things worse than not remembering your own story after all, things much, much worse.

I don't want to think about who put her there or why, I don't want to think of what happened to her or where she is now. I don't want to think about Mr. Connor with his rage and his unsettling eyes, or the stories of his sinister son.

I must go to the police but I'm afraid they still won't take me seriously. It would be so easy for them to suspect I was making it up or more likely imagining things, particularly someone with my history.

It doesn't help that there's no trace of the room now, only the rubbings I took from the walls. At least the number is still there, safe beneath the carpet in my office. I can't recall if I even mentioned the hair clip before. I hope I did otherwise it would be too easy to suggest that I saw it in the photo and then conveniently inserted it into my tale. I wish they'd written everything down and had a proper record of what I said before. I wish I'd kept the hair clip and not thrown it away.

I drive into town and park in my usual place, the car park behind the church. I pull into a space a little way away from the other cars so I can sit quietly and plan what I want to say. I need to get this right. I can't afford a repeat of last time or rather the Graingers can't. They're relying on me, the least reliable person I know.

I lock up the car and walk through the little alleyway at the side of the church. It's almost dark now and some of the lights aren't working. There are long pockets of shadow which flicker and teem with hidden movement so I'm glad to reach the high street. A fine drizzle has begun to fall, almost like mist, which rings each streetlamp with an orange halo. I pull up my collar around my ears and hurry toward the police station.

All appears to be in darkness. I try the heavy blue doors to the front but they're firmly locked. I ring the bell to no response. I don't know what to do now; it's been less than an hour and already I'm breaking my promise to the Graingers.

An elderly man materializes out of the gloom.

"You won't be getting any luck there, love. They close this one at five, it's the cuts. The only one that's manned overnight now is the new station out on the main road. If it's urgent you'll either be driving out there or it's a 999 call. This government doesn't give a damn about law and order despite what they tell us."

He tuts and shakes his head before moving on down the street.

I want to get this dealt with. I want to hand the responsibility for Rachel over to someone else but it's hardly an emergency. She's waited twelve years so another twelve hours can hardly matter. I could drive out to the new headquarters but it's not as though they'll do anything tonight. I can feel myself slipping and sliding into a loop of indecisiveness, of shall I, shan't I. This could mean me standing here for hours, locked in a circle of doubt.

I promised I'd phone Matthew after I'd seen the Graingers. I quickly ring him now and he picks up almost immediately, his voice like a balm to me. I tell him what I've learned or rather had confirmed, and he agrees with me that of course it can wait until tomorrow. I hear the gentle concern in his voice as he asks where exactly I am at the moment and what I'm doing. If I'm okay.

My decision's made and I feel calmer after speaking to him.

It's my art class tonight. I'm tempted not to go but I can hardly let them down. It may help to have something else to occupy my mind, otherwise I'm just going to go over and over the things I've found out, everything running on that endless spool of thoughts. I'll just worry away at it all until I go mad.

Everything with the Graingers has taken longer than I thought. I realize I don't have time to get home and back again before class is due to start. Actually, come to think about it there's nothing to go home for. I don't think I could face Tom's mildly accusatory presence tonight. He's moved on from his whipped pup phase. His tail is out from between his legs and now it seems I'm the one that's being unreasonable by not accepting his mistake and letting things "get back to normal." He's pointedly made the point that after all I'm "hardly blameless" in all this either. No, I'll not go home. Instead I decide to go to Carter's. I need to pick up some paint. I need Titanium White and Hooker's Green, and some new brushes.

I love Carter's shop, both the smell and the feel of it. It's housed in an ancient building and everything about it is steeped in history and atmosphere; everything from the smooth dips in the oak floorboards to the antique till with its engraved casing and enamel keys. The air inside is redolent, rich with the smell of linseed and turpentine. The shelves are laden with paints and media, and every kind of brush and knife. I can browse here for hours. It exudes such peace I sometimes think I'd like to move in if Paul and Leanne would let me, bedded down in a sleeping bag under the counter, their resident bag lady.

I leave Carter's with my bag of purchases. As usual I've bought things I don't really need, like some metallic paint I'll probably never, ever use and an extra-long palette knife with a cranked steel blade.

I glance at the clock on the town hall; it's still too early for my class. I could walk round to the school and wait but I've hardly eaten today. I can feel that my blood sugar is in my boots. I'm finding it hard to concentrate and am even more jittery than usual.

I settle on the Bluebird Café, which is warm and steamy and comforting. They thoughtfully have newspapers and magazines for the solitary diner so we don't have to spend half an hour studiously avoiding one another's eyes. I opt for a blueberry muffin, swelling over its paper case, and a decaf latte—caffeine is the last thing I need right now.

I take a copy of the local paper and settle at one of the high stools by the window, looking out onto the street. The glass is misted over and there's the faint outline of entwined initials, a declaration of love left by one of the schoolgirls who normally frequent the window seats. I'm seized by a childish urge to join them by drawing a heart encircling "I. W. and M. W." pierced by cupid's arrow. Needless to say, I resist and realize with a jolt that already in my mind I'm Isabel Weir again.

The muffin is homemade and wonderfully fresh but I fight to force it down. The adrenaline has closed my throat and I struggle not to gag at its cloying sweetness.

I finish my coffee and pick at the pieces of muffin crusting the fluted paper. The newspaper sits unread on the counter. I've tried but my eyes just skim the words not taking anything in. I shake myself. This won't do. I have a class to teach so I pick up my things and make my way round to the primary school.

Moira is already there huddled in the rain, which has increased from a fine mist to a heavy drizzle. She looks relieved and waits patiently as I fumble with the keys to the hall, and then scuttles away to set up her easel and workspace. Lorna and Colin are next to turn up and come in puffing and flapping and stamping their feet as though they've braved flood and tempest just to get here. I must be a bad person for they irritate me more than they deserve.

As though to make me feel guilty Lorna looks at me with genuine concern and asks, "Are you okay love? You really don't look well tonight, you're so pale." She then goes on to tell me, "There's flu about at the moment and that reminds me, Walter phoned, he's gone down with it so won't be coming tonight. You look as though you could be brewing something."

At the moment I wish it was a strong beer.

I smile in what I hope is a reassuring way and reply completely honestly, "I don't know, I think I'm fine. Just a little tired that's all."

The lights in the hall seem harsh. They make me squint and I detect the early start of a headache. I feel spacey and a bit disoriented, as though I'm not entirely here.

The others eventually roll in although there's no sign of Daniel yet. The usual "hellos" and the ripple and burble of chatter circles the hall as they greet each other and get themselves sorted out.

I'm finding it increasingly difficult to focus and find myself zoning out, retreating back inside my own head. Their voices are coming to me as if from a distance and I suddenly become aware that it's gone quiet. I pull myself back into the room and they're all looking at me. I realize Mark has been speaking to me.

"Sorry Mark," I say, "I was miles away. What did you say?"

"I was just asking if you'd had a good Christmas, that's all."

He cocks his head and frowns.

"Are you sure you're okay?"

God, are they all going to ask me that? I need to pull myself together.

"Yes, I'm fine, honestly. Right, come on you lot let's get started." I take a deep breath. "Last time we talked about warming up or cooling down your landscape by the color of your underpainting. Now you've got your canvases prepped you need to lay out your structure, where you want your horizon, trees, buildings. We're looking for balance in the composition. You can use your photos but feel free to experiment with the different elements. We don't want empty spots but equally it mustn't feel cluttered."

Their eyes watch me. Blink, blink, blink.

"Then you need to think about your lights and darks. Remember last time we discussed a bit about tonal extremes."

A row of heads each bend toward their canvases and at that moment the door flies opens and Daniel rushes in. He comes over to me.

"Sorry, I'm late, someone had broken down out on the main road, held us all up for ages."

He smiles at me apologetically and I feel a small flicker of gratitude that he's here, a familiar face that's a bit more than a casual acquaintance.

The evening drags. I walk the room trying to engage and stay with them but my mind keeps spiraling back to my meeting with the Graingers. I can close my eyes and see Rachel's smiling face looking out at me, that daisy sparkling in her hair. I can still feel the tension reverberating in that room when the mother realized what she was holding, those numbers that told so much.

I usually enjoy my class but tonight I can't wait for it to end and my mood affects my students. They're usually chatty and buoyant, tonight they're subdued. I catch them looking at me; particularly Laurence with his hooded watchful eyes, and Mark with his air of quiet concern.

I'm glad when it's finally over and breathe a sigh of relief as they pack up their things and make their way out of the hall. No one suggests the pub tonight. I've put such a damper on things that they all just want to get home. I just want to get home too. Home to bed and to sleep, the sooner it'll be morning.

The burden of what I know sits heavily on me and I feel a sense of urgency to safely deliver it to someone who can do something about it. I'm haunted by the fear that I'll fail. That something will prevent me getting to the police or that something will happen to me to stop me telling my story. I know it's irrational; most of my fears are.

I gather up my handbag and my shopping and follow the others out of the building. The rain's stopped but there's still a fine mist hanging in the air. Moira's the last to leave and the droplets cling on her coat and hair, making her shimmer in the streetlight.

By the time I've locked the door everyone has drifted away. I'm left to make my own way back to the car park alone. The weather has kept people indoors and the alleyway back to the church is deserted. It's even darker than before. I'm sure there's another light out and my footsteps echo loud and solitary in the night air. I'm seized by a sudden urge to run and break into a clumsy uneven trot back to my car.

Or not. The space where I'm sure I left it is empty. I look wildly around the car park in case I'm mistaken but my car has gone.

I feel a rising swell of panic. I scan the empty rows and unknown vehicles, and the familiar tingling starts in my fingertips. I mustn't panic. I'm safe. It's just coincidence that this has happened tonight of all nights. I just need to ring Tom and he'll come and get me. Even now I know he'll still do that for me. I can wait for him back in the high street, back in the light.

I go to the island in the middle of the car park and stand in the cone of orange light falling from the single streetlamp. I fumble in my bag but my phone's not there. It must be. I used it earlier to phone Matthew so I know it was there. My chest feels tight and I start to rummage frantically in my bag. Tissues and lip gloss and old receipts fall to the ground. It isn't there. I check the bag from Carter's just in case I put it in there by mistake. There's nothing.

I feel the spiraling terror. I can't do this. I need a plan, I need control. I can't be adrift like this. I count to ten and fight to slow my overbreathing. I can do this. All I need to do is walk back to the high street and find a pay phone, or if all else fails go to The Swan and use theirs.

My heartbeat slowly calms and I bend to pick up my belongings scattered in the damp at my feet. As I do, I am overwhelmed by a sense of impending danger and I run. Despite the weakness in my right leg I move as quickly as I can back into the alleyway toward light and safety.

I hurtle round the corner and run into someone. A man, coming in the other direction, and a strangled sob escapes from my throat. He grabs my arm to steady me and with a rush of relief I realize it's Daniel.

"Hey, Isabel, what on earth's wrong? What's happened?"

For a moment I can't speak and instead bury my face in the wool of his jacket. Some random, detached part of my brain registers that he smells nice, citrus and expensive. My words fall over themselves.

"My car's gone. It's been stolen and I can't find my phone. I can't get home."

"Hey," he says gently. "Calm down, it's okay. You're okay now. I'll take you home. My car's just round in the car park, I can drive you back. It's all right."

Even in the semidarkness I can see the look of confusion on his face, his bafflement at the extent of my distress.

"Come on you," he says, "you're fine. Let's get you home. You're not going to be there alone are you? Is Tom there?"

I nod, feeling foolish and weak with relief. Is this really all it takes to make me lose my grip? Am I really this fragile still?

He takes my arm and leads me back toward the deserted car park. There's quite literally not a soul about and mine is hammering against my ribcage to escape.

He hands me a tissue from his pocket.

"Look, before we go are you absolutely sure where you parked it? Are you positive it's not here?"

He bends his head toward mine and tries to jolly me along.

"Come on, we've all done it, suddenly forgotten completely where we parked. We'll just have a look around to be sure."

I silently point to where I know my VW was parked. The rectangle of tarmac is slightly drier than the area around it.

"It was there, definitely. I know where it was."

"Okay, I believe you. Come on, let's get you home."

We walk to a silver Audi parked near the light and I hear it unlock with a small reassuring click. He holds the door for me and I gratefully slip inside.

50

"An end in terror is preferable to terror without end"
—Sophie Scholl

The inside of Daniel's car is warm and spotlessly clean and bar the faint smell of his aftershave, it hardly feels used. Mine has sweet wrappers and tissues, water bottles and sunglasses. His is neat and unlived-in.

I settle in the seat and stow my handbag and shopping safely in the footwell. I lean back and close my eyes. Today has shaken me. I sometimes think I define myself too much by what happened to me and then I unravel like I have today and realize I am defined by it, like it or not. I feel the beginnings of self-pity, which I push away, distasteful, self-indulgent emotion that it is.

I notice how quiet Daniel is as he drives. I'm grateful to him for giving me space to recover and gather my wits. I wonder if he knows about me, if Zoe told him her sister's story.

I glance sideways at him and there's something about his profile that startles me for a moment. There's a flicker of familiarity that feels misplaced, almost as though he's someone else. We're out on the main road from town now, and the streetlights are lighting his face as we pass. Light, dark, light, dark, strobing. For a fleeting second there's a trick of the light and he looks as though he has hair. More hair, dark and floppy on his brow and I feel a sudden spurt of fear.

Something feels wrong. *I* feel wrong and I remember Dr. Stedman's words. What if he's right after all and my mind is slipping its moorings; what if the knowledge I have is too much for my fragile brain to hold. I clasp my hands in my lap and concentrate on looking out of the windshield at the houses and the cars as they pass. I mustn't think like this.

The houses begin to thin out and the streetlights are more widely spaced. We're getting into the countryside now and I'm sure we've missed the turn I usually take. I feel like we're heading away from home. I turn to Daniel with a question on my lips but before I can speak he seems to read my mind.

"Don't worry, it's quicker this way. If you've lived around here for as long as I have you know all the back lanes and cut-throughs. I'll have you where you need to be in no time."

I relax back into my seat and try to ignore the niggling doubt and sense of anxiety that's playing at the edges of my brain. To use Tom's oft-used words, I'm just being silly. This is Daniel. I know him so why do I feel so afraid?

The stretch of highway we're on now is in darkness. There's nothing to see except the mesmerizing rush of white line and tarmac illuminated in the cones of light from the headlamps. The world either side is black and deserted.

I steal another look at Daniel. The car's too dark to read his expression but I sense a certain tension coming off him that finds an answering resonance in me. I'm sure we can't get home this way. I'm sure I remember Zoe or Amy saying he wasn't from around here and had lived abroad, so why did he say he knew the area so well? I feel the trill of fear building again. The adrenaline is drying my mouth and making it hard to swallow.

I hear the sudden tink-tink of the indicators and the car quietly slides off the main road onto an unlit track. In the arc of the headlights' beam as we turn, I see the sign to Marston clay pits. The headlights dip to sidelights, abruptly casting the track into semidarkness. Something is very, very wrong.

I find my voice, which comes out small and squeaky in the darkness. A mouse's roar.

"Daniel, where are we going? This isn't the way home."

He turns to look at me, taking his eyes from the road for a moment and the car bumps and lurches across the rough terrain.

"You really don't know what's going on, do you? You really are the same stupid bitch you always were."

I recoil from the venom in his voice and my mind clouds with confusion. I don't understand what he's saying. A part of me registers danger, clear and present, but I don't know why.

I try to mask the tremor in my voice, "Daniel, I don't know what you're doing or why but I need you to take me home right now. This isn't funny."

"Oh, but it is, Izzy Weir, it is," he says, and I wonder why he's calling me that; that isn't the name he knows me by. "You were unfinished business and you didn't even know it."

He raises his voice to a shrill, mocking falsetto, "Oh Daniel, please help me, please take me home."

He laughs maliciously. "I took you home once before and we both know how that ended. Oh, wait Izzy, of course you don't remember do you, you don't have a clue."

He isn't making any sense. My fear is clouding my understanding and I'm losing my perception of things. He's never taken me home before. I've never been in this car in my life. I try but I'm finding it difficult to grasp what he's saying.

He continues in a voice that's hard and hate laden and strangely familiar.

"You've been poking around thinking you're so fucking clever but all the time you've been playing my game, and fun though it's been, it's over now. You overstepped the line today going to the . . . Graingers!"

He shouts the last word, making me jump and I feel the hot wetness of his spit on the back of my hand.

Slowly through the fog of obfuscation I start to realize this has something to do with Rachel and the room in the coach house. The fear makes me almost release my bladder. I go to speak but I can't get my lips to move; I'm not just adrift, I'm drowning.

He starts to talk in a quiet, conversational voice that's even more frightening than when he shouted.

"There's a symmetry to things, you see Izzy, a meaning beyond the everyday. You were here on borrowed time but it couldn't continue. The clock ticks, the hands turn, and things find their rightful place. You were upsetting the balance, so you've had to come full circle to where you're meant to be. You and Rachel together."

He looks across at me again and I see the glitter of his eyes.

"Oh Izzy, you were my first, my one bird with a stone. You escaped but poor Rachel wasn't so lucky."

He's talking in riddles and I begin to suspect that he's not who he says he is; that he's dangerous and insane.

I can smell tires burning and there's a taste of sulphur and rubber in my throat. It makes me think of fire and brimstone. Of damnation. The buzzing in my head has become a roar. I mustn't fit or pass out. If I do, it's over. His voice has become a meaningless jumble of words and sounds, and I fight to regain control. Think white noise, focus. One thought at a time.

I become aware of the Carter's bag against my shin. I concentrate on the feel of it, the rustle of paper against my leg. I try to calmly visualize its contents, metallic silver paint, Hooker's Green, Titanium White. I picture the fat white tubes with their colored labels, the curve of the cursive spelling their names. The smell of Carter's shop like a meditation. The palette knife with its wooden handle and its shining steel blade.

The palette knife . . .

I prise my tongue from the roof of my mouth and find my voice.

"Where are you taking me, why are you doing this, where are we going . . ."

I let a torrent of words flow from my mouth while my hand slips into the bag and closes around the handle of the knife. Dear God, don't let him see.

The distraction works. I quietly slide it into the warm depth of my pocket and am nearly sick with the relief of it.

We drive deeper into the dark hollows of the trees and Daniel begins to whistle a low tune that jangles and scratches at my nerves. I recognize The Smiths' "This Charming Man" and remember the silent phone calls with this record softly playing at the end of the line. A piece clicks into place.

He turns to me and I see the startling white of his teeth as he smiles and breaks into song.

My terror gives way to a sudden rage, emboldened no doubt by the weapon now concealed in my coat and I scream at him, "Shut up, shut up . . ."

But he just laughs and goes back to whistling that same tune, low and mockingly. Hateful.

"What's wrong Izzy, don't you like a bit of music anymore?"

The trees either side of the track start to give way to low bushes and there's a break in the clouds which gives sufficient light to see we've reached the clay pits. We're in a grassy clearing punctuated by scrubby undergrowth beyond which there's an inky blackness that makes me shiver.

My head is still roaring but the smell and the taste have receded and I'm not going anywhere. I'm angry. I haven't lived through what I've lived through to die here and now. Not when I've got so much to live for. It's funny, so much of my life has been dominated by fear and dread, dread of my attacker, dread of the unknown, but now it's here there's almost a relief. Fuck it, bring it on. Let's get this over with at last. The thoughts ping and fizz in my head like popping candy.

Daniel, or whoever the hell he is, swings the car around and brings it to a halt and I see there's another vehicle here. Although I can't be sure in this light I think it might be mine. The door is slightly ajar and the windows glow a dull yellow, like a candle in the darkness calling me home.

Daniel opens the car door and in the glimmer of the interior light I can see his eyes. They're glittering and manic and my fleeting bravado retreats. My heart thunders in my chest, pushing its way up into my throat, making it hard to breathe.

"Welcome to Marston clay pits," he says, as though us being here is the most normal thing in the world. "Did you know it was brick from here that built our house?"

Another piece falls into place and my terror accelerates; I know who this is.

My voice is barely a whisper, constricted and hoarse. "Grant Connor, my God, you're Grant Connor."

He throws his head back and laughs, clapping his hands together in delight.

"Bingo, a point to player one, but sadly it's too late for the late Izzy Weir."

I fumble desperately at the door handle. It won't open. Either he's done something to the mechanism or my fear has made me feeble. I must stay calm, I must. If I panic now I'm lost.

"You're really not my type, not anymore," he says, grimacing and lifting a handful of my hair. I flinch at his touch.

"I prefer the golden and glittering personally, so we need to look at this more like . . ." He hesitates and puts his finger to his lips pretending to think. ". . . putting out the garbage, that's it. My real fun will start after you've gone, after poor old Izzy's 'suicide.'"

He makes "inverted commas" around the word with his fingertips in the air. "When I'm comforting that delicious little sister of yours, letting her have her after-Christmas surprise. I might even find time to fit in the other one. I know how much they like to play their dirty little games together."

His tongue flicks, shiny and moist, across his lips and he smiles at me as he pulls a crumpled sheet of paper from his pocket. The feeble light makes me slow but then I realize with a rush of horror that it's Laurence's picture, the one he did of Zoe. I see there are two dark holes gouged where her eyes should be.

Unbidden tears rush to my eyes. Dear God no, not Zoe. Not Amy. I think of Rachel Grainger's photo and the similarity between her and the twins in coloring and looks and in that certain sense of vitality. Involuntarily my stomach heaves at the thought of it, a retch catching in my throat.

His hand flies out suddenly catching the side of my face and my head smacks hard back against the headrest.

"Don't be sick in my fucking car you filthy bitch. You're responsible. It's all your fault so don't play the injured party now. And after all you did, you have the fucking nerve to buy my house, poke around in my life."

I swallow a sob, silent tears coursing down my cheeks. I've no idea what he's talking about. I only know I'm never going to get out of here. I'm going to die here in this godforsaken place and there's nothing I can do about it.

I realize he's holding something else out to me and I see it's my phone. Instinctively I reach for it but he snatches it away.

"While you were giving us the benefit of your meager little talent I took this from your bag. It's too late now but you really ought to have been more careful with your things. First your car keys, now your phone. You really shouldn't be allowed out on your own."

He presses a button and lights up the screen where there's a message waiting to send.

"It's your suicide note, Izzy," he says and he reads it out to me.

"My dear Tom, It breaks my heart to do this to you but I can't go on anymore. I'm so, so sorry but it's all too much, life is too

much, so I need to let it go now. Please don't blame yourself, I know things haven't been good recently, but this isn't about you, it's about me. I feel everything unraveling and I'm just too tired to keep on trying to hold it all together. This is an inevitability that was meant to happen years ago and I know now that you can't cheat fate. Know that I loved you and that I'm finally at peace so be happy my darling.

Please forgive me. Izzy"

He looks at me, his face a gray disk in the light of the screen, and he presses send.

My heart constricts. He has everything planned. For weeks while I've made him welcome in my home he's been watching me, planning and plotting this. I realize all the things that have happened, Mina's murder and the magpie, my missing keys, all of it was him.

He gets out of the car, stretching and flexing his arms before coming round to my side and wrenching the door open. I scrabble away from him and clutch at the edge of the seat. I feel the pain of my nails ripping and tearing against the leather. He's too strong. Even without my weakness, without my disability, I'd never be able to fight him off.

He pulls me from the car and I fall to the ground, the grass drenching the knees of my jeans. He grabs my hair and starts to pull me toward the blackness.

I desperately flail my legs, squirming and twisting against his grip, anything to stop him dragging me away into the night. I claw at the earth trying to find a purchase but I can't hold on. My hands slip and slide on the wet grass, the cold numbing my fingers.

He grunts and swears under his breath and heaves me to my feet. His arm is around my throat cutting off my air so that sparks fly before my eyes. He forces me to walk into the darkness, his knees pressing into the backs of mine, propelling me forward.

The grass thins and I feel the crunch of clay and gravel beneath my feet. We must be near the edge. I try to lock my legs, bracing my feet into the dirt and I buck and push back against him. I can feel his breath hot on my neck and a flicker of memory surfaces, that fleeting déjà vu I've felt so many times before. My thoughts crowd and jostle each other, fighting for attention.

His grip loosens for a moment letting the air rush into my lungs. I feel his shoulder flex as my phone flies out in an arc over my head, its screen a silver flash against the night sky. There are seconds of silence before a faint splash sounds somewhere ahead and below us.

I grasp how this is intended to look; as though I drove here after class, sent my message to Tom then hurled myself to oblivion into the freezing water. I imagine the members of my group unwittingly compounding the lie with their tales of how ill and distracted I seemed.

I panic at the thought that no one will ever know the truth about me—or about Rachel Grainger. Not unless Matthew finishes what I've started. At the thought of Matthew my heart squeezes itself into a tight little fist of grief.

I have only seconds before this is all over. If I go over the edge and fall down into the icy water I'm lost. I can almost feel the cold slowing my limbs and my desperate fingers scrabbling at the wall of clay. I can't let that happen.

I slide my left hand down into the warm depth of my pocket and close my fingers over the handle of the palette knife. Its blade is sharp edged and strong, like a chisel. I pray it's enough.

I pull it from my pocket, grasping it in my hand with the blade pointing upward. I bring my arm up and thrust blindly over my shoulder. There's a judder as the blade makes contact, with what I'm not sure. I pull my arm downward as hard as I'm able, driving it into him. The resistance gives like spearing a steak and there's a sound like the tearing of canvas, close by my ear. I feel a hot rush of wetness on my hand and the metallic scent of fresh blood steams into my nostrils.

He lets out a sound that's half howl, half grunt, a chilling inhuman sound and he releases his hold on me. I lurch forward away from his grasp and toward the light from my car. I feel his hands claw at my back as I go but I'm free.

I stumble toward the car and can feel him behind me, the breath rasping and bubbling in his throat. My feet slip and slither on the wet turf and I fight to keep my balance.

I'm almost there before he claims me. I feel his hand closing on my arm and my soul screams out. The other hand comes around my head to clutch at my face, his fingers catching the side of my mouth. He pulls, using my lips and jaw to twist my head back and stop me.

I can't let this happen.

My teeth find his flesh and I bite. Hard, feral, desperate. I feel my teeth ripping, grinding, down to the bone. I'll tear his finger from his hand if I have to. Like a dog. Brutal. Nothing else matters, only escape.

He cries out, instinctively wrenching his hand from my mouth, leaving behind shreds of his skin. I twist from his grasp and suddenly I'm away. Iron floods my mouth and I gag as I run. Scrabbling, stumbling toward my car.

As I grab for the open door my feet slide out from under me and I half fall onto the driver's seat. Once more he's on me. I feel fingers close around my ankle and see his hand stained red with his blood, clutching at my foot. I kick out with my free leg and feel my heel make contact with the soft flesh of his face, crunching and gristly. Once, twice I pound my foot into him until I feel his grip slacken and he falls away into the grass.

I haul myself into the car and almost sob with relief as I see my keys there in the ignition, the keys I thought I'd lost. I pull the door closed. My fingers find the key and turn. I hold my breath. Don't let the light have drained the life from the battery. Don't let us be dead. The key turns, the engine fires into life and the relief rolls like a breaker, the tears coursing down my face.

I can't see where Grant is now. He must be lying out there somewhere in the darkness and I wonder for a moment whether I've killed
him. A hard amoral little part of my brain, over which I have no
control, hopes that I have.

The car slips into drive and I pull away, the engine shrieking as I
over-rev. The wheels spin on the wet ground. I register the thud of
something against the wing but I don't stop, I don't look, instead I
turn on the headlights and drive toward the clearing in the bushes
where I know the route back to the main road begins. I skid onto the
hard-core surface of the track, the car bouncing and lurching over dips
and potholes. Twice the undercarriage hits ridges and rocks and the
steering wheel bucks under my hands. I must slow down; I must get
back to the safety of the main road.

In terror my eyes flick to the rearview mirror, dreading the sight
of his headlights coming for me. There's only darkness. In front the
branches arch over the track clawing at the night sky. I feel that I'm
hurtling down a tunnel; one which suddenly ends, and the car flies out
onto the main road before I have chance to hit the brakes. I wrench the
wheel to the left to stop the car overshooting the carriageway entirely
and swing round into the path of oncoming traffic. For a moment
lights dazzle me and there's the blast of a horn before I swerve back
onto my side of the road barely missing the car in the other lane.

My brain is still processing and I hear Alan Harris's voice in my
head playing over and over. "She looked just like you, she looked
just like you." There's something else here, I can feel it just out of
my reach.

Images crowd my brain: Grant with a head of dark hair. The Lodge
sun-kissed and sparkling. My old kitchen brooding and ominous, the
tiles on the floor. Me running through trees for all that I'm worth.
My breath is coming in ragged gasps, too fast and I'm afraid I'm
hyperventilating.

My concentration lapses and suddenly the car bumps off the road and onto the verge. I fight to regain control but too late as the wheels crash into a gulley leaving the car floundering at an angle with the front off-side wheel spinning crazily in the air.

Other headlights come to a stop alongside me. I hear the slam of a car door in the darkness.

I struggle to get out of the car but the door keeps falling back onto me, trapping me inside. I have to get away. I finally get myself free of the vehicle and clamber to my feet. There's a tall figure silhouetted at the edge of the road and just as I think I'll lose control completely a woman's voice calls, "Hello? Are you okay? What happened, are you hurt?"

I sink to my knees there on the verge and feel the final piece falling into place. It's coming home and making me whole again.

I realize my mouth is open and I'm screaming, over and over, "I remember, I remember."

51

1994

*"Everyone is a moon, and has a dark side which
he never shows to anybody"*
—Mark Twain

He didn't want to be there. In fact, if he really thought about it, he didn't want to be anywhere, not feeling how he did. He wanted to be gone, to be other, to feel something real and hard and true. To feel the thing that was out of his reach, sharp-edged and glittering. Sometimes he'd almost felt it, lurking hidden in the crush of bone or the acrid singe of fur, just out of his reach.

He'd tried cutting himself to see if it would release the nameless something he felt inside. It didn't help. Once he'd bitten his own arm so hard he'd drawn blood. He'd tasted the iron and the salt of himself but nothing brought the release he craved.

Sometimes the way he felt and the thoughts that came unbidden into his mind frightened him but there was nothing he could do; it had always been so.

Once he'd craved to be like them, his parents and his sister. Instead he was always on the outside watching, observing, trying to make sense of what they were and what they felt. And he knew that they knew or at least sensed his otherness. Now they circled the wagons and kept him at bay, the coyote in their midst.

He'd heard his mother that morning, her tone all hushed and urgent.

"Please take him with you Richard, I can't deal with him this morning. You don't know what it's like when you're not here, he watches me. I know it sounds silly, but he unnerves me so."

He'd pictured her face, all pinched and nervous, her fingers anxiously twisting a strand of her white-blonde hair.

His father had sighed, his voice heavy with defeat. "Eleanor, I'm sorry but you're being ridiculous. I know he can be a bit, oh I don't know, intense sometimes but it's just his age. He's seventeen going on eighteen, boys are all a bit odd at that age. You make too much of it."

So that's how they saw him, an oddity, some kind of weirdo.

"Please Richard, just for today. I've got to go out at ten anyway, I've got that hospital appointment, remember?"

He'd heard the whine in her voice. Plaintive, on the point of begging.

"You'll only be a few hours. He can sit in the library and do some revision. God knows he needs to do more than he's doing at the moment if he wants to be sure of a place. If he stays here while I'm out he'll only flop about in his room all day listening to music."

A place, the place, his place, always going on about the fucking place. He didn't want to go to King's anyway. He didn't want to follow in his father's footsteps. Why did they all think he wanted to be like them? He was nothing like them, he was a changeling and so much for the better.

As usual she'd got her way. He'd been sent off with his father with a can of Coke and a bag of crisps like some fucking kid. He was seventeen not seven and there was no way he was spending his morning in the library of some fucking girls' school while his father got off on their little white teeth.

The thought of their moist little mouths, all pink and visceral, almost made him hard for a moment but that didn't work anymore. It didn't provide the release he needed. It made him think of his mother and the sounds that she made in the night. It left him feeling dirty and squirming inside. She'd always made him feel odd. When he was little she'd cuddle him and stroke his hair, when all he wanted was for her to leave him alone. Her touching him made him feel strange and wrong somehow. Sometimes he wanted to hurt her. He didn't know why but he did and sometimes he thought she sensed it too.

Today he'd persuaded his father to drop him off in the village, promising he'd walk back to the school afterward and wait in the car. He'd happily sit there and look through his books. He was not going to the library, no way. His father had relented and given him the keys to the Jag, "under no account are you to drive it," and they now sat heavy with promise in his pocket. His father always gave in; he seeped weakness like pus.

The village had been shit, so now he was sitting on the grass by the playing fields listening to his Walkman. The Smiths' *Meat is Murder*, the best-ever album in the universe, totally mega.

His father had parked miles away from the school. You couldn't even see the buildings from there, hidden beyond the pitches and the stand of trees. Probably wanted it where no one would touch it, the "Jaguar XJ6 X-300, air-conditioning and tinted power windows," his father's pride and joy. A scratch or a dent and he'd probably slit his wrists. Now there was a thought.

A red admiral settled on the grass nearby and he cupped it with his hand, feeling the flutter of its wings against his palm. He pressed his hand into the ground until the movement stopped, crushing the butterfly into the soil. The iridescent dust of its wings shimmered like gold in the sunlight and he ran his tongue across the glimmer on his thumb. God he was bored; existence was boring and fleeting and pointless. He lay back and looked up at the sky, staring into the bleached infinity until his eyes ached with the need to focus.

He sat up and saw a girl had appeared by the pavilion. She was dark haired and elfin, aimlessly scuffing her shoes in the dirt. She looked about as bored as he was. He sat very still and watched her. She seemed to be looking for something in the grass.

Isabel had seen the boy but she pretended not to. She kept her head down, watching him from under the length of her lashes; watching him watching her. In her innocence she saw only that he was beautiful so missed his air of menace and mistook the predatory nature of his gaze.

God, she so wished Maria was there. There were never boys at the school, certainly not ones like that. This was like totally weird. She scuffed around in the grass looking for her bracelet, keeping one eye on the boy. He really was cool-looking, with dark jeans, a tight white T-shirt and a Walkman plugged into his ears. His black leather jacket was rolled up on the grass where he'd been using it as a pillow. She wondered if he would speak to her and felt a shiver of excitement. She moved a bit nearer to him, trying to appear as though she hadn't seen him yet.

He slowly stood up, unfolding his long legs, and strolled toward her. Oh my God, he was probably the most gorgeous boy she'd ever seen. He was like someone out of a magazine.

He leaned against the side of the school pavilion, arms folded, and watched her for a while. He inspected her from head to toe, noting her dark hair loosely wound in a clip, the too-short skirt and the tie carelessly knotted over an open neck. He watched her bend to pick something up from the grass and let his eyes linger on the dark V shadowing the top of her bare thighs. A word hissed into his mind, "gusset,"and he liked the dirty feel of it. He felt the thrill of something slowly uncoiling inside him.

Eventually he spoke, "Hey there, what you looking for?"

She looked directly into his eyes, gray meeting brown. "Hi," she said.

He had the most incredible eyes, the darkest brown so that the black of the pupils bled into the irises. They were discs of fathomless obsidian that could see right into her. She felt the color blooming up her neck.

"Just looking for a bracelet I lost, that's all. Thought I'd found it but I haven't."

"You at the school or what?"

He knew he was asking the bleeding obvious but just wanted a way to talk to her. Alleviate his boredom for a while and maybe have a bit of fun with her.

"Yeah, 'course, otherwise I wouldn't be wearing this would I," she said, indicating her uniform with a gesture of contempt.

He liked her attitude. She made him want to rise to the challenge. Of quite what he wasn't sure but she interested him.

"Cool. I'm away at St. Bart's doing my As but I hate it. It's like total shit and I can't wait to get out. What's it like being here?"

"S'alright I suppose. Can be dead boring sometimes though. We have to board and it's okay if you're sharing with someone cool, like me with my mate Maria, but not if you get put with one of the saddos. And if you end up getting stuck here all summer like I'm going to be, then it really sucks."

Maria was never going to believe this. Isabel tried to take in every detail to tell her friend. He was tall and lean with dark hair flopping forward in his eyes, and he gave off an edgy electric energy.

"Anyway," she said, "what're you doing here?"

He realized from the way she spoke that she was younger than him, fifteen at most. He switched his tone to match hers, the better to win her over. He ignored her question. He was hardly going to tell her he was there waiting for daddy like some baby.

"God, that really sucks. Why can't you go home for the summer?"

"My parents are in America and they don't want me with them. I wanted to go but there was no way they were taking me. You ever been there?"

"Yeah, once when we were kids," he said, pulling his cigarettes from his pocket. "Smoke?"

"Wow, that's so cool, what was it like?"

She casually took a cigarette from his hand. No big deal, she and Maria smoked all the time.

He bent forward to light her, his dark head almost touching hers, his eyes carefully watching.

"Loads better than here, we went to Disney World and did all that kids' shit but went to Miami as well and down on the Keys. That was dead cool. Did scuba diving, saw where Hemingway hung out and everything. I didn't ever want to come home."

They flopped down on the grass together, her head resting on his jacket.

"God, I'd die to go there. My Dad's got shed loads of money and everything but I never get to go anywhere. They're always too busy. They let me come to Boston once on a business trip. That was cool but mostly they leave me here and do their own shit."

She leaned back, amazed at her own daring. She'd wished for something to happen, something out of the ordinary to break up the dull monotony of the summer. Perhaps he was it.

"What's that on your T-shirt?" she asked, more to prolong the moment than anything else. She stretched out a hand as though to touch him but bottled it at the last moment.

"What, you mean you've never heard of The Smiths? Best band ever. They were, like, so nihilistic. They really got it."

She laughed up at him. "But they're ancient, even my dad likes them."

Her teasing annoyed him but he didn't let it show, instead he thrust his chest toward her to show her his T-shirt, daring her to touch him.

"It's one of their album covers, the title's on his helmet, *Meat is Murder* and anyway, they're not ancient," he said, "they're iconic. Morrissey's had an album in the charts this year. Better than the shit you probably listen to."

He nudged her, hard but disguised as playful. "Bet you love Take That and Boyzone. Here, listen to some real music."

He leaned across and pushed one of the earbuds into her ear, his hand deliberately brushing the soft skin of her face. Probing the dusky velvet of her lobe. He smiled to himself as he registered her involuntary shiver.

They lay back together on the grass and listened to the crooning cadence of the lead singer's voice as it echoed their private rebellions. There in the sun they talked of old bands and new. Of The Damned and The Style Council, of Oasis and Blur. He found himself oddly at peace, as though she could push the dark feelings aside for a while.

He turned to her. "We don't even know each other's name," he said, "I'm Grant," and he held out his hand.

"Hello Grant, I'm Isabel, Izzy Weir," she replied, calmly placing her small hand in his.

"Tell you what Izzy Weir, let's go for a drive. We can stop off at mine and I'll put The Smiths on and we can watch TV or something."

On the "or something" he raised his eyebrows at her, his eyes both hard and humorous.

"Come on, I've got the car, you'll be back before anyone misses you." He enticingly waggled the keys to the Jag and nudged her on the arm. "Come on, unless of course you're scared."

Isabel paused. This was all a bit too much. She'd never bunked off without Maria. Then again this wasn't the sort of thing that happened every day. The thought of it frightened her a bit but after the briefest of hesitations she answered, "Yeah, shit why not."

They didn't know it then, but they stood on the sun-baked banks of the Rubicon and the crossing they were about to take would change both of their lives forever.

52

1994

"Stars, hide your fires;
Let not light see my black and deep desires."
—William Shakespeare, *Macbeth*

The car sped through the lanes and with each passing mile Isabel's apprehension increased. What had started off like a cool adventure was beginning to feel just plain stupid and scary. After all she had no idea who he was, not really, and no one had any idea where she was. She'd tried to change her mind at the last moment but he'd been so insistent and had sort of bundled her into the car before she'd had a chance to say no. He'd seemed angry almost and had frightened her a bit.

She stole a sideways look at him. He was dead good looking but there was something about him that didn't feel right. The white of his knuckles tensed on the steering wheel made her feel uncomfortable somehow.

God, what if he thought she was going to have sex with him. The sweat prickled on her scalp at the thought of that and she started to feel properly afraid. She really wished they could turn back but she couldn't ask again. She didn't want to look like a stupid kid. Anyway, she knew he'd say no and she didn't want to make him angry. She fleetingly thought of opening the door and rolling out like she'd seen on TV but she'd heard him lock the doors, and they were moving too fast. She'd probably kill herself if she even tried. She was just going to have to go with it and hope it was okay.

They turned off the country road into a lane flanked with fields on one side. On the other, dense trees arched over the road blotting out the sunlight. She wished she knew where he was taking her.

Eventually the car swung through tall gates and onto a gravel driveway which opened out onto lawns in front of a red brick house. She felt a surge of relief. If they were going to his house like he'd said then surely nothing bad could happen. His parents might even be there or perhaps a brother or little sister.

Grant opened the front door and stood back with a flourish to let her go in. He felt a strange mixture of excitement and something nameless that hovered at the edge of his mind like a hunger. As she passed he blew gently on the back of her neck lifting the small tendrils of hair that lay there, slightly damp against her skin. There was something vulnerable about the back of her neck, all pink and helpless, that made him want to bite it. She turned to look at him with eyes wide like a startled animal and he sensed a flicker of fear; a flicker of fear which awoke the nameless something in him. He ran into the hall grabbing her hand as he passed.

"Come on Izzy Weir," he said, twirling her round and pulling her into the sitting room, "don't let me down."

Isabel let herself be led into the sitting room although every instinct was telling her she should never have come. The house was empty, she was sure of it, and his nervous energy was making her scared. She sat on the edge of the sofa and watched him as he went to put on an album.

"This one's from way back, *Hatful of Hollow*. There's some brilliant tracks on it."

He looked over at her perched on the sofa as though she was about to take flight. What the fuck. She'd wanted to come here so why was she looking like that, as though he was doing something wrong? He felt a flicker of annoyance. God, she looked just like his sister with her small face all pinched and wary. He could smell the fear coming off her. If she wanted something to be scared about then he could see to that. She had no idea what he was capable of. He sat down next to her on the sofa and roughly pulled her back into the crook of his armpit.

"What's wrong Izzy Weir, starting to wish you hadn't come? Maybe this'll cheer you up." He placed his hand over the small mound of her breast, firm beneath her shirt and squeezed—hard.

In the background Morrissey's voice questioned where his intentions lay, and the delicious irony of it wasn't lost on him.

Izzy leaped to her feet, pushing his hand away and tears rushed to her eyes. She was really, really frightened now.

"Please stop it," she said. "Take me back. Please. You've got the wrong idea. I don't want to do this."

He laughed at that. "I was only teasing, we're not going to *do* anything. Don't look so scared, you're perfectly safe with me."

At that he growled low in his throat and made a lunge as though to grab her. He laughed again as she sprang back terrified. Her fear made him feel spiteful and nasty.

"Come on, don't be such a baby. Let's have a coffee. I'm sorry, I didn't mean it. Okay?"

He ran the nail of his little finger down her cheek and she stopped herself from flinching but only just.

Isabel had no choice. She followed him through to the kitchen, her heart scampering like a mouse in a wheel. If she just had a coffee with him and listened to his music maybe he'd leave her alone and take her back to school. She'd even help him make the coffee—anything to keep him sweet. She should never have done this. God, what was she thinking, she was so stupid. She could feel the sob quivering in her throat and fought back the tears.

He went to the cupboard to get two mugs. He was starting to get properly pissed off now. She'd led him on. Letting him think that she liked him when really she was just like all the others. He could feel the nameless thing more strongly now, that hunger that ached to be fed.

The bright sharp edge of it made him breathless. He watched her at the sink filling the kettle all in a rush. He sensed her wanting to get away from him as soon as she could and his anger started to build. He realized he was trembling. She'd tricked him so she deserved to be afraid. She deserved to be hurt. She owed him.

He crept up behind her and put his hand on her mouth. His hot palm pressed her lips to her teeth, hurting. He ground her hard against the edge of the sink with his hardness, hurting. This was better, so much better.

"What are you?" he whispered, his mouth hot and wet against her ear. "I'll tell you what, you're a teasing—Bitch!"

He shouted the single word making her jump, and the kettle crashed and clattered into the sink. She tried to turn round but still he kept her pinned, his face pressed into her hair. His hot breath released the scent of it and he felt his excitement mounting. Shit, he could do anything he wanted, anything at all. He felt the irregular trembling of her body against his groin and realized she was crying. It made him feel happy and sad and regretful and weird all at the same time.

He wanted to kiss her. He wanted the taste of her on his tongue. She owed him that. He spun her round and pressed his lips to hers, his tongue burrowing between her teeth, rough and wet. She gagged convulsively, wrenching free from his grasp, and ran for the door. She had no idea where she was going but she had to get away. She must. The door was only seconds away but it felt like her lifetime.

The hunger beat against his skull. This was what he was. He felt his control slide away as his mind skittered to somewhere dark. He didn't care. It felt so good. A shred of humanity somewhere inside him knew it was wrong but his other self was stronger, urging him on.

He launched himself at her as she reached for the door. Her fingertips grazed the knob but her fear made her clumsy and she was too slow. He knocked her down, grinding the skin of her cheek against the tiles and pressing the air from her lungs. His hands were in her hair now and he pulled. He didn't know how this would end, all he knew was he could no more stop it than die. She screamed and then the answer came. He needed to see her bleed.

As he dragged her back from the door, a movement caught at the edge of his vision, fleeting and fast. For an instant a face appeared at the window, wide-eyed and ashen. For a second, time froze and then it was gone.

What the fuck. He sat perfectly still for a moment, holding a fistful of hair while she sobbed, her eyes fixed on the window. He wanted to howl with frustration; instead he waited. He needed to be careful now. He needed control. Slowly his rage left him and the aching hollow settled in his chest once again, as the moment of wonder slipped away. He knew the answer had been in his grasp. He'd glimpsed it, that point where he'd finally be alive and now it was snatched from him, lost and gone.

He let his loss carry him across the space to the door and into the garden. The girl was momentarily forgotten.

Alan was raking up leaves, slowly and deliberately, his face averted away from the house. Careful now. He wasn't even going to look. He'd seen nothing, heard nothing, nothing at all. If he didn't look then he wasn't there. Then there was nothing to fear.

Grant moved to silently stand beside him, close beside him. He was in control again. He was channeling his energy somewhere else. To somewhere it had been before, many, many times. He slowed his breathing and closed his eyes. He could almost feel the heat of Alan's body and smell his fear, warm and vinegary on the air. He knew Alan would eventually turn to face him. He always did. Grant could bend and snap his feeble will any time he chose. God the fun they'd had for a while back as kids, but this wasn't fun now.

He heard the raking slow to a stop and snapped his eyes open.

"What the fuck were you doing spying on me, you pervert? I saw you. You got a thing about little girls or something, you fucking weirdo?" He whispered it with quiet and deliberate menace. He found that always did the job. Even the boys at school found that hard to ignore.

Soft lips and chin quivered and twitched with a life of their own.

"Look at me when I'm talking to you, you retard, or you know what'll happen."

Alan's eyes met his and Grant saw the familiar terror there burning bright. It was little consolation compared to what he'd nearly had, but it still held a small tingle of pleasure. A pleasure he thought he'd outgrown.

"You've had it now," he hissed, low and hard. "They're finally going to lock you up for this. I'm going to have to kill that girl now and it's all your fault. You've made it happen, you know that? You say one word, just one word to anybody and I'll tell them you did it, that I saw you, and who do you think they're going to believe? Everyone knows you're fucking weird, everybody hates people like you. They'll take you away from that old slag of a mother and she'll go to prison too—if I don't get to her first and give her what she's got coming."

Grant saw the tears well up in the vacant child-eyes and had to tamp down the urge to hurt him, really hurt him this time. There was no time for that, he had her to deal with. Anyway, he preferred to linger over his games with Alan, and to leave no marks.

He suddenly raised his voice and shouted, the spit flying from his mouth and landing on Alan's cheek.

"I'll tell them I caught you with her, that you were hurting her and I tried to stop you but couldn't. Then when you're safely locked up I'll go to that shithole of yours and I'll do for your junkie mummy nice and slow. You know what I'm capable of and it'll all be your fault. They'll both be dead because of you."

He grabbed the rake and jabbed at Alan's face, catching the skin by his eye and ripping a ragged and bloody streak down his cheek.

"Now look what you've made me do. I did that to try and stop you. You made me."

The young man finally spoke, his voice imploring and surprisingly deep.

"Leave me alone, I ain't done nothing. I was just doing the hedges and burning the leaves like what I was told."

Tears ran from his eyes and snot bubbled at the tip of his nose. Grant smashed his fist into the side of his head, knocking him to the ground. He followed it up with a well-aimed kick to the groin then watched with satisfaction as a hot stain spread outward, darkening the blue of Alan's jeans.

"God, you're fucking disgusting. You think anyone would ever believe a cunt like you over me? Look at you, you've pissed yourself, you pervert. You ever come back here again or say one word to anyone about what you saw, I'll make sure they know you did it. That it was you who killed her."

Alan pulled his knees to his chest, gasping for breath, his hands pressed to his crotch. With eyes closed he began to hum, louder and louder, anything to block out the voice that'd tormented his teenage years. It belonged to the monster that hurt him and scared him.

"I should just kill you too. You know what? I'd probably get a medal, you worthless piece of shit. Get up off the fucking ground and stop blubbering, you baby. Go on. Go home before I change my mind and remember, not a word."

He slapped him hard on his torn cheek and caught the hot scent of blood. One day he'd finish the game.

"Go on, run home piggy. Run before I get you."

He watched as the fat arse wobbled from view and turned back to the house. He had nothing to fear there, that pleasure had always been his for his taking.

The girl was a different matter. He felt scared now. He didn't understand where it all went wrong. He'd thought he liked her and that she liked him so why did it all fall apart. Sometimes the way he felt and the thoughts he had frightened him but never anything like this; never so wonderfully dangerous and real. He'd have to take her back. He had no choice really, not now Alan had seen them. He was afraid for himself. God what if she told somebody. He'd never meant to hurt her and never would've, not really—or that's what he had to make her believe.

Isabel hadn't moved. She'd seen the face at the window and for a moment she'd hoped she was saved. Then she'd heard their voices and had heard what he'd said and now her fear paralyzed her. Instead of running for help she stayed on the floor curled tight in a ball, sobbing. She was hurting and scared. God, she'd never been so scared.

She'd been afraid before, at school in the beginning. At night in the dark of the dorm when her parents had left her but nothing like this. That was fear, this was terror. She knew she should run but had nowhere to go. She didn't even know where she was or how she could get back to school.

Grant looked down at her. Fuck, he needed her gone. Tormenting Alan was one thing, he was an animal and he deserved it. This was something else entirely. He didn't want to think about how good it had felt, how glittering and true. He'd save that for later when he was alone. He'd stroke that memory alone in the darkness. For now he was in deep shit and had to get out of it somehow. He needed her to keep her mouth shut, that above all else.

He reached out and touched her hair, feeling her quiver and flinch.

"Look, I'm really sorry about what just happened, okay? It all went kind of weird but I wasn't going to hurt you or anything, honest."

He felt lost, all drained and empty. Tears of self-pity pricked at his eyes and he hated her.

"Look, please just stop crying. I'll take you back and we can forget this ever happened. Just shut the fuck up. Please."

Her tears were beginning to get to him. He could never deal with emotion, he hated it. He just needed to get her out of there, into the car and away. They'd only been gone for an hour or so. Hopefully she hadn't been missed. He tilted her chin up and smiled at her, flattery might just get her on side.

"You were just so pretty and sexy."

God, now she was making him sound a right prick. It made him want to punch her in her puffy face.

"I just got a bit carried away, that's all. I'm sorry."

She disgusted him, her face wide-eyed and slack with terror, all slimed with snot and tears. He shuddered, this wasn't what he'd wanted, no way.

Isabel nodded. She didn't care what he said. She couldn't look at him and didn't trust herself to speak. She'd heard what he'd said about killing her, she just needed to get away from him and back to the safety of school. She tried to shrink into herself, to make herself small and deflect his attentions and anger away.

They sat in leather-scented silence as the car ate up the miles, back to the school and to safety. Isabel felt as though she was holding her breath. She was willing him to keep going, not to stop on the way or take her anywhere else. Waves of panic washed over her at the thought and a silent mantra ran on a loop in her mind, "Please take me back, please take me back," over and over again. She could feel the rush of her blood in her ears.

As they neared the school the crushing fear gradually gave way to relief, then to shame and finally to anger. Once the welcome roofs of Thorpwood House hove into view her mantra changed, "Nearly there, nearly there," and she summoned the courage to steal him a sidelong look. He was mental, a total sicko, to scare her like that. He wasn't even attractive, not really. He was creepy and weird.

She had to tell someone even though that meant owning up to bunking off. She'd be in the shit and she'd go on report but she didn't care. They'd be on her case all summer and she wouldn't get to do anything but it didn't matter. If she didn't tell he might come back and get her, actually hurt her this time. God, what if he was really dangerous, what if he'd killed her? At the thought she was run through with a new spike of fear and fresh tears found their way to her eyes. She had no choice, she had to tell them what he'd done and take the consequences. She couldn't afford not to.

They were on the sweep of Thorpwood's drive now, the climb through the trees to the playing fields. Nearly there, nearly there, nearly safe.

Grant swung the car into the same spot as before; it couldn't look as though it'd moved. Luckily there were no security cameras this far out from the building and the thick canopy of trees sheltered them from prying eyes. They'd passed no one on the drive in. If he could just make sure she kept her mouth shut he'd be okay.

He'd felt the shift in her on the way back, the gradual transition from fear to anger. He could feel her now. Her cold little eyes boring into him. Those flat gray pebbles watching him.

Flattery hadn't done him much good so now he was going to have to scare her into silence. She deserved it anyway. Looking at him all hostile like that with those shark eyes. What'd he even been thinking, taking her home? She didn't deserve someone like him, not at all. He'd liked her and this was how she repaid him.

He turned to her but before he could speak the door was open and she was out. She was off, running for the cover of the trees and the playing fields beyond, as though her life depended on it. Away she ran, to safety, her hair flying loose and wild behind her, her legs pumping.

Fuck, he couldn't just let her go. He had to stop her, make her see she couldn't say anything, not ever. Grant half fell, half leapt from the car and set off in pursuit. He had to get to her before she cleared the cover of trees, before she was out in the open and away.

Isabel could hear him behind her crashing and breaking through the undergrowth and her legs turned to water. She couldn't let him catch her. He was gaining ground. She could feel the rush of his fingertips grasping for her hair. Just one last push and she'd reach the path. Nearly there, nearly there.

So close, then her foot caught a root and she fell. Before she could save herself her head hit the ground and from somewhere far away she heard a crack like gunfire. The world spun with a firmament of dizzying stars and then he had her.

Grant looked at the girl on the ground, with her unfocused eyes and her arms and legs twitching and flailing, trying to stand. Lyrics from the Smiths, "Barbarism Begins at Home," played in his mind, telling him what to do. He felt electrified and wild. There was no going back now. He couldn't let her get away, not after this. He'd be blamed for hurting her and everything would turn to shit.

He saw the streak of blood, red at her temple, like a message just for him and he knew what he had to do. Another crack on the head was what she needed. He picked up the rock that she'd hit when she fell and he hit her. Hard. He watched as her eyes went milky and wide and he hit her again. The blood splattered the carpet of leaves and her limbs stopped their striving. She didn't cry out, not really. She just made animal grunts and splutters as her head bucked and rolled. He tried not to laugh at how stupid she looked.

The wood was silent save the birds singing high in the branches. Grant stood with the rock in his hand and felt the munificence of the universe. It had gifted him with the answer at last. He strived for the word to describe how it felt—transcendent. He was at peace. The calmness flowed through him all sleepy and warm and he looked at the smooth round stone and the blood on his hand as if from far away. Slowly, as though in a dream, he wiped his hand on the grass and wrapped the rock in his jacket. He would keep it. It was his talisman.

His juju. His totem. The magic charm that'd made him whole. He was Mors, God of Death.

He was not the man she thought he was.

He knelt in the leaves and whispered, "You really should've known that girls like you make graves."

It was a shame she couldn't hear him, that she'd never hear anything anymore. He felt a surge of love for her. He'd known she was special the moment he saw her. She'd given her life to show him the shape of his.

He walked the short distance back to the car. He was tired now, so very tired, weighed down with her life force. He stuffed his jacket into his bag with his books; he'd think about that later, safely back in his room. Right now he needed to sleep. He lay across the back seat and despite the heat of the day he pulled the travel rug over himself. He fell into a deep and dreamless sleep but not before he'd cleaned his hand, like a cat. He licked the last briny traces of blood from his fingers, using his teeth to get under his nails.

He opened his eyes to the sound of voices. Instinct told him not to move, to stay where he was, enfolded in the darkness of the blanket. The memory of what he'd done came flooding back like joy. He had to clamp his lips tight shut to stop himself from shouting it aloud.

The voices came closer. He could pick out his father's stentorian tones and that of a woman.

"Thank you so much Mr. Connor, it's always lovely to see you. We'll be in touch with the surgery about the two girls that need to come in for treatment and I'll wait to hear from you regarding the other lass."

"I really do think it's best if she sees my colleague in London. I'll do the letter today and hopefully hear back next week. I'll let you know as soon as I do."

He heard the click of the boot and his father sliding in his bags. He stayed low. She mustn't know he was there.

"Well thank you again. It's always so helpful you coming to the school."

Pleasantries over, he heard the sound of her footsteps receding across the gravel and the boot closing. He waited until the footsteps had faded away and only then sat up as his father reached the door.

He felt sunny and kindly disposed. "Hi Dad," he said, smiling the smile he usually reserved for special occasions.

His father looked at him with his habitual disappointment and sighed.

"Don't tell me you were asleep. I thought you were supposed to be revising. What have your mother and I always said? You're not going to get very far you know if you're not prepared to work at it."

Grant felt the familiar bubble of dislike rising to the surface but he smiled sleepily. He could let it all wash over him now. Yes, he had been sleeping, now he was awakened. He could afford to be benevolent for they had no idea what he was, or how powerful he'd just become.

He stretched and yawned before his languid reply. "Sorry Dad, it was hot and it made me sleepy. I dozed off, no big deal, okay? Please tell me we're going home now, I'm absolutely starving."

His father started the car.

Somewhere in the cool shade of the trees Isabel's fingers began plucking and twitching.

Epilogue

My life is changing. I'm changing. I'm no longer the people I've been before; nor am I who I'll be in the future.

It's been over a year since my mind gave up its secrets, those mysteries that lay hidden in the deep sulci of my brain.

It's been over a year since I killed a man and several months since I was cleared of any crime. It's still strange to think I've taken a life. That I've sent a soul spinning to who knows where, albeit "without intent and in self-defense." It's strange to think my literal stab in the dark sliced deep into the meat of his carotid and that he bled out in the very place where he intended my life to end. It's one of those things too massive to comprehend and when I've tried, really tried, to grasp the essence of it, my mind shies and skitters away from the thought. Then, when I'm not thinking of it, I find it humming like a tuning fork in my brain. I hope one day to be free of it.

His sister Gemma was there that last day in court. She was pale and composed in a light gray suit with a solemn-faced man at her side. Her husband I presumed. We didn't speak but when we passed in the long corridor outside the courtroom, she stopped, and our eyes met. She fleetingly placed her hand on my arm in a gesture I couldn't read. The look on her face was strangely like pleading; for what I'm not sure. Forgiveness perhaps, or understanding? I saw no hostility lurking in her cool gray eyes. I often wonder if she ever told her father. I hope not, for I sometimes think of that sad confused old man, haunted by his suspicions about his son and conflicted by his loyalty and love. I have to believe that's how it was and that he didn't know or hide the truth of it.

⸰◌◌⸰

Zoe is fine, thankfully. Her heart wasn't broken. She had begun to be wary of Grant, or Daniel as she knew him. A little afraid of his intensity and of a certain strangeness the rest of us never got to see—not until the very end when I saw enough of it to last a lifetime. She was trying to end it. I haven't told her what he said, what he had planned for her and her sister. I don't want his thoughts to be in her head or for him to become the nightmare that haunts her dark places.

The investigation into Grant Connor is ongoing, both here and across the Atlantic, but no other crimes have yet come to light. It seems he was a wealthy man, running a pioneering dental technology firm in the US. He had no wife or family and few, if any, true friends. Apparently, it's a picture that's typical of a high-functioning psychopath—and even those words make me shudder.

I have tried in a small way to undo a tiny bit of the harm he did to others, to pay it forward if you will, and so I went back to the Harrises'. When Alan's mother finally agreed to let me in I sat on their sagging sofa with his plump, moist hand in mine and told him that I *was* that girl who looked like me and that I didn't die. I told him he'd done nothing wrong and that Grant Connor had gone now, so we were both safe again. He watched me from those wary hooded eyes and I hope he believed what I was telling him. I think he did for when I stood to leave he stood with me and gently put his finger to the scar at my temple. His mother thanked me as I left, both for coming and for finally setting her mind at rest. She'd nursed a secret fear for years, that the girl found at the school was somehow linked to her son's story. Her bony hand clutched mine as she struggled to find those unfamiliar words of gratitude, her face pinched tight to hold back unshed tears. My heart went out to her and her fierce protection of her damaged son.

Rachel Grainger eventually came home. Her body was found on a late spring day there in the woodland behind the coach house, close to the boundary with Stour Cottage. For a week the forensic team, the SOCOs, swarmed over our land with their aerial photographs, their ground-penetrating radar and cadaver dogs. All the tools of their tragic trade. Tom and I were politely asked to go to a hotel for the duration but I point-blank refused. I needed to see this thing through to the very end, so we stayed. Tom following me with his haunted, guilty eyes. We were assigned a Family Liaison Officer, the firm but gentle Judith. Ostensibly to support us; in reality to keep us contained.

I had no wish to witness Rachel's disinterment, no desire to see the inhumanity of her remains wrenched from the earth, but it seemed I had no choice. I found I was drawn to where they worked as though pulled there by my deepest self. As each area of interest came to light I would try to slip unseen from the house and stand silently in the trees, a respectful distance from where they searched. I saw them amidst the woodland in their protective Tyvek suits, marking their gridlines and sampling the soil. The crime scene tapes gaily fluttering in the breeze.

I was there unseen on the day that they found her. I heard the single elated shout that carried on the wind and the murmur of urgent voices. I saw the white tent go up and I knew. I stood there for hours until my feet were numb and suddenly I felt the coolest breeze waft past me. Gentle, with the hint of a fragrance, soft like daisies. It was in that moment that I realized I was clenching my hands into fists, my nails biting into my skin. As I released them I looked down and saw the indentation left there in the soft flesh of my palm, a strange mark in the shape of a key. To think of it even now makes the goosebumps roll and ripple and my scalp contract.

I have wondered—but not in Grant Connor's mad way—whether there is a pattern to things, for if you really think about it what were the odds, the one in a million that I would go to live in that particular house. What coincidence was it that brought us to The Lodge? What twist of fate made it the house of Tom's dreams?

I don't like to dwell on it, for although it could be comforting to feel there's a reason behind the randomness and a natural justice to things, it's also slightly frightening to think we're preordained. That no matter what we do our paths are fixed, and there's no free will. I like to push the thought aside.

There was no doubt that it was Rachel. The dental records confirmed it, those dental records from Mr. Connor's old practice. She and her family had been patients of his and it's likely that it was there that Grant first saw her. I was told he worked there with his father as a dental technician before he went abroad.

She was buried alongside her father on a clear bright day flooded with sunshine and attended by birdsong. Her mother invited me to the funeral and I quietly stood there at the back, with my collar of concealment pulled up around my neck. A hat shaded my face and my tears, as the cameras snapped and the police cordon held back the ravening press. Both mother and grandmother were dry-eyed and dignified but at the end, as she turned away, I saw the white radiance of her grief blazing in Mrs. Grainger's eyes. I hope she can find some kind of closure now. She went to thank me but I stopped her. There was no need for thanks because in finding Rachel, Rachel helped me find me.

Tom and I are getting divorced. He asked me one last time if there was any chance for us. The answer was still no. It isn't because I met Matthew, nor is it because of his infidelity. In fact, now that I view it from the distance of time, I think I could've forgiven him his indiscretion if we'd been happy before, but we weren't. Not for a while. The thing we can't fix and mend is his view of me. His lack of faith in who and what I am. I've tried so hard to explain this to him. He still doesn't see it and therein lies the rub. He's met someone new now, Fiona, a lawyer from his firm. Fair-haired and feisty, firm and

forthright; I think she'll be good for him. It's early days but I do so
hope he's found his happiness.

He's still living at The Lodge while the sale goes through. We've
done what he planned. We've had deeds drawn up for the coach house
with a parcel of its own land. It includes the woods where Rachel
lay, and we're selling it separately. The house itself is under offer, the
coach house is yet to go. I suspect its recent history doesn't help, but
it's so lovely a spot I know someone will eventually come along and
love it as I did.

As for me, I'm back in London. I'm renting a one bedroom flat on
the ground floor of a white stucco terrace in Little Venice. It's cool
and tranquil with high coved ceilings and tall shuttered windows that
look out through black railings and onto the street. I see the window
boxes are springing to life now with purple crocuses and dwarf narcissi
raising their heads. They're a flash of welcome color. The walls inside
my home are all in shades of white and the sitting room has a silver
and crystal chandelier that tinkles gently in the slightest breeze.

The kitchen opens onto a courtyard garden of Japanese acers and
cherry blossom trees, which are presently spreading their petals like a
blush of snow. There's a small pond with cool water trickling through
bamboo pipes and silent fish gliding golden under the lily pads. It's
healing. Even the animals are calmed. Both Major and Hugo drift
through the rooms in tranquil docility, or curl at the foot of my bed
together, asleep.

I live here alone for the moment, until The Lodge is sold and I
decide where to go. Matthew and I are still together; we see each
other once or twice a week and for the time that he's here my heart's
not my own. He hasn't moved in because I don't need to rush things.
I need time to be myself now I finally know who I am.

The initial flame of our attraction hasn't dimmed. It has blazed and
crackled into something warmer and rounder, a fire to come home to.
We're slowly getting to know each other and the more I know him the

more I love him. We have no secrets from each other, no hidden shallows to slowly drown us in the future. No need to control or be controlled. I now know where he went that first Christmas when I sensed the evasiveness in his words; he was visiting his late wife's parents and didn't want to let me know just yet. In case it complicated everything or I misread his motivation. Her father has multiple sclerosis so every year Matthew helps put up their Christmas tree and cuts their holly. It's nothing more and I'm fine with it.

I'm fine with lots of things now. I know I'll never be like other people, not entirely. I'll be like me and that suits me just fine. I'm calmer too. I no longer squawk and flap at every sound or see danger lurking round every corner. Also my bitterness has leached away.

My art has changed with me, it's softer now. In part because I use brushes more—I've lost my love of spatula and knife. There's also a calmness in my pictures that was never there before. The woman who bought my last piece said she found it restful. I liked that, the thought that I could be a calming presence and not a raw bundle of jagged nerves, all jangling and discordant in the world.

I've rented a unit in a converted warehouse and that's where I work. There are five of us there; Aaron, a sculptor, Shakira, a silversmith, Anna and Clare, both artists, and me. I try to go there most days if I can. If I can't, if it's a bad day, I take it in my stride and stay home, safe in the knowledge that tomorrow will be better again. I've finally learnt how to be kind to myself. Dear Anton would be proud of me at last.

I am so rinsed of all bitterness I've even made peace with my mother. I've given her one last chance to be a mother to me and a grandmother to my child.

I run my hand over the smooth mound of my belly and my heart swells with the wonder of it until I think it will burst. If I close my eyes I can see her tiny hands like starfish. The chubby fold of flesh at her wrist, the soft creases of her palm already formed. Her tiny nails like shells. If I concentrate I can almost feel the grip of her hand on my finger anchoring me to the world and holding me fast. She is my miracle.

Will I be a fit mother? Who knows? Possibly not all the time but Matthew will be there when we need him.

Will I do my best and love this child with all my heart? Yes, with every fiber of my being and that will be enough.

I know she is a girl. I have no doubt. She's a little girl with soft brown hair like her parents' hair and she has her father's chocolate eyes. And her name is Rachel.

There are those who would find it morbid, or unlucky even, to name my child for a murdered girl but to me it's a remembrance, a pure act of love. A recognition of what she did for me for without Rachel I'd be unaltered, still lost and adrift. Instead I'm whole again.

I close my eyes against the bright whiteness of the room and make a vow; a vow that I will love this Rachel with each and every beat of my heart. I will do all that I can to give her the life the other Rachel didn't get the chance to live. My Rachel will laugh, love, live life in its every moment to the full. Everything she does will be both for herself and for her namesake.

As I open my eyes there's the softest movement in the air of the room, a gentle shift like a breath and for a fleeting moment the crystals of my chandelier shiver with a sound like distant bells.